SH▮FT

HAPPENS

A Novel of Awakenings

Shift Happens
A Novel of Awakenings
by
Jerry Thomas Boyd

Original Story Copyright © 2003

First Edition
Copyright © 2010 by Jerry Thomas Boyd

Contact the Author at
www.thatjerryboyd.com
Art, Visionary Fiction and More

ISBN 978-0-944370-05-6

Synchronicity Press
Box 1154
Waynesboro, VA 22980
www.synchronicitypress.com
Synchronicity - the sense of significance beyond chance

Book Design by Elisabeth Y Fitzhugh
www.altered-e-art.com

Cover Art Photograph
Mount Shasta by Jane English

Author Photo by Peter Urban 1995

Printed in the United States of America

SHIFT

HAPPENS

A Novel of Awakenings

Jerry Thomas Boyd

2010

SYNCHRONICITY PRESS
Waynesboro, Virginia

To all those unfortunate souls who have grown
up without knowledge of the magical realism
that surrounds them.

Some things have to be believed
before they can be seen.

"M-m-m-m, love the Spielberg effects."

ONE

Andy grabbed the phone, pounded out Richard's number, listened and waited. After the fourth ring, the message machine picked up and told him,

"Hi, this is Richard. Sorry, I can't think of another cute answering machine message so just leave your message for me after the beep – blah, blah, blah – I'm sure you've done this before. Thanks."

Andy heard the beep then jumped right in. "Hello, Richard, this is Andy. I know it's the middle of the night, but I really, really have to talk to you now so please pick up the phone. I'm going to keep talking until you do, so please pick up the phone now, okay? I'm sorry to wake you up at ... what time is it? Oh, shit! It's 3:38, sorry. But this is important. There's nothing wrong; I'm okay, but you're the only one I can talk to about what just happened to me, Richard. Richard? C'mon! I'll call back and let it ring some more if this isn't waking you up. Richard, hello, hello-o-o-o!"

Finally he heard the click of the pickup on the other end. "Alright, alright, I'm awake. What is so goddamn important?"

"They tried to contact me again!"

"Yeah? Andy, what the hell are you talking about? Who tried to contact you again?"

"I still don't know exactly who they are. They haven't told me. I asked them to tell me, but they ..."

"Wait, wait, slow down. Is this some more of your X-Files shit?"

Andy staggered over the speed bump of Richard's honest question and slowed down to deliver his retort. "Yes, Richard, this is some more of my X-Files shit. So. Now that you've registered your usual token expression of disbelief, may I continue, or do you, perhaps, need to heap some more scorn and ridicule on me? Hmmmm?"

"I'm sorry, go ahead, go ahead; I'll shut up."

Andy said, thank you and resumed speed, "I woke up about an hour ago. What woke me was that feverish thing I've told you about: you know, that thing you made me get an HIV test about when I told you I was sure I was negative but you insisted..."

"Yeah, yeah, I know, just go ahead and tell me what this is all about, okay?"

"Okay, so this feverish thing was starting to happen and it woke me up. I got up, got a drink of water, went to the bathroom, cooled down, went back to bed and tried to go back to sleep. I was just drifting off when I heard this knock on the door – but it wasn't my door – it was a sound in my head. It was loud enough to startle me awake again, and I knew, instantly, they were knocking on the door, you know – symbolically, metaphorically, whatever – to get my attention. So I gave them permission, like I learned from Riegel, and I spoke out loud to them."

"What did you say?"

"I said, 'Come in."

"Okay, right, and did they?"

"No! Dammit! I said to them, "You can come in but you have to tell me who you are and you have to be aligned with the Light."

"So what did they say?"

"Nothing. I waited and tried to keep myself open to receiving their message but nothing came through. And I'm really upset about it!"

"Why is that, babe?"

"Because I don't know if they just can't get it right yet on their end, or if, somehow, I'm still not ready for contact. I'm trying to be open, but maybe I'm still blocking with unacknowledged or unexpressed fear or ... or maybe – and this is what really does kind of scare me – maybe they aren't aligned with the Light."

"Andy? You know I love you, don't you?"

"Yeah."

"You know how I want to be supportive of you, even with this X-Files 'stuff,' okay?"

"Yeah, but?"

Richard exhaled a thoughtful sigh before continuing, "But it is kind of scary, Andy. I mean it's weird scary. It's spooky. And I'm trying to act like it doesn't freak me out, but, you've got to admit ...."

"C'mon, Richard, level with me. Do you think I'm crazy?"

"No, I don't. You are a little ... 'eccentric' ...."

"Andy interrupted him, "I like to think of it more as 'queer,' actually."

"Very queer, sweetheart, and most charmingly so, I might add. No, I don't think you're crazy, but sometimes I wonder if you aren't maybe ... just a little ... shall we say, 'overly-imaginative'?"

There was a sigh of resignation on Andy's end followed by a pause before he sincerely and humbly replied, "I'm sorry, Richard. I really shouldn't have bothered you at this...."

"No, no, Andy, please ... !"

"No, that's alright! I know I'm pushing it. You are very sweet to put up with this. I guess it could have waited 'til morning after all."

"Andy? You want me to come over?"

"Aw, I don't know. I can't ask you to do that. I feel really stupid now."

"Stop it. I'm coming over."

"What for? I'm okay now, really."

"Maybe I can make it better than okay. Would you like that? Hmm?"

"Let's not compound my guilt. I think I should just let you go back to sleep and we'll ...."

"Hey, I am wide awake now, baby butt!"

"So am I, but, I'm not sure. I mean, emotionally, I'm a little shook up, and I don't think sex is what ...."

"We can do it over the phone."

"Richard, please! I'm serious."

"C'mon, tell me what you're wearing."

"No!"

"Are you naked or are you wearing your bathrobe? You're buck naked, aren't you?"

"You pig!"

"Yeah, that's right, call me names. Talk dirty to me, baby!"

"Okay, okay, that's enough. I'm amused. I'm laughing. I'm over it. I'm fine. Really, I am."

"Well, I'm not. I'm all hot and bothered now. May I please come over?"

"Do you know why I love you, Richard? Because you are a gentleman and an animal."

Before Richard could provide a suitable comeback, he heard a startled Andy exclaim, "Jeesuz H. Christ!"

"Andy, what is it?" There was no response.

"Andy? Are you alright?" He waited and still nothing.

"Andy! Talk to me, goddammit!"

"Richard, I think they're here."

"What? Who? Are you joking?"

"M-m-m-m, love the Spielberg effects. Very nice."

"C'mon, babe, what are you talking about? Who are you talking to?"

"They're here alright and I guess they are aligned with the Light because it is amazingly bright in here."

"Andy, don't kid me; don't play around with this, okay?"

He heard Andy say, with a strangely dreamy and unintentionally dismissive tone, "Richard, sweetheart, I really have to go now."

And then the telephone went dead. Completely dead. He frantically banged the disconnect button until he got a dial tone. He tried to call back and got a busy signal. He hung up and tried again and again, always getting a busy signal. It was a waste of time. He yanked on some clothes and was out the door in two minutes.

He made it from his house on Telegraph Hill to Andy's Potrero Hill flat in under twenty minutes. His mind raced but he drove his '94 Volvo station wagon sensibly. He was frantic with worry but kept to the legal speed limit and didn't run a single stop sign. The last thing he wanted was to get stopped by the police.

"This is not like Andy," he thought. "Sure, he has a great sense of humor, but he hates practical jokes. And he knows I do too. He just couldn't be playing a joke on me. Not in the middle of the night. No, dammit! Not ever! He just doesn't do bullshit like that! But he'd sure as hell better be there or I don't know what the fuck I'm gonna do!"

He turned off Vermont Street and saw that the sidewalk in front of Andy's funky, three-flat building was conveniently empty. "Thank you, Parking Goddess, I owe you one." He switched off his lights and turned off the ignition. Before he got out he took a long look around. There were no lights on in any of the buildings on the street, including Andy's. It was very quiet except for occasional gusts of wind. There was no one to be seen on the street, no homeless wanderer, not even an insomniac dog walker in McKinley Square.

He had to use his own set of keys first, to let himself into the building and then into Andy's top floor flat. Although it was dark, there was plenty of light coming through the apartment's large windows. Richard found his way by the glow from the lights of downtown San Francisco alone. In his estimation, Andy paid too much rent just for that gorgeous view. He made his way down the railroad entry hall, a gallery for eighteen of Andy's extensive collection of movie star portraits of the forties and fifties. Most of the 8x10 glossies, both in color and black and white, were autographed. Richard had heard most of the stories behind the pictures and their subjects, more, really, than he had ever wanted to know about Hollywood and its sociology and gossip. He took Andy's word for it when he said it was a valuable collection even though it included more B-movie stars, like Maria Montez and Guy Madison, and character actors like Eric Blore and Beulah Bondi, than the better known Stars like Lana Turner and William Holden. Tonight Richard ignored the nevertheless abundant star power and went straight to Andy's bedroom.

Yes, the bed had been slept in; no, he hadn't taken either his black leather motorcycle jacket or his jeans. The jeans were folded and draped over the chair next to his bed, just as he always left them, even when he slept over at Richard's. He checked the pockets. Wallet and keys were still in them. "What the hell is going on here!? Where could he have gone without his clothes?"

Clinging desperately to the practical joke explanation, untenable as it was, he looked in the closet and under the bed. He checked the closet in the entry hall and the shower in the bathroom. He checked the second bedroom, Andy's office and occasional painting studio. Carefully and quietly, he made his way through the living room and kitchen to the back door which let out onto the deck and the outside back stairs. It was locked. He opened it, trying to make as little noise as possible, and stepped outside. The wood creaked and groaned under his weight. The deck was in shadow but the stairs were brushed by the light of the streetlamp shining through the leaves of the trees in the side yard, the light and shadow sweeping back and forth with the wind. The sight left Richard desolate. Andy was gone alright. Through clenched teeth he whispered, "Dammit, Andy! This isn't funny!" He went inside, re-locked the door, leaned back against it and let out a desperate sigh.

"What the hell do I do now? Every minute I don't call the police looks suspicious. But what am I going to tell them? 'Help, officer! Aliens just kidnapped my boyfriend! Quick, do something! Go after them!' I can't call the cops, I just can't. Oh, Christ! Get a grip, Richard!"

Richard Lang, the ex-Marine, six foot three and a solid two hundred twenty pounds, did not look as though he could be frightened easily. He was a Vietnam vet, had run his own building contracting business before settling into middle age with his own real estate agency. He was self-reliant and self-confident. At forty nine, he had survived a lot. He knew how to take care of himself. But he was shaken and he needed a moment to figure out what he was going to do next. There was another wall of Andy's movie stars in the living room just off the kitchen and the back door.

They gazed down on him from their Hollywood Heaven, serenely secure, assured of their place in that firmament as immortal sex gods and goddesses. They caught his eye for a moment. The implication in their perfect faces and bodies and in their glamorous poses tried to mock him. It didn't work. It didn't even register. He looked away. But what finally unnerved him were the blinking red lights of all the appliance clocks, silently winking at him, signaling to him that the electricity had gone off and come back on. The fright rolled in on him like a tidal wave; he could spot it coming. He bolted for the front door, moving as quickly and quietly as possible. He locked the door behind him and hurriedly crept down the stairs to the outside door at the front of the house.

"Oh, shit! I just left my fingerprints all over the door!"

He hurriedly crept back upstairs and wiped the door knob with his bandana. Then he remembered the back door to the deck and, muttering self-berating curses, had to let himself back in to wipe his prints off it as well. He wiped them from the doorknob of the building's entrance too, and eased himself outside. Finished covering his trail, he looked up and down the street to be sure it was still empty, then strode quickly to his car and got in. He drove off slowly, deliberately leaving his headlights off until he turned onto the next street and was headed downhill.

An agonizing hour later, sipping coffee on his deck, Richard stared at the light of dawn rising in the sky over the Oakland hills. But he didn't really notice it until the sun peeked over the ridge and threw a shaft of light into his eyes, momentarily blinding him. He winced but, being lost in thought, he went on formulating his plan.

"I've got to stall for time. Maybe Andy will return before anyone misses him. So I never got a call from him in the middle of the night. I don't know anything. I'll go about my business as always. I can't act in any way that might be suspicious."

After saying that to himself, he got up to erase Andy's message from his answering machine. But when he reached it and was about to hit the rewind button, he hesitated. "What if this is the last message I ever get from him?" It was a chilling, morbid thought, he admitted it, but he had to cover all the bases. He pulled out the tape and put it in the pocket of his jeans. Suspicious behavior or not, he didn't want to lose it and it must not fall into the wrong hands, namely the police. "God help me if it comes to that." He took up his coffee mug and began to pace as he continued formulating his plan.

"As far as I know, nothing's wrong. I'll call him at work, quarter past nine as usual, and he'll be there. That's all there is to it. He'll be there. Or not! Shit! I can't stand this!"

He picked up his cordless phone and speed dialed Andy's apartment. The busy signal was gone but there was no answer and the machine did not pick up. He broke the connection after five rings. "No use waking the neighbors by letting the phone ring off the hook." But he also thought, "It's time for him to be getting ready for work. What if he's in the shower?" He waited five minutes and dialed again. Same thing. He disconnected after four rings.

Another five minutes of pacing and he was about to try again when he received the vision. Floating in front of his eyes, like some holographic projection, was the image of a towering, snow-capped mountain, rising above a broad, flat plain, and shimmering like a heat mirage. He blinked, he squeezed his eyes shut, he rubbed them, but it would not leave. It hovered in front of his face for a full nine or ten seconds and disappeared only when he identified it with the spoken words, 'Mount Shasta.' He didn't know where the thought came from. He'd never been there, never seen Mount Shasta himself. He just knew that it was Mount Shasta.

He felt like he needed to sit down so he sank into the nearest available chair. When the stunned skeptic returned to the here-and-now, he again spoke aloud, "So? What about it? Is Andy on his way to Mount Shasta? Is that it?"

Confirmation, if that's what it was, came in the form of a chill down his spine. He shivered and gasped and sat stark still, holding his breath until he had to exhale. He shot to his feet, took two steps for the door and stopped abruptly. The electric impulse prodding him to get in his car and drive to Mount Shasta cut off as suddenly as it had jerked him to his feet.

In an agony of indecision, he began to pace again, faster, and talk to himself, "I gotta be nuts! What the hell am I doing? What am I fucking around for? I should just call the police and report .... No! Oh, no! I must be losing it. It's too soon. Besides, I can't call the police! I'm too nuts. In fact," he added, with bitter sarcasm, "I'm hysterical, goddammit!" He sat down in his armchair, leaned forward, elbows on his knees, his face in his hands and wanted to cry. He tried to let tears come but they wouldn't. Every time he thought of being hysterical, he thought of the police and he thought of Billy. And he couldn't cry over Billy anymore.

And he thought of how Billy died so helplessly and needlessly and how the policemen accused him, Richard, of being hysterical, as if it was a crime to be hysterical for your lover of ten years who just took a blow from a baseball bat to the back of the head and who was obviously dying in your arms while the goddamn cop radioed for an ambulance with that disgusting, maddening smirk on his face as he reported just another, routine case of domestic violence between a couple of faggots – one 'in bad shape' and the other one – the 'hysterical' one – with a broken arm.

And he thought of how the smirking cops had taken him into custody while they let the real, mother-fucking murderer get away. Or murderers. Sure, it had only been one of them with a bat, but the other two were accomplices who held him down and broke his arm. No witness ever stepped forward, and by the time he was cleared, they couldn't have tracked down the bashers even if they'd wanted to. But that was the whole point: they didn't want to, they didn't try, they didn't care. Well, he made them pay in court but it wasn't enough, it would never be enough. It wasn't enough he had to carry with him forever losing Billy, he also had to carry the rage – the paralyzing fear and mistrust – the police now evoked.

"My God, that was twelve years ago, Richard, and it still makes you nuts," he told himself. That was not quite true and he knew it. Seven of those twelve years had been spent in therapy and AA and NA. He knew it was the current crisis that was really making him nuts, tapping into his penchant for paranoia, making him see hallucinations. He needed to calm himself down. This was no time to go to pieces. His buddy was missing and he had to deal with it, like a man.

"Andy, just don't leave me. Please. I want you back. I'll do whatever it takes, whatever I have to do. Just don't leave."

At 6:35 a.m. he had had enough of waiting and doubting and feeling helpless. He made his decision. It might later be construed as running away, but he kept coming back to his vision. He was going to Mount Shasta. Maybe it would seal his fate but he didn't care. He called his office and left a message for Phyllis, his officious administrative assistant, asking her to clear his schedule for the day. He made up something vague about needing to check on his mother in Sebastopol and said he'd call in later to check on 'things'. If she found out, Phyllis wouldn't like his playing hooky, and Phyllis could be 'difficult', but he had an idea that just might spare him her lecturing. He'd been planning to give her a raise and saving it for just such a time when he might need a bit of leverage. If she squawked too much, as she was likely to do, he felt certain he could shut her up with a salary increase.

At 7:00 he was crossing the fog-shrouded Golden Gate Bridge and calling his mother on his car phone, knowing she would have been up since 5:30 anyway. Joan Lang was a chipper and spry eighty-five year old widow, still active as the CEO of the winery she started with her husband. Although she no longer lived on the estate near Calistoga, (Richard's younger brother had taken over that part of the business) she continued to run the vineyard from her cottage and garden in Sebastopol. A tough, no-nonsense businesswoman, she was first and foremost a properly gracious and tasteful Welsh matriarch. She sponsored two college students from Wales so that she would have some live-in companionship, but also so that she would have someone with whom she could speak in her native tongue. She missed that, especially since Tom died, although she complained that nowadays 'these kids' don't speak the language very well. She loved the cell phone Richard had given her for Mother's Day and, at this hour on a sunny morning, she was probably having tea on the terrace with the phone by her side.

"Good morning, Ma."

"Dickie! What a pleasant surprise! Good morning to you, too."

"Are you outside on the terrace?"

"Oh yes, dear. The sun is already blazing. I think it's going to be a hot one today. What's it like down there in the City?"

"Oh, the usual fog. Listen, Ma, I'm playing hooky today and I gave you as my excuse to Phyllis. I said I had to check up on you, so if it ever comes up, remember, I spent today with you."

"Sounds like an alibi to me. What are you really doing, if I may ask?'

"I'm driving up to Mount Shasta for the day."

"You and Andy?"

"No, Ma. Andy isn't with me."

"Oh? Anything wrong?" Joan approved of Andy, but she was well aware of the rocky road to romance her son had traveled ever since Billy. She tried to stay neutral, but Richard had kept company with so many men and they all came and went so quickly from his life, or so it seemed to her. Andy was comparatively new. After only three months, Dickie and Andy still were not even talking about living together, so she always half expected to hear of their breakup.

"No, we're fine, Ma."

"Well, what on earth are you going to Mount Shasta for?"

"I can't really explain right now, but I will. I promise."

"Well, be careful, darling. It's a long drive. Are you going up Route Five?"

"Yeah."

"Well, don't drive too fast and watch out for those trucks."

"Yes, Ma. I'll be careful." Richard paused thoughtfully then continued, "Ma? Do you believe in UFO's?"

"Believe in them? I don't like that term, 'believe in.' One believes in Roman Catholicism or the New York Times or the weather report. I believe they could be real, if that's what you mean, although I've certainly never seen one. But, my dear, you're asking the same crazy old lady who talks to her dead husband every day."

"Thanks, Ma. That's all I really wanted to know."

"This doesn't have anything to do with Andy's interest in channeling and the occult, does it?"

"It might, Ma. I'll let you know when all this gets sorted out, I promise. Thanks. You've given me something to think about. Especially the channeling part. Bye-bye, love."

"Good-bye, darling."

Richard took the first exit for Corte Madera and pulled into the parking lot of a fast food restaurant. He dialed directory assistance and got the number for Sarah Fitzsimmons in San Rafael. "Hello, Sarah? This is Andy Gage's friend, Richard Lang. Sorry to be calling so early."

"That's alright, the kids just left for school. What can I do for you?"

"Its about Andy. I'm in Corte Madera. May I stop by for a few minutes?"

"Sure. I have a client at ten o'clock but I'm free until then. This is urgent, isn't it? Is Andy alright?"

"Yeah, but I'd rather talk to you in person."

"Alright. Do you remember where I live? 1187 Alta Vista?"

"Yes, I do."

"Good. See you in, what? About ten, fifteen minutes?"

"Sounds about right, yeah. Thanks."

Richard easily found the house of Andy's friend and the channel for the collective entity known as Riegel. It was on a tree-lined street in a quiet, older, residential part of San Rafael. He recognized the tall front yard fence covered with bougainvillea. He let himself in, stepping through the hole in the flowering vine created by the gate. A light morning fog, unusual in this part of Marin County, cast a soft, diffused light over the short stretch of front yard. The house looked deceptively small from the front, no more than a cottage, really, but it extended almost to the back of a deep lot. Richard had been here twice before, with Andy. He knew it was actually two large cottages connected by a glassed-in garden room.

An attractive woman in her late thirties, with fine features and a halo of curly blond hair, greeted him warmly at the door with Archie, the Jack Russell Terrier. Archie quickly sized-up Richard and, after a few low, harrumphing barks, permitted him to enter. Sarah led him through the house and atrium, as she called it, to the kitchen in back. In her Thai silk caftan, the color of burnt orange, she almost seemed to float rather than walk, her feet barely visible beneath the floor-length hem. Archie was expectantly trotting circles around Richard's ankles, a lime-green tennis ball clamped confidently between his jaws. It was a nice try, but Sarah, in one fluid, well rehearsed motion, walked him directly to the back door and let him outside. She came back to Richard and said, "Please, sit down. Would you like some breakfast? Fruit salad? A bagel? Some coffee? The pot's fresh."

"Just a cup of coffee, thanks. Black." He took a seat at one end of a long, antique oak table. She poured his coffee into a Far Side™ cartoon mug and set it before him, then got her own hand-thrown mug of herbal tea and sat down next to him on his right. This was the cue for her cat, Mehitabel, to jump onto her lap. Mehitabel was mostly Siamese and mostly black with charcoal gray shadings around her face, paws, and the points of her ears. Richard remembered her. He thought she was the most spookily gorgeous cat he had ever seen.

Sarah was a single mom whose late husband (and her in-laws) had left her this house and a hefty inheritance, as well as trust funds for twelve-year-old Callie and nine-year-old Danny. The clients for whom she used her 'gift,' her ability to channel, paid her on a sliding scale. Richard had already judged that, if she was a charlatan, she wasn't in it for the money.

"No coffee for you?" he asked, trying to make conversation.

"I had my quota earlier. Besides, I really can't be too wired on caffeine and channel too. So, what's on your mind?"

Richard had no idea how to begin. He tried just jumping in, "Well, I was wondering ... hoping you might ... I know this is presumptuous of me, but ...."

"What is it?"

"Would you channel for me? I'd like to talk to Riegel."

"You mean right now, don't you?"

"Well, ... yes."

"And this is about Andy, isn't it?"

"Yeah." Richard took in her reaction uncomfortably. She looked peeved.

She frowned and fidgeted and Mehitabel jumped off her lap. She cocked her head, aiming the gaze from her large, brown eyes at him and began, "I know you have your doubts about the channeling phenomenon, so I'm afraid I don't quite understand what it is you are after. But I can tell you that I do not pull Riegel out of my subconscious like a rabbit out of a hat. Riegel is a committee of separate entities and a free agent. And as such, they are not necessarily available on command."

"I'm sorry. I didn't mean any disrespect."

"Okay, apology accepted, but there's something else. I've known Andy for almost three years. I'm enormously fond of him. He's a good and dear friend. If there is something wrong, I want to know about it. Speak to me about it first, understand?"

"Yes. Of course. Sure." Richard nodded, looked down into his coffee mug, then dropped the bomb. "Andy has disappeared."

"Disappeared?"

"About 4:30 this morning."

"How? I mean, how do you know he's ... gone?"

Although somewhat disjointed, Richard rushed out a one-minute version of the last three and a half hours that, nevertheless, managed to be an accurate rendition of Andy's disappearance. Sarah listened, sitting forward, bent over the table, never taking her eyes off him, not daring to move until he sputtered to a stop. And even then she waited in case there was more. When she realized there wasn't, she sat back, still staring at him, mouth slightly open, brow furrowed, as she ferociously tried to make sense of being told her friend had been abducted by aliens from outer space. Richard wasn't prepared for disbelief from a channeler.

"Well, what if he's at work when you make your usual call at 9:15?"

"I'll be relieved, of course, but I'm afraid that's just wishful thinking. Tell me, do you think he'll be there?"

"Hmmm. Not really. Why don't you call right now?"

"But I always call at 9:15."

"Honey, don't sweat it. Work with me. Let's put some energy out there, okay?"

She handed him the phone and he dialed the number of Coffee A-Go-Go, the coffee bar Andy managed at the Embarcadero Center. It was the height of the coffee-on-the-way-to-work rush and the young woman who answered sounded stressed. There was a lot of background noise and she had to speak loudly to make herself heard.

"Hello, Coffee A-Go-Go, Embarcadero!" Richard shouted back, "Hello, may I speak to Andy Gage?"

"Just a minute!"

Richard's eyebrows shot up and he looked at Sarah hopefully, but before he could explain what was happening, the girl came back on.

"Sorry, he's not in yet! Any message?"

"No. No thanks." The girl clicked off immediately, without a good-bye. Sarah didn't have to be a psychic to read the situation in Richard's face. He slowly replaced the telephone handset without looking at her.

"So, he's not there. Okay. Give me ten minutes. I'll see what I can find out." She left Richard in the kitchen and went to the atrium, the room where she customarily channeled. In the midst of all the plants, geodes, and crystals was a grouping of comfortable furniture: a large sofa, a loveseat, and two

16

armchairs. She lit several candles and a stick of incense, as her private ritual dictated, then took a seat in one of the armchairs and made herself relaxed and comfortable. She shut her eyes to begin then opened them and called out to Richard, "Hey! You can join me in here, you know!"

When Richard sat down on the sofa her eyes were closed again. She took several relaxing, deep breaths; her chin dipped down to her chest. When she brought her head up, eyes still closed, and sat up straight, Richard sensed a change in her. He had seen her channel a couple of times and had been surprised at how quickly she went into a trance and how easily Riegel seemed to slide into her body. The skeptical part of him thought it was too easy, another part of him found it eerie. But that subtle change was undeniable. And then there was the voice.

"Good day, Richard."

"Good morning, Riegel."

"And what is it you seek from us this morning?" Sarah's voice was not so subtly altered. She did not sound like herself at all. Riegel spoke through her vocal chords in a politely formal manner, in a vaguely British, vaguely Hindi accent. During his first two visits, Richard had found the voice corny and theatrical. He was still impatient with all this, but could not help but respond to Riegel's serenity with the same well-mannered respectfulness. In fact, he actually became shy in the presence of Riegel and he replied haltingly, like Dorothy before the Great and Powerful Oz.

"My friend ... Andy ... has ... disappeared. And I hoped ... you might be able to tell me if he is alright ... and where he is. Please. And ... that's all."

"Yes. Well. Of course we understand you are concerned because this involves dimensions and realms not of your experience." (Riegel used the imperial, third person, 'we' not for effect but because, as Sarah said, Riegel was actually the combined wisdom of as many as seven entities.) There was a thoughtful pause before 'they' continued.

"We would like to assure you that Ahn Dee is in perfectly safe surroundings and with beings of friendly, caring intentions. He has courageously volunteered to link, in a spirit of good will, with those not only from another world but from what you would call another dimension, another reality. This linking, this exchange, is of mutual benefit and has been agreed upon in advance. This is not what is called in your culture an 'alien abduction'. There is no fear and no harm in this event. Ah! Yes. Yes, your tears are good. Let them go, let them flow freely. No harm will come to Ahn Dee, nor to yourself. We see around you a strong fear of wrongful accusation and we will tell you this is not part of the present situation. Let go of this fear. It does not serve you anymore. May we assist you in this healing?"

Richard had no idea what they were getting at but, operating on pure instinct, he nodded yes. They responded, "Very well. Thank you."

Sarah/Riegel brought a hand up, palm facing Richard, and exhaled loudly and forcefully in his direction. Richard choked back a couple of sobs, and buried his face in his bandana. He was stunned by the breath which hit him like an intense gust of wind and went right through his body. In the midst of so many emotions, he was amazed to feel such visceral comfort. And he was also amazed by Riegel's insight. He had never divulged the full story of Billy's death to Andy, had never told him about the lawsuit against the San Francisco Police Department nor revealed his lingering paranoia concerning the police. Sarah could not possibly have known about all this.

Riegel continued, "We hope that is better. Now then, you already know where to find Ahn Dee. Your intuition, your vision, is correct. The mountain is where you will be reunited. Today. This afternoon. So, go there, as you are already intending to do. But remember to drive carefully. There. You see, we make a little joke. Is there more we can tell you?'

Richard was having difficulty thinking, he was so overwhelmed. Not least of all by his own acceptance of Riegel's information. He felt relieved, encouraged, heartened; and he didn't know why. Why should he believe a woman with her eyes closed talking in another voice? Why should he believe that voice came from disembodied beings? Intellectually it was not to be believed. He should be questioning, indeed protesting, this whole experience. But he could only think of one more question at the moment.

"Where on the mountain will I find him?"

"Do not be concerned about that. Just go. He will find you and you will find him. You'll know where to go. Trust yourself, Richard. Honor yourself and honor your knowingness. It will not lead you astray. It will not betray you. And now, if you will excuse us, we will be going. This one needs a bit of rest and quiet until we return later. We thank you for allowing us to be – or what we hope has been – some assistance to you. And we wish to remind you to honor yourself also for the courageous step you have taken in seeking the perspective of such as we. We understand that many in your world, your culture, would consider this kind of communication incredible and invalid, and are not open to the possibilities of sharing knowledge in this manner. We will go now. Good-bye."

Richard said good-bye, although he felt a little silly doing so. After all, the body that had spoken the words was still there. Sarah coughed and her eyelids fluttered open. She reached for a glass of water on the table beside her and took a long drink. Setting down the glass, she spoke in her own voice, "Well, I feel better about all this now, don't you?"

Unlike many channelers, Sarah did not go completely 'out' when she channeled. She always knew what had been said during her sessions. She usually taped them for her clients' benefit but it wasn't necessary this time. She continued, "I'm glad to know he's alright and that he'll be back today. And I'm very grateful to you."

"Yes? Why?"

"For coming to us with this and for going to get Andy."

Richard smiled, "Well .... Thanks. Thank you too." Before this morning, he had met Sarah twice. He found her pretentious and he knew she thought he was condescending. Richard realized they had yet to really warm up to each other. Maybe this adventure would bring a friendship into focus.

"Will you bring him back here? Or at least call me, won't you?"

"Yes, I will. It might be pretty late by the time we get back, but I'll call you as soon as I've found him. Well, I've got a lot of driving to do, so I'd better be going. Don't get up, I'll let myself out." He took a couple of steps, stopped, then turned back to ask her, "Before I go, one more thing. Where's your bathroom?"

TWO

Nearly four hours of driving on the Interstate had severely eroded the sense of confidence Richard had taken away from his session with Riegel. With nothing to do but drive and think, that exhilaration was now a memory. He was almost as wracked with anxiety and doubt as before. At least he was grateful to be driving, to be doing anything rather than sitting at his desk in his office, trying to make himself concentrate on work. Hours of cruising up the sun-baked Sacramento Valley, past mile after mile of irrigated farmland, gave him plenty of time to stew.

He remembered his other sessions with Sarah and Riegel; how, at Andy's gentle insistence, he had consented to see what the phenomenon of channeling was all about. The first time had been with a group of eight or ten other wackos; the second time with Andy alone. He made an effort to be respectful while it was going on, but he'd given Andy a pretty hard time after the group session. Couldn't he see that Sarah was an actress, a very good one, admittedly, but an actress nevertheless? "And what was all that didn't-you-notice-the-change-in-energy crap? Did the lights dim? No. Did the candles flicker? No. He remembered how Andy sat calmly and patiently in the passenger seat of the car and just let Richard go on about the flaky, meaningless New Age jargon, like 'energy' and 'expanded consciousness' and the widely touted, so-called magical powers of crystals and herbal infusions and acupuncture and acupressure and tai chi and Reiki and so on and so forth until he ran out of spleen. He had been surprised at himself, by how galled he was about it, but he just kept 'heaping on the ridicule'.

He caught glimpses of Andy listening to his rant, his eyes wide open and focused intently on Richard, and he thought, didn't he have an ego? He should have been hurt and angry, but he was apparently unflappable. And when Richard finished, Andy's only comment was, "Boy! You really need to be in control of your mind, don't you? But that's okay. In fact, I love that about you." Richard was so utterly taken aback, he remembered wondering about Andy's sincerity. He doubted anyone could really love him after such a cynical tirade. But Andy's remark, whether sincere or sarcastic, had completely disarmed him, and the tension, apparently all of it his own, had evaporated instantly. He shook is head in disbelief at the memory.

During his second contact with Riegel he kept his skeptical defenses up. He told himself he was only there because Andy wanted him to be. He didn't address Riegel at all. He sat there quietly in 'the presence' and just listened. It was Andy's agenda all the way. And what an agenda it turned out to be! Andy spoke of the disquieting dreams and meditation experiences he had been having of late. He thought his desire for conscious contact with friendly extraterrestrials was actually being answered. From 'their' so-called 'multi-dimensional' perspective, Riegel confirmed that it was indeed so. Richard could barely contain his shock at what he was hearing. He remembered thinking, "This is utterly ridiculous! This is beyond belief!" It was all he could do to keep his mouth shut. But although he managed to keep quiet, he couldn't keep still. He fidgeted and chewed his fingernails until Andy gave him a puzzled look. Another scornful rant was definitely building inside him for the ride home. And yet . . . .

Just before the end of the session, Riegel surprised him, acknowledging his presence by asking him directly if he had any questions. "No, thank you," was his terse reply. And then they said something like, "We wish to honor you for being here tonight with Ahn Dee. This is a courageous and loyal and loving gift you give to him. We encourage you to trust your own innate powers of discrimination, for you are a very discerning person and this will serve the both of you in your future together. You have much to learn from each other and much to share." What a helluva thing to say! Richard had never been addressed in that way before.

He felt as though Riegel or Sarah had seen right through him, and while they or she could have chosen to mock him, even the cynic in him could not discern the slightest trace of sarcasm. Instead they spoke of honoring him. The ride home that night was remarkable for Richard's silence. Disarmed again, he simply couldn't think of a reply when Andy said, "I thought Riegel's comment to you was very accurate. I think it was very validating too, especially of us as a couple." Richard smiled wanly and nodded. This time it was Richard's reticence that proved to be unsettling to Andy.

Later, back at Richard's, Andy could not begin lovemaking until he got some reassurance that Richard was okay, or at least coping, with all this crazy paranormal stuff. When it came to openly discussing his psychic beliefs, and his 'sensitivities' or his 'tendencies' (as he also put it), he was well aware of the fear and ridicule the unexplainable could elicit.

"You know," he said, "back where I come from in Indiana, they would say that I am a blasphemer and that I am working with Satan. And they would not say such things in irony." He said his trust in an expanded awareness made him a spiritual outlaw and outsider as surely as being gay made him a social and sexual pariah. Andy felt there was a genuine need for discretion and he hoped Richard would understand that. He said that, for him, sharing this side of himself was like having to come out all over again at age thirty-seven. He told Richard he certainly didn't expect him to 'convert' to his spiritual perspective, but he was afraid of losing Richard's respect.

As he spilled his guts that evening, he said he was worried that Richard felt threatened to have their relationship validated in such an unconventional manner. And today, as Richard replayed the scene in his memory, the hairs

23

on the back of his neck stood up when he remembered Andy saying, "Maybe I'm going places you can't go." Then he confessed that he would understand if Richard were having second thoughts about it. He wouldn't even blame him if he wanted to bail out of their fledgling relationship. It was the most heartfelt, honest, and longest monologue Andy had ever laid on Richard, and it too disarmed him.

His response to what Andy had to say that night was carefully thought out and 'edited.' He could not allow himself to say that he doubted he would ever take it as seriously as Andy, and he was glad now that he hadn't. But what he did say, as far as it went, was an honest account of how he felt. Crazy or not, Andy was the best thing that had come Richard's way in a long, long time. Richard was adamant when it came to sticking with the relationship. He said he had no intentions whatsoever of bailing out and he meant it then as he meant it now. But he remembered admitting his discomfort, his disbelief and his distrust, especially his distrust of Sarah.

And he had to ask himself, why was he trusting Sarah now? Sure, when she channeled Riegel, something felt different: something was different. It was maddeningly ineffable, and yet undeniable. But, like today, it didn't seem to last outside of her presence and, in his cynicism, he jumped on that. Was she practicing some sort of subtle, cult-like mind control? What about that scary incident in Japan where that cult leader told his followers to release toxic gas in the Tokyo subway?

For a moment that thought made him very uneasy, and then he felt very foolish. Sarah, the mind-controlling leader of a suicide cult? Sarah, some sort of Minion of Satan? Something inside him could not, rationally, make either one of those accusations stick. He certainly had no hard evidence. What was the proof? He didn't always know if he believed in God, let alone in Satan. Maybe Andy was right, he really did have to keep a tight lid on his mind. Look where it went when he didn't.

But here he was on his way to Mount Shasta, all because of a bizarrely unexplainable disappearance and at the prompting of a bizarrely unexplainable vision, now sanctioned by a bizarrely unexplainable voice. How could any of this be real?

No matter how he looked at it, it was surreal. It was crazy. And how could he accept this unreality? Or was he crazy? Or was Andy crazy? No, no. That was just fear talking. It was sane to be questioning all this, wasn't it? No, he hadn't lost it yet. But he was going to if he didn't start thinking more positively. So he tried to direct his thoughts to more pleasant associations, like the first weekend he and Andy spent at his mother's. He was nervous about having them meet. Ma didn't usually have much patience with the men he brought home to her. Her bullshit meter was finely tuned. And, annoyingly, it usually turned out to be highly accurate. If Ma didn't like someone, they usually didn't last long before Richard found out she was right about them. But even worse, Ma could be really obnoxious when she got on her high horse. It was best not to show any fear or self doubt around her. And it was probably because it never occurred to Andy to be afraid that they clicked. They hit it off so well, in fact, she even let Andy help her cook Saturday night's dinner.

Listening to the two of them talk as they worked, Richard saw each of them in a pleasant new light, learned new things about both of them, nothing major, just stories he hadn't heard either one of them tell before. It was wonderful to listen to the two of them pulling things out of each other in the sweet, trusting safety zone of their instant fondness for each other. Later, after dinner, around the fire, Andy got all three of them to share personal accounts of the supernatural. Andy told of an encounter with a 'ghost' back in Chicago, and his mother told about his father's near death experience, an event that had taken place well before Richard or his brother and sister were born and which genuinely shocked him when he heard it that night for the first time.

And finally Richard was surprised to hear himself tell of the battle premonition, the warning of danger that had saved his life in Vietnam. He'd never told anyone about it before, not even Billy, because he'd put it out of his mind as too crazy or else blamed it on the drugs. He'd definitely been stoned out of his gourd, tripping his brains out when it happened. He was surprised he could even remember it. He hadn't even thought about it in years. It came back to him that evening and he shared it in the warm, accepting company of the two people he cared about the most. And it was Andy who almost convinced him it was something other than drugs that opened his eyes and guided him out of harm's way. Certainly Ma was convinced. That Sunday night on the drive back to San Francisco, Andy remarked, "I really like your mom, you know."

"Yeah. I think it's mutual."

"I wish my mom were more like her." Richard heard the pain under that veiled expression of regret. Andy had nothing to say about his family. Richard knew better than to try to get him to talk about his brother, mother and father back in Madison, Indiana, so he simply acknowledged the compliment. "That's nice to hear. But, you know, most people don't like her. At least, not at first. She's kind of tough, direct, opinionated. Sometimes she's downright confrontational. And I guess you noticed that she's not a gusher, even though she liked you."

"Oh, I noticed. She's a piece of work, alright. You know, she looks amazingly like Barbara Stanwyck. Fantastic cheekbones. She even has some of Stanwyck's mannerisms, that feisty, brittle, crustiness that's so prominent in her later films. And she's got Stanwyck's shifty, beady eyes. I love that sharp, always thinking, gleam in them."

"It's a good thing you didn't mention it to Ma, she hates the comparison. Lots of people see it and tell her, and she's not always very gracious about it."

"I had a hunch it wasn't the thing to say. And how do you suppose I knew that? Mere coincidence? I think not!"

Richard chuckled at the memory. Andy talked a lot about synchronicity, unseen forces conspiring to bring people, objects, events together. But he also had a way of poking fun at the occult, he didn't always take it or himself very seriously. Then he remembered what else Andy had said, "I don't suppose your mother would go to Halloween in the Castro with us, would she?"

"Oh-oh. What do you have in mind?"

"Well, I was just thinking: dress her up in a gaucho hat, a suede bolero jacket with a matching maxi skirt, put her in boots with spurs, hand her a riding crop and she's Victoria Barkley in 'The Big Valley.' The queens would go wild!"

"Or flee in terror," Andy added as an afterthought. "But wouldn't it be a hoot?"

Richard did think it would be a hoot. And, indeed, they hooted. The more they thought about it, the more they laughed. They tried to get their hysterics under control but every time they thought they were done laughing, another convulsion shook the car. And then Andy set them off once more with, "Oh, please stop me before I think again!"

The memory made Richard beam. He admired a good sense of humor in anyone, but in a lover it was essential. Billy had been great at mock pomposity and bursting the bubble of pretentiousness, as was Andy. But Andy ran the gamut of humor from dry self-mockery to outrageous non sequitur. What is funny, like what is beautiful, is in the eye of the beholder. It was Richard's great good fortune to have found someone who not only shared many of his ideas of what was funny, but expanded on them in bright and often unexpected ways. Richard did not consider himself to be particularly funny, but he knew he was an appreciative audience for Andy.

He probably didn't know that it was also Andy's great good fortune to have found someone who he could so easily and readily entertain.

But, of course, their relationship wasn't all laughs. And Richard was well aware of that. Andy could be quite serious as well as funny. His reticence wasn't always placid. Sometimes there were darker concerns going through his mind, thoughts to which Richard was not granted access. Neither one had entered the relationship a starry-eyed romantic. They were both older men with dead lovers in their pasts. They were both survivors of the great pandemic, but it had personally touched Andy much more deeply than Richard. Or so it seemed to Richard. And there was twelve years' difference in their ages: they were practically from different generations. While they were both recovering substance abusers, their patterns of abuse were different. So too their methods of healing. They'd had different life experiences: they came from different social backgrounds, even from different parts of the country. Consequently, they held differing opinions about many things.

They weren't even gay in the same way. Andy was much more liberal. He was more accepting of the diversity in the gay community. At least he gave more lip service to it. He was more 'out' than Richard could ever conceive of being except when it came to public displays of affection. Richard was used to it from living in San Francisco for twenty-five years. Andy still carried something of the small town closet with him, despite more than a decade living in Chicago's Boy's Town. He was as contradictory as anyone he'd ever known and Richard often didn't have any idea what Andy was about. But he had Richard using the word 'queer' in the new, contemporary way that all the 'kids' were using it, the way that was supposed to defuse the negative, pejorative connotation, even if he wasn't wholly comfortable with it and thought it was a bit arrogant and in-your-face.

And then there was that whole damn, getting-in-touch-with-your-feminine-self thing. That was something Richard just could not find humorous. Richard had always been a devotee of the leather and Levi segment of the gay population. Drag queens got on his nerves. Only last month Andy had said something to him that had really upset him. He was explaining how it had not been possible for him to accept the evidence of his own growing psychic abilities until he'd learned more fully to accept and 'embrace' (as he put it) his homosexuality. He went on to say, "If intuition is feminine, then it certainly helps to be gay."

Well, that just set Richard off. He remembered how he'd cringed when he heard that, how they had their first real argument over Richard's don't-put-yourself-down-you-aren't-effeminate reply. It was the first time he had seen the usually sweet-tempered Andy get really pissed off. He accused him of being "some kind of homophobic misogynist." Andy insisted neither 'feminine' nor 'effeminate' was an insult. Gender 'affectations,' as he called them, had little or nothing to do with sexuality. Gender was 'a societal construct' of what, by consensus, society considered to be masculine or feminine. Gender was about appearances and therefore 'fluid' and not to be confused with sexual orientation or affectional preference. His harangue ended with a bang as a very agitated Andy exploded, "I know, I know you don't get it! But you will! Someday you will. Someday you'll understand that gender is not about genitals ... or ... or ... rather that it's only about genitals! And all that means is who gets to plant the seed and who gets to grow the baby!" Richard remembered how shocking it was to witness Andy's passion unleashed. He was completely unprepared for what came next.

When Andy paused to take a breath, and saw the look of astonishment on Richard's face, he burst out laughing. Richard, seeing it was alright, began laughing too. He told Andy, "Boy, you really had me there for a minute! I thought you were serious."

Then Andy laughed even harder and said, "I was serious! I am serious! That's what's so funny!" It was great that Andy could laugh at himself, but Richard still didn't get it.

Oh, well. So he had to admit, after three months, there was still a lot he didn't know about Andy. He didn't understand why their sex life was so inconsistent. When it was good. it was out of this world! But sometimes Andy just wasn't there, just wasn't approachable for sex. Of course, that only made Richard want him more. He enjoyed the seduction, the chase, the catch. He loved the foreplay as much as the Big 'O'. And he really enjoyed breaking in a new partner. But he couldn't really say what Andy enjoyed. Sometimes that bothered him, but not for long. After all, Richard had nothing but confidence in his own sexual prowess. He had always been 'the Man,' 'the Top,' and he knew he could still go into any bar in San Francisco and go home with whomever he pleased. If Andy wasn't always responsive, well, it just made it more interesting, because he genuinely enjoyed the challenge of finding out what made another man tick. Yes, Andy was often a mystery to him, but a tantalizing one.

He still didn't really understand those three times when Andy had decided to stop seeing him. He just said they were going too fast. So why did that mean they had to stop seeing each other? Richard just accepted the relationship. Andy seemed to fight it. Okay, that was another way they didn't agree on things. But Richard had known a lot of gay men, 'known' in every sense of the word, and he could always just agree to disagree and let it go at that. He had long ago given up either expecting or wanting a congruent lifestyle with his partner of the moment. So if Andy wanted to take it slowly, that was okay. If he wanted to talk to extraterrestrials, that was okay. If he identified with his feminine side, that was just fine too, as long as he didn't go too far with it. Personally, he felt that Andy's trouble in bed was his conflict over his masculine and feminine selves. "If he'd give me the chance, I could straighten that out for him, real good."

It was just north of Red Bluff. The temperature outside the car was 100 degrees Fahrenheit. Richard didn't know it was that hot, but he knew he needed more cold air in the car. He interrupted his erotic roadway reverie to turn up the air conditioning. When he looked back to the road, he was startled by what he only now noticed looming over the horizon before him. Although at least seventy-five miles away, the mountain so dominated the landscape it seemed to be coming to meet him. The chill of recognition again took a slither down his back. He stared at it, transfixed, until he almost rear-ended an old pickup truck crawling along at 60 m.p.h.. With no one on his tail he was able to brake in time to avoid a collision, but his mother's (and Riegel's) admonition to drive carefully came back to him and he muttered, "Sorry, Ma," before he stepped on the gas, passed the pickup and resumed his 75 m.p.h. cruising speed.

He kept his eyes on the road but could not help but glance up at frequent intervals to look at the majestic peak. He didn't know why this one was so uniquely distracting. The roadmap told him it was 14,162 feet high. But he'd seen plenty of mountains as tall or taller. Of course, they had been part of whole mountain ranges of equally impressive stature. He could see there were mountains to the west of Shasta, but none of them was tall enough to be capped by snow. In this grand-scale, big sky California landscape, Mount Shasta simply stuck out like the proverbial sore thumb. There were a few cloud puffs scattered randomly across the hot forenoon sky.

Occasionally Richard noticed the heat waves coming off the road, and off the hood of his car. That's when he saw the mountain wrinkling, waving, unfurling like a flag in a lazy breeze, like a filmy transparency, an optical illusion. But looking beyond the heat waves, he saw the solid, three dimensional cone of a dormant volcano. And beyond that, the sleeping power, the unselfconscious power that is oblivious to its own strength; the unlimited and immeasurable power of a force of nature.

When he began to pass exits for Redding he checked his gas gauge and was surprised to see the indicator, not just on low but, on reserve. His stomach reminded him he needed fuel as well, and, though he didn't really want to stop, not even for food and gasoline, he took the next exit off I-5 and turned into the first Unocal station he saw. Behind the self-serve pumps was a full-service repair garage with a routine assortment of cars and trucks parked around the edge of the tarmac and two on the lifts. There was one other car at the pumps, the driver nowhere to be seen. He stepped out of the car and into a blast furnace. His face and bare arms felt the heat immediately, but the car's coolness lingered just on the surface, a momentary buffer, micro millimeters thin, that he could also feel as he moved to the gas nozzle. By the time he'd filled his tank, sweat was dampening his T-shirt, denim jeans, underwear, even his socks.

As he approached the office to pay for his gas, he noticed it was full of customers. Richard assumed they were all escaping the heat. But, oddly, they were all clustered around one wall-sized window looking toward the mountain. Once inside the office, blessedly air-conditioned, he discovered they were also listening to the radio turned up loud. It was tuned to a local call-in show. A female caller was talking, and Richard was not paying any particular attention because he just wanted to pay for his gas and get going, when he was grabbed by the voice saying, "They sure are puttin' on a show over Shasta today! I've seen 'em before, but nothin' like this; and not in broad daylight either. They're just zoomin' around up there like the Blue Angels or somethin'. The star bursts are my favorite. And the formations! Well, I counted twenty-five in one diamond shape alone."

Richard gave his credit card to the chunky redheaded mechanic with the red goatee who stepped away from the window to attend to business and told him he was pump number five. The guy checked the amount of the purchase and filled in a blank receipt. Richard asked, "What's going on out there?"

"UFO's over Mount Shasta," he pointed at the window wall behind him, but the guys were crowded together and Richard couldn't see a thing. He wanted to run over and push them aside to see, but instead, he just smiled from behind his sunglasses and said, "Is that right? UFO's, huh?" He even added a bemused chuckle to emphasize his cool.

"This here's the fifth or sixth call about it. They got a TV crew headin' up there now, but I'll bet you they disappear before they can get 'em on film." Richard listened and impatiently tapped his foot while the mechanic ran his card through the machine. The mechanic handed him his receipt to sign, Richard signed it, handed it back to the mechanic who tore off his copy and handed it back to him with his card. Richard put both in his wallet and said, "Thanks. I'm heading up that way. Guess I'll go check it out."

"Well, good luck," the mechanic grinned. "Don't let 'em getcha."

Playing it cool, resisting the urge to look at the mountain, he sauntered back to his car, got in, buckled up quickly and started the engine. Then he looked. He saw nothing, not even a cloud, near the mountain peak. He glanced at the office. They were all still looking at the mountain. He looked again and still there was nothing. Could they see something he couldn't? He turned on the radio, and when he found the call-in show, put the car in gear and took off.

Back on the Interstate, another caller was droning on about the peace and quiet of the area being destroyed by all the 'crackpots and New Age dipsy doodles.' Though he used his grandfather's vocabulary, the voice was that of a young man. Somehow, his logic blamed the 'weirdoes' for 'attracting the flying saucers.' It wasn't the strange phenomenon that bothered him, but the strange people he blamed for 'causing it.' The edge of defiance in his tone led Richard to dismiss him as just another redneck, dumber than dirt and proud of it. He was about to turn him off in disgust when the caller, apparently watching the sky as he talked, shouted, "Wow! There's some more!"

Richard looked and this time he saw something. The lights formed a scraggly V wedge-like a formation of migrating geese. They were small but bright as mirror reflections. He counted twelve of them moving from left to right, making a pass over the mountain. As they flew east, the scraggly V snapped into a sharp, precise, and symmetrical V which unsettlingly pointed west while continuing to move east. Once they had gone past the mountain's peak, they reversed the whole procedure, ending up as a scraggly V pointing east while moving west. When they reached the spot in the sky from which they had started out, the lights simply blinked off. "So that's what UFO's look like," he thought. "Top secret military aircraft on maneuvers? Highly unlikely." Those were very 'public' maneuvers like he'd never seen any plane do before. What was it supposed to mean? Was it some sort of signal?

One thing was obvious to Richard: it was a display of aerodynamic virtuosity designed to impress watchers on the ground. And Richard was impressed, alright. But he was also disappointed. Somehow the reality of distant tiny lights flying around in the sky didn't seem as awesome as the idea of flying saucers from outer space. Certainly not as they were portrayed in the movies of his boyhood; movies like: 'Invaders From Mars,' or 'Earth vs. The Flying Saucers.' They may have been 1950's era Hollywood special effects, but he remembered the look fondly. They were totally cool! To his then unsophisticated teen brain, they were also completely believable, and utterly fantastic. What did one of these 'lights,' one of these 'UFOs,' look like? He just had to see one up close. Well, maybe not too close. He didn't want to be like the fools in those movies who took risks and got too close and got incinerated by the aliens' heat ray. Okay, he knew that was being silly, but it did lead him to wonder what the extraterrestrials who had taken Andy were like. He decided not to think about that. Instead he scanned the sky for more of those strange lights. Apparently the lights took a fifteen or twenty minute intermission between shows.

Richard kept driving, even pushing up the speed limit set by his cruise control. The mountain was getting closer. He crossed Shasta Lake on Shasta Dam and watched twenty or more single lights materialize in a vast ring around the mountain. He saw them rush in, at breathtaking speed, to converge into a single light above the summit only to fly back out, at the same 'faster than a speeding bullet' velocity, to their original positions, rotate two spaces, then repeat the maneuver. Traffic on the highway had thinned out dramatically. Richard drove past roadside rest areas and scenic overlooks jammed with cars, RV's, trucks of every kind, their drivers and passengers standing beside them looking toward the mountain. After another suitable intermission, the lights were back in what gave the illusion of being a sort of stacked, three dimensional tic-tac-toe formation. As he drove and watched, he saw this arrangement collapse into one flat square, a single plane comprised of twenty-seven lights. 'They' – the alien pilots – even tilted the plane to show how flat it was. This plane of lights then gave the illusion of flying through the mountain, appearing to slice the cone of Mount Shasta, like a giant razor blade, at an angle parallel to the ground. This maneuver was repeated three more times, the slice coming from all major points of the compass. The effect was astonishing: were the lights that disappeared actually going through the mountain? Richard was not the only one saying to himself, "How the hell did they do that?"

Watching for the return of the lights, he almost missed the exit for the town of Mount Shasta. He slammed on the brakes and skidded into the turnoff. If the scare he'd given himself hadn't, the two lane road into town forced him to drive more slowly. The fields and trees, the occasional house or out-building, passing by on either side of the road, slowed him down inside too, calming him, bringing him down to earth after the flying he'd been doing on the Interstate. His growling stomach also brought him back to earth and he decided to look for a place to pick up some food, as he'd meant to do in Redding. Not eating was making him 'edgy.' He looked at his watch and saw it was almost 12:50. He hated to do it but, he thought he'd better check in with Phyllis, before she went to lunch.

"Good afternoon, All The Best Realty, this is Phyllis speaking, how may I help you?'

"Hi, Phyllis, it's me, just checking in. How's everything going?"

"Oh, just fine, Mr. Lang. Ron and Mitzi have taken care of your morning clients, so everything's under control here. And how is your mother?"

"She's okay. She sounded a little down on the phone last night, so I thought I'd pay her a surprise visit. I think she's fine now. I took her to breakfast and I'm running some errands for her." ("Whoa! Easy, Richard," he told himself. "Watch the embellishments, you don't want to get yourself too deeply into this lie.")

"Uh-huh. Well, that's nice. I'm glad to hear she's doing fine." She didn't believe him for a minute. He winced and frowned at the unctuous tone in her poisonously honeyed voice. Honestly, sometimes he just wanted to slap her.

She continued, "Oh, by the way, do you know your answering machine at home is broken?"

"Uh, yeah, the tape broke and I haven't had a chance to replace it."

"Uh-huh. Well then ... I guess this means you won't be coming in later this afternoon, am I right?"

"Yes, Phyllis, I won't be coming in later this afternoon. Why? Is there something that needs my attention?"

"Oh, no, no. Mitzi and Ron are doing a fine job, an excellent job. And I can reshuffle Jack's schedule so he can take your three and four o'clock appointments."

She was so cheerful, so very accommodating, she practically sang, "I was just checking." ("You were just prying, you mean. And trying to spread a layer of guilt at the same time.") Richard showed her that he could smile through clenched teeth too. "Okay then! I'll see you tomorrow, Phyllis. Thanks for holding down the fort."

"You're welcome. Have a nice afternoon, Mr. Lang, whatever you do."

"Right! Thanks. Same to you, Phyllis." ("God, what a bitch! And just why, exactly, did she try my home phone when I said I'd be with my mother?") This was precisely the reason he had never given her the number of his car phone. In fact, he had never even told her he had a car phone, although he wouldn't be surprised if she knew about it anyway. He thought about calling his mother to see if she had been grilled by Phyllis, but when he tried, there was no answer. "Oh, hell! I can't let Phyllis worry me now."

True enough, but the woman was impossible to ignore. She was so entrenched, and so well-versed, in passive-aggressive behavior, that this conversation was, like many conversations with Phyllis, a thinly-veiled contest of wills. In his life, Richard had endured a lot of control queens, but she could give lessons to some of the neurotic faggots he'd known. A divorced (no surprise), single mother of twin girls (age 10), Phyllis came from a very small Midwestern town, he didn't remember where, but it was apparently the kind of town where it is possible to perfect the smiling backstab to an astonishing degree. Her behavior was an almost constant source of friction around the office. She liked to keep things stirred up. It proved impossible to discipline her because she had an uncanny sense of just how far she could go and just how hard to push things. And she was also smart enough and devious enough to always keep her butt covered. Richard knew he should get rid of her. But her efficiency and attention to detail, while maddening at times, were essential and, he knew, absolutely reliable. She ran the office so well, it was difficult to conceive of any one person replacing her. Well, it was difficult for Richard, and, after all, he was the boss. Right?

His stomach growled and, mercifully, just around the next bend in the road was a grocery store surrounded by a gravel parking lot. The building, with its gray, weathered wood exterior, looked to be of 1920's vintage or earlier. Hanging from the roof of the covered porch was an artfully carved wooden sign, painted in bright and fresh colors, the art nouveau letters proclaiming, "Nature's Way Organic Foods, est. 1974." There were no cars parked in front and only two pickup trucks in back in the shade of a stand of fir trees. One of the trucks was the store truck with the same lettering on the door as the hanging sign, although dust almost obscured the message. The other truck, without wheels, was mounted on cement blocks and the hood was raised. There was no engine inside.

When he got out of the car, Richard immediately noticed the air temperature. It was cooler, by maybe ten degrees, than it had been in Redding. Though still quite hot, a little altitude made a big difference. He strolled inside, letting the screen door bang shut behind him, perched his sunglasses on his head and began to look around. He paced the aisles methodically, his gaze went everywhere, quickly scanning the shelves. He wanted a snack but he didn't have time to waste shopping. He chose quickly only those items that instantly grabbed his attention. He helped himself to a pound of trail mix and picked out a beautiful pair of red delicious apples. He snatched a liter bottle of spring water from the cooler, then impulsively lifted an additional gallon jug. He wrestled this armload to the checkout counter, but it wasn't until he plopped it all down by the cash register that he noticed there was no one to wait on him.

"Hello? Anybody here?" He waited and listened. There was no response. All he could hear was the quiet whir of a ceiling fan and the hum of the refrigeration units. "Hey! I'd like to buy some food! Anybody here?" Richard slammed the service bell rapidly several times with his palm, filling the store with sharp, nerve jangling reverberations that quickly faded to the same electric silence. A wasp, perhaps awakened by the noisy outburst, came buzzing out of nowhere, circled Richard's head once, ominously, then flew off back to nowhere. There was still no human response.

"Well, what the hell ...?" he muttered and pulled out his wallet. He tossed a five on the counter and gathered his purchases. As he was putting them in a large, double-strength, brown paper bag, he saw a display of big, fat, rich-looking 'all natural' brownies with nuts. They seemed to say, or rather, scream, "Buy us for Andy! Buy us for Andy!" He picked up two and added them to his take-out lunch. He decided that three were even better, so he tossed another one in the bag. He briefly debated whether or not to leave more money, then decided not to: "Serves 'em right for leaving the place unattended."

He opened the passenger-side front door and put the bag on the seat for easy access. On his way around to the driver's side, he felt a tingle, like static electricity, all over his body. He opened his door but hesitated to get in. He didn't know why, but he decided to look up at the sky, directly overhead. Row after row of lights, in flying wedge formation, were passing over as if in review. They were much closer now, much larger, though he still could not make out any detail. They were round and they were dazzlingly bright but that was the extent of it. The sight caused him to suck in his breath and exhale. "Ho - ly shit!" he hissed. He tried to count them but the number in each row varied, though most of them seemed to contain seven, and the number of rows was hard to count because of the movement. He stopped trying after ten rows. They crossed the sky majestically from northwest to southeast, as if heading for Mount Lassen. But the eerily silent procession was strangely climaxed as, one by one, front to back, the rows of lights blinked off, as if disappearing into some invisible time warp. The message this time? It was clear to Richard: "Show's over, folks, thanks for watching." But if 'they' were leaving, then he had to work fast to find Andy. He peeled out of the parking lot, throwing a rooster tail of dust and gravel.

Driving along as fast as the road would allow, he guzzled water and chewed handfuls of trail mix, wondering, "Where is it?, where is it?" He was frantic to find the way up the mountain. He made up his plan on the spot: he would head up the mountain as far as his car would take him. That was as much of a plan as he could manage. He knew that Riegel had said not to worry about how he was going to find Andy, but he couldn't help it, he had to have a plan, no matter how lame. He kept himself alert, thinking that any minute he might get a clue or a hunch, maybe even another vision, about where he would find Andy.

The speed limit dropped to twenty-five miles an hour. He was now driving through downtown Mount Shasta. He saw vans, cars and pickup trucks parked along the street but he didn't see any people. He cruised along slowly, watching for a road sign that would direct him up the mountain, which now filled almost half the sky to his right. When he did begin to see people, they were in twos and threes and it was puzzling: some looked stricken – a woman was sobbing in the arms of a man – and others looked excitedly happy, as if they were playing hooky to go to the circus. They seemed either to be going to or coming from a patch of green lawn visible a block ahead on the right. A sign announcing the Alpine Meadow indicated a right turn. Richard spontaneously followed the suggestion and found himself at what he took to be the town square.

He hit the brake and slowed to a crawl. Roughly three hundred people filled the square, most were milling around or standing around, waiting for something more to happen. Ahead of him was his destination, the immense, rugged cone of Mount Shasta. But between him and his destination was a sight that made him brake to a dead stop. At the end of the square was a roadblock, and there were police cars, with lights slowly flashing. There were also three cars ahead of his. Anxiously, he looked for an exit, a side street, an alley, anything, as long as it was a way out. There was a TV mobile news van parked on the grass with its satellite dish and a twenty-foot antenna deployed on top. Folks crossed back and forth, walking on the street in front, beside, and behind his car. In the rearview mirror he saw two more cars behind him. He was trapped now. He could only go forward. He saw another crying woman being comforted by two men and a pale little girl. Three boys on dirt bikes tore across the square, weaving between stands of people and trees, followed by three romping mutts: small, medium, and large. They managed to avoid a group of about twenty-five people in a circle, holding hands, eyes closed and heads bowed. How could performing lights in the sky cause such a range of responses? Richard hadn't expected anything like this.

What had happened to warrant this roadblock and this skittish throng? The underlying mood of the mob was uneasy, and Richard felt it turning up the heat under his own simmering pot of apprehension and dread.

He pulled ahead slowly and stopped again. The state police were now only two cars away. They seemed to be sending cars to the right instead of straight ahead toward the mountain. He looked left and right. He was beginning to sweat, in spite of the air conditioning. Between the news van and the police cars, in the far ground beyond the roadblock, he saw some kind of relief tent where a military transport truck was unloading four people. They were two young men and two young women dressed in hiking gear, but without backpacks. He couldn't read anything into their neutral expressions, but then, they were almost thirty yards away.

Richard looked farther to his left, to the news van. Beside it, a pretty, dark-haired Latina was brightly lit and holding a microphone, which she periodically stuck under the mouth of a police officer standing next to her. Because the officer was wearing a uniform different from the California Highway Patrol or the Park Service, he guessed it was a representative of the county police, possibly the local sheriff, who was being interviewed. Was she being broadcast live, or merely recorded for the news at 11:00? Did lights in the sky really merit this kind of emergency response and media coverage? Or had something else happened? What was waiting for him on Mount Shasta? He inched ahead one more car space.

More importantly, how was he going to get by this roadblock and get up the mountain that loomed even more dramatically before him? Then he literally jumped to attention in his seat belt when he saw three more men climb off the olive-drab transport. The last one off could have been Andy, same lanky build and reddish blonde coloring, and Richard had to stare very hard and long before he was satisfied that it wasn't his guy. He felt like a plug had been pulled as all his enthusiasm just seemed to drain away. His stomach was in knots so he took a swig of water. He wiped the sweat from his face and neck with his bandana. The car ahead turned right. The helmeted cop motioned him forward.

The butterflies in his stomach churned up his gut in a frantic attempt to either escape or commit suicide trying. The big man felt pretty small and helpless inside, but he did what he always did when he felt like he was in over his head. He rolled down his window and turned on the charm. He noted the name tag, gave officer Wilson his most laid back, macho grin, and began to speak, but so did the officer, and they both spoke at once, on top of each other.

"Hey, what's happening, officer?"

"You can't go up the mountain, sir."

They both stopped speaking simultaneously too and looked at each other for a few tense seconds, one's sun-glassed gaze reflected in the other's sun-glassed gaze. The stocky, tanned, clean-shaven, square-jawed, twenty-something officer Wilson caused Richard a momentary flashback to a motorcycle cop fetishist of his acquaintance, from his distant, South of Market, heavy-into-leather past. It was so far in his past it was before Billy. It was before cop uniforms had become triggers for his rage and his fear. The very desirable policeman was a living mixed metaphor. It momentarily threw Richard off. Then the officer began to speak in his rich, bass baritone voice. "Sorry, sir, but you'll have to turn off here, we aren't letting anyone up the mountain at this time."

Turn off? Turn away? Give up his search? Richard gripped the steering wheel and shifted nervously in his seat. Somebody or something had pulled the plug on his bravado too. He didn't have a clue about what to say next. Things were getting hazy, he felt a little light-headed. Was he going to pass out? But no!

There was Andy's look-alike, walking around behind officer Wilson, looking closer than ever and, as if in a dream, he heard himself stammering, "Well-uh, well gee. I mean ...." And then, with surprising candor and conviction, he simply stated, "Look, officer, my buddy's up there and I was supposed to meet him. I've got to find him. Couldn't I just go up and take a look around?"

"Well, you see, sir, we've evacuated most of the campers and hikers. Maybe you should check at that tent over there. Your buddy may already be down here." Richard saw himself clearly in the policeman's standard-issue mirrored sunglasses. He was faltering. He couldn't help it. The man was looking at him intensely, but it was impossible to read his eyes and, therefore, impossible to know what the intensity signified. And inside himself Richard was fighting to erase the sneering look of mockery from his nightmare past that was bleeding into the present moment. There are times when we are never aware of the gut-wrenching courage it takes for someone to say something as simple as, "But I've already checked and he's not there. Let me go look for him." He hoped and prayed it hadn't sounded impertinent, or desperate, or, God forbid, 'faggy.'

Officer Wilson leaned closer, almost sticking his head inside Richard's car. "Sir, my orders are ...." he paused and then said, with a compassionate tone that stunned Richard, " ... let him go." He snapped back, stood up straight, and affirmed loudly, for all his colleagues to hear, "It's okay, let this guy go through." He turned back to Richard and added, in a low, conspiratorial voice, "Check back here, with me, when you've found him. I'll be taking down your license number, so don't forget. Now get going. And drive carefully!"

"Thank you! Thank you very much!"

He took off as carefully as his euphoria would let him. It wasn't exactly a jackrabbit start, but he threw a few stones as he accelerated on through. In the rearview mirror he could see Officer Wilson looking after him and writing on a small pad. He shook his head and said to himself, "What the hell was that all about? I don't believe it! I stuck it out, I faced him down!"

Momentarily proud of himself, when he let it sink in, he knew that wasn't what had happened at all. And he thought, "But why? Why did he? And what about the way he said, 'let him go'? It was like he was talking to somebody else. Was he wearing some kind of tiny earphone? Was there a headset in his helmet? But who was telling him to let me go?" It was useless to try to figure it out. He threw his head back and laughed. "Ha! Unbelievable! In-fucking-credible! I don't know but I don't care! I'm on my way again!"

Along with his great relief, Richard was revisiting the same exhilaration and elation he had taken away from his session with Sarah and Riegel. He was absolutely certain now that he was right on course, and that it would be only a matter of minutes before he'd find Andy. Alone on the winding road, focused on the task before him, he navigated with care each hairpin turn, his car in low gear and straining against the force of gravity. He ignored spectacular, sweeping vistas to keep his eyes on the mountain road. As he passed the snowline, he glanced up at the snowy mountain crags and sky above, half hoping to see a hovering UFO. All he saw was a large, white cloud gathering at the summit, swirling ominously and beginning to obscure the mountain top.

The last altitude marker he would remember informed him that it was now 10,616 feet above sea level. Within seconds his car's transmission began sputtering. "What the hell is this? Not car trouble, please! Not now!" None of the cautionary lights on the dashboard display were lit. There was no indication that anything was going wrong. Still the car was losing power and slowing down. The transmission cut out entirely just in time to coast into a scenic overlook. "Dammit!"

He ground the ignition several times but it was no use: the engine would not turn over. "Damn! Shit! Damn!" He hit the steering wheel with his fist and was about to bang on the dashboard, when a wave of nausea hit him and he broke out in a cold sweat. He desperately needed air and tried to roll down the window. But he moved very slowly and, of course, the electric window button did nothing. Another wave of nausea rolled over him, and he grabbed the door handle so he could barf outside, but then he felt himself falling forward, and saw the steering wheel rushing toward his face in a weird kind of slow motion as everything faded to black.

"Is that one of my T-shirts?" "No, it's an ET-shirt."

THREE

The first sensation of which he became conscious was his right cheek resting comfortably on his right forearm. He was slumped over the steering wheel, his torso twisted to the left and his right arm cradled his head, as if he'd just paused by the side of the road for a catnap. A tiny trickle of something warm and wet had dripped onto both his hands. He was slowly climbing out of a dark well of sedation, so his first thought was that he might be bleeding. That should have been alarming enough for him but he also thought, bleeding or else it was – "Oh, no! I puked on myself." Now that was sufficiently alarming so that he tried to sit up fast. Well, it felt abrupt to him, but he really only managed to do the reverse of the slow motion crumple which had put him in this position in the first place.

He paused, thinking he had successfully regained a sitting position now, his hands bracing himself against his knees, propping himself up. Eyes still closed, he felt as though he must be towering over the steering wheel. He was almost afraid to look. Somehow his sunglasses had been either knocked or fallen off and the sunlight, even through closed eyelids, seemed painfully bright. He opened his eyes a tiny bit, and through the slits, looked at his hands. They didn't look so far away after all. He was reassured to see that the liquid was only saliva. He slowly and laboriously wiped his hands dry on his jeans and wondered how long he'd been out. But, what the hell, what did it matter, he was intact. He wasn't bleeding and he hadn't puked. He felt good, a little light-headed maybe, but he wasn't nauseous. He revised his estimation. In fact, he was beginning to feel great.

However, it seemed really hot in the car and he reflexively reached for the window button. The window was down and he was enjoying the fresh air before he realized the car's electrical system was working again. That meant the engine was running. So that's what that humming vibration was. He thought that was very odd, still, he was too fuzzy-headed to care. He thought he ought to get going and look for Andy, but knew he was in no shape to drive. Not just yet anyway. Besides, all the urgency was gone. He thought that was odd, too, but he just needed to rest. He leaned back, managed to adjust the seat backward, and stretched out his legs. He was just spent, utterly drained. But it kind of felt good. A minute's rest was all he needed. He wanted to enjoy this feeling of being so relaxed, so care free.

And that light-headed feeling? It was more than that. It felt good too. How would he describe it? Well, it was definitely trippy: an easy, liquid trippy, like psilocybin, not a speedy trippy like LSD. But man, that sun was bright! He adjusted the seatback to its original position and leaned forward. Straining against his seatbelt harness, he bent over to fumble around on the car floor for his sunglasses. He must have moved too fast because it made him dizzy and just a little nauseous. And his muscles weren't responding in the usual way: they wouldn't quite do what he wanted them to do. For instance, he couldn't seem to grip the steering wheel firmly at all. Nor could he hold on to his sunglasses, which fell out of his hand onto his lap. He picked them up several times and was amused to watch them 'drip' through his fingers every time. Oh, he was tripping, alright, and he laughed at himself. And he said out loud, "Far out! I've turned into silly putty!"

"Not you too?" said a voice in mock dismay from the back seat. Richard didn't need to turn around, he knew the voice. "Ahn-Dee" sounded in his head like a bell tone and the echo came out his mouth as he exclaimed, "Ahn-Dee! I mean Andy!" Well, of course it was Andy. There he was in the rearview mirror, sitting in back of the shotgun seat. In his excitement to reach over the seatback, Richard, still moving in slow motion, turned, rose and practically choked himself on his seat harness. He faced forward to release himself, and was reaching back to Andy again, when Andy said, "Wait! Don't touch me! Not just yet."

Richard froze, restrained from crawling into the back seat as if by an unseen hand. He didn't like that. He pouted. He made a sour face. Then Andy continued, "Just for a minute, okay? Let's just relax for a bit."

Richard unwound and slowly slid back down into his seat. He faced forward and rested his head back, in compliance with his buddy's request. He could still see Andy in the rearview mirror. He could see that, somehow, he had gotten Andy back. He had accomplished his mission. The pouty face softened into a self-satisfied smile. They sat in silence for a minute or more.

"Andy?"

"Yeah?"

"Are you ... you know, ... alright?"

"Oh yeah."

Richard looked at his pal, taking him in visually, voraciously, just as he longed to take him in his arms. He was satisfied that Andy was physically okay, but he noticed his fine, straight, medium length, reddish-blonde hair was having a bad day. And what was that covering his trim, five-foot ten inch, one hundred seventy-five pound body? It looked like an ordinary, extra large, plain white, short-sleeved T-shirt. He craned his neck to see more of his buddy. It was such a large T-shirt it fit Andy like a tunic, reaching down almost to his knees.

"Is that one of my T-shirts?"

"No."

It seemed understood, but Richard felt foolish for asking, "Did you get it on the ...you know?"

"Yeah. It's not mine. And it's not a T-shirt. It's an ET shirt, as in extra-terrestrial." Andy quipped.

"Is that all you're wearing?"

"Now don't get all seductive with me, okay?"

"You mean you were naked? You were naked ... up there?"

"Well, I'm sorry, but I didn't have a lot of time to pack."

"I know, but naked?"

"Good thing I'm stoned," Richard thought, "or I'd be really upset about that." After a long pause, while he debated with himself whether or not he should ask, he decided he had to. "Andy?"

"Yeah."

"Did they hurt you?"

"No. It wasn't like that at all."

The sun was hot on Andy's face and shoulder. He rolled down his window. The cross-ventilating breeze came from over the snow banks. It seemed gradually to refresh them both. Andy put his head back and closed his eyes. Richard continued to look at him with the loving ache of wanting to hold him.

"Andy?"

"Yeah?"

"You look really good, man."

Richard felt his eyes fill with tears but his voice did not betray his emotion and the tears did not roll down his cheeks. "I'm really glad I found you." That seemed to say it all; so, satisfied, he closed his eyes again and continued his rest. Andy smiled and mumbled, "Thanks." Soon tears welled up in his closed eyes, but his voice did not betray his emotion, when he replied.

"Richard?"

"Yeah?"

"I'm really glad you came to get me."

Andy was wiping his eyes, cheeks and chin when Richard shouted, "What?!"

Startled, Andy barked back, "What, 'What!'?"

Andy opened one eye and was about to repeat himself, when Richard interrupted with another shout, "Andy? Was that you?" Richard answered himself before Andy could respond, "No, of course that wasn't you!"

"Was that me what?" Andy wanted to know.

"We have *got* to get out of here." Richard spoke gravely, with an urgent resolve, as he moved his seat forward, rolled up his window and refastened his seat belt. He wiped the dew from his eyes, put on his sunglasses as he snapped out of his dreamy malaise and took charge with a renewed vigor bordering on mania. He quickly discovered that, in an emergency, you could come down from this new kind of trip as fast as from the old kind. He revved the engine, put her in gear, and peeled out. The tires squealed as he spun the station wagon around and screeched as he shot off back down the mountain. Andy was wide-eyed as the centrifugal force threw him first against the car door, then back against the seat.

But Andy was still so wrapped in mellowness that he hummed to himself, "Mm-mm, this is kind of fun." And he thought to himself, "Yeah, I'm definitely back on Earth, alright. Gravity: blessing or curse? You decide."

Richard's dilemma also had something to do with gravity. He was in a great and terrible hurry, yet he could not drive too fast and risk losing control of the car. Still, he took the curves at top speed, fast enough to make the tires squeal and slide Andy around the back seat. He fought gravity and the steering wheel, braked and shifted gears up and down like a madman, and still managed to carry on an intense conversation with his laid-back rider.

"Oh, Richard? Why are we going so fast?"

"Because the voice said, 'Get going – Now!' with a distinct emphasis on the word 'Now'!"

"Really? You hearing voices? That's great! See, remember what I said, once you open yourself to the possibility that there is an expanded awareness available to you, reality starts to look and sound a little different, doesn't it?"

"Shut up."

"I'll bet the voice you heard was Lohr."

"Who?!" Richard practically shrieked.

"Long story. Tell ya later."

"Oh, yeah? The hell you say! Well the voice just now told me we have to get off this mountain, pronto!"

"Did he really say 'pronto'?"

Richard scowled at him in the rearview mirror and said, "Fasten your seat belt, would you please?"

"Okay, okay." Andy tried several times to get the belt clasped, but gave up to stare out the window. Then he saw something and burst out, much louder than he'd intended, with, "Hey!"

He startled Richard who again practically shrieked, "What?"

"You can really see a lot from up on a mountain, can't you?" Richard rolled his eyes as Andy continued, "I'll bet that's Mount Lassen way over there. Got to be at least a hundred miles away."

"I thought I told you to fasten your seat belt."

Andy obediently made another attempt to buckle up. "Did you know that Lassen and Shasta are both dormant volcanoes?" He banged the ends of the seat belt together several times very loudly in frustration, then gave up again. "They could erupt at any ...." He stopped mid-sentence. In Andy's mellow, quasi-altered state of mind, he came up with a possibility that he just couldn't express with the proper concern, so he finished his sentence with a flat, barely audible, "Oh, my god. Are we on ... ?"

"No!" Richard answered emphatically.

"What?!" Andy yelled back.

"Not that! It's not gonna blow!"

"Oh, okay, then."

The discussion in the careening car had reached a high decibel level. While it was appropriate to the controlled hysteria that Richard was experiencing, Andy was merely matching him, decibel for decibel, because he thought it was what he was supposed to do. He wasn't the least bit worried or frightened. He had an unshakable faith that everything was absolutely, unquestionably, and incontrovertibly correct, just as God intended it to be. So he was simply being curious when he yelled, "How do you know?!"

"Because it wouldn't dare blow up while I'm having a nervous breakdown!" As he made his point, Richard's voice did that near shriek thing again. It made Andy wince but he recovered. He caught the sarcasm and decided to run with it, "That's right! Because God never burdens us with more than we are able to bear!"

Richard glared at Andy in the rearview mirror and said, "Oh, would you shut up! And fasten that seat belt, dammit!"

Andy whined, "I caa-a-an't!" He tried it one more time and heard the click of a perfect connection. Surprised, he said, "Oh," just as Richard swerved to miss a fallen rock on the road, and struggled briefly to maintain control.

"Andy, who is this talking in my ear?!"

"I told you. It's Lohr!"

"Well, this 'Lohr' is telling me it's not the volcano that's gonna blow!"

"That's good! Right?!"

"I guess there's no time to explain, he's just saying, 'go, go, go!'"
Andy spoke quietly, to himself, "That's Lohr alright, annoyingly prone to withhold information."

As they neared the base of the mountain, the road was less winding and the angle of descent not as steep. Accordingly, Richard increased speed on the straight-aways while he braked and skidded sharply around the turns.

Andy unsnapped his seat belt and leaned forward, his hands on the back of the front seat.

"What are you doing?! You just got that seat belt fastened!"

"I want to sit in front with you!"

"Not now, Andy! Not while I'm ... !" Richard saw it coming and only just managed to push the bag of groceries onto the floor. Andy dove forward, head first, spilling over onto the shotgun seat. His legs swung around and hit Richard's shoulder, causing his hand to jerk the steering wheel, and causing the car to swerve dramatically, dangerously, into the other lane.

"For God's sake, Andy! Watch out!"

As the car fishtailed and Richard, with steely determination, wrestled to keep it under control, Andy scrambled wildly to seat himself right side up.

"Get over there and sit down!" Richard hollered as he took several spastic kicks from Andy, who paused, out of breath, to sit on his right hip with his right leg folded underneath him.

"I'm sorry, I'm sorry," he gasped as he moved slowly, with great, exaggerated care, to swing his left leg around and put his left foot on the floor without hitting Richard again.

"Well, dammit, we could have been killed! And don't step on the grocery bag!"

"Groceries? There's food? I'm starved! And so-o-o-o thirsty, too. Is there anything to drink in there?" He leaned forward to rummage in the bag, but Richard barked at him again.

"Not 'til you fasten that lousy seatbelt!'

"Well, then I won't be able to reach the sack."

"Look, we have to get through a roadblock coming up any minute now and you have to be fastened in or we're in violation of the law, get it?"

"Got it."

"Good."

Andy muttered, "Boy, are you strict." He soothed his slightly bruised ego while making an elaborate show of smoothing out the ET-shirt, as if he were straightening a skirt. By the time he was satisfied that he wasn't sitting on any twisted or bunched fabric, and had snapped his seat belt and shoulder harness, he had forgiven Richard. He longingly eyed the out-of-reach food in the grocery bag his legs were straddling, and asked, "So why is there a roadblock?"

"They aren't letting anyone go up the mountain."

"Why?"

"Because of UFO's."

That pulled Andy's attention away from the food bag, and he looked at Richard to ask, "Really? What'd they look like?"

"Lights, that's all, just lights, flying around the mountain in wild formations."

"Did you see them?"

"Yes. But not up close. I wanted to see one up close, you know, see what shape it was. I wondered if they were really saucer shaped."

"Oh, they're saucer shaped, alright. Mostly."

Richard glanced questioningly at Andy. "Oh, really?"

Andy resumed, "Of course, I don't know if the ones you saw were saucers." He paused, offering no further explanation before changing the subject. "How did you get through the roadblock?"

"I told them I had to find my buddy up on the mountain and, for some reason, this California Highway Patrol hunk let me go through. But we have to check back in with him on our way out."

"Have to?"

"He's got my license plate number."

Before they could discuss it further, the roadblock was there, just ahead of them, waiting for them. From this side of the roadblock, there were no other cars waiting to leave the area. To Richard, everything was reversed: the relief

54

tent, the transport truck, the TV van, all now on his right. His car would be deflected to the left; that is, if they let him go through again.

He looked hard for Officer Wilson in the group of patrolmen clustered around the checkpoint. He drove up as close as he could and stopped. Just as he rolled down his window, Officer Wilson broke away from his cohorts and walked toward the car. The officer wasn't smiling, but he lifted his head and raised one hand, a gesture barely discernible as either a wave of recognition or a greeting.

"Is everything okay?" he asked in a friendly tone that belied the serious expression on his face. He leaned down and looked in the car to check out Andy.

"Just great, thanks. I found him just fine and he's ... just fine."

If Officer Wilson had noticed that Andy was barefoot and pantless, and if he was suspicious, he nevertheless gave no indication from behind his sunglasses. He nodded his head encouragingly as he commented, "Well, that's good. Good ...." This was followed by five seconds of excruciatingly awkward silence. Richard couldn't stand it anymore and broke the tension by speaking.

"Listen, thanks a lot for letting me go up there. I really mean it. So…we're going to, you know, go on home now. Okay?"

"Well, yeah, sure ...." he drawled. He raised his right arm and slowly scratched the back of his neck. Andy could see right up Officer Wilson's short sleeved shirt to a sexy patch of blonde armpit hair. The officer was stretching it out, and it was obvious that he was trying to figure out how to say "no" to them. Finally, he just came out with it.

"Would you guys step over to that tent, first, and talk to the doctors? They just want to ask you a few questions, you know, about what you saw up there. It won't take long."

Doctors? Richard and Andy locked eyes for a second in a charged look that silently whimpered to each other, "What do we do now?" But Richard quickly recovered his bravado and turned back to face the policeman. It was the battle of the sunglassed stares all over again.

Richard took a deep breath and exhaled, then began, "Listen, officer, we didn't see anything up there."

"Did you see that cloud?"

"What cloud? No, we didn't see any cloud." He turned to Andy to ask, "Did we see a cloud? Did you see a cloud?"

Andy shook his head, no.

"We didn't see any cloud. And we'd really like to get going. So, do we have to go see the doctors?"

Richard was trying for a tone this time that was respectful of authority but whine-free, challenging but not cocky and not glib. He was worried that his last sentence was a tad lame. It must have worked because, after a moment's thought, the highway patrolman abruptly straightened up and said, "Aw, what the hell. They've got plenty of folks over there to talk to. Forget it. You go ahead, get going."

"Are you sure?'

"Yeah, go on." He gave them a big smile and a friendly pat on the car roof as they drove off.

"Whew!" Richard loudly exhaled as he turned left. "Another close shave," he beamed.

But Andy was thinking and he had to ask, "I wonder why he let us go?"

"I don't know. I'm still trying to figure out why he let me through in the first place. You know, it was so weird, like he heard some voice in ...." Richard's jaw dropped open, just enough to register his surprise as he made a connection. He looked at Andy. Andy looked at him. And they spoke in unison. "Lohr!"

Richard dithered, "Oh, no, no, no. It can't be. Do you think so?"

"I don't know," Andy shrugged, "but it could have been."

"But just now I, me, myself, didn't hear anything."

"He wasn't talking to you."

"I still don't hear anything."

"He's still not talking to you," Andy offered patiently.

"Well, frankly, I hope he doesn't talk to me ever again."

"Oh, c'mon. He's just trying to help."

"Help? Oh, yeah? Then what was that big rush to get us off the mountain all about?"

"Listen."

"No, I'm serious! Seriously annoyed!"

"Do you hear that?"

Andy was picking up on a distant throbbing sound, backed by a steady drone. Richard listened.

"Oh. You mean, do I hear that noise? The one that's rapidly getting closer?"

Andy was rolling down his window when the noise exploded over them, and he had to shout his identification, "Helicopters!"

But Richard already knew. He knew there were three helicopters, flying low and flying fast, skimming the treetops. The whipping blades vibrated, the sound peaking at a deafening roar as they passed directly overhead. Andy leaned right and stuck his head out, looking up and behind the car, catching a glimpse as they flew away "Three of them," he reported, "Military, I think. At least two of them were, you know, green? But the third one was black." Richard tensed his shoulders and shivered. A profound discomfort gripped him. A low, barely audible moan of "Oh, god." escaped from deep in his throat.

He was meandering: turning right, then left, then right again, instinctively deploying evasive action to throw someone off their trail. Even distracted, he seemed to know where they should be going. He turned left onto the main road, the one headed back to the Interstate. And as he drove, he unconsciously accelerated. Andy looked at him and asked, "Now do you know?"

"Know what?"

"Why we had to get out of there."

"Yes," he answered reluctantly. Then he protested, "No! No, Andy, I don't know! I don't know anything! Everything's changed. What happened to you? What's happening here? What the hell is this all about? It's just nuts! And why am I having premonitions and audio-visual hallucinations, like LSD flashbacks?"

"You mean like that time in Vietnam?"

Richard nodded yes, then added cryptically, "Evil riding in a black helicopter."

Andy didn't like the faraway look in his eyes. Just when he was feeling like he was finally back in reality, he didn't want to see Richard go tripping off somewhere else.

"This isn't Vietnam, Richard, okay? You got that?"

"It was one of our own, wasn't it, Andy?"

"You are really starting to bum me out. Listen to me: you are fine, there's nothing wrong with you, or with me. I'm fine too. I'm okay, you're okay, even the evil black helicopter is okay. Why? Because he's supposed to be evil, just like we're supposed to be afraid of him. Just like we're supposed to obey the speed limit. Would you please slow down?"

Richard glanced at the speedometer. He was doing sixty-five miles per hour where the posted limit was forty.

"I'm speeding, aren't I? I'm sorry." He stepped on the anti-lock brake to slow down gently; five, then fifteen miles per hour. When he had braked down to fifty, that seemed slow enough to him. "After all," he thought, "what's a forty mile per hour getaway? How puny is that?" He stole a glance at Andy. "Forgive me. I didn't mean to scare you. I'll try to get a grip here. I guess I'm a little spooked. I'm sorry."

"I know. I'm sorry too. Me and my X-files shit."

"You can't help it, can you?" Richard said affectionately. It was more of an affirmation than a question. But his tone turned serious when he asked, "What happened to you, Andy? Do you want to talk about it?"

"No. Not yet. I need some time to take it all in, sort it out. I don't know, I just need time, that's all."

"Well, it's a long drive back to San Francisco. Oh, I almost forgot." He handed the car phone to Andy. "Call Sarah. I told her I'd call when I found you." This simple, factual statement seemed to disorient Andy.

"When you 'found' me? You talked to Sarah?"

"Yes. This morning. And Riegel too."

"Riegel too? Wait a minute. What time is it now? Is it Wednesday?"

"'It's a little after three and, yes, it's still Wednesday. You were only gone about ten hours."

Despite a couple of adrenaline rushes, Andy was awakening slowly. It was just beginning to sink in: the usually taken-for-granted awareness of his time and place had been interrupted. He was mildly shocked to realize he couldn't accurately connect this time and place to the time and place from which he had just returned. He needed confirmation of where he was in the universe, and he needed it now.

"And where are we? What mountain was that?"

"Northern California, Mount Shasta. I just assumed you knew that."
It was Andy's turn to be struck dumb. He stared at the dashboard like he was trying to see through it. "Ten hours? Gone? I was 'gone'?" He sat there staring, mouth open, until his stomach loudly protested its emptiness. He gulped some air and belched it.

"Excuse me. Okay, I'm back. When do we eat?"

"Call Sarah first."

"Yeah-yeah, but then can we stop somewhere?"

"There's food in the bag!"

"I know, I know. I mean, can we stop somewhere, stop the car, stop moving, so I can eat it?"

"Oh, okay. Sure."

As Andy dialed Sarah, Richard continued his unconsciously evasive driving: he turned at the next right off the road headed back to the Interstate. He proceeded on a winding, tree-lined back road, not at all sure of where it went. He just thought he was looking for a nice place to have a picnic. Behind him, in the rearview mirror, he saw a police car tear past the turnoff for the road he was now on. The siren was off, but the lights were flashing, a sign of some urgency. Richard noticed it and placed it in the wonder-what-that-means file, then easily dismissed it.

Andy waited through Sarah's outgoing message, then began talking after the beep. "Hello, Sarah? It's me, Andy, are you ...?"

Sarah broke in excitedly, "Andy! I thought it might be you! You're alright?"

"Yes. Yes, I am."

"Are you with Richard?"

"What are you, psychic?" he joked. "Yes, I am."

"Very funny. Where are you? Are you coming here?"

"We're near Mount Shasta. Let me check." He asked Richard, "Are we going to Sarah's?"

"Up to you."

"Yeah, Sarah, I want to see you. We'll be there ... uh ...." He asked Richard, "What time do you think we'll get there?"

"Let me talk to her." Andy passed the phone to him. "Hi, Sarah. I just had a thought. It's been kinda weird up here, UFO's, roadblocks and stuff, and I think we're going to take the long way home, you know, down the coast maybe."

"What's wrong?" Sarah snapped urgently.

"Probably nothing, but I'd just like to play it cool and careful, keep a low profile, at least for the time being. There was a mobile news van up there so you might watch the news tonight to see what they say about UFO sightings around Mount Shasta."

"Good, I will. But when should I expect you?"

"Down the coast might take us six or seven hours, so I don't know." He puzzled it over, looking at his watch and checking it against the car's clock, both of which agreed it was three fifteen. "It's about three fifteen now, so I ...."

"No, it's not, it's ten 'til four."

"Are you sure?"

"Yes, the kids just got home from summer school about three thirty, as usual, and that was about twenty minutes ago. Better let me look. Hold on. Yes, my kitchen clock says 3:52."

"Uh ... okay, my clocks are wrong here." Richard, momentarily flustered by the time discrepancy, stopped speaking.

Sarah completed the calculations and spoke up, "Then it might not be until ten or eleven before you show up here, right?"

"Yeah, right. Sure. Uh ... is that too late?"

"Not for me!" she chirped.

Richard checked with Andy. "We might not reach San Rafael until ten or eleven tonight, is that too late for you? Do you want to just go back to San Francisco?"

"No, I want to talk to Sarah. Do you mind?"

"No, no. That's fine with me." He assured Sarah they'd be there as close to ten as possible, then they said good-bye and disconnected. "Oh, I'm sorry, did you want to talk to her some more, just now?"

Andy's stomach, outraged and insistent, growled again. He looked askance at Richard, then down at his stomach. "Not really. We're more interested in eating at the moment."

"Soon. I promise," Richard placated. He turned right onto a gravel road and they rolled up their windows against the dust. Andy felt no inclination to question the detour. They rode along in silence through the rolling, grassy landscape for a mile or so, until they came to a shallow, rocky stream bed, its banks heavily populated with birches and aspens. A wood and steel bridge spanned the fast-moving water. Richard drove the car over the bridge, cut left off the road into the grass, and came to a stop under the trees in an unhesitating maneuver, as fluid as if this had been the destination for their drive all the time.

He turned off the engine, undid his seatbelt, and opened his door. Andy did the same. They both sat for a few moments, savoring the breeze, the shade, the quiet stillness of no longer hurtling down roads strapped into a machine, letting all the urgency of the last thirty minutes melt away. All, that is, except the urgency to satisfy hunger and thirst. Somebody had to move, so Andy slowly reached down for the bag of groceries between his feet and hoisted it onto his lap. As he swiveled to get out of the car, Richard did the same.

Andy felt the weight of gravity anew. On bare feet, he carefully picked his steps as he lugged the bag over to a grassy, shady stretch of the stream's bank. He was sure it must weigh twenty pounds if it weighed an ounce. Richard was rummaging around in the back of the car, and he soon followed carrying an old quilt and his gym bag. Together they spread out the quilt and Andy kneeled over the grocery bag and began pulling out its contents. Richard sat and pulled off his construction boots, then reached for some trail mix. Andy sipped from the liter bottle while digging deeper into the bag. He chuckled, exclaiming happily, "Oh, hey! Brownies! Nature's most perfect food! And there's three of them! Bravo, Richard!"

"One of them is for me, okay?"

"Oh? Well, sure, okay. Say, where did you get all this stuff?"

"A little organic food store just outside of town. We passed it a few miles back. We can stop for a real meal later on."

"This is perfect, just what I would have chosen for myself. Very thoughtful of you, Richard. Thanks." Andy chose an apple and bit into it. To him it was an apple as luscious as the first apple on the first day of creation.

"Mmmmmmmm," he hummed in a tone of sensual, almost erotic, delight. Some juice ran down his chin and Richard leaned over and very quickly – and very thoroughly – licked the juice off his face.

"I'm sorry. Is it alright to touch you now?"

"Let's hope so."

They looked in each other's eyes and they both felt the spark and the jolt. Richard closed his eyes and pulled Andy to him to give him a kiss, but Andy gently squirmed free of the embrace and pushed him away.

"No. Sorry. Not here. Not now. I can't." Richard turned away, although not before Andy saw the pained expression of disappointment on his face. He felt a strong tug of guilt. He wanted to make it go away. He wanted to make it alright with Richard. But what could he say that would do that, what part of the truth would Richard find acceptable?

Andy tried to explain to Richard's back. "Right now, I feel like I'm in several places at once. I mean it literally, both physically and emotionally. I guess what I'm trying to say is I'm a little mixed up, a little unsteady. But I know sex won't clarify anything for me." There was an awkward pause before Andy asked, "Richard? Did you hear me?"

He nodded affirmatively. "It's okay. I'm sorry. Let's forget it."

That wasn't quite enough for Andy, so he had to make one more point. "Maybe you won't believe this, but, for me, it's enough just to be here with you by my side. I don't always know why or how, but I love you. You know that, don't you?" He nodded yes again, and when he turned back to face Andy, there was a hint of a smile, very sheepish, and very charming. All he said was, "Shut up and pass me an apple."

"Here 'Adam'."

"Thanks 'Steve'."

When Andy was finished snacking, he stretched himself out on his back, closed his eyes and took three deep, measured breaths, exhaling each one forcefully, but slowly, through the mouth. He stretched and flexed his legs and arms, his neck, shoulders, hands, and feet, took another breath and concentrated on relaxing and centering himself. As he exhaled, he felt the Earth holding him, supporting and uplifting him, as if in Her giant hands.

Richard finished the liter of water, then rolled over onto his stomach. The temperature was still hot, but here in the grass, in the shade, in the breeze, it was more than bearable: it was refreshing. He was physically comfortable, but still keyed up. He needed something to relax his mind. He found some success as he watched a raptor – a hawk, perhaps, or maybe even an eagle – circling high in the sky over the rolling hills and distant woods, a mile or so away. Richard gazed, mesmerized, as the great bird soared, occasionally swooping low, lazily looping back and forth, rising to ride the air currents, patiently looking for prey.

Andy felt the sun-dappled light on his face, watched the changing light patterns on his eyelids, as the breeze moved through the tree branches. He listened to the rising and falling whisper of the breeze through the grass and the leaves against the background of white noise from the rushing water. He heard the far off caw of a crow and, nearby, the twittery nattering of smaller birds. All Creation was alive and breathing and he was part of it. It might be any summer day, in any year, in any place on Earth. He could be back home in Indiana, in Clifty Falls State Park, in 1965. He could be on a hillside in Tuscany in 1587. On the web of All-There-Is, he was suspended out of time, connected to all time, everywhere, to every lazy summer day that had ever been in the history of the World.

But Richard reminded him that he was in Northern California in 1995 when he cautioned him, "Don't go to sleep, we should get back on the road soon." Andy let himself come back slowly then opened his eyes. "You're right. I could sure use a nap though."

"You can sleep in the car. Here, try these on." Richard took a pair of his own, formerly neon orange, now faded, trunks out of his gym bag and handed them to Andy. "I know my shoes don't fit you, but I've got some extra socks here too; for when it gets cooler later tonight. I know how your feet get cold."

"You are so prepared. Are you sure you were never a Boy Scout?"

Richard chuckled, "No." Then he changed it. "I mean, yes. Yes, I'm sure I was never a Boy Scout." He put his boots back on, pitched the apple cores into the stream and began packing up. Andy stood on the grass and modestly turned his back while he pulled on the trunks. He smoothed out the ET shirt over the trunks, barely an inch of which showed beneath the hem of the shirt. They were stowing everything in the back of the car, when they heard a lone chopper in the distance. They both looked up to see if it was visible.

"There," Richard pointed, "just over those trees. I think it's moving southeast, away from us, don't you?"

Andy noticed it wasn't moving away very fast, but agreed, "Yeah. Do you think they're looking for us?"

"I don't know why they would be, but we should behave as if they are. That's the reason we're heading down the coast. By the way, we've got a stretch of Interstate to get over before we can head west. Why don't you get in the back seat and, while we're on I-5, you can just lie down back there under the quilt?"

"Is that really necessary?"

"Maybe, maybe not. But I think we should be careful."

"Well, that doesn't sound like much fun," Andy playfully teased. "I mean if we get stopped again I can't just hide in the back seat. How about if I were to pose as your wife? You got any cute drag in your gym bag?"

"Hey, mister, you'll find no drag in my gym bag!"

"And no wonder. My, you're a big girl!"

"Watch it."

"Maybe you should shop at Lane Bryant? Of course, they're rather – 'stodgy' – well, okay, 'traditional' – but I'm sure they could fit a girl your size."

"That's enough!" Richard may have loved Andy's sense of humor, but he didn't always appreciate it when it took a turn into the realm of "camp."

But Andy was on a roll now, as one of his favorite alter egos came out to play. This one was Felicia, who lived to puncture inflated egos. "Then again, maybe 'stodgy' is what you're going for."

"Now stop it!"

So Andy switched to Rip, his Valley-Boy Jock persona. "Wull – like – okay, Coach, but does this mean – like –I have to stay after practice –like – again?" Richard threw the quilt at his head and Andy caught it with one arm. "Get in the back seat, Sybil! I'm warning you, right now I'm in no mood for your multiple personality disorder!"

He meant it. And Andy knew he meant it. So he complied, but not without muttering to himself – himself as Rip, that is. "Sybil? Like whoa! Totally brutal, dude."

"What was that?"

"Nothing. And it's not just a disorder, it's also a defense mechanism."

Under the quilt in the back seat, Andy was asleep before they reached the on ramp to the Interstate.

"He hoped none of them looked like cockroaches."

FOUR

It was snowing light – tiny flakes of white light – in Andy's bedroom. Glittering chips of white gold seemed to be congealing out of the air. Andy, in his living room talking to Richard on the phone, did a double take when he spotted the phenomenon across the hall.

"Jeesuz H. Christ!"

More and more flakes were arriving. They kept swirling while suspended in the air, like the glitter in a shaken paperweight. As he watched, this snowstorm of light was quickly becoming a blizzard. And yet, odder still, he noticed there was no wind to blow these shimmering flecks around. He felt no draft in the apartment. Nothing else in the bedroom was disturbed; it was as quiet and still as held breath.

"Richard, I think they're here."

Curiosity drew Andy a few tentative steps forward to get a better look. He saw the dancing flakes forming two spirals: one swirling clockwise from the ceiling to the floor and the other the reverse. One spiral of light intertwined with the other like strands of DNA. He dreamily murmured to himself, "M-m-m-m, love the Spielberg effects. Very nice."

The condensing light was now so intense, everything in his room – curtains, bed, desk, bookcases, lamps – was outlined in a shallow, black shadow, flattened into low relief. The blizzard approached whiteout. Andy had to squint.

"They're here alright and I guess they are aligned with the Light because it is amazingly bright in here."

Richard said something but Andy didn't really hear him. He just knew it was time to go. "Richard, sweetheart, I really have to go now." He distractedly replaced the handset on the already dead phone. He was mesmerized, and yet completely conscious that he was mesmerized. He stepped over the threshold into his bedroom and was pulled into the light column.

He could feel the whirlpools of light grazing the surface of his naked body. The currents were gently brushing and squeezing, caressing and embracing him. Fluid but not wet, windy but not cool, they pulled at him both up and down. It was not an unpleasant sensation, much like being tickled. But he had a fleeting notion that he was now trapped, and although it was ominous, he was unafraid.

Then the sound came, distant at first, which he characterized as the howling wind of a hundred harmonized accordions. It grew so dense it formed a sustained tone surrounding his body. As the volume increased, he felt both the sound and light currents simultaneously entering his body, moving inside the skin, flowing through the tissue, around the very molecules of his being, setting them to the vibrational level of the tone. It wasn't exactly multiple orgasms but it was euphoric, a 'buzz' that was almost ravishing. The currents whirled and hummed around his spine and in his head, always in opposing up and down directions. It was dizzying but he wasn't just lightheaded: he swore he actually felt lighter – literally – bodily lighter.

And yet, when the upward pull won the tug of war, took control, and tried to snatch him up, he felt the drifting-off-to-sleep sensation of falling and his body convulsed to catch itself. At that exact moment a surging pulse was added to the tone. This instantly counteracted the adrenaline rush and a soothing feeling flooded his body, encouraged by a disembodied voice resonating in every cell. It was fortunate for Andy the panic response had been neutralized. The voice, mostly monotone, had difficulty getting the volume right. Quiet at first, it exploded into stupefying loudness several times before finding a moderate range.

It said, or sometimes screamed, "Please do NOT LEAVE YOUR BODY. REMAIN conscious. The UNPLEASANT SENSations will quickly pass. You are in the most loving of God's hands. DO NOT BE Afraid. No harm WILL COME to you. Maintain your focus: here and now."

While his reverie remained essentially undisturbed, each time the volume shot up, Andy grimaced and shuddered. He was more annoyed than destroyed by the sonic blasts since his whole body and not just his ears took the brunt. But the advice was most welcome. He was on the verge of being overwhelmed. He was struggling to keep from passing out. So he paid close attention to the Resonance and forced himself to breathe and to focus on that breathing.

And when he felt his feet leave the floor for the second time, he breathed deeper and faster. In his dreams, Andy could fly upright, his body vertical just like this. In his dreams, simply by kicking his feet, he could rise straight up like a helicopter. Now, with eyes squinty open, but without kicking his feet, he rose up to the ceiling. The Voice said something that sounded like, 'Peter Pan,' and somehow, in a blink, he was through the roof and rising above his apartment in a column of light. "Good thing I live on the top floor," he thought. And when he smiled, he sensed laughter around him. Up he went, suspended in the single beam formed by the opposing light vortices. For a moment he closed his eyes and sensed bodies gently bumping into him, nudging him, and helping to lift him higher. The light kept spinning around him and inside him, and combined with the tone and the pulse, here he was, defying gravity.

The tangible Voice, the Resonance, said, "Look up." He obeyed and his eyes widened. In the night sky above was a gigantic eye: a gray, elliptical shape, easily the length of a football field, with a darker gray circle in the middle like a pupil, and a bright dot of light in the middle of that. It looked back at Andy from some indeterminate distance high above. His view of the eye was sometimes partially obscured by fog, shredded pieces of clouds, flying by on the wind. He could not feel this wind. He could only gaze wonderingly as he rode a beam of light into God's Eye. Was he going straight into the Mind of God? And he thought, "Am I dying?" And he sensed the laughter again, and the Resonance said, "This is not dying. There is no dying, there is only transformation." And he thought, "Am I transforming?" And the response was, "This is not transformation. This is traveling, traveling between, from one density to another."

"Fascinating," he thought. "Absolutely fascinating!" But Andy just could not focus on a dialogue while 'traveling between' so that answer satisfactorily ended the conversation. He looked to the expanding hole of light above but there was nothing or nobody to be seen up there. He looked down. He was higher than he thought, much higher. He saw the column of light reaching down to the roof over his bedroom. He saw the lights of cars moving on the streets, the expressways, and the Oakland Bay Bridge. He knew he was dangling precariously in midair and wondered if anyone in the cars could see him or the column of light or the Eye of God above him. The pulsing stopped. The next thing he knew, he was sinking. He was concerned about this, - yes, he was, - but he just couldn't summon the proper degree of sink-or-swim panic.

To counteract this regression, the Resonance decided to open up the dialogue again coaching him with, "You have to help us. Please, just breathe and look up. You can propel yourself."

"With my feet?"

"With your thoughts."

"Oh, I get it!" he thought, "Peter Pan again." His mind's eye played a rerun of a scene from the Disney animated version where Wendy, Peter,

John, and Michael soar above the clouds in the night sky over Edwardian London. As soon as he did that, as soon as he went from 'being carried' upward, to 'flying' upward, in other words, from passive to active, he shot up and through the light hole like water sucked up a straw. He whooped and hollered and was inside the Eye so fast it left him laughing helplessly.

"Oh! Oh, please!" he gasped, giddy with the thrill of his arrival on board. His laughter dwindled to a chuckle. A big grin stayed on his face as he began to check out where he was. He was sitting, or lying, in a plush, upholstered pocket in a huge, hand-shaped chair, like a big, maroon catcher's mitt. He couldn't be sure about the sitting or lying part because, although the sound and light were gone, he still felt very lightweight, very insubstantial, as if he was barely making a dent in the 'palm' of this chair. The grin faded. Now it struck him how utterly, seriously strange his circumstances were. He was inside a flying saucer, 'on board' a spaceship, that had come from who knows how many light years away. He wondered what these intergalactic space travelers looked like. And just how friendly would they be?

As he pondered all this, he noticed that he was in a lens shaped room; anywhere from thirty to sixty feet in diameter. He really had a hard time judging distances but he tried very hard to make definitive assessments of such things so that he could make some sense of his environment. There were no doors or windows in this lenticular room, and only one 'corner' – the seam where the curved, concave bowl of the 'ceiling' met the curved, concave bowl of the 'floor.' But which was which? Both surfaces were the same color and texture: an apparent brushed aluminum. The lighting, what there was of it, was so indirect that its source could not be detected. With no strong sense of gravity and little in the way of visual clues, he was beginning to wonder if he and the chair were stuck on the ceiling. He froze, unwilling to move, lest it might result in a fall. Whether it would be a fall up or a fall down, he had no idea.

Just when he'd concluded he was trapped, his chair began to move. Simultaneously, a thick plane of smoky, highly-polished glass emerged from one side of the room's single 'corner' edge, soundlessly slicing the space into two hemispheres. The chair freakishly slid slowly down the curve of the newly-created wall and righted itself where the wall met the darkly-mirrored floor. Although Andy felt no change in the force of gravity (or lack thereof), he could now relate to up and down, at least visually, which he found enormously reassuring. With the chair in place, a single tone sounded, like a sustained note played by rubbing the wet rim of a fine crystal glass. When the vibration died away, a door, a mere sliver of an opening, appeared on the far side of the dome, directly opposite Andy. It appeared to be a welcoming committee of one.

There, poised to enter was what looked to him to be a fashion model. Her large feet were solidly planted, aligned beneath her somewhat wide shoulders. Arms akimbo, her large hands rested on slender hips. She wore a black mini skirt and a glittering, sapphire blue, beaded and sequined jacket with three quarter length sleeves. And even from this distance, he could tell she was smiling at him. She dropped the pose and, with a saucy toss of her head, launched herself toward him. She crossed the floor, striding confidently, commandingly, 'working it' in the playful, carefree manner of a professional runway model. The echo of her black, three inch heels, clicking on the glass, was the only sound. Her coppery auburn hair was cut in a sculpted Dutch boy bob. A single button secured the jacket. The resulting décolletage revealed a bare chest and a tantalizing glimpse of cleavage. She was lavishly but tastefully accessorized with diamonds: dangly earrings, a three strand bracelet, and a matching choker that set off her graceful but muscular neck. Sheer black stockings sheathed her long, shapely legs. "That is one helluva dish," Andy thought.

Ten feet from him she stopped and assumed her earlier pose. While she was getting a good look at him, she turned up the wattage on her smile. This plus-size demigoddess gave off a palpable, shimmering radiance powered by something more than personality. She glowed from within and, at the same time, seemed to be standing in her own personal spotlight. She quite literally lit up the room.

Andy was speechless, completely enthralled. They stared at each other, the eons ticking off, one by one. She cocked her head slightly, tucking her chin, and her smile took on an impish quality, as if she had a secret and was daring him to guess what it was. "Don't I know you?" Andy thought, "I feel like I should know who you are." He studied her face for an answer. Her make-up was perfectly executed. It was not a mask to conceal but, rather, was rendered to skillfully bring out and enhance the natural, exotic beauty of her face. Her subtly shaded eyelids accented large eyes that matched the color and sparkle of her tailored jacket. Her mouth seemed small until her plum red lips parted in a Cinemascope smile that showed off dazzlingly white, gloriously perfect teeth.

That smile! What was it about that smile? A second, even more nagging, suspicion was intruding on the first. The question of 'Who is she?' was being nudged aside by the question of "What is she?' Like words that elude the tongue, trying to come up with the answer to either question was beginning to induce in Andy an agony of self-torture. What new goddess of movie star glamour was this? She was too stunning, too 'drop dead gorgeous' – a phrase Andy used with the utmost judiciousness in the age of AIDS – to be what he was thinking.

That was when he found out just how stunning she actually was as she pulled off her hair, tossed it aside, and revealed that she was, indeed, a man. Andy gasped. He'd seen a lot of drag queens in his day but had rarely, if ever, been so completely deceived. He'd been unconsciously holding his breath and he now exhaled with a whistle. Even in full make-up, the face, now framed by a very short, boyish haircut, was unmistakably masculine. Could a wig really make that much difference? Or had the planes of the face subtly changed somehow? A shock of reddish blonde hair fell with boyish, unruly charm over the forehead, just above the right eye of this still glowing being.

"Call me Lohr," he/she offered in a husky contralto. Even the voice defied precise gender identification. Andy was dumbstruck and not even sure he could speak. But he tried and succeeded.

"Lohr. My name is Andy. You are so, so-o-o-o-o …beautiful!" How odd, he thought, that "pretty" really described her but 'handsome' was the only appropriate word for him. And 'beautiful' was definitely the word to describe both. He/She smiled his/her thanks and Andy babbled on, "If I was a woman, I'd want to look just like you do … did … do!"

"Don't worry, honey, you have and you will," Lohr responded cheerfully if somewhat cryptically. The voice slipped down a notch, becoming less ambiguous. He continued to beam that impish grin at Andy and asked, "Have you figured out yet who I am?"

Andy stared hard at this big, handsome creature, but, as usual, his mind turned to oatmeal in the presence of such a gorgeous man. "No, I'm afraid I don't know who you are, even though I feel . . . ," he hesitated then guiltily affirmed, "I mean I know I should know. But I don't."

"It's not important now. Don't worry about it. Besides, it's been a very long time for you. Stand up and let me get a look."

Andy slid himself off the oversized chair and was relieved that his feet stayed on the floor where they landed. However, while looking down at his bare feet, he realized that the rest of him was bare too. He started to blush and reluctantly raised his gaze to look Lohr in the face. That's when he discovered just how tall Lohr was. Even allowing for the three-inch heels, he was taller than Richard's six feet two inches. He had to be six eight or six six at the very least.

"Oh! You are really tall," Andy remarked stupidly.

Lohr smiled down at him lovingly. "Yes, I am. And you are really — "

"Short?"

"I was going to say 'beautiful'," Lohr continued, "beautiful in your splendid and innocent nakedness."

Andy's blush deepened beyond mere modesty. He thought he detected something more than a compliment in Lohr's statement. He knew it was sincere and not in the least sarcastic. In fact, it was almost reverential. Could Lohr be coming on to him? But that's what bothered him. Sincere compliments always made him very self-conscious.

Andy was far from secure in his sex appeal. He suffered varying degrees of embarrassment whenever the topic came up and was, obviously, the most vulnerable when nude. He was glad for the low, indirect lighting in this strange meeting place. Nevertheless it did not hide his discomfort with his unexceptional body. He could deal with rejection. Rejection could be stoically endured, cushioned by indignation, but flirtation, even the merest hint of sexual attraction, had been known to completely unnerve him. That's why he hated gay bars: he was just as uncomfortable being desired as ignored. Sooner or later, in all his past relationships, the issue of his attractiveness had to be faced and overcome. Fortunately, Richard had enough sexual self-assurance for both of them.

Something about the expression on Lohr's face lured Andy away from his momentary discomfort. He was drawn to the beautiful countenance by a compelling curiosity and the irresistible desire to understand the mystery of it. And he found amazing depth there. Lohr's smile was not lecherous: there was more in it of the secret longing of the heart, the longing to nurture and protect, than of the lust to consume. And as he stared up into Lohr's eyes, he heard Lohr's voice speak to him though his lips were not moving. It was a quieter, more tender, more intimate version of the voice that had coached him into this spaceship.

He was saying, "Our connection goes deep. I understand you, my friend. I understand your feelings, your perceptions. I even understand your poignant misperceptions. Yes, you are correct. It is true I would love to bring us both to that rarely achieved level of bliss, of communion. And I deeply regret that you do not consider yourself worthy. But I assure you, that kind of communion is not on our agenda today. Here we want to encourage you to communicate with us on every level, especially the emotional, to feel your feelings and to express them. Soon you will meet others. Don't be put off, turned off, by the erotic. It is a wonderful emotion, a powerfully creative emotion. Don't be afraid of it. Use it. Have fun with it. Enjoy it. And trust yourself. It is not in control of you. You have the power."

Andy's heart melted. His eyes filled with tears. The words of Lohr's last sentence touched him deeply. Five years ago, when his therapist said those very words to him, they were the most important words he had yet heard in his life. They gave him the permission to heal. And coming from Lohr, they gave him the permission to be himself. They were also a signal for acceptance. He was safe. Lohr could be trusted. Man or woman, friend or lover, Lohr emanated a pure love, undiluted, and unconditional.

Lohr spoke aloud, "Now that you're here, let's open up. Let's open fully." Andy nodded his consent. The area around Lohr's heart chakra began to glow. He gathered and focused his Love Ray. It flowed from his heart area and pierced Andy's. Andy felt it like a cool heat that rippled through his body. He began to tremble inside. His face scrunched up to cry. And he did indeed open up, sobbing silently, shaking with the release of wave after wave of emotion – emotion in all its fullness – drawn from the depths of his soul. First came the tears of frustration and anger, the tears of forced repression. Then, in even more abundance, came the tears of regret and sorrow until he could no longer see Lohr through the deluge. Lohr gently placed a handkerchief in Andy's hands and he buried his face in it as he choked out his thanks. He could not see that Lohr was crying with him but he heard the compassion in his voice.

"Yes, yes, I know but first the forgiveness and then the gratitude."

"But there's so much to forgive," Andy blubbered.

"Of course there is; you are connected to the whole world's sorrow."

"And the world is a very unforgiving place right now."

"Yes, and that's why forgiveness starts with you; why you can't forgive others, and they can't forgive you, until you forgive yourself."

"I know…I know," Andy said, wiping his eyes, gasping for breath between the wracking sobs.

Lohr wiped his own eyes and dried his own cheeks with his hands.

"I know that you know," he smiled. "Just as you know the same is true of love and compassion. It all begins with you. You have to take the first step."

"But knowing and doing are two different things and I still fail to live the lessons I've learned." This admission of his humanity renewed the deluge of tears for Andy. Lohr was there to comfort him with, "It is inevitable that we will stumble. You, dear one, have succeeded far more often than you have failed. And, you must remember, you are a co-creator – you are not solely responsible for what happens between you and others in your life. Believe me, you are making wonderful progress; progress so wonderful, it is nothing short of miraculous."

The words seemed to help. Andy smiled bravely through his disappointment with himself. The tears subsided. Lohr gently grasped Andy's shoulders and leaned over so that he looked deeply into Andy's wet, red eyes. Tenderly he spoke, "I am so proud, so infinitely, so eternally proud, of you."

Mirrored in Lohr's adoration, Andy was inspired to speak on his own behalf, "I guess I have learned a few lessons this time around. Haven't I?"

Lohr stood up and stepped back, but he did not withdraw the heart connection. He continued to speak reassuringly, "Be grateful that you are not shut down completely, that your heart is strong and true and open to all the possibilities that Life brings to you. The world needs your forgiveness and your compassion. It needs all your emotions. You must allow yourself to have your emotions, feel them, all of them, to be fully alive. What is Life without feeling? To have Life in all its abundance: that's what Prime Source wants for everyone and that's what Prime Source gives to everyone."

At the mere mention of the name Prime Source, Andy's tears dried up; the storm had passed and the waters were placid again. He felt wondrously refreshed and cleansed inside, as if he was starting over with the proverbial 'clean slate.' For the moment, there seemed to be nothing more to say but Andy felt comfort and ease in the silence. Blissed out, he smiled at Lohr for a long time, or for what he supposed was a long time, as he was also spaced out on Lohr's earrings. They were twinkling. Like mirrored flags they were sparkling and flashing, lazily and hypnotically, madly signaling from some distant mountaintop.

"Are these too much?" Lohr asked out loud, touching and fingering both earrings. "A little distracting, are they?"

"Maybe a little, but I love them."

"How about this?" He touched his choker.

"Its okay. On you it's kind of sexy, actually."

Lohr looked at Andy expectantly and asked, "You're hesitant. What is it? I sense it but you need to tell me."

There was a definite twinkle in Andy's eye as he replied, "It's just that . . . well, next to you, I'm feeling just a bit . . . how shall I put it? . . . underdressed?"

"Aha! Yes. I see what you mean. Let me try to even us up for you."

Lohr took off the high heeled pumps and carefully placed them in front of the discarded wig. Then he shimmied out of the skirt and, less carefully, added it to the pile which now looked to Andy as though some Transgendered Fashion Witch had vanished by melting into the floor. Even though the pantyhose he wore already afforded him sufficient modesty, he straightened the jacket and pulled it down.

"Is this better?"

Now it was Andy's look that was expectant; and it seemed to say exactly what he was thinking, "Is that it? Is that all?"

"Oh!," thought Lohr, and plucked off the earrings and the choker and put them in the pocket of his jacket. "Better?" he asked aloud.

"Very nice, yes," Andy replied, politely reining in his penchant for the sarcastic, "but actually, well, you see, instead of undressing you, I was hoping we could dress me."

"Oh, but of course! And dress you we shall, my little bodhisattva cupcake! In fact, if all goes according to plan, you'll be going to a party later on so we can really lay on the 'glam' then. I mean, if you like, that is. But before that you've got a meeting with the Contact Committee and they are a rather austere bunch. Oh, don't get me wrong, they're very nice, nothing to be afraid of, it's just that they're all business. So, yes, you must be dressed for them. Now they have a lot to tell you and it's all very important so, remember to take it seriously and pay close attention; you won't be allowed to take notes. Oh! Such a face! Am I hurting you? I'm terribly sorry, I meant no harm; I was just kidding about taking notes, it won't really be necessary, you'll remember everything just fine. Really. Don't worry."

Andy was bewildered by Lohr's barrage. "A party? A meeting? The Contact Committee? What is this all about? I just wanted to meet some extraterrestrials; you know, come onboard, say 'Hi, Howya doin'? Welcome to Earth', 'Please don't kill us', that sort of thing; that's all."

"And you shall. All in good time. (What a quaint little phrase that is!) But first, let's go to my quarters and we'll get you ready for your audience." Lohr picked up the wig, the skirt, and the shoes, turned and started to walk away.

"Now you wait just a darn minute!" Andy practically shouted.

Lohr stopped and looked back over his shoulder. "What is it?'

"I have a lot of questions, that's 'what is it?'!"

"Well, come along and ask them and I will do my best to answer them – at least the relevant ones – but we've got to get you dressed."

The self-opening sliver of a doorway appeared in front of Lohr and he continued walking toward it. Andy hesitated, then began following, taking several quick steps to catch up, and finding that he moved much more easily in a lighter-weight body. At the opening he hesitated again so that he could check out the tunnel-like hallway Lohr was leading him into. Octagonal and also indirectly lighted, it did not seem particularly forbidding to Andy. He didn't want to parade himself through the ship naked, but his curiosity canceled any misgivings he might have had and he stepped into the hallway and turned right to follow his guide.

The walk to Lohr's quarters took less than five minutes. The grade of the floor rose and fell in increments so minute they were barely perceptible. The hall branched several times and Lohr took a right here and a left there, seemingly at random. There was nothing to distinguish one branch from another: there were no words, numbers, or markings of any kind, and no visible doors. Neither the lighting nor the mauve coloring of the walls varied significantly. Andy was completely at the mercy of Lohr in such a labyrinth, but he wasn't concerned about it. He was more interested in other forms of orientation.

"Is this a spaceship?'

"Yes, it is."

"Is it moving?"

"Yes, it is."

"Where is everybody?"

"Exactly where they are supposed to be, I hope."

"I meant, why haven't we met anybody in this hallway?"

"Partly because of what I just said and partly because you are being protected from sensory overload and the others are avoiding us."

"Oh. Are they scary looking?"

"Some of them." Lohr indicated they were taking a left turn.

"How many different kinds of alien beings are on this ship?"

"Approximately seventy."

"Seventy?!"

"Approximately."

"Is this the Mother Ship?"

"No."

"You mean there are bigger ships with more aliens?!"

"Yes."

"Cool."

"Does that mean you are impressed or that you are not warm enough?"

"I'm impressed."

"Are you warm enough?"

"Now that you mention it," Andy paused to give it some thought. Then continued, "Yes, I'm fine, thanks."

"Good." Lohr indicated a right turn.

"Where is this ship going?"

"Oh, wa-a-ay out into space, to rendezvous with the rest of the fleet, and then back to Earth."

"The fleet? How big a fleet is it?"

"Very big."

"How big is that?"

"Thousands of ships."

"Why? Are you invading?"

"Oh, no, no, no. Of course not. Entities from all over this part of the universe, representatives from many galaxies and many star systems, are here for generally one of two reasons." Lohr indicated another left turn.

"And those would be ... ?"

"Either to observe Earth's Ascension into a higher plane, or vibration, or to facilitate the Ascension. But I thought you knew that."

"Well, that is the gist of much of the channeled information I've read or heard. But a guy just doesn't know what to believe nowadays."

"Here we are."

Apparently doors on this ship were kept invisible until someone wanted to use them. A round 'hole,' eight feet in diameter, appeared in the wall to their left, a wall with no discernible thickness, and Andy followed Lohr into his room. It was a generous, trapezoidal space, where walls, floor, and ceiling curved, flowed, and blended into one another. There wasn't a right angle to be seen. The room seemed to have been molded rather than constructed. And every surface was upholstered or padded, even the pillowy sofa and chairs that grew like mushrooms from the floor. Recessed, spot lighting revealed the area was washed in several colors: deep shades of olive, gold, and turquoise. There were no visible windows or doors, no pictures on the walls, no nick-knacks, no plants, no pets, no television, no books on shelves, in fact, there were no shelves. Clean but unadorned, without any personal touches whatsoever, it was, to Andy's taste, somewhat sterile.

"Please, be seated. This is where I live. It is, perhaps, a simpler aesthetic than you might otherwise prefer," Lohr offered.

Andy sat in a sculpted chair, so padded it felt like sitting on a cloud, or so the cliché automatically sprang to his mind. "I love the colors, and the . . . ," his hands moved in small, expressive swoops and circles, as if feeling the contours of the room, "walls and floor, so . . . sculptural, so . . . organic." Andy was grateful for his art school vocabulary; at a time like this it really came in handy.

"But ... ?"

"But ... , well, it's kind of impersonal, kind of undistinguished. I mean, what makes this room *your* room? Where are your favorite photos or works of art? Don't you like to decorate?"

Lohr laughed, "I see what you mean. I used to like to be surrounded by things, to have cherished objects where I could see them and enjoy them. I liked having my memories and my senses stimulated. But lately I find all that can be distracting, too. I do have treasures. I just don't have them here on display. Besides, you would ask me questions about them, and they would not be relevant questions, and I would have to refuse to answer them. So, you see how it goes.

"Now, clothes for you. I'm going to change, too, so please, excuse me. I'll try to make it quick." Lohr stepped up to a wall, it opened and he stepped through. Andy caught a glimpse of a well-stocked walk-in closet before the 'door' closed behind his host.

There was nothing for Andy to do but sit still and wait. He wanted to poke around but there was nothing to poke into. He liked the smooth texture of the chair he sat on, like the softest suede. That was nice. And he noticed it was quiet. It was perfectly silent in Lohr's room. That was nice. And a little weird. And there was a lingering scent in the air. It was subtle, but there it was: a dusky, woodsy floral base with a clean, citrus highlight. (Andy once dated a guy who was the fragrance buyer at Marshall Field's. Less often, that vocabulary came in handy, too.) Maybe it was Lohr's favorite cologne that delicately permeated the room. Or maybe his body odor was as beautiful as he was. Better not follow that thought path; it too would surely be deemed 'irrelevant.'

But Andy grew bored. He wondered what 'wa-a-y out into space' meant, especially to intergalactic travelers like Lohr. And he wondered just how scary some of Lohr's fellow travelers were. He fervently hoped none of them looked like cockroaches, that might make him sick. Then again, if they looked like parakeets, that might make him laugh. Neither response, he was certain, would be looked upon as polite. And, although he wasn't particularly hungry or thirsty, he wondered if they would serve him snacks or beverages, and, if so, should he accept them. What if they served crudités at the party? He hated crudités. Or alcohol? How do you explain being in recovery to aliens? But then, he reasoned, surely they would accept a polite no, thank you. And what was this party about? Plucked from San Francisco, to go to a party on a flying saucer? This was turning into one bizarre abduction experience. As if there were non-bizarre abduction experiences!

Lohr emerged from his closet dressed in an off-white, long-sleeved, pullover tunic, worn belted and over white leggings. He wore pearl gray, low-heeled boots that came just above his ankles. He handed Andy a short-sleeved version of the tunic, a belt, a pair of the leggings, and a pair of the boots. "This is pretty much the uniform around here. At least for humanoids. These should fit you."

Andy pulled on the leggings. The drawstring waist – very low-tech – provided a perfect, non-binding, fit. The tunic was essentially an extra large T-shirt, although the jersey fabric was a heavier weave than most T-shirts on Earth. The belt, identical to scouting or military belts, was a sturdy web weave that fastened with a brass-like buckle. Andy noticed that Lohr had a small pouch strung on his belt which probably served the same purpose as a fanny pack. Everything, including the boots, fit him just as Lohr said.

"I'm sorry its not flashier attire – we could really have fun playing dress-up, I've got some great drag! – but its not a good idea to flash the Contact Committee. Although I must say, that looks very nice on you."

"Thank you," Andy replied. "It probably looked better on Luke Skywalker but I like it, too. It's very comfortable. Is it cotton?"

"It's much like cotton, yes; a plant fiber."

"And the boots? Animal skin?"

"Yes."

"And the animal? Much like a cow?"

"Not particularly."

"From what planet?"

With a wry smile and twinkling eyes, Lohr answered, "The planet K-Mart." It was Lohr's way of saying, "sorry, but you don't really need to know that."

Andy smiled back, "Irrelevant, right?"

"Yes, that's right." Lohr laughed, "I like you; you catch on fast."

"Thanks," Andy acknowledged the compliment with a shy grin and a nod of his head and sat down.

"Will you excuse me for a few moments? I have to check in and see if the Contact Committee is ready for us."

"Sure. Go right ahead."

Lohr turned his back to Andy, took a deep breath, and exhaled. There was a pause of silence for about half a minute, and then he began speaking in muffled tones as if to himself and as if he didn't want Andy to hear. Andy thought that was a little silly; one of them could have stepped outside if confidentiality was an issue. He was wondering whether or not he should mention it, when he clearly heard the word 'greys' in his head. And the word flashed subliminally in his consciousness so that he also clearly knew that it wasn't 'graze', that thing that cows do. He knew all about the Greys. They were the little bastards responsible for most of the scary abductions in UFO literature. Andy braced himself for the possibility that this exquisite adventure could easily turn ugly.

Lohr's mumbling took on a stern, insistent tone, the volume rising and falling between long pauses. Finally finished, he took another breath and turned to face Andy with a strangely unreadable smile on his face.

"Well, we are just about all set. After I give you my briefing it will be time to go to the meeting place."

"What about the Greys?"

"My, you are clever!" Lohr sat down across from Andy. He kept smiling while he stalled a moment before replying. "There will be no Greys at this meeting. None were invited but, at the last minute, they petitioned to send some observers. I had them bumped. It's kind of a personal thing, I admit I'm prejudiced, but there really isn't any good reason for them to be there."

"I'm relieved. Thanks. I don't think I'd want to meet any of them, even if they were part of the Committee."

"They aren't exactly warm and fuzzy, are they? But then, they are making an effort to correct their mistakes and improve the races. You know, they used to be very much like Earth humans. However, they destroyed their planet, had to move underground and lost the ability to have a full range of emotions, even in the face of reproductive sterility. They are desperately trying to give themselves a future."

"Well, I guess they have at least one emotion we can all relate to: desperation."

"Yes. And the desire for a future."

There was a slightly uncomfortable pause; Andy was aware of a poignant subtext in the conversation. He wondered if the Earth would survive its present course. He wondered if enough people were desperate for a future; not just a short-term future for themselves, but a long-term future for all their descendants.

"It might interest you to know," Lohr continued, "that, since approximately 1992 of your time system, the Galactic Federation has prohibited further experimentation by the Zeta Reticuli. First, they must substantiate their claims of progress and, second, before they can resume experimentation, they must implement less invasive, more cooperative procedures."

"Is it true that abductees have made unconscious agreements to submit to these experiments?"

"Yes, and many of the abductees are recognizing some rewards, some benefits, in terms of spiritual growth, that their cooperation has brought them. However, a plateau was reached and the next benefits, for both Zetas and Earth humans, will only come about with increased honesty in the contract.

"You see, at first it was an honest mistake, a simple misunderstanding. The Zetas asked for help to rebuild their species and the Earthlings said, yes, we will help you, without either side delineating their needs and their limits.

86

What I find objectionable is that, while many of the Earthlings may have been ignorant and naive, many of the Greys were exploitive and quick to take advantage of the miscommunication. There must be no more victims of this kind of treachery. That is why the Galactic Federation proclaimed a moratorium on the whole affair."

"Is it working? I mean, can they be trusted? Can the Galactic Federation police them?'

"I'm told it is mostly working but, personally, I don't believe they can be trusted. After all, once betrayed, a trust must be earned, or re-earned. And that takes time and repeated demonstrations of trustworthiness, of reliability, and responsibility. To answer your last question, officially there is nothing the Federation can do to police the situation. Unofficially is another matter, but I am not authorized to comment on the various 'pressures' that might be brought to bear on the Zeta Reticuli."

"Not even off the record?"

"You'll have to read about it in the Enquirer."

Oddly enough, that statement did not sound like irony to Andy. Before he could figure out what Lohr meant, Lohr launched into his briefing.

"The Contact Committee wishes to communicate with you for two reasons: to continue your gradual awakening into the Light and thus expand your role in the Ascension of the planet, and to impart to you vital information that will accomplish this further expansion of your personal and planetary reality.

"As to protocol, I will be present as your guide and advocate. The information will be given to you via dialogue, holographic imagery, and direct links to your subconscious. As I mentioned, you are not required to take notes. I would advise you not to try to memorize the experience but to 'have' the experience, to be fully present and aware. I would encourage you to relax, to watch and listen, to be yourself, and to speak candidly when asked to share your thoughts. Otherwise, I must ask you to, please, keep questions to a minimum. After the meeting I will be glad to answer any you find particularly compelling. Provided they are relevant, of course.

"The Committee will consist of as many as nine entities, only seven of which might be visible to you, and only three or four of those are likely to interact with you directly. They will all, however, cooperatively assist in the presentation. While I cannot provide you with any details regarding this meeting and presentation, I have been asked to introduce two words for your consideration. They are: interspecies communication."

A delightful image of himself swimming with dolphins, laughing, squeaking, and clicking, wafted through Andy's head. But he could not reconcile that carefree vision with the apprehensive feeling that wrapped itself around him like a slithery tentacle. Hugging himself, he absentmindedly caressed his shoulders, as if trying to wipe away the ominous sensation and stared, with a worried frown, past Lohr's left shoulder.

Lohr correctly gauged Andy's body language. "One last thing: if, at any time, for any reason, you require an end to the proceedings, simply look at me and say so. If you need the experience modified in any way, just ask it. None of this could take place, none of this is possible, without your consent. Remember: you have the power to control this experience."

He waited until he saw Andy relax, then finished the briefing, "I think that just about covers it. So, are you ready to make Contact?"

Now that the moment was here, Andy was not one hundred percent certain, but he made it sound convincing when he answered, "Sure, let's go."

F⬇VE

He kept a California roadmap tucked between his seat and the console, but he'd already decided to get off the Interstate and head west on State Road 299 through the Trinity National Forest. The exit was well-marked. Once on SR 299, he breathed a little more easily knowing his very traceable car was now off the state's major north-south artery. Maybe it was silly of him, but he felt safer, less conspicuous, taking the 'back roads.'

When Richard was satisfied that Andy had fallen asleep in the back seat, he turned on the radio and kept it at a low volume. The station to which he was already tuned had replaced the call-in show with hard rock, so he wandered the stations hoping to find an all-news-all-the-time format. When he failed to find any news at all on either AM or FM, he returned to an FM station playing light rock and left it there. The station broke for news highlights at 4:00 o'clock (which reminded him he needed to reset his car clock and his watch).

There was no mention of UFO activity over Mount Shasta so he quickly scanned for some more substantial news from some other station. He caught the tail end of one news-on-the-hour broadcast. Unfortunately he could monitor only one station at a time. By the time he listened to one broadcast, the news on any other station would also be over. At least he could identify a Redding station which would be the most likely to run a report on the Shasta flap. After the news, they settled in for an hour of oldies devoted exclusively to the top forty hits of the Seventies. The hits just kept on coming and Richard had a connection to every one of them. Each song came with a story and reminded him of a place, a time or a lover. This kept Richard engaged enough so that he wasn't thinking every ten minutes about waking Andy and forcing him to spill everything about his encounter with alien life forms.

He was lip-syncing all the parts to one of his favorites when, around a bend, he came upon a parked state trooper's car. He tensed up guiltily and checked his speed. He was just under the posted limit but he slowed and drove by nervously, trying not to look into the car. He got enough of a glimpse to know it wasn't Officer Wilson. The trooper looked down as if reading something and paid no attention to Richard's passing car. Five miles later he felt like he could relax again. Five miles after that, he was trying to get into a lip-synch performance of another favorite when the police car, lights flashing wildly, appeared in his rearview mirror bearing down on him with alarming speed.

"Oh, shit!" he thought, and slowed the car to pull over. Before he could get off the road, the trooper tore around him, leaving him relieved as he watched the lights slowly shrink into the far distance and vanish abruptly around another bend in the road. He let out a long sigh and accelerated. He thought, "Maybe they aren't looking for us after all. But then, maybe we were just lucky this time."

At five o'clock Richard listened in vain for any news of UFO's over Mount Shasta, then quickly tuned to find the end of another news broadcast. When the second station identified itself as "Redding's Home for News and Sports," he decided to stay with this one for awhile. It turned out not to be the all-news format he was hoping for, but he resigned himself to stay with it even though it was playing current top forty hits. Richard didn't care for most contemporary pop music. It tried too hard to be grown up, cynical, rebelliously shocking, and, musically it was boring, formulaic, synthetic, and

90

just plain stale. He knew he wasn't being fair, that he was being an old fogy, but he felt out of the loop and took out some of his resentment at being almost fifty on the 'kids.' But after the second nerve-wracking song he turned off the radio altogether rather than get himself all worked up over ageism and the deplorable state of teen-driven pop culture.

In the town of Douglas City he stopped to go to the bathroom, reset his wrist watch and car clock, and to pick up some extra-strength pain reliever for his rapidly expanding headache. He didn't have the heart to wake up Andy who slept intensely with a furrowed brow, his cheek pressed against the seat and the quilt thrown aside.

He was determined to let him sleep at least until they reached Mendocino, where he planned to stop for a decent meal. He consulted the roadmap and further decided that, even though SR 299 looked like a better road, he would head southwesterly on SR 3, then pick up Highway 101. He suspected this was going to take longer than either he or Sarah had figured.

Now that he had Andy back with him, he frankly didn't care how long it might take. Compared to the mad dash to the rescue up Interstate 5 or the 'Escape From Mount Shasta,' this drive was relaxing, a breather, a triumphant victory lap. This winding, dual lane, state road was not heavily traveled, so while it would be a longer journey, it would be a much more enjoyable one. He could just sit back and, as his mother used to urge him to do on long, family road trips as a child, 'drink in the scenery.'

But as he drove, even the abundant natural beauty of the land could not keep his mind tranquil. He barely gave his own blackout on the mountain a second thought. It was just one more inexplicable link in this baffling chain of events. He desperately wanted to make sense of it all, but his thoughts kept leading back to Andy. What had he been through? Richard's mind was eager to fill in a scenario and it now seemed stuck on one fact: Andy was returned naked from the waist down. Why? And thinking about Andy pantless – so exposed, so vulnerable – with, God only knows, what kind of creepy, slimy creatures around him, slobbering, drooling, touching him, poking him, prodding him, groping him, … . Well, it just infuriated Richard. He had to know what they did to Andy! Not knowing was sheer torture!

Sure, he seemed fine. He said he was okay. But what did he really remember? Maybe it would take hypnosis to reveal the truth; a truth so horrible, so traumatic, that Andy had to bury it deep in his unconscious. He would need therapy. He would need a medical examination, the sooner the better! Dammit! It should have been his first thought, his first priority! Richard grabbed his car phone and thumb-dialed the office number for his best friend and personal physician, Dr. David Forsythe. Dave would help. He'd know what to do.

There were five doctors in Dr. Forsythe's office on Bush Street in San Francisco. All of them were either gay or gay-friendly. Dr. Dave himself was gay, in his late forties and very handsome. (In certain circles, he was also sometimes referred to as Dr. Dreamboat.) As a gay internist, a substantial part of his practice was with AIDS patients, but he also treated a core clientele, now diminished and still dwindling, of loyal friends who, like Richard, had thus far survived the epidemic. He and Richard had met, through Billy, in the late Seventies. The doctor too had lost a partner, not to gay bashing or AIDS but to cancer. He and his present companion, Chuck, had been together nine years. Since Richard and Andy had started dating in March, they had seen them socially on several occasions. In fact, it was at their New Year's Eve party that Richard met Andy. Andy was part of the catering crew that night at a sit-down dinner for twelve. At any rate, the foursome seemed to enjoy each other's company but Andy was still 'the new guy.' Perhaps Chuck and Dave were just being gracious and polite while waiting to see if Andy was going to work out as Richard's life mate. Like Richard's mother, they had seen a lot of boyfriends come and go. But they were good friends and Dave would do this for him without hesitation.

"Doctors' office, Fran speaking, how may I direct your call?" Fran, the office manager and head nurse, was busy. She was brusque and in automatic business mode. But, as usual, as soon as Richard identified himself, she brightened right up.

"Oh, I'm afraid Dr. Forsythe is with a patient right now, Mr. Lang, can he call you right back?"

"I'm not in my office, … ." Richard started to explain as Fran, throwing protocol out the window, cheerfully cut him off.

"Oh, that's okay, just hold a sec' and I'll ring him for you."

"I don't want to bother … ."

"Oh, no bother!" she chirped as she cut him off again and placed him on hold. When the doctor came on the line, a scant fifteen seconds later, he was dismissing his patient. Over the phone Richard could hear his voice echoing off the walls of his examination room. Then he spoke directly into the mouthpiece with his usual concerned greeting, "Richard, hi, is everything okay?"

"Sorry to bother you, but, … ." Richard was once again cut off.

"No, no! No bother at all. I was finished. That was my last patient of the day. What's up?"

Richard looked in the rearview mirror at Andy's sleeping form. "I was wondering if you would examine Andy."

"Of course, but Fran could have given you an appointment; why are you asking me? Is it urgent?"

"Dave, it's kind of silly, I suppose. No, it's not exactly an emergency but… , could we see you tomorrow morning?"

"Why don't you come in at ten, I'll see you first thing. But what seems to be the problem? What are his symptoms?"

"There are no real symptoms. Look, this is kind of awkward for me, Dave, even with you. Can we talk about it tomorrow?"

"Sure. Sure we can."

"Thanks. I'll let you go then."

Dr. Forsythe was puzzled and a little confused by Richard's brush off. "Well. Fine, if you say so, but if you … ."

"Say hi to Chuck for me, will you?"

"Uh, yeah, right. I will. Fine, then. See you guys tomorrow at ten."

Dr. Dave knew many very private things about Richard, not the least of which was his medical history. Beyond the professional, he knew the personal things that Richard told him, voluntarily, confidentially, friend to friend. Dr. Dave never pried; he didn't have to. He was a great listener: attentive, empathetic and compassionate; you just wanted to confide in him. And he could be trusted; he could be counted on to be discreet. Richard knew this because, in the past, he had tried to get Dr. Dave to let down his guard and divulge something, anything, about Billy. It never worked. Dr. Dave was cool, the coolest. Richard needed that now.

As he drove, the late afternoon sunlight flashing through the trees, he was trying to be hopeful. He told himself, "So he will examine Andy for signs of … of ... physical trauma and that will clear up this whole stupid idea of . . . about the possibility that … Andy was … was ... abused." It was extremely difficult for him to navigate around the real thought he was thinking, to avoid the word 'rape.' He winced when he realized the exam just might confirm his worst fear. Richard's face took on a very grim cast, one that Andy had never seen, quickly tightening into an angry mask of hate. His firm grip on the steering wheel became the crushing grip on the alien gook bastard's neck and he squeezed until his hands hurt. For the second or third time today he told himself to get a grip. Then he noticed his white knuckles and got the joke. He laughed bitterly, then ironically, did just the opposite: he relaxed his grip. Before he could dredge up anything else to stew about, he remembered to turn on the radio.

His timing was uncanny. The signal from the Redding radio station was beginning to fade but the six o'clock news was clear enough to hear the report for which Richard had been waiting. He turned up the volume to hear the announcer say:

"Hundreds of people claim they saw UFO's over Mount Shasta today. Park Service Rangers along with state and county police were on hand to maintain order in what is being called a full-blown outbreak of mass hysteria. Local, commercial, and military aviation spokesmen maintain the skies over Shasta were clear of man-made aircraft. However, for a period of about four hours, from approximately ten a.m. to two p.m., one hundred fifteen reports of strange lights flying in bizarre formations over the majestic peak were received by authorities. A temporary evacuation of the surrounding camping, hiking, and recreational areas was carried out for reasons of safety and security.

Cameras from our sister station, TV Five, were on hand to record the light show which strangely failed to show up on video tape, even though news anchor, Paula Perez, and her crew insist they themselves could clearly see the lights. The fact that many other potential witnesses could not is the reason why psychologist Dean Pennington, from Cal' State, Chico, is calling this one a classic case of mass hysteria.

While many residents would just as soon forget the odd occurrence, many others are already adding this story to the wealth of legends and myths surrounding the mystical, dormant volcano. The weather is next, followed by sports, after this word from . . . ."

Richard turned off the radio. So, the 'experts' were writing this off as some kind of mental aberration, delusions and hallucinations on a mass scale. "Just how does something like that work?" Richard asked himself. "Didn't they claim that mass religious hysteria in the Middle Ages was the result of villagers eating moldy bread and getting high on it? But now? 1995? What would cause such a reaction?" he wondered, "Contaminated drinking water?"

Until today he might have agreed with the experts about mass sightings of UFO's. Their explanation was plausible, certainly, but he had seen them himself. Hadn't he? Of course he had! And he had seen crowds of people who had seen them too. But why was there no mention of the military presence? That certainly threw up red flags all over this weird event. Or was the military the actual cause of this hysteria with the leak of some top secret, experimental nerve gas?

Anything was possible, of course, but somehow Richard thought that was straining toward the preposterous. Who was covering up and why? No, it was too fantastic, too tabloid shocking. Yet, even if the mass hysteria hypothesis were correct and he himself had fallen victim to the same psychosis, that didn't account for Andy's disappearance and re-appearance ten hours and two hundred fifty miles later.

Conspiracy theories and hallucinations; Richard frowned. Did he really know anymore what was preposterous and what wasn't? He looked in the rearview mirror at his sleeping prince. His head throbbed and he popped another extra-strength pain reliever.

"The pyramid glowed like rose alabaster lit from within."

S⫶X

Lohr and Andy were silent as they made their way through the deserted passages of the starship. Their booted feet clumped softly as they strode briskly along on a floor that resembled more the padded suede of Lohr's furniture than carpeting and was identical to the seven other walls of the octagonal corridor. Andy was wound up, giddy as a ten-year-old on a field trip from school. At one point he even tried to skip, but the floor was too springy for that. Lohr paid no attention to him when he started reaching out to touch, slap, and pat the leathery walls and the hollow-ribbed supports that maintained the hall's octagonal shape.

After a short while in the labyrinth, Andy sensed their progress was spiraling to the right. The grade rose and fell but his perception was that they were ascending. He imagined they were circling the outer edge of the saucer, gradually homing in on the top center of the ship. He marveled again at how light his body felt and how easy it was to keep up the power-walking pace set by Lohr even on this flexible flooring. Still he hoped it wouldn't be too much farther. The suspense, the anticipation, was the real cause of his breathlessness, not the exertion of matching steps with Lohr's long legs.

Without warning those long legs stopped abruptly, and Andy almost ran into Lohr, who turned, smiled, and announced, "Here we are." Again, there was no discernible distinguishing mark to indicate a doorway. Lohr just seemed to know intuitively where the rooms were and the magic commands to open their doors. He did his thing and a round hole, eight feet in diameter, grew in the wall, some invisible technology wondrously causing it to expand like a camera's iris. Through the hole came a wavering, shimmery glow, that as light reflected through water, illuminated the passageway and danced on their faces. Andy stepped closer to the threshold for a better look and actually felt his mind blow. The detonation was gentle, but it still provoked a gasp at the sight of what lay beyond the opening.

Through the doorway was the infinite vastness of the Universe, the black, eternal night of outer space, a night sky strewn with a diamond field of stars, constellations, planets, comets, suns, and moons. Looking down, he saw the horizon of an equally vast ocean. It was as though he saw all this from a platform in that same sky. Vertigo made him step back. And he got down on his knees and peered over the edge of the threshold.

In the middle of the dark, purple and teal ocean was an atoll of white sand on pastel coral. The sand seemed to glow or shine like reflective tape. A gentle breeze caught the tops of the palm trees. The surf coming in from an infinite horizon broke quietly, majestically, on the reef which surrounded and protected a small tropical island. A volcanic cone dominated the jungle-covered landmass. From its summit either a cloud or a plume of smoke smeared off to the right.

Prominently featured in the middle of the lush greenery, on the long axis of the island from the white sand beach to the towering volcano, was a four-sided step pyramid of Mayan design. A steep stairway on each side climbed to the top. And on the top was a small, cubical structure, really no more than a covered room with large windows and front and back door openings. The pyramid glowed like rose alabaster lit from within. Andy looked at Lohr who surveyed the scene with obvious delight. But Andy's mind was radically boggled and it took him some time before he could put together a question, and another moment before he could speak it.

"Is that in the ship?"

"Technically speaking, yes. Actually, no. You are looking at another dimension, another reality contained within the ship, or rather, for which the ship is a gateway." Lohr's answer didn't quite satisfy Andy, but he had no idea what further information would clarify it. So he went on to his next question.

"Is that where ...?"

"Yes, that's where you will meet the Contact Committee."

Andy could not help noticing that they were really high up above the island, maybe as much as two thousand feet, and that there was no stairway, elevator, cable car, rope ladder, there was nothing, no way at all to get down to the island from where they were. So his next question was, "How?"

"We jump."

"Are you kidding me?"

"No. We just jump in. We'll be stepping off into reality number two of your extraterrestrial adventure. Are you ready?"

"Hey! Whoa! Wait a minute here. Not so fast."

"You don't want me to push you, do you?"

"Of course not! But ... geez, Lohr, that's a long way down! That's ... that's a 'void' we're talking about! That's the 'abyss'!"

"And you don't think you can fly? How do you think you got here in the first place?"

Andy snapped back emphatically, "Damned if I know!"

"Did you or did you not levitate? Did you or did you not defy gravity?"

Andy thought about it for a moment then replied, "Well ... Okay, I suppose you have a point. But let's just do it before I change my mind."

"Excellent! Give me your hand. Now, on the count of three, we'll step off together and you'll see how easy it is."

Andy took a very deep breath as Lohr counted. On three Lohr stepped forward and had to pull Andy after him. Holding his breath meant his scream was muffled, but he quickly discovered he was not plummeting. Andy was shocked to feel them both floating slowly downward. It was like sinking in water only this 'air' was much more buoyant. Their descent was startling for its slowness. There was something else about the 'air' that was unusual. Andy noticed ripple-like distortions, as if they were immersed in a crystalline clear, viscous fluid. When he could hold his breath no longer, he gasped and found, to his further astonishment, that he could breathe normally without the slightest sensation of suffocation.

Lohr let go of his hand and Andy watched him kick himself into a downward, diving position to show him how they could swim in it. Amazingly, though it supported them better than water, it was not wet. Andy's shock turned to delight and he swam after Lohr. As they descended, he made another pleasant discovery: there was no increase in pressure as there would be under water. And it didn't take half the muscle power of swimming! "This is what they do in cartoons," he thought. He became so enraptured he turned his free fall into a romp and began doing lazy underwater-ballet circles, twists and arcs. He was proudest of his corkscrew spins.

Lohr's swimming strokes had, indeed, increased his momentum, so he had to slow his headlong descent toward the beach. From a hundred feet ahead, Lohr called back, "Watch me land! Watch how I do it!" Kicking himself into a feet first position, steering and stabilizing himself with his arms, he touched down on the fine, white sand and turned around to check on Andy's approach.

"That's it, that's right! You're doing fine!" Lohr shouted encouragement. It was so easy that Andy felt as if he'd done this before, as if he'd known how to do this all his life. He made a clean, low impact landing, grinning with sheer joy and unadulterated pride at his newfound grace. Had he ever before known what it was like to feel so perfectly un-clumsy?

"Hey! I did it!" he shouted jubilantly, "I did it! I flew!"

Lohr happily embraced him in a congratulatory hug and the two of them spontaneously let out a long, harmonic howl of joy. They let go, stepped back and laughed at each other's goofy grins.

"Wow! That was so much FUN!" Andy stole a glance at the top of the pyramid, his grin wavered for a split second, but he charged on. "Hey! Can we fly up too?" Before he got an answer, he ran a few feet and tried a Superman leap and went sailing straight up about ten feet.

Lohr smiled and called after him, "Just swim! Its harder going up, but you should be able to do it."

Instead, Andy let himself sink back down again.

"Sorry. I got a little carried away. I'm ... uh, ... just a bit nervous. I guess I'd rather play than get down to business."

"I understand," Lohr said sympathetically. "But, come, follow me." He turned and walked toward the pink pyramid, his footsteps shifting in the sparkling, sugar sand. Andy followed dutifully. He told himself to behave. It would not do to meet his otherworldly brothers – or sisters – giggling hysterically. He let the seriousness, the importance, of what was about to happen to him settle inside, and he thought of how honored he was to be getting his wish. Peripherally, to his right, he detected some movement; just a shadow, really, but when he looked there was nothing there. The jungle was, for a moment, quiet and still.

But a balmy breeze soon rustled the forest leaves and palm fronds. The muffled crashing of the surf on the reef, and the occasional, distant bits of whale song, cast a calming, centering spell over his anxious spirit. At the base of the pyramid, Lohr turned around to check on Andy's progress. Andy caught up and, looking up the steps, asked, "Well, shall we go up?"

"Yes, in a minute. We're waiting for someone, a friend of mine. Then we will ascend together."

"Oh," was all Andy could think of to say. Waiting was the last thing he wanted to be doing at this point. Biding his time, he looked around and decided to take mental notes of what he saw. He scanned the sky for the opening from which they'd jumped. Of course, it was gone. How could one jump through a hole in the sky? Or swim through the air, for that matter? Miles away, out over the dark ocean, was a line of stormy looking, cumulus clouds. He saw several flashes of lightning but it was so far off the sound of thunder never reached him. He noticed how the palm trees, Lohr, and he, himself, cast pale, noontime shadows on the sand.

The midnight sky, though ablaze with celestial lights, could not account for the near daylight brightness of the island. Like Lohr, everything seemed to be infused with its own light, shining from inside out, casting subtle auras of varying intensity around each tree, rock, and blade of grass. He imagined this aura included every drop of water and grain of sand. And he noticed in the fluid rippling of the liquid air, the now-and-then glint of glitter flakes, just like the light he'd first seen in his bedroom. In more ways than one, this was an incredible spot in which to be.

All this had to be a dream. Didn't it? But never before had he dreamed in such detail, nor had his senses been so acutely aware in the dream-state. And, so far, at least, this wasn't nearly as bizarre as some of the psychedelic trips of his youth. Well, maybe that was debatable. Still, everything was so extraordinarily vivid it was beyond real; it was hyper real. He wondered how much he would remember when he woke up, if he woke up. That's why he wanted to look and remember as much of what he saw as he could.

This was a startling, new reality that he found himself in, alright, but what was the use of trying to figure it out? He refused to be distracted from admiring the perfection, the unnatural natural beauty of this cosmic Tahiti. He loved this place! He felt its beauty in his heart as if only now was he coming home after many, many lifetimes. At last, he had finally found the place where he belonged. He already felt a tug of regret for the moment when he knew he would have to leave. "Stop it," he thought, and chided himself for future-tripping, a strict no-no in the recovery community. As his mind was beginning to wander into speculation again, a gust of breeze puffed the back of his head, and the stirring leaves announced the arrival of another sentience.

He completed a three-quarter-turn and saw a figure, unmistakably female, walk out of the undergrowth. She seemed not to notice him but, instead, beamed the same friendly light at Lohr that Lohr had beamed at him. And, even obliquely, Andy was intrigued and captivated by the energy. Graceful as a dancer, regal of bearing, she was an exquisite woman of mixed race. He thought her the most beautiful possible blend of Asia and Africa. She glided over the sand, barely disturbing the surface. As she drew closer, Andy took in more details.

She was buxom in her pink, scooped-neck, short-sleeved jersey tunic. A silky sarong, an abstract print in rainbow hues, was wrapped around her waist and tucked above her left hip. Her flawless complexion was of the palest café-au-lait'. Her shiny, wavy, blue-black hair was swept to the back of her head and held in place by a golden, spiked clip. Gold disc earrings the size of quarters and a necklace of garnet beads set off her graceful neck. Rings adorned most of her fingers and toes whose manicured and pedicured nails were lacquered blood red. And then there was her scintillating fragrance; sweet but decidedly spicy. He knew he'd smelled it before, though it had never seemed as lovely as now, but he couldn't name it. Strong at first, it soon retreated into the background of sensory impressions.

She stopped five feet from Lohr and they each placed their hands, in an attitude of prayer, over their heart and bowed deeply. They beamed at each other, speaking not a word, clearly happy to be in each other's company. Then Lohr spoke to her, "Allow me to introduce to you our guest from the third density ."

She turned to Andy to give him her full, welcoming attention. The radiance, though different in kind from Lohr's, was equally affecting. Her good will was sustaining after he was jolted by a close-up look at her face.

Her sharply prominent cheek bones, her huge, shadowed, almond eyes, opaque black and set at an exaggerated slant, the tiny bump of a nose above the generous mouth with full, rouged lips, and the pointed chin; all of it , the total effect of her, set an unearthly standard of beauty.

"This is Andy," Lohr said.

She bowed. Andy bowed. She reached for his hands and took them in hers. He saw himself reflected in her eyes. He could not read any emotion in them. Still, the rest of her face was smiling, and she spoke in an appealing way when she said, "Andy, I am Reiko. I am so pleased to finally meet you. I am here, with my dear friend Lohr, to be your supporting, balancing energy. As you have seen, I am of mixed lineage, part human and part ... well, let me just say ... part star being. I am an empath, much like yourself. We are those who are receptive and sensitive deeply and innately, beyond that which is called empathy. I will be a gatekeeper for your energy, a kind of transformer and interpreter all in one." To Lohr she asked, "Did you explain about the breathing?" He shook his head, no, and she turned back to Andy. "Briefly then, for you to be here with us, for you to be present in this reality or density, requires you to be in an altered state of consciousness. You see, not every sentient being resides in your three-dimensional version of reality.

"There are many levels of density, although 'levels' implies a hierarchy, which would be somewhat misleading. To come aboard our star vehicle, you entered an altered state similar to R.E.M. sleep. In R.E.M. sleep you have access to most of the other dimensions. Lohr greeted you in the fifth dimension. I am speaking to you now in the seventh dimension. Some members of the Contact Committee are from higher densities and would not be able to function comfortably below seventh. We will be helping your consciousness to achieve ninth dimension for the purpose of greater receptivity to the messages from the Contact Committee. I can see you have a very good question in mind, so let me try to explain further."

"You are correct. It is true, we could have conducted this meeting while you slept in your bed. That would have meant an out of body experience for you in the dream-state, at which you are quite adept, by the way. You look surprised but you are. Your disbelief is precisely why we did not use that method this time."

The implications of what Reiko was telling Andy disturbed him. She spoke familiarly, clinically, of his unconscious life, the life he didn't usually want to know about. What had he done while in this other state? He shifted his weight and leaned closer to Lohr, as if just from proximity to his trusted guide, he could shore up the security Reiko was benignly eroding.

"It is a common tendency for you to discredit and discount the validity of your life in the dream-state, as if it is significant of nothing more than random electro-biochemical firings among the neurons of the human brain." Andy could accept that his spirit was busy at night on other levels of reality, but he didn't want to know about it. He never wanted the two lives to overlap.

"Excuse me. When I said 'you,' I meant the human race in general and not necessarily you specifically." She glanced at Lohr and continued, "I know there is a part of you that understands this and supports your participation in this contact scenario…" She looked back at Andy and went on, " … even if that part is not always in full communication with your consciousness.

"I promised to be brief and I'm afraid I have not been. Forgive me. I assure you I am trying to complete this as quickly as possible. The Committee is waiting. So that you would embrace this experience and not dismiss it as a figment of your dream imagination, it was necessary to bring your body along with your consciousness, you complete and all together, out of third and into ninth dimension. To be fully receptive you must be both completely relaxed and completely alert. So, as we climb the pyramid, each step will include a breath and exhalation. By the time we reach the top, you will be in perfect synch with their dimensional energies and receptive to dialogue with the Contact Committee.

"This will use more of your brain than you have ever used before. Your awareness will be more expanded than it has ever been before. This will stretch your mind so far that it will never be able to return to the level of understanding it once had. Don't be afraid. We are absolutely certain you are ready and able to assimilate this experience. It will not be without difficulty, but it will also not be without reward."

Andy nodded as though he understood, but he really didn't have any idea how all this was going to go. He was glad for the dream explanation (as far as that went), but he had a comical, tortured picture of his head expanding like a balloon being inflated. Yet, even when it popped, he felt optimistic. Hadn't he always handled, for better or for worse, whatever came his way? He would trust in and embrace the 'now' and let each moment take care of itself. Besides, he had Lohr and Reiko for support.

He liked Reiko, even though her eyes seriously freaked him out. Were they some kind of protective contact lenses or what? Still, she was no scary monster, in spite of her 'lineage.' She exuded strength, compassion, and a knowing quality, an all-around competence, that inspired confidence in Andy, much like a good and kind nurse would. And he (or maybe it was the playful Felicia) mentally joked, "If I had boobs like hers, I could rule the world." He was quite startled to hear an immediate response of "Thank you." He looked at Reiko but she was looking expectantly to the top of the pyramid. He looked at Lohr, who shrugged with a silly, don't-look-at-me, expression on his handsome face.

"Did one of you just say something?"

"I thanked you for your compliments," Rieko replied matter-of-factly, neither amused nor offended by Andy's reference to her breasts.

Lohr interjected, "She's an excellent empath, wouldn't you agree?"

Andy, quite red-faced, nodded yes. A very amused Lohr took his arm and gently urged, "Come, O Transparent One, let's go embrace the 'Now'." Too nervous and excited to stay embarrassed, Andy began the ascent with Lohr on his left and Reiko on his right. They carefully instructed him to inhale on the step up and to exhale on the rise: breathe, step, exhale – it all became a fluid motion. Slowly at first, then building momentum, they climbed together. After the first dozen steps the trio fell into perfect synchronization: breathe, step, exhale, together – became one fluid motion. In spite of the unusually high rise of the steps, their progress had a natural ease, their breathing effortless and unforced.

As he knew he would, Andy entered a trance state. It was not a trance of sleep but one of heightened wakefulness. His senses sharpened, his body grew more robust. It was functioning on levels of efficiency, ease and harmony that he'd never felt before. His perceptions were so magnified that when he closed his eyes, it was almost as if he could still see but with his whole body, through his skin.

He heard Lohr and Reiko reciting, in unison, an invocation to God, the Prime Source of All-There-Is, asking for blessings of understanding, cleansing, healing and forgiveness – all on behalf of that which is of the most benefit to all of Creation. And he recognized some of the words. He knew them as surely as he knew the Lord's Prayer, though he was just as sure he'd never heard them before in this, his current life. As he listened and as they climbed, the last remnants of Andy's self-distracting mental static, thoughts such as, "Boy, I am really working the Steps now," simply evaporated as his mind entered the same rarefied state as his body. His ego didn't disappear, it merely shut up and smiled at him. He felt himself, his essential self, skewing first to the right and then to the left, drifting slightly outside the boundaries of his body. Reiko and Lohr were there to nudge him gently back inside.

The higher they went, the more the synchronized stepping became a dance, keeping time to the pounding surf and the soft, thudding explosions of the flukes of sounding whales. Soon the whales were singing a beautiful, joyous counterpoint to Lohr's and Reiko's invocation, sometimes lapsing into a call-and-response rhythm with each other. Another distant voice, a crying, bird-like call, added an occasional grace note.

Andy felt an ecstatic crescendo building within him and without. They were gracefully floating, bounding in slow motion up the steps. And now Lohr and Reiko were no longer invoking but were vocalizing, toning harmoniously, riffing on the Song of the Universe. Rapturously, Andy added his singular note to the Symphony of All-There-Is. He opened his mouth wide and each exhalation of breath produced a perfectly resplendent tone. His throat and diaphragm vibrated with such joy and purity he felt light shoot out the top of his head. As the trio hit the top step, Andy's feet left the ground and Reiko and Lohr, holding on to him, had to keep him from climbing higher into the air. The soles of his boots touched down on the pinnacle of the pyramid and the crescendo peaked. The celestial harmony converged and the sound was sucked up and away in an instant. For three or four seconds there was a residual echo and then the quiet was there, a quiet as lush and rich, as transporting, as the music had been.

Light continued spouting from his crown chakra, pulsing with each breath and heartbeat, overflowing, enveloping his body in its holy glow. He felt the tingling of this energy flow inside his body, too. It was very much like his experience of being levitated aboard the UFO, the sound and light setting his molecules to the same vibrational pitch that left him feeling lighter than air. The difference this time was that he actively participated in creating this state, while before, it had been imposed on him from without. And now it was a constant glow inside him, ebbing and flowing with his breathing, but a constant nevertheless. He recognized that he was living in the Light.

It was time to open his eyes. There on the flat top of the pyramid, more than a hundred feet in the air, he stood. Before him was the cubical room. Through an open double doorway he saw an unusually large snowy owl peering at him with its wide-eyed, bewildered-looking gaze. Behind it he saw three cloaked figures standing with their backs to him. Each robe was a different color, highly saturated hues of purple, blue and green. Andy got the distinct impression, erroneous or not, that the Contact Committee was expecting him to appear from the opposite stairway. He wanted to call out to them, "Hey! Here we are! Behind you!" But, of course, he did not.

He stared at the back of the central figure's covered head, the one in blue. He stared for two strangely elongated, time-bending seconds at the back of that head. When the head turned, showing a profile and making eye contact over its left shoulder, Andy's gushing fountain of light spluttered to a dribble. He heard Reiko moan, knowing instinctively it was both a warning and a tone of protection. Struck by a vicious one-two psychic punch, he gave an agonized gasp as he felt something bite into his guts and give a yank that pulled him off his feet. He was blacked out cold by the time he hit the pink floor.

"We've all shifted. And we can't go back."

SEVEN

"Andy? Andy? Are you okay? C'mon, wake up, Andy. Wake up."

"Hmmmm? Yeah? What? I'm 'wake."

"I hated to wake you, but we're in Mendocino."

"Yeah? California, isn't it?"

"You were really having a good sleep, weren't you? I'm sorry, buddy. But I'm starved and I need to eat. I thought you might need a real meal about now too."

Andy yawned and let out a long, heavy sigh. Richard waited. Andy did not continue the dialogue Richard was trying to start. He swallowed another yawn and still said nothing.

"C'mon, how about it? Want some dinner?"

"Hmm? Food? Oh, god! I don't know." He struggled painfully to sit up in the back seat. "Ow. I have the mother of all headaches. You don't happen to have any aspirin, do you?"

"So happens I do." He handed him the green plastic bottle. Andy squinted at the label.

"Extra-Strength. Bless you." He fumbled with the lid, got it off just as Richard was about to offer to help, and shook out three fat pills into his palm. Richard handed him the gallon jug of water. He took it and slugged them back. After gulping the water, he took a couple of deep breaths and groaned,

"Let me get in front with you." There was no crawling over the front seat this time. He dragged his butt across the back seat, gripped the door handle, lifted and pushed with all his weight behind it, as if opening a bank vault. Taking a lurching step outside the car, he saw the floodlit sign and discovered that they were in the parking lot of 'Pegeen's Oceanside Restaurant,' a quaint, restored, many-gabled Victorian house with flower-bordered walks around and through a manicured lawn. There were four cars, including Richard's, in the lot, which was really just a widened driveway for the house. It could have held at least four more cars. A restored carriage house, now a two-car garage, separated them from a spectacular view of the red sky over the Pacific.

Andy took it all in at a glance, opened the front car door, and slid inside. "What time is it? I mean besides sunset." The sun had only just set and the fiery afterglow was softening. The sky was changing to delicious shades of peach and cherry.

"It's a beauty, isn't it?' Richard admired. "No fog, clear and calm."

Andy slouched in his seat and shaded his eyes as if the sunset were blinding him. He gestured feebly toward the dashboard clock, which indicated 8:35, and asked, "Is that right ... now?"

Richard quietly said "Yes," then said no more. Andy sat, head down, with his hand over his eyes. Eventually he noticed that Richard wasn't talking and looked over to see the concern on the face of his ardent champion. Richard mustered a tired, half-smile.

"Besides the headache, how ya doin'?"

"I am wiped. I am beat meat."

"You know, maybe a little food on the stomach would help; 'might give you your second wind. What do you say?"

"I don't think so. But I'll go in with you. I can have a soda or something while you eat."

Richard got out and opened the rear door. He reached into his gym bag on the floor and tossed a pair of socks to Andy.

"You're going to have to wear a pair of my gym shoes too. They'll be floppy on you but at least you'll pass the dress code."

He put on a heather gray, crew-neck sweater then pulled out a windbreaker and threw it onto the front seat next to Andy. "Here. You might want this too. It's chilly."

He led the way up the gravel path to Pegeen's while Andy scuffled along beside but slightly behind him. Andy was quietly grateful when Richard put his arm around his shoulder, patiently, tenderly, rounding up his little, bedraggled buckaroo and helping him up the steps.

The restaurant was far from busy. Two middle-aged couples occupied one table, two younger couples, not together, sat at separate tables, and at a fourth table was a family with three pre-teen kids. A young waitress in a Kelly-green, uniform dress with a white bib apron was lighting the hurricane lamps at the occupied tables. A pleasantly smiling, fortyish looking woman in a similar uniform appeared with a tray and greeted them as she hustled past, "Hi, fellas! C'mon in. You can just sit anywhere." In this room, in the room next to it (which led into the bar), and on the enclosed porch, there were plenty of tables from which to choose.

Richard spoke to Andy, "Let's eat on the porch. Do you mind?" Andy grunted his "Fine-by-me." Richard hesitated. There was no one else seated out on the porch, so he thought he should check with the matronly waitress on her way back to the kitchen with her empty tray.

"Is it okay if we sit out there?"

"Oh, sure, hon'! Best seats in the house. I'll be right with you."

They found a table for two next to the wall of the house and sat. True to her word, the waitress, Ellen on her name tag, was right behind them with menus. She established that this was to be on one check then asked, "What can I get you boys to drink?"

Andy asked if they had ginger ale. They did. He ordered it. Richard asked for coffee. And water. She wrote it down and left to get their beverages.

"Oh, ma-a-a-an!" Andy wailed, coming momentarily to life.

Richard was alarmed, "What is it?"

"You ordering coffee just reminded me."

"About what?"

"I never called in sick. Oh God, I hope I still have a job! Damn! Hell! I've just got to go in to work tomorrow, that's all there is to it. And I feel like homemade shit!"

"You don't have to go in to work tomorrow."

"What do you mean?"

"While you were conked out, I called in for you. I left a message that you were not feeling well, and that you had a doctor's appointment for 10:00 a.m. and that you would call in afterwards. I hope that's okay."

Too tired and achy to fully register his surprise, Andy just stared at him.

"Is it okay?" Richard needed to know.

"Uh ... well ... sure, I guess so."

"I know you'll hate this, but I also made an appointment for you with Dr. Dave. So you really do have a doctor's appointment for 10:00 a.m.."

"You didn't."

"I did."

"Richard! Why? I'm fine. Okay, so maybe I do feel like I just went over Niagara Falls in a barrel, but I just need a little rest. I'm fine! Dammit! Really."

"Sorry, babe, but I want a medical opinion. I don't want to take any chances with your ...."

"My what?"

"Your health. You know, your well-being."

"Well. I just don't know quite what to say. I mean, thank you for your concern, but .... You know something? That really ticks me off, Richard! You are really very ...."

"Controlling? Manipulative?"

"Oh, we know all that. I was going to say 'presumptuous'."

"How about bossy?"

"Oh, yeah."

"Meddlesome?"

"That, too, but the best word – although it's way overworked in your case – is 'pushy'. You are pushy, Richard. Very, very pushy."

Richard, with an ease that usually both amazed and appalled Andy, switched on the macho charm and flashed his cocky-stud smile. "How about ...." he paused for effect, 'masterful'?"

"Oh, please!"

"Then don't forget: 'crazy about you'." Under the table his knee met Andy's. Andy did not recoil. At least not until Ellen broke it up.

"Here we go." She set down their drinks and asked, "Are we ready to order?" They said no, so she happily conceded them some more time and left. They were silent as they sipped their drinks. Andy turned sideways in his seat and leaned back against the wall. He looked out at the deepening night and missed Richard's knee and his attempt to take up where he'd left off before Ellen interrupted. He couldn't touch his buddy. His buddy had turned away. There was no connection there. The rejection, though unintentional, was still vaguely humiliating to Richard, so he dismissed it and retreated behind his menu. It wasn't an extensive menu. He studied it, made his decision, put it down, and then studied Andy instead.

"So you feel like you went over Niagara Falls in a barrel, huh?"

Andy continued looking out the window as he answered, "Were you ever in an automobile accident or had a bad fall? You know how, afterwards, you feel strained muscles you didn't even know you had? Well, it's like that. My

114

arms and legs, my chest, my back – they all ache. My head really aches and my stomach hurts like I'd just done a hundred sit ups. It's like some kind of full body hangover."

"I could kiss it and make it better."

Andy had already fallen into the habit of ignoring Richard's often inappropriate and distracting sexual come-ons, but he was saved the trouble when Ellen showed up again.

"Are we ready now?"

Richard asked, "What's the soup today?"

"Two kinds, both homemade: chicken noodle and cream of mushroom."

"I'll have the sirloin tips, with fries, the grilled garden vegetable medley, and a cup of the chicken noodle soup."

"Uh-huh. And how about you, sir?"

"Nothing for me."

"Not even some chicken noodle soup?" Richard urged.

"It really is homemade," Ellen tempted. "It's got lots of chicken in it, too."

"Go on, just try some," Richard gently prodded. Reluctantly, Andy said okay.

"Will that be a cup or a bowl?"

They answered together: Andy requesting the cup and Richard ordering the bowl. But he backed down and gestured toward Andy who reiterated, "The cup." As Ellen turned to leave, Andy thought of one more thing. "Oh, wait! May I have a side order of cottage cheese?"

She did a little quick step as she halted, nodded yes, wrote on the check, then charged off to the kitchen.

After swallowing the first spoonful of soup Andy had a feeling this was not a good idea. He wondered if he was going to keep it down. But the soup was delicious and he was hungry, so he ate slowly. He swallowed spoonfuls between long, soulful looks out into the night sky over the ocean. Richard ate voraciously, but kept glancing at his silent dinner partner. His own headache was not completely gone, but it was not bothersome. Andy, on the other hand, was clearly suffering: the pain was visible in his face, the strain showing around the eyes and in the set of his mouth. His nap had not been restorative.

Andy took a couple of bites of cottage cheese and put his spoon down. He was finished eating. He stared out the window, oblivious to Richard's scrutiny. The sky was a study in deep blue, the horizon barely discernible. He got up and walked over to the window, the glass outside wall of the porch, and stood. He did not speak. Richard gave him a couple of minutes to tell him what he was doing. Finally, he had to ask.

"What do you see out there?"

Andy looked at him. "Do you see that light?" He gestured due west, indicating a bright dot about twenty degrees above the horizon, then continued, "That's them. They're watching me."

This sent a chill through Richard, but he kept his composure and seamlessly held up his part of the dialogue. "How do you know that? It looks like the evening star to me, probably Venus."

"You're right; it could be." He thought about this for a moment. "It could be. Although ...." he hesitated, pausing for the effect, "maybe that's the evening star instead." He pointed out a light of equal size and brilliance sixty degrees above the horizon and off to the south-southwest. Neither light twinkled and neither was moving, but they were the most prominent lights in the entire panorama of the western sky. Richard stubbornly ignored his goose-bumps and took another bite of meat. He looked up again and the first light, the one due west, blinked off. He dropped his fork and stared harder, he strained to look at the spot in the sky where the light had just been. He prayed it would come back on, but it didn't. It was gone. Andy was satisfied. He returned to his seat, now untroubled as though released from a hypnotic spell, but he read the alarm just under the surface of Richard's composure. Richard stuffed a few more French fries into his mouth.

Andy said, "Probably some clouds or fog moving in." He tried to give Richard a reason, an excuse, to disbelieve what they both knew was the truth. He nodded as if in agreement with Andy, but he was not convinced.

Ellen appeared and quietly refilled Richard's coffee cup. She seemed to have lost some sparkle. She walked away without saying a word. Richard continued eating. Between mouthfuls he told Andy what he'd heard on the radio. Whether from fatigue or discomfort, Andy was interested but unwilling to get excited about it. He said he wasn't surprised that it was neatly explained away as mass hysteria, but he did not understand why so much energy was put into denying the obvious and putting off the inevitable. Richard put down his fork and picked up his coffee. When he couldn't stand it anymore, he asked, "What's inevitable?"

At first Andy pretended not to hear the question. "What? Oh, I don't know. Contact, I guess." It wasn't a guess and Richard knew it. But he didn't know why Andy was being evasive. He didn't know what, exactly, was behind Andy's strange mood. Richard didn't like it though. The thought that Andy was keeping things from him had been nagging him since they left Mount Shasta. He was struggling again to keep from grilling Andy about his abduction, but just did not dare risk making Andy shut him out completely. Richard had quit smoking eleven years ago but this was one of those times when he really wanted a cigarette. Or a drink.

Richard paid the check, left a tip, and met Andy outside the men's room. After his own pit stop they headed for the car. At 9:30 they were the last to leave the restaurant which officially closed at 10:00. At the door they passed three young guys headed for the bar. The bar was definitely filling up. As they left they heard the TV sports audio mixed with the buzz of bar conversation punctuated by a loud burst of laughter. Outside, the parking lot and street curb were packed with cars. Without any warning, Andy doubled over and heaved on the edge of the gravel path. He groaned from the pain then, still bent over, hurled the rest of his stomach's contents. "Ow," he complained, then added, "Cripes! All over the freakin' begonias. Why couldn't I do this back in the john?" He spit a couple times then straightened up, groaning again.

"Are you okay?"

"Yeah, I'll live."

"You gonna do that again?"

"I hope not. No. I don't think so. Honestly, I don't feel sick. My stomach's not really upset. Hey, c'mon, quit looking at me. I was as surprised as you looked. This is your fault: you made me eat when I didn't want to."

They got into the car, got themselves belted in, and Richard started the engine. As they pulled out onto Highway 1, Andy said, "You know what?" Richard hit the brakes, swerved over on to the berm and barked orders at Andy, "Not in the car! Quick, get out!"

"Take it easy, would you!? I'm not going to be sick!"

"You're not?"

Andy shook his head no.

"Oh, well then, what were you going to say?"

"I was going to say that I changed my mind, and I just want to go home and sleep in my own bed tonight."

Richard beamed, "That's great! That sounds awfully good to me, too!"

"I knew you'd like that."

Richard was relieved. This was more like the old Andy; this made sense.

"Are you gonna drive or what?"

Richard put the car in gear and pulled back onto the blacktop. Andy called to tell Sarah they wouldn't be stopping and that he'd call her tomorrow. He told her what Richard had heard on the radio. She assured him she would watch the TV news. In fact, she and the kids had three VCR's and TV's among them and she planned to tape three different broadcasts. She also confirmed that there had been nothing in that afternoon's San Francisco Examiner. Yes, as self-appointed media watchdog, she would be sure to let them know if any mention of the Shasta UFO sightings turned up.

They got on Highway 101 in Willets. Around Ukiah, Richard picked up a news broadcast out of Santa Rosa. They heard nothing about what Richard, Andy, and Sarah had dubbed, 'The Shasta Incident.' Andy's stomach was now a little upset. He thought it was from the headache. They stopped at a convenience store and got Andy some ginger ale. That seemed to help his stomach and it stayed calm.

As they drove through the night in silence, Andy replayed his experience on board the spaceship. He was still trying to decide how much to tell Richard. It was so awesomely thrilling to think about what had just happened to him, about what he'd been told, what he'd seen and done, who he'd met and talked to, and at the same time it was truly preposterous. It was too beautiful and too special to share, to put before the world and watch it be reduced to a joke. And if he told what he had learned about Richard, he might not think it was a very funny joke at that. Well, Andy didn't exactly think that part of it was very funny either.

Near Healdsburg he felt well enough to drive. He offered and Richard took him up on it. Richard was apparently too wired on caffeine to sleep but he put the seat back, stretched out and reveled in not having to watch the road. The radio was tuned to a country station which neither one paid any attention to for about half an hour until Andy decided he'd had enough and found some jazz fusion and some romantic, 'quiet storm' R & B. The music put him in a mellow mood. It made Andy reconsider Richard. He got the yearning and it seemed like it wouldn't go away. It was sexual, but it hovered more around his heart than his loins. He wasn't going to do anything about it so he dismissed it and it went away. They passed Sebastopol and all the exits for Santa Rosa.

The night was dark without a moon. There wasn't a lot of traffic in either direction. From time to time Andy checked on Richard who just stared out his side window looking only at the occasional house lights up in the hills. He was certain he saw him nod off a couple of times, but he didn't stay asleep long. They lost the jazz fusion, R & B station but found a classic rock program to keep them company until Petaluma. It was just south of there that Andy saw another beacon in the sky, this time in the east. He looked over at Richard, who did not see it, then back at the light. He thought it best not to mention it. He watched it move in closer and trail them just above the hills to his left. Though it meandered some, it stayed with them, visible in some part of the eastern sky, all the way to Sausalito.

The Golden Gate Bridge was wrapped in fog but the sky over the City was mostly clear. Driving through the Marina Andy saw other lights over the Bay but he knew none of them was his. His light was gone, yet he knew it would return.

They pulled up in front of Andy's flat about 12:15 a.m., nearly twenty hours after Richard had last been there. Two exhausted travelers, they sat in the car, each waiting for the other to make the first move. Andy looked at the handsome and sexy older man beside him and easily pictured him as the irresistible young stud he must have been, the King of the Castro Clones.

"Are you coming up?" Andy asked.

"Am I staying over?" Richard countered.

"Are you expecting sex?"

"Do I look capable?'

In spite of his headache, Andy grinned through gritted teeth. "No, you don't. But then, I remember our second night together when we were both so-o-o-o tired. You didn't look especially capable that night either. Do I need to remind you what happened then?"

"Well, in that case, I guess I'd better go home." Richard tried to leer as he said it but it was a tired attempt.

120

"You don't have to. I'd really like it if you'd stay over. How about it?"

"In the same bed? Or do I get the couch?"

"Same bed, if you can behave yourself. I don't want to promise what I can't deliver. I've still got the headache. Which reminds me, I'm due for some more pain reliever. But anyway, I just wanted you to understand that it's not an invitation for some hot, sweaty, monkey love. Okay with you?"

Richard bristled and frowned. He was shocked and repulsed by the sound of the phrase, "hot, sweaty, monkey love," and he squirmed when he heard it. He didn't know why it should upset him. After all, it was his own pet phrase. Perhaps it was a reminder of his ugly, weird disgust with the possibility that Andy had been molested by his abductors. But that never entered his head. Still he must have had a stricken look on his face.

"What's the matter?"

"Huh? Oh, nothing. Nothing."

Andy wondered what in the hell was going on. All he wanted was a little reassuring physical closeness. Richard probably just wanted 'the Good Cookie.' Was the man really incapable of intimacy that didn't lead to orgasm? Andy seethed. "He can go home and beat off for all I care," he thought, half hoping Richard could read his mind. He struggled to hide his annoyance and remain civil on the outside.

"Look, let's just forget about it. It was a bad idea. I'm not even sure I can sleep with this headache. Why don't you go home, get some rest, pick me up tomorrow and take me to my appointment. How does that sound?"

"Yeah, sure. Okay."

Andy leaned over to give him a kiss. Richard didn't turn to accept his offer but awkwardly took a peck on the cheek. Andy was disappointed. And hurt. And now he was more than a little angry.

"Are you mad at me, Richard?"

"No, I'm not mad at you. Don't be silly."

"Then do I get a rain check on the monkey love?"

Richard cringed. There it was again, a sharp twinge of emotion, a powerful combination of jealousy, regret and guilt. Richard hesitated too long before he answered, "Of course you can."

Andy didn't need to see the cringe or the fleeting look of discomfort on Richard's face. He got the vibe whether he liked it or not. And he didn't like it. "So what the hell is going on with him tonight?" he thought. "I think he's actually turned off by the mere suggestion of having uninhibited intercourse with me! I don't get it. The relentless Studly-Do-Me, who always gets his man, not interested in sex? Why? How come every time I propose or initiate sex, Richard loses interest? Okay, that's not exactly fair, but it sure seems like it, and it is especially odd tonight. We can 'process' our mistimed, mismatched, sexual agendas some other time. But dammit, that really pisses me off, especially considering what I just found out on the starship about him. Oh, what the hell do I care? I'm too tired and I really do have a headache." They sat in silence during Andy's internal monologue. Finally he opened his door and got out. Richard did the same and came around to get into the driver's seat. Andy began disrobing in the street.

"What are you doing?"

"Here, I'm giving you your shoes and socks back. And your windbreaker. And you might as well take your shorts." He handed each item, one at a time, to Richard, stacking everything in his outstretched, dumbly receiving arms. "Oh, wait! That reminds me, I don't have my keys, you'll have to let me in."

Richard threw his arm-load of clothes into the back seat and humbly followed him to the front door, digging out his set of Andy's keys on the way. Andy stood aside to let him open the door and curtly said, "Thank you!" before entering in front of Richard. Now it was Richard's turn to 'read the vibes.' He got the annoyed attitude, alright, but wasn't sure from where it was coming. "Is he somehow reading my mind?" Richard thought. "Is that why he's pissed at me? No, that's impossible. That couldn't be it. I must be paranoid. Okay, paranoid and maybe feeling just a little bit guilty."

Meanwhile, Andy paraded his ET-shirt-covered-ass up the stairs, passive-aggressively flaunting it in front of Richard, scornfully willing him to eat his heart out. That wasn't lost on Richard either.

On the top floor, he unlocked the door and Andy again curtly said, "Thank you." He crossed the threshold, turned, and looked at Richard. Neither one of them knew what to say or do next. They looked at each other for several moments. Andy tried to project an impatient and defiant smirk. But it was hard in the face of Richard's wistfully pleading expression. He was silently begging Andy to forgive him. He wasn't going to ask out loud and Andy knew it. That would be admitting something was wrong. And so Andy forgave him. For now, anyway. He stepped back over the threshold, embraced Richard and said, "Get some rest, you big palooka. I love you. Now get the hell out of here." He went inside, shut the door and Richard went home alone.

Andy was back where he started, home again, and far from sleepy. He went to the bathroom and got his own extra-strength pain reliever. In the kitchen for a glass of water, he noticed the blinking lights of the appliance clocks. He took his pain reliever, but passed on fixing the clocks. What he needed first was a nice, hot bath. He went to his bedroom and removed his ET shirt and put it on the chair, on top of his jeans. From his closet he grabbed his terry cloth robe, and put it on. He saw himself in the mirror on the inside of the closet door, did a quick take, then took a longer look. Seeing the reflection of himself here in his room with the ET shirt behind him, made him stop for a moment and think. He slowly turned around and surveyed the room. The furniture, the clothes, the toys, the posters, the 8x10 glossies, the walls, the floor, the ceiling – all looked the same as when he left. The bed was still unmade. The windows were still open a few inches. There may have been a few more dust kitties than before, but essentially, nothing had changed since the vortex of light had entered this space and taken him away. Nothing in the room gave any indication that something quite beyond the ordinary had taken place here. Even Beans, his one-eyed T-bear, still guarded a pile of papers on the desk.

"What's that, Beans? No, I don't know if they are coming back. No, I don't know if I'm going away with them again." Andy walked over to the desk and picked up his old toy. The reddish-brown bear had been with Andy for thirty-two of his thirty-seven years. "Well, I'm sorry, Beans. I'm sorry they scared you. Was it what? Was it real? Was it a dream? What happened to me? That's the big question, isn't it? And you know what? I don't know what to tell you. But I know one thing: nothing is going to be the same. Not even you and not even this room. Oh, I know you all look the same. On the surface. But you're different. You're just slightly ... 'off'.

"You can all look as innocent as you like, but it's changed, all of it. We've all shifted. And we can't go back. I'm sorry, but that's the way it's going to be. Hey! What can I say? Shift happens." He walked Beans over to the bed and put him down on his pillow. "Sleep with me tonight, okay, pal? And don't worry. That awful, mean Richard's not sleeping over; he won't throw you on the floor." Andy put Beans down on his pillow and just stood by the bed, looking at his ET shirt, thinking. And when what he thought began to freak him out, he shook his head to clear it and headed for the bathroom. On his way, he passed the telephone and noticed the message light blinking furiously. It made him smile.

"Well, well, well. Desperate to be noticed?" he said to the blinking light, "I can relate." He counted the number of blinks.

"Wow, nine messages! Since when am I so popular?" He pressed the button and listened to the whir of the tape rewinding. It seemed to take more than nine messages worth of time. It finally stopped, clicked and began the first message with the customary beep.

"Um, Hi, um, ... this is Chrissy? Um ... how do you open ...? What do you call it? Oh, um, never mind, okay?"

*** "Yes, uh, Andy, this is Alan Feltscher. Uh, please give me a call. As soon as, uh, possible. Thanks."

*** "Hi. It's Sky. I'm at work. Feltscher said you didn't call in. So, like, where are you, man? Give me a call."

*** "Hi. It's Sky. It's 3:30 and I'm about to leave work. Are you okay or what? Leave a message on my home machine."

*** "Hi. It's Sky. I'm home now and there is still no message from you. Call me as soon as you get my messages, alright? I don't care how late. Although I am going out tonight, I'm not sure when ... or when I'll be back. I think I'm meeting Carlos at the Box. So ..., I don't know, ... but, ... leave me a message, man, I mean it. Okay?"

*** "Hi, Andy, this is Kelsey, calling about a catering gig for Saturday. Sorry for the short notice, but you know, blah, blah, blah. Anyway, it's a reception, twelve bucks an hour, at the Oakland Museum, start time is 5:30, or 4:00 if you want to set up. Give me a call, A.S.A.P. Thanks! G'bye."

*** "Hi. It's Sky. Listen, I stopped by your house after my deliveries and you didn't answer your door. Guess you really are gone. But where? Oh, and I was gonna call Richard but I don't remember his last name. Is your machine working? Can you pick up your calls from where you are? So ... anyway, ... where are you? Like, dammit."

*** "Yess, I'll leef a messsage. Lissten care-foolly. If you know vaht iss good for you, you vill not talk about your 'trip' to Mount Sshassta. To ANYVUN! Ziss iss not a joke call. Do you undersstand? Good."

Andy hit the stop button. What the hell?! He hit the rewind then stopped it again and hit play. "Like, dammit." *** "Yess, I'll leef a messsage." Andy let it play through, trying to identify the strange voice with the sibilant S's, and the Bela Lugosi accent. He stopped it and thought a moment. It was nobody he knew, that's for sure. He played it again.

It would have been comical, except for the fact that it was an out-and-out threat. The voice faded in and out, and there was an eerie, whiny static in the background. It sounded exactly like the message was coming in over a short-wave radio, but from where? Andy thought, "This is totally bizarre! Can't wait to play this for Richard and Sarah. Whew!" He shook his head and went ahead and played the last message.

*** "Hi. It's Sky. Uh, okay. Listen, I'm still going out. But you can still leave a message, so call me anytime. And, um, I know you are definitely not at San Francisco General Hospital, but if I don't get a message from you by the time I get in, I'm going to call somebody. I mean it. Really."

Well, poor Sky! It was sweet of him to be so concerned. Andy decided he'd better call him immediately. He got Sky's answering machine and the outgoing message was the same one he'd had for at least the year that Andy had known him.

"Hi. It's Sky. Leave a message after the beep."

"You can call off the investigation, I'm not in any of the hospitals and I'm not in any of the morgues. Yes, this is Andy. I'm home and finally returning your calls. Sorry to cause you all that concern. I'm okay but it is a long story. And it's about 12:30 now so don't call me tonight, I'm going to bed. And I won't be in to work tomorrow either. How about if I call you at home tomorrow after work? I mean today, which is what? Thursday? And who is Carlos? Sounds like you have some stories for me, too. That's it, talk to you later."

When Sky began working at Coffee A-Go-Go, a little over a year ago, he quickly became Andy's right hand man. He proved himself to be competent and reliable. He also demonstrated a commodity at work which Andy found to be frighteningly rare in 1995: common sense. Those were qualities that appealed to Andy and he soon became a friend of Sky's outside of work. No one was more surprised by that than Andy. Ordinarily he wouldn't expect to find that he had anything in common with the likes of Schuyler Orson

126

Blaustein, a twenty-year old, prep school dropout from Darien, Connecticut. When the handsome, dark-eyed Jewish prince got his driver's license in 1991, he also got his own car. The day after, he drove his brand new Acura Legend to San Francisco. He never went back to Darien or to prep school. Whether he was cut off from his family, or did the cutting off himself, was never clear, but Andy, who was still not close to his own family back in Indiana, had been there and done that too. Though they rarely spoke about their respective familial estrangements, for Andy it was indeed a silent and sympathetic bond.

Andy admired and respected Sky's self-reliance. On his resume he listed that he had gotten his GED, been an office temp, a bike messenger, and a video store clerk, all since moving to San Francisco. Later, in strict confidence, he mentioned to Andy that, from time to time, he was also a dancer in the gay clubs South-of-Market and implied that it could be a pretty lucrative gig. He often invited Andy to come and see him perform at the End Up. Andy refused. He wasn't quite comfortable with the possibility that his young friend might be hooking on the side, so he offered to get him catering work if he really needed the money. He took on the catering jobs, but didn't give up the dancing. He was endlessly intriguing to Andy, who may have been uncomfortable with his bad-boy persona, but was equally attracted to it. He was also alternately charmed or amused by his youthful earnestness and sincerity. Schuyler took himself very seriously. He was a poet, an artist, or at least he was sure he had the soul of one. He took guitar lessons and tried to play flamenco. He attended auditions for theater and dance companies. He was looking for an acting teacher. He felt everything very deeply, but always kept his reserve behind a thin, protective shell. He insisted that he be called Skyler Bluestone, vowing that when he turned twenty-one and inherited his trust fund, he would have it changed legally. When he was famous, he wanted to be known as Sky Blue. And he said this with a perfectly straight face.

Apart from a sixteen-year age difference, there was another reason why it was unusual that a friendship had developed between the two. Skyler had an enduring crush on Andy. Andy tried not to encourage this, although privately his feelings were ambivalent. (After all, who among us would find it easy to resist the adoring attentions of a hunky, albeit callow, youth?) Being the manager of an underling with a crush on you could easily have become a sticky situation. But it hadn't. At least not so far. This was due in large part to Sky who professed to know that he was way too young to even think about settling down with just one man. From the stories he told, he clearly seemed to enjoy a very active social life, and indeed, did not appear to be pining for Andy. And yet he also continued to be perfectly frank about his feelings, keeping his crush so out-in-the-open, that they both could (and did) tease each other about it.

Richard met Sky early on. Andy insisted he considered him a little brother and was no threat whatsoever to Richard. But Richard had eyes. He didn't need to be told what the deal was. He just didn't like Sky. Or so he claimed. He referred to Sky as 'the kid.' Sky referred to Richard as 'Andy's old man.' When Andy was present, they were civil to each other, but just barely. Alone with Andy, Richard would tell him, "The kid acts like he doesn't like me, but he really has the hots for me." Which is precisely what Sky maintained was going on with Richard: "He's not just jealous of me, you know, he really wants me and he knows he can't have me." Andy called their relationship a "mutual aggravation society" and he had no qualms about laughing out loud when listening to their silliness. Even now he smiled as he realized he takes far more pleasure from hearing the two of them diss each other than he should.

Andy made a couple of quick calls and prudently left a couple of brief messages: one, to turn down Kelsey's offer for catering work, and the other, to let Alan Feltscher hear first-hand from Andy himself, that he would call him that morning after his doctor's appointment. He remembered the blinking appliance clocks and decided to fix them now and finish the job.

He called the telephone Time Operator, and as she announced the correct time in her pre-recorded voice, he glanced at the microwave clock in the kitchen. She said, "At the tone the time will be one oh five a.m. and ten seconds." When the tone sounded in his ear, the clock on the microwave reset itself to 1:05 and quit blinking. Suffering from wonder fatigue, Andy could only ask himself, "How does that work?" Walking into the living room he saw that the VCR clock and the clock on the coffee maker had also reset themselves. He thought about calling Richard. He could always just say it was to see that he'd gotten home alright, and then tell him about how the clocks had reset themselves. But that would be too much like the night before. He decided that was too freaky, better to let him get his rest instead.

Now he could finally complete his trip to the bathroom where he began drawing his bath. He tossed a generous handful of aromatic bath salts into the water, then lit some candles and a stick of incense and turned out the overhead light. He got into the tub while the water was still shallow so he could run it as hot as he could stand. As the hot water gradually engulfed him, he closed his eyes and began his breathing meditation. When he had himself centered, he began focusing on his lingering headache. Between the technique and the pain reliever he'd taken half an hour ago, the headache was greatly diminished. However, it stubbornly refused to go away completely.

He ran some more hot water. The soothing, penetrating moist heat melted away most of the aches in his arms, legs, shoulders and neck. He inhaled the fragrant steaminess and exhaled a long, tension-releasing sigh. At least his body was starting to feel good about being back home. Now if it could just convince the rest of him.

A Medical Opinion and Suspicious Minds

E¦GHT

Doctor Dave entered the examining room at exactly 10:10. Richard and Andy had been waiting for only five minutes so that did not really explain their sullen faces. Cheerful but professional, the doctor wasted no time in idle pleasantries. "Good morning, gentlemen. And to what do I owe your visit this morning?" Andy and Richard eyed each other frostily while remaining tight-lipped, so the doctor tried another tack. "Richard? I believe this was your idea, so why don't you start."

Richard squirmed uneasily in the molded Formica seat. He chewed on the corner of his mouth, his arms folded over his chest. He looked at the floor, he looked at Andy, but he made no attempt whatsoever to explain himself. The doctor interjected, "Gentlemen, I should probably remind you that I have a full schedule of patients to see today and, while I would love to be able to give you as much as an hour of time, that just isn't possible, so would one of you, either of you, please be so kind as to tell me what the purpose of this visit is?" He waited a polite but brief interval for an answer. It was time to be direct. "Richard, you said that you wanted me to examine Andy. Now, please, what am I to examine him for?"

"Dave, it's a delicate matter."

"I'm sure it is, but I don't have time to play guessing games."

Richard hung his head. He looked defeated. From his seat on the examining table Andy spoke up, his quiet voice strained through his anger, "He wants you to find out if I've had sex in the last twenty-four hours."

"Oh, god," Richard moaned. He hid his face in his hands, avoiding Dr. Dave's incredulous look.

"Richard? Is that what this is all about?"

Richard lifted his head to speak up in his own defense, "Well, that's not entirely true, Dave, I mean, there's more to it than that."

"Such as?"

"Such as ... well ... uh, such as ... the thing with ... you tell him, Andy."

"Oh, for crying out loud! What Richard is getting at, or rather what he is too chicken-shit and too embarrassed to get at, – as if I'm not, as if I just couldn't wait to be dragged here and make a fool of myself – is that ... well, okay,". Andy hesitated as his courage momentarily flagged, but then he pulled himself back into the task and continued. "I believe, ... 'we' believe," he added looking at Richard, " ... that yesterday morning, about 4:00 a.m., I was taken aboard a space ship, flying saucer, whatever, and that I met these ... I spoke to some ... I mean, I made contact with ... well, obviously they were ... extra ... terres ... trials. And they let me off on Mount Shasta, which was where he picked me up, ... yesterday afternoon ... about 2:30. Or maybe 3:00, I don't know, because the clock in the car and his watch got screwed up and lost some time and so I .... Richard, please stop saying 'Oh, god, Oh, god." Andy decided he'd said enough. He looked pleadingly at Dr. Dave, begging for some sympathy. All he saw was the quizzical, but far from shocked, expression of the sincerely interested professional.

"Okay, I get it now. What Richard wants to know is whether or not there is any physical evidence of this experience, whether or not there was any trauma suffered by the body during this experience. Am I right?" Richard closed his eyes and nodded yes. Andy's jaw dropped in outraged disbelief. "So, Andy. Do you recall any such trauma? Was there some sort of ...?"

"Did you hear what I just said? How can you stand there and ask me questions about what I just said to you, what I just confessed to you, as if I had just told you I broke a nail or stubbed my toe or something?! Geez-o-Pete's!"

"Easy, Andy. Yes, I know what you are saying, but I'm a physician, not a psychiatrist. I'm in no position to question your story or challenge your sanity. Of course I'd be happy to refer you to an excellent psychiatrist if that's what you'd like, but right now I'm only going to try to evaluate your physical health. If that's alright with you. Richard, please stop saying, 'Oh, god, Oh, god.' In fact, why don't you wait for Andy out by the front desk? I'll talk to you in a bit. Alright?"

Richard got up and left the room without saying another word. Before Dr. Forsythe began his exam, he wanted to know some more about the experience which Andy was reluctantly claiming had befallen him.

"Andy, was this an abduction?"

"No, it was strictly voluntary. That's what I've been trying to get Richard to understand. I'm sure you've probably heard stories of alien abductions, but this wasn't one. There was no force involved. And there was no physical exam, no alien probes or microchips, nothing, absolutely nothing, was embedded or inserted into me! Anywhere! I swear!"

"Alright, take it easy now. Is it possible that you were not conscious while something of that nature was done to you?"

"I was completely conscious the entire time."

There was a pause while Dr. Forsythe thought about that. Andy was certain he saw doubt in his face. "Have you had any symptoms at all, anything unusual, any aches or pains, any trouble urinating, anything like that?" Dr. Forsythe scribbled some notes as he listened for Andy's answers.

Andy said nothing. Not only was he embarrassed, he was appalled with himself because he had already lied about the losing consciousness part. Even though he was sure nothing had happened to him, it was impossible to expect anyone else to believe him. There was nothing believable about this experience. A part of him just wanted to deny everything strongly and get up and leave. Dr. Forsythe's scribbling stopped.

"Andy?"

"Do you have any idea how humiliating this is? Don't you think I know how this sounds?"

"Please don't be embarrassed. I really do want to help and I think I can understand what this must be like for you. You seem perfectly rational to me. Whether or not such a thing happened to you, whether or not such a thing is possible, doesn't really matter here. The important thing is that you believe it happened. That's good enough for me. And Richard believes it happened or he wouldn't be concerned for you. So my role here is strictly to cover all the bases from a medical standpoint. That's just common sense. Something out of the ordinary happens and you have to try to make some sense of it, right? What do you think? You yourself must be curious or you wouldn't have let Richard drag you in here. Am I right?"

Andy knew what Dr. Forsythe was saying was true. He nodded in the affirmative, though still reluctant to agree with him outright.

"Now, how 'bout it? Any symptoms you care to tell me about?"

"I have had a headache for most of the last twelve hours. Aspirin helps, but it hasn't gone away completely. I do have some body aches, although they are much better this morning. I had a little trouble keeping down some food last night. However, my breakfast coffee and bagel and fruit salad seem to be doing okay. That's all I can think of."

"What medications are you currently taking?"

"Besides the aspirin, none."

"You look tired. How are you sleeping?"

"Well, last night was not so hot. I got about five hours all together. But before yesterday, generally okay."

"Any falls in the last week or so? Have you struck your head in any way?"

"No. Nothing like that."

"And I can assume that no recreational drugs were involved?"

"Yes, you can. I assure you I have not lapsed. Clean and sober since 1986. And besides you can check me for that."

"Okay, then, Andy. We'll get some urine and blood from you for the usual tests. I want to send you across the street to Saint Francis Hospital for some tests, too. You are fully insured, right?"

Andy nodded yes. His Coffee A-Go-GO benefits package included one of the best medical insurance plans in California.

"Good, then I want a CAT scan and an MRI. If you'll undress to your shorts, I'll be back in a minute to look you over."

Andy nodded his still reluctant agreement and Dr. Dave left the room. Andy spat out a silent, "Damn!" then sighed. He hated all this fuss. He hated being "looked over." He stalled for a minute, then muttered "Oh, screw it," and began to take off his shirt, shoes and pants. He hated medical tests. But he would cooperate because he knew, just like the doctor said, they had to cover all the bases. It would be worth it to prove to Richard that he hadn't been violated. Actually, to go through all this wasn't so unreasonable. One day he might be called on to prove what had happened really had happened. In that case, he would need to be able to say he'd had all this checked out. And yet he didn't want to talk about it. He especially didn't want to see a psychiatrist. He'd spent years in therapy. He didn't want to talk about himself anymore. He was as fully integrated as he was ever going to be, dammit! He didn't want to spend any more time justifying his existence, convincing some shrink that he was 'normal.' It would feel like being sent back to square one. And to think about that made him very angry.

Dr. Forsythe knocked, paused, then stepped back inside the room. "I've given Richard the name of my shrink, Dr. Walker, Calvin Walker. He's a psychiatrist. He can prescribe medication for you if that's necessary. There's no hurry in making an appointment. He'll want the results of the tests, anyway and they probably won't be able to schedule you for the CAT and the MRI before next Monday. I'm going to treat this like a head injury for the time being, so please let me know if you experience any further symptoms like dizziness, blurred vision, nausea, anything at all. Do you have any questions?"

Now, stripped down to his Hanes briefs, he felt utterly and excruciatingly self-conscious. He was secretly hoping he could just disappear so, at the moment, he had no questions whatsoever. It was bad enough he had to get naked, let alone in front of Dr. Dreamboat. He wondered if a straight guy would be as nervous if their doctor was as beautiful a woman as Dr. Forsythe was a man. The doctor's exam was routine but thorough. Andy felt as though he were under a microscope. He was checked for bruises and tender spots, his eyes, ears, nose and throat were checked, then he was asked to drop his shorts. Andy made a faint protest, something about 'is this really how you treat a possible head injury,' but did as he was told. Then he was told to turn around and bend over. Under different circumstances he'd be only too happy to oblige, but was this really necessary? He was sure Richard must have been the one to order the anal and then the – oh, damn – urethral cultures, damn him! Dr. Dave was wonderfully gentle, which was nice, but Andy grew warm and flushed by the combination of embarrassment and sexual turn-on caused by the exam. And he was quite obviously turned on. He shut his eyes tightly in a vain attempt to make it all go away. He had to remind himself that not only was Dr. Dave a professional, he was also a personal friend of Richard's. Finally the ordeal was over and he was told he could put his clothes back on. He felt a major snit coming on.

Dr. Forsythe handed him a plastic cup and told him to see Fran, who would see to getting the specimen and that the blood was drawn. She would also make his appointments for the tests at Saint Francis. "You're a bit dehydrated, but except for that and the fatigue, you seem perfectly healthy to me. I hope you won't worry about all these tests. We're just ..."

"I know, 'covering all the bases'. And what about the sex angle? Can we rule out rape?"

"Yes, I believe we can."

"Then I hope you'll tell that to Richard."

"Yes, of course. But that reminds me, uh, just for the record, when was the last time you and Richard had sex?"

"Oh, right, you have to know that. Just for the record. Well, then, I suppose I'll have to tell you. Just for the record, it was last Sunday."

"Thanks. I know that's personal, I appreciate your honesty."

"Yeah, well, maybe you can appreciate my dishonesty. I need to ask you for a favor. I need a doctor's note for my employer. See, I failed to call in to work yesterday and I need to convince them that I was really sick. Would you lie for me? In writing?"

"I have no problem with that."

"Well, I've been thinking about this and maybe we can go with the head injury thing. I mean, like maybe I fell at home in the middle of the night and took myself to the emergency room, forgetting to call in. You don't need to go into detail in your note, but if you are looking for a head injury, I can make that plausible when I talk to them."

"Sure, I'll write that up in a minute and you can get it from Fran on your way out. Do you want to stay off work the rest of the week? Just let me know, I can get you off as long as you want."

"No, thanks. I'd like to go back to work tomorrow, if that's alright."

"Okay, but you really should be taking it easy. I mean it about telling me if you notice any other symptoms. Understand?"

Andy answered, "Yeah, alright."

"I'm going to talk to Richard in a bit and see what I can get from him. In fact, I'm going to check him over, too. And Andy, I would really like to hear the whole story, as much of it as you are willing to share. In fact, I'm going to suggest that you and Richard come over to our house and join Chuck and me for dinner tonight. Will you do that?"

"I don't know. Right now I really don't feel like talking about it."

"So just come have dinner with us."

"Thank you for the invitation, I'll think about it, okay?"

"Okay. At any rate, I will let you know what your blood and urine test results show, and then let's see you again after the hospital's test results are in." Dr. Forsythe opened the door for Andy and let him step out into the hall first. In the doorway he thought of something more to add. "Oh, and Andy, don't be too hard on Richard. We all know what an overbearing asshole he can be, but he does care about you, you know. Hope to see you tonight. Take care." He smiled, turned and took the charts from the file holder on the wall next to another examining room, then knocked on the door, opened it and went inside. Andy was making his way back to Fran and the front desk when he saw Richard being shown into another room.

Richard asked, "How'd it go?"

"Okay, I guess. I have to give them some samples, get my note from the doctor, and get some appointments for some tests at Saint Francis."

"I don't know what he wants with me, but it shouldn't take long. I'll meet you out in the waiting room, okay?"

"No. I'm just going to go on home by myself. I need to make some phone calls and maybe take a nap."

"Andy, please don't be mad at me."

"No Richard, you back off. I'm trying, okay? I'm doing the best I can. You know, this is the second time, in our still young relationship, when you have managed to humiliate me and somehow make me feel unclean by asking me to submit to medical exams for reasons distinctly having to do with your insecurities and your uncertainty about what you think my sexual history is, or has been. And you know as well as I do, that if one of us has any reason whatsoever to be jealous of the other's past or present sex life, it should be me!"

"What? First of all, I've told you, that is not the only reason I wanted to have you see Dave. Okay, alright, I know I'm a jealous lover, but ..."

"No, it's not the only reason, but it is the reason why you don't want to have sex with me until you can be sure I didn't screw some ET, isn't it." Fran came up to Andy and interrupted the rapidly escalating 'discussion.'

"Excuse me. Mr. Lang, just take a seat in that room and Dr. Forsythe will be with you in a minute. Mr. Gage, if you'll just take this cup into this room right here, when you finish let me know and we'll draw some blood." She breezed on by and Richard and Andy both looked at her with the same 'damn-the-jolly-nurse' expression. Then Andy stepped over the threshold into the bathroom and Richard grabbed his shoulder.

"Will you have dinner with me tonight?" Richard implored. Andy shrugged his shoulder. Richard let go. Andy emphatically answered, "I don't know. Call me later when I'm not so ticked off at you."

"At least wait for me in the waiting room and I'll give you a ride home."

"No, thank you. I'd rather do some walking." Andy closed the door to the bathroom behind him, and on the conversation with Richard.

When he came back to the examining room, Dr. Dave found Richard staring out the window, watching Andy walk away down Bush Street toward Polk. "Okay, do you want to tell me what's going on here?"

"I was hoping you could tell me."

"He said the last time you and he had sex was last Sunday. Is that true?"

"Yes, that is true."

"Are you two having trouble?"

"I didn't think so, at least until this morning."

"Well, I can tell you that I found no evidence of any recent sexual activity, traumatic or otherwise. I also see no evidence of any trauma to the head, although we are going to look into that further. He appears to be perfectly rational, a little tired maybe, but I am going ahead with the usual drug tests, blood tests and cultures just to be sure we have a clear picture of his physical condition. And I am also going to take a look at you."

"Me? What for?"

"The same reasons. Now, would you like to tell me if you are experiencing any unusual symptoms?"

"Dave, get serious. I am perfectly fine."

"Andy tells me you lost some time on Mount Shasta. Is that true?"

"Yes, about half an hour. I was passed out in the car. I recovered. What's the big deal?"

"Maybe nothing. You tell me."

"Oh, c'mon, Dave. There's nothing to tell."

"Then tell me about what Andy thinks happened to him."

"All I can really tell you about, the only thing I can verify, is that he disappeared from his flat early yesterday morning, and that I found him later the same day at a scenic overlook on Mount Shasta."

Dr. Dave allowed himself to be a little bit surprised by this statement. He raised his eyebrows to show it. He waited to hear more, but Richard was not forthcoming. "So do you believe his story about being taken aboard a flying saucer?"

"I don't know what to believe anymore. I have no logical explanation for what happened. I do know it has changed our relationship. He is tuning me out. He doesn't want to talk about it with me."

"Forgive me, Richard, but can you blame him? Whatever happened to him, he clearly needs some time to come to terms with it."

"I know. I want to give him some space, really I do. But it scares me when he withdraws like that."

"Richard, my friend. We've known each other a long time. I like Andy. I think you make a good match. I'd like to see you two in a committed relationship. I hope to God, for both your sakes, that he is not going off the deep end. This is pretty weird stuff, I admit, and I certainly don't have any idea what really happened, to either of you, but I don't yet see any evidence that there's anything seriously wrong with him. Although frankly, I do see some of the same old evidence of your tendency to micromanage a partner right out the door. You are just going to have to bite the bullet and back off this time. I mean it."

"You're right, of course, dammit. Do you have any ideas about how I do that? Lock me in a room and don't let me out, no matter how much I beg and plead?" Richard was only half joking.

"Don't be so hard on yourself. That's precisely why you're so hard on your boyfriends. Now, I've got to check on another patient, but I do want to examine you. So, when I come back, I want to see you stripped naked. You got that, tough guy?"

"Okay, smooth talker." Richard began to unbutton his shirt enthusiastically. Dr. Dave winked at him on his way out the door.

Andy crossed Polk Street on his way to Van Ness. His mind was brimming with concerns. Watch out for traffic. Don't look at the panhandler. Don't forget to call Feltscher. And Sky. And Sarah. "You've got to talk to her about what happened," he thought. "She'll help you sort it all out. And you've got to sort out what to say, just how much of this to tell people. Especially Richard. He is trying to be good about this, but I'm not at all sure this isn't going to completely freak him out. And why not? Why shouldn't it? Parts of it freak me out, too. Hell, who am I kidding, all of it freaks me out. It would probably be best to let the whole thing drop and never mention it again. But, no matter how much I would like to say it was 'just a dream,' I know it is only the most fantastic and incredible experience I've ever had, asleep or awake, and I cannot pretend it never happened. Richard experienced it too, at least in part, so we have to talk about it sometime. And we have to talk about where our relationship is or is not going. Oh, man! It is all just way too much for me to think about right now. That's why my headache is coming back, dammit!"

Waiting for the light to change so he could cross Van Ness, Andy was startled by a vintage, black Cadillac limousine that recklessly, tires screeching, jumped the curb in front of him as if swooping in to intercept him — which was exactly its purpose. Andy hopped back several feet to avoid being run over. The limo, oddly parked half off, half on the sidewalk, sat there for a second. Then the back seat window was rolled down with some difficulty, hurriedly, jerkily, to reveal an oriental-looking man wearing a large, black felt fedora and huge, opaque sunglasses. His long, wispy, gray mustache and stringy chin hairs were obviously hastily glued on. His too large, black suit coat hung on his frame and his too small, wrinkled white shirt, buttoned to the top button and looking painfully snug, seemed to be intended to hide a long neck. The outfit was completed by a black shoelace which was given a peculiar knot and hung around his neck like a string tie. Andy was too astonished to be afraid.

Even before the window was down the man began haranguing him in a loud, piercing, strangled voice. His Chinese accent might have been as fake as his beard, but his anger was pretty genuine. To top it all off, Andy noticed the definite dank and musty odor of a damp basement coming from the man. "You not tell! You not tell! You tell, you die! We kill you if you tell! You understand? You know nothing! You are nothing! You are crazy person!" Andy had to laugh, he could not help himself. This really annoyed the man in black, who shook with rage, while his long bony fingers clutched the rolled down window and he screamed even louder.

"You not laugh! You not laugh at us! You will see! You talk crazy about flying saucers! You not know! You talk and you will pay the price. You not live to see another day! I guarantee it!" The word 'guarantee' was amusingly garbled and Andy's stifled laugh broke out again. The man added, "Not

141

funny! You die!" and then the car's unseen driver must have floored it because the limo shot off, bouncing back onto the pavement and laying fifteen feet of rubber on Van Ness as it streaked off north toward the Bay.

Andy watched it disappear, weaving up Van Ness, taking note of the fact there was no license plate on the car. He also noticed there was a strange lull in the traffic. At that moment there were no other cars around to interfere with the getaway. And when he looked around, there were no other pedestrians nearby, there was no one else within a hundred feet who might have witnessed the spectacle. "Now how did they do that?" he wondered. "How did they find me on a busy street in broad daylight and at the exact moment when no other pedestrians were around?" Just turning up out of nowhere, that was unsettling. That was a little too eerie, a little too 'in-your-face.' Were they capable of controlling reality like that? Maybe they weren't just shouting idle threats at him to scare him. That, more than anything, wiped the smile off his face.

His paranoia box now opened, he hurried on across the street and down a block to catch a bus and get on home. But as he waited, he was restless, watchful. The pay phone near the bus shelter looked like it was intact and working, so he decided to call his boss and get that out of the way. He dreaded talking to Feltscher. The man, ten years Andy's junior, was a blatant misogynist and homophobe, and could be counted on to let unwanted, unwarranted, snide sexual innuendoes pepper his conversations. It was only a matter of time before this guy was going to be the subject of a sexual harassment suit. Andy was hoping to get the bastard's voice mail but he was not so lucky. "Feltscher."

"Uh, yeah. Hi, Alan. It's Andy Gage."

"Well, well. Where have you been? I got your boyfriend's message. You two finally get unstuck?" Andy seethed, but he went ahead, ignoring the comment as best he could. "I just saw the doctor and thought I'd let you know what the story is, like I said in my message last night. Remember? You did get my message, didn't you?"

"Yeah, yeah. So what did the urologist say? Is it the clap again?"

"Not funny, Alan. Do you want to hear this or not?"

"Okay, okay. What's wrong with you and when you comin' back to work?"

"It looks as though I might have a slight concussion, from a fall I had in my apartment night before last. I knocked myself out and when I woke up I took myself to the ER. By the time I was done there and got home, I was really ready for a nap and I forgot to call you. I'm sorry. I think you will agree that I am not usually so irresponsible."

"Yeah, yeah. What did the doctor say?"

"I'm having some tests run next week at Saint Francis. He says to take it easy and let him know if I have any symptoms. Oh, my god!"

"What?"

Andy spotted the limo coming back down Van Ness. It did not stop but slowed down as it passed by. While the tinted window stayed up, he could feel the accusing look of the man in black without actually seeing it.

"Uh, nothing. I'm calling from a pay phone on Van Ness and a strange car just drove by."

"So when did he say you could come back to work?"

"I'll be in tomorrow morning, but I have to take it easy. I've got a headache and it isn't in any hurry to go away, so, just so you know, I may have to leave work early, if it gets too bad."

"You'll be fine. You got a release from the doctor, didn't you?"

"Yes, of course."

"Good. Just bring it to work with you. I'll stop by the store tomorrow and get it. I've got another call coming in. Talk to you later." Feltscher disconnected before Andy could say good-bye. It was rude but it was typical and Andy was glad the exchange was over.

"Well, that's done," he thought. "I did my duty. He seemed to buy it, that's the main thing. But what the hell is with that car and that creep in black? Are those guys going to follow me around and harass me everywhere I go? The Contact Committee could have at least warned me about these intergalactic Tong gangsters. They might even have told me how to deal with them. But, no! That would be too helpful!"

Andy looked to the clear, blue sky and wondered if anybody from 'his side' was watching out for him. There wasn't a UFO to be seen. A standing-room-only bus pulled up but it was not the one he needed. Muni buses usually ran in packs, in total disregard of all posted schedules, and this one was no exception. Three more buses came crowding in behind, letting off a trickle of passengers and letting on a disgruntled crowd of twenty or more. The bus Andy wanted was not among these either. From past experience he knew it could be as long as a half hour before his bus came along. He loved not having to worry about the cost and maintenance of a car, but public transportation was often a big fat, annoying compromise. He always hated waiting. And he hated it even more now that he seemed to be a sitting duck for alien drive-by threats. One by one the buses pulled away. He felt exposed. Should he start walking or stay put? He was feeling more vulnerable than usual out here on the street. It may be just another highly evolved survival tool of gay people, but sometimes he could do without the paranoia.

Richard arrived at his office on Union Street before 11:30, but, as far as Phyllis was concerned, he was late. She smiled when she saw him, of course, but the first words out of her mouth were, "Oh, there you are," as if she had been looking for him all morning. She was dressed in her usual outfit, a crisp cotton, shirtwaist (this one the color 'peach'), complete with pearls and high heels. Andy's first impression of her had caused him to ask Richard, "It's the Nineties, for god's sake, where in the world does she find shirtwaists?" The answer was that she herself made all her own and her daughters' clothes. With her auburn hair in bangs and a French twist, she was straight out of a Fifties sitcom minus only the winged, rhinestone-encrusted eyeglasses on a chain. Why a thirty-five year old woman had adopted a style that she could have seen only on TV was anybody's guess. But Andy ultimately understood — after all she was from the Midwest, wasn't she? Besides, "if you're going to dress like a cartoon, San Francisco is the place for you."

"You are supposed to meet the Faders at their property at noon. And some gentleman from the United States Air Force has called twice for you. He refuses to state his name, his business or leave a number where he can be reached. Oh, and was everything alright at the doctor's office?"

"Thank you, Phyllis. Yes, everything is fine. Did the man from the Air Force say when, or if, he might call back?"

"No, Mr. Lang, he did not. I'm sorry but he was most abrupt and uncooperative." There was a distinctly peevish tone to her voice. She almost stamped her foot. Nobody gets around Phyllis Dean like that! The nerve of that man! Richard headed for his desk and Phyllis for hers, but she remembered something else that just had to be said. "Oh, and Mr. Lang, one other thing."

"Yes?"

"If you tell me what kind to get, I would be happy to replace your broken answering machine tape on my lunch hour."

"My what?"

"Your home answering machine? Remember, the tape broke?"

"Oh, yes, yes. That's nice of you, Phyllis, but, silly me, I don't know what kind I need. I'll have to look when I get home. Thanks, anyway." Richard made a detour over to the coffee pot and poured himself a mug. "She's in rare form this morning," he thought, "probably already tried to call me at home. But I'm glad she reminded me. I forgot to replace that tape, didn't I? Now what did I do with it? It must still be in my jeans."

He sat down at his desk in his private office and began gathering the papers he would need for the Faders. Today it felt great to be back in the office. Today he needed the distraction of work. Phyllis had a typed schedule for him on his desk. He had called a meeting for brokers and agents several days ago and that was setup for 3:00 today. Before and after the meeting he was visiting sites and clients. At 5:00 Mitzi had requested a private consultation, probably about that property on Vallejo. He hoped it wasn't another complaint about Phyllis. Just the kind of varied day he liked. He took a slug of hot coffee just as she buzzed his line. A bit jumpy, he almost spilled some on his cream colored silk shirt, but quickly recovered and picked up his phone.

"That man from the Air Force is on the line again. Do you want to speak to him now?" Richard hadn't expected to have to deal with the military quite so soon, but he didn't hesitate to respond. "Yes, sure, put him on." There was a click as the line was opened for the incoming call. Richard spoke up, "Good morning, this is Richard Lang speaking. How may I help you?"

"Mr. Lang? Mr. Richard Lang, who drives a 1994 dark green Volvo station wagon?"

"Yes, that's right."

"Shall we verify the license number?"

"I don't think that will be necessary. Who is this, please?"

"This is Lt. Colonel Doyle, of the United States Air Force, and I have it on the best authority that you were present yesterday in the town of Mount Shasta, in northern California. Would you care to confirm or deny that authority?"

"Would you care to first tell me what this is all about?"

"Mr. Lang, I think we both know what this is about and I think we both know that you were allowed to leave a military quarantine area without the proper exit interview. I think we both know that, as a federal offense, such an action has serious legal consequences."

146

"Are you threatening me?"

"The threat, sir, is to national security. Now, I do not threaten, but I strongly suggest that you cooperate with me and we can clear this up very quickly with just this one phone call. Shall we do that, Mr. Lang?"

"Alright, Colonel Doyle."

"That's Lt. Colonel."

"Alright then, Lt. Colonel Doyle, how do I cooperate with you?"

"By answering, and answering correctly, two very important questions. The first one is, just what exactly did you see while you were on the mountain yesterday?" The man waited for an answer. Richard was very pissed. He had a few questions of his own, like 'who the hell is this guy to threaten me over the phone? And how do I know he is who he says he is?'

"And the second question?"

"And just what, exactly, did your friend in the car with you see on the mountain yesterday?" The nerve of this guy! But how did he know? How did he know about Andy? It must have something to do with Officer Wilson? But he's civilian. My god, what did they do to him?

"I'm still waiting for my answers, Mr. Lang."

"And if I don't answer correctly?"

"In matters of national security, Mr. Lang, we have the authority to see that potential threats are removed, or perhaps a better word would be, eliminated. Someone with false stories to tell might disappear, vanish from the face of the earth, and never return, never be seen or heard from again. I believe that answers your question. Now, how about answering mine?"

"I suppose the answer you're looking for here is that we saw nothing on the mountain. Am I right?"

"Yes, that is correct. And you saw nothing in the skies over Mount Shasta either, did you?"

"Not a thing. Not even a cloud."

"Very well put. Now can I trust you to pass along my message to your friend, Mr. Gage?"

Richard's internal reaction was: "Holy shit! They know Andy's name too? How the hell could they know that? That's impossible! That just can't be!" Richard was shocked but kept control of his voice when he replied, "Oh, I can assure you, my friend will be only too happy to say he saw nothing. I mean, he *knows* he saw nothing, so what else is he going to say?"

"That's exactly right. So I see we understand each other. Good. Good. Then I see no reason to detain you further." Click, dial tone, end of message. Phyllis was right: he was very abrupt.

His impulse was to call Andy. But the more he thought about it, the more he thought maybe he should just keep quiet. Andy was under enough pressure. It was better to spare him the shakedown scenario. "But what if they decide to threaten him anyway? Shouldn't he be warned? My god, if they have to call everybody who was up there yesterday and threaten them .... why, what a colossal waste of taxpayers' money!" The more he thought about it the angrier he got. He had half a mind to call Dianne Feinstein, or Nancy Pelosi, or Barbara Boxer and voice a complaint. It wasn't an idle threat. They knew who he was, he'd worked on the campaigns of all three of them, so he had some clout. "Hell, I'll call them all!" Then Phyllis buzzed him and interrupted his revenge fantasy.

"Yes?"

"Mr. Fader just called to say they are running late. He and Mrs. Fader will meet you on site, but it's going to be closer to 12:30, if that's alright with you. "

"Oh, okay. That's fine. Thanks."

"And did you help the man from the Air Force?"

"I'm afraid not, Phyllis. We don't have a thing in his price range."

"...bring it up ... and I will categorically deny it."

N⬇NE

By the time Andy got back to his flat, successfully avoiding any more run-ins with hostile ETs in limousines, it was noon. He was ravenous and confident that food was still his friend after the welcome reception given his meager breakfast. He fixed himself his favorite lunch: a sliced breast of turkey sandwich with red-leafed lettuce and a generous dab of mango chutney. He opened a bottle of raspberry-flavored seltzer and downed a couple of extra-strength pain relievers. Then he settled in his most comfortable chair and happily munched away, admiring his view of downtown San Francisco. The sky was clear, the sun bright. The usual stiff breeze kicked up whitecaps on the bay. The panorama was alive with movement. A huge cargo ship piled with containers slid beneath the Bay Bridge. A medical helicopter scooted east sweeping rapidly toward Oakland. The cars and trucks, the blood in the arteries of Interstates 101, 80, and 280, were moving steadily and speedily along. He heard a gust of wind surprise and shake the trees in the side yard. He felt pretty good. He felt centered again, almost content. He felt tuned in, in synch, in touch with All-There-Is.

For a moment or two, he sensed he was on the verge of that cosmic rhythm meld, about to step between the veils into hyperconsciousness. Were they close by? He wondered whether he was going to see his light in the sky. He wanted to see it again. He longed to see it again. But apparently it was not to be. He belched and the feeling passed. And so he thought, "Oh, well."

He wanted to call Sarah and arrange getting together for a long talk about the Shasta Incident, the Men-In-Black, and Richard. Maybe she could come into the city tomorrow and they could have dinner together. After checking in with her, he was going to indulge in the luxury of an afternoon nap. He was tired, sleepy, and his body felt sluggish and still a little achy. If he didn't know better, he'd swear he'd had decaf' coffee for breakfast. And there was that nagging, low-grade pain, right in the middle of his head, that not even extra-strength aspirin could mollify. It would feel great to stretch out on his bed in the afternoon sun and catch up on all those lost Z's. When he finished eating, he took his plate and bottle to the kitchen, then went to the phone. The light on his message machine was blinking in repeating sequences of three. He pressed the play button and waited through the rewind.

*** "Hi, it's Sky. Got your message. Thanks. Glad to hear you're back. Call me at home after work, and before I go out to make my Open Hand deliveries. If you can. Otherwise I'd say call me tonight but then I'll probably go to bed early. So if you don't get me after work, I guess I'll see you tomorrow morning at the Go-Go. Yeah. I guess that's a plan, right? You are coming in to work, aren't you? Hope so, I'm really psyched to get your story. Like where were you, man? And you're right, I've got a story or two to tell myself. Later, dude." Andy smiled at the thought, "You don't know the half of it, Sky."

Next on the tape, a familiar female voice chimed right in. *** "So how ya doin'? Feeling better? Listen, there was nothing on the news last night, absolutely nada, about the Shasta Incident. I even forced myself to watch several of the local happy morning news shows. Not a word. And nothing in this morning's Chronicle either. What does that tell us? Media blackout? Big time cover-up? All of the above? I'm going out to grocery shop at 1:00, but call me, guy. I want to talk to you! Love you!"

"Good," Andy thought to himself, "I was just going to call you anyway, Sarah." Then he braced himself for the last message, expecting either Fu

150

Manchu or Count Dracula to deliver another threat. He was close. Only it was more like the Invisible Man or rather the equivalent, silent version. The beep sounded and was followed by twenty seconds of silence. Well, it was not total silence. There was some kind of ambient noise in the background but Andy couldn't make it out. There was sporadic hissing and several brief garbled mumbles that were faint, muffled, and disguised by static and the short-wave radio whine. Then the message tape clicked off. Andy winced. He knew it was another attempt to scare him into silence. All it lacked was the heavy breathing. "Ha!" he thought, "They probably don't breathe." He did not like having his personal space violated by threatening messages anymore than he enjoyed receiving solicitations from telemarketers. But, bold as they were, telemarketers didn't accost you on the street. At least not yet. So far they had generously left that to the panhandlers. With this attempt to scare him he was more annoyed than frightened. But he also had to smile when he was reminded of the 1930's Buster Crabbe movie serials, with their ridiculously fake smoking spaceships and clunky, jukebox version of 'Tele-Vision.' This latest message from the campy M-I-B might easily have been the background soundtrack for Ming, the Merciless, transmitting his doomsday ultimatum to Flash Gordon.

He saved these messages as he had last night's and then called Sarah. She picked up on the second ring. "Hello?"

"The saucer has landed."

"Andy! Did you get my message?"

"I was going to call you anyway, but, yes, I just got your message. And one from the planet, Mongo, too, I think."

"What?"

"I'm already being harassed by Men-In-Black."

"Oh, dear! Are you alright?"

"Mostly, yes."

"I've read about them. They seem to be an integral part of the close-encounter phenomenon. Kind of scary, though, aren't they?"

"They would be if they weren't such scenery chewing klutzes. I honestly don't know how seriously to take them. I just got another threat on my answering machine, the second of two so far. And about an hour ago, one of them in a black Cadillac limo almost ran me over on Van Ness."

"Oooh, sweetheart, be careful!"

"Well, let me get to the point. Are you free to meet me for dinner tomorrow, here in the City?"

"Dinner is problematic unless I can get a sitter. How about lunch instead, or do you have to work?"

"Hmmm-m-m-m-m, I am going to work tomorrow. But I told them I may have a concussion, and that, if I wasn't feeling better, I might have to leave early. So, good, leave early it is. Where and when would you like to meet?"

"How about 11:30 at Akashic Books and Tapes?"

"Sounds fine. That way I can get out of the cafe before the lunch crowd hits. Where would you like to do lunch? I'm thinking Green Goddess. How about it?"

"Now you're talkin'! I love Green Goddess and it's been ages. And to think, all I was going to do tomorrow was clean house."

"I've got so much to tell you that I don't have any idea where to begin. You know, I'm completely overwhelmed by this, Sarah. And having to deal with Richard is making it even more difficult. He dragged me off to Dr. Dreamboat this morning to see if I'd been buggered by the ETs."

"You're kidding?!"

"I wish I was. Of course it served several other purposes as well, but that's what was really bothering him. I know he means well, but when he gets wound up like this, I don't know.... Sometimes he just wears me out."

"So what did the doctor say?"

"I'm fine. But we're treating this like it might be a head injury. Because of the headache, I guess. Anyway, enough about all that. From your message it sounds like a blackout regarding the Shasta Incident. Since the media want nothing to do with it, have any of your metaphysical sources had anything to say yet about Shasta? I know this sort of thing usually has some wide repercussions. I may not have been the only one being contacted yesterday. Have you heard anything on the paranormal grapevine?"

"No, not yet, but we'll have to wait and see what comes out. I've got an interesting client coming in Saturday morning, maybe Riegel will make reference to it then. If so, I'll let you know what I can; otherwise client/channel privilege and all that…you understand?"

"Sure, I understand. Well, I'm going to ring off now. I'll see you tomorrow."

"Hey! Wait! Hold the phone! Aren't you going to tell me anything right now about your contact experience? Can't you toss me just a few crumbs? C'mon. What d'ya say? Please?"

"Oh, … alright, let me see …. Uh, I met a reptiloid, a pharaoh, and a goddess, and some guys, one of whom I used to know, who are now dead. And there was someone else there, someone who I think you know. Oh, yeah, and I'm on a mission from God. How's that?"

"Wow! Honey, I said a few crumbs, not the whole cake. I think you better go lie down now."

"Trust me, that's not the whole cake. Anyway, a nap is precisely what I had in mind. Take care, see you tomorrow."

"Okay. Bye-bye."

In his bedroom the partially-opened windows faced west. Although there was a stiff ocean breeze coming down off Twin Peaks, he knew direct sunshine would turn his room into a sweat lodge, so he lowered his shades against the afternoon sun. And he closed the window opposite his bed, leaving the other one open for cooling ventilation. To gain the maximum in comfort, he took off his shoes and pants. He leaned over to put the pants on the chair by his bed. But he dropped them on the floor when he noticed that his ET shirt was no longer on the chair where he'd left it. He was sure it was there this morning. Where was it? Where had it gone? Had Lohr somehow retrieved it? But why? He'd given his permission to keep it. Was some other entity responsible, some elemental, a nature deva, a gnome, some kind of household gremlin? Or was this the work of the irritating M-I-B? Whatever mischievous spirit was to blame Andy was ticked! He hated practical jokes! How rude! How invasive!

Once again his private and personal space had been violated and he was livid. Giving voice to his displeasure, he shouted to the room, "Alright, alright! I don't care who took my ET shirt, but I want it back! Do you hear me? Very funny, yeah, ha ha ha, but the joke's over! I want it returned NOW! A.S.A.P.! That means As Soon As Possible! Got that?" He muttered some more displeasure under his breath and decided that was enough. This would NOT spoil his nap. He was determined to relax, so it was dismissed. He'd get the shirt back. That's all there was to it.

He picked up his jeans and laid them on the chair, then put on a relaxation/meditation tape: 'Journey to the End of the Universe' by Orchestra Galactica, a silly title but, as out-of-this-world sounds go, the music was highly accurate. At least it seemed so to him, if he could call his own out-of-this-world experience accurate. He made sure a coverlet was close by in case the breeze got too cool. Then he stretched out on his bed, tried several positions to find the most comfortable one and, between the music and his conscious breathing technique, he soon put all his cares and concerns in an imaginary paper bag, drop kicked it off a cliff, and descended into the Afternoon Valley of Peaceful Sleep.

The office for All the Best Realty was located in the ground floor of an apartment house near the Presidio end of Union Street. It was not far from the property that Lawrence and Bernice Fader wished to look at one more time, a Victorian townhouse, on Pacific at Steiner. To Phyllis, the all-knowing, it was a done deal. She was so sure they would buy it she already called it 'their' property. Richard met the Faders at 12:30 as scheduled, and they made one last inspection. The Faders were perfect clients. They took their time coming to a decision, but they weren't skittish. They knew what they wanted, were forthright about it, could easily afford it, and Richard didn't have to schmooze them into buying. It was an easy sale for which he personally received in excess of $100,000.

He got back to the office at 1:45, in plenty of time to eat a sandwich at his desk before his meeting at 3:00. It was to be a routine, strictly informational meeting. His three brokers and four agents needed to be made aware of certain revised real estate codes and other changes recently mandated by the state of California and the City and County of San Francisco. He set the deli bag down on his desk, pulled out a can of soda, and was about to pop it open when his phone rang. It was his mother.

"Oh, good! You are there and I didn't have to speak to Phyllis. Is she around?"

"No, Ma, she's at lunch. Why?"

"Are you in trouble with her?"

"About yesterday? No. I don't think so. Why?"

"I tried to call you at your home number last night but your message machine didn't seem to be working. I wanted to warn you that she may suspect you did not spend the day with me."

"Did she call you?"

"Yes. About 11:00. She took me by surprise and I'm afraid I didn't lie very convincingly. I think I said you were out, I don't remember saying where. I asked if you needed to call her and she said that wasn't necessary, but she sounded very suspicious behind her cheerfulness. I'm sorry, dear. I'm a miserable excuse for an alibi. And why does she have to talk to me like I'm an idiot?"

"She talks to everybody that way. It's alright, Ma. I don't think you gave it away. I called her later and said I was running errands for you, so that jibes."

"You know, dear, she really is a dreadful creature. Couldn't you find a nice person to replace her?"

"I have given that idea some thought, Ma, believe me."

"Well, perhaps you should give it some more thought. I'm not trying to tell you how to run your business. I don't mean to be critical. I'm sure you will do the right thing. But don't underestimate the damage a person like that can inflict on office morale."

"You're right, Ma."

"I know you're busy so I won't keep you, but how did your trip go yesterday? Did you accomplish what you set out to do?"

"Yes, I did. And while I still can't tell you about it, at least not today, let's talk over the weekend."

"That would be lovely. Come visit, why don't you? And bring Andy."

"We'll see if we can't work that out. Bye for now."

"Bye-bye, dear."

Richard pulled out his sandwich and unwrapped it, but he didn't start to eat it. He stared off into space, thinking about what his mother had told him. When he called Phyllis from Mount Shasta, she had already spoken to his mother and she never said a word about it. Thought she could trip me up. The conniving, little bitch! She apparently didn't have enough evidence on him or she would have struck first thing this morning, the minute he walked in the door. He would play her little game, but it was unnecessary and tiresome. It was also demeaning, which was why he now had to beat her at it. It had become a point of pride, of honor. Well, okay, maybe it really was more like a dishonorable point of competitive egotism, but, "One way or another," he

156

silently vowed, "I'll have the last word on this." He didn't want to dwell on it. He wanted to relax a moment, enjoy his lunch in peace and leisurely bring himself up to speed for the meeting. He began eating his roast-beef-on-rye while he read the handouts Phyllis had copied and left on his desk.

She had also taken a telephone message and placed the pink paper form neatly alongside the handouts. However, Richard had placed his lunch on top of it and only discovered the message after he was finished eating. The caller's name, Travis Wilson, shouldn't have been familiar to Richard, but he knew immediately who it was. He sipped his soda while he eagerly read the brief and simple message, complete with Phyllis' comments.

"From: Mr. Travis Wilson. ('Very polite') Time Called: 12:48 p.m. Left Message: Personal Business ('?') Believes you will know what this is in reference to. Declined ('Courteously') to comment further. Claims he met you yesterday on Mount Shasta. ('!!!') ('??????') Urgent. Please call him A.S.A.P."

"Oh, god! Oh, god! Dammit to hell!" he thought. "Here's her evidence! How am I going to weasel my way out of this now? Even if I pretend Officer Wilson is another client, like I did with Lt. Col. Doyle, I still have to explain meeting him in Mount Shasta. I suppose I could just tell her the truth. What am I thinking? The truthful approach is out of the question. Think, Richard, think! Why would I meet a client clandestinely in Mount Shasta? And anyway, a client wouldn't leave a 'personal' message. So what is this all about? Why a personal message? What does Officer Wilson want with me? I guess there's only one way to find out."

Richard dialed the number with the 916 area code, wondering just where in northern California Officer Wilson, Officer Travis Wilson, was. After two rings someone picked up and he heard the familiar deep baritone of the hunky highway patrolman answer tentatively, questioningly, "Hullo?"

"Hello. This is Richard Lang." He was going to say 'returning your call' but didn't have the chance. Officer Wilson broke in with a combination of relief and enthusiasm verging on mania.

"Hey, alright! How ya doin', buddy? Listen, I'm coming down to San Francisco, and I was wondering if we could get together. What d'ya say? Is that alright with you? How 'bout it?"

Richard was floored. "Uh, ...well, ...uh, when would you...?"

"How about tonight?"

"Tonight?!" Richard gasped.

"Too soon? Okay, sorry, why don't I give you a call later and we'll work something out. You are going to be around, aren't you? I mean you aren't going out of town or anything like that, are you? I really want to see you, we really need to talk, we've got a lot to catch up on, buddy."

"No, no, I'll be here, but would you ...?"

"Great, then! I'll talk to you soon. I've gotta go, buddy, so long!"

After the click of the disconnection, Richard finished his sentence speaking to the dial tone, " ... please tell me what in the hell this is all about? 'Buddy'?" Before he could make any sense out of Officer Wilson's torrential monologue, Phyllis knocked on his door. She waltzed right in without waiting for permission to enter, with a perky, I've-got-you-now kind of smirk on her face, and announced, "I'm back from lunch and I thought I'd make sure you saw that phone message I left you."

"Yes. Yes, I did, thank you."

"Did you understand the message?"

"Frankly, no. At least not all of it."

"I thought there must be some mistake, because he said he met you yesterday in Mount Shasta, and you weren't up there at all, were you? You were in Sebastopol, visiting your mother, all day. Weren't you?"

"Phyllis, please close the door and come over here. I want to talk to you. Privately."

She turned around and did as he asked, then twirled and flounced eagerly back to his desk. The smirk didn't vary but the gleam in her eyes intensified. He could almost hear her unspoken, 'Oh, Goodie Goodie', and picture her clapping her hands in childish glee. She plopped herself down in a chair before his desk and sat up straight and tall; alert and ready to hang on every word of his confession.

He began slowly, speaking quietly, choosing his words carefully. "I suppose, by now, you know that I was not with my mother in Sebastopol yesterday." The expression on her face, feigned surprise, concern, and confusion, was so insincere it was a burlesque, a vaudeville turn, a parody of melodramatic bad acting. If Phyllis had been a light-hearted jokester, it would have been funny. But she wasn't, and it wasn't. Richard was stalling while he tried to feel his way through this. He didn't know what he was going to say next, until he saw that look of mock surprise on her face. Then something inside him snapped, some kind of doorway clicked opened, and the words began to flow. His words, spoken with calculated ease and deliberate restraint, were not propelled by anger. They came from someplace where he was both in touch with his displeasure and above it. And most amazingly, he was beyond all fear of a confrontation with Phyllis.

"Where I was yesterday, and who I was with, is my business and my business alone. As far as you are concerned, I *was* with my mother in Sebastopol. I'd like to keep it that way. If anyone should ask, that is all you know. That is all you need to know and all you are going to know." Richard was firm but hardly scolding. Still, Phyllis stiffened and squared her shoulders. She clearly didn't like the tone he was taking here. Her head slowly tilted back, her nose went up, nostrils flared, mouth tightened, and her eyes narrowed.

Letting himself be guided by this new and strange inner muse, Richard countered her indignation and continued, smoothly changing tack. "Tell me, Phyllis, how long have you worked for me?" Genuine surprise momentarily

159

clouded her insulted glare and she answered cautiously in a low, deeply serious voice, "I believe it will be one year in July." She wanted to ask him why, but he didn't give her the opportunity.

"And would you say you enjoy working here? Be honest, please."

"Yes, of course, I do."

"Good. Good. I'm glad to hear that. And tell me, how are your little girls?" Changing the subject again confused her even more, making her even more suspicious. "They're fine."

"What are their names again?"

"Jessica and Jennifer."

"Oh, yes, that's right. Twins aren't they?'

"Yes," Phyllis answered firmly. She and Richard had been through all this chit-chat before, the last time being six months ago during her end-of-probation review. She was fiercely protective of her daughters and did not know why he had dragged them into this conversation.

"How old are they now?"

She heaved a sigh of exasperation and said, "Almost eleven."

"That's an expensive age, no doubt. School is expensive, all the extras they need. The kids must have those new shoes, new clothes. The kids have got to have those designer clothes nowadays, don't they? Maybe even braces." She was fuming now, waiting for him to get to the point. "I appreciate your concern, but, if you don't mind ...."

"Yes, of course, what does all this have to do with my being in Mount Shasta yesterday? Let me be frank to the point of bluntness. As I said, why I was in Mount Shasta yesterday is my business and my business alone. Personal business is just that. I neither owe you an explanation nor do I intend to offer one. My only mistake was in dishonestly trying to keep my personal business private. Obviously I never intended for you to know in the first place. It is only because of Mr. Wilson's call that you do know. That is unfortunate, but that is the reason we are having this discussion. So I find that I am in the awkward position of having to ask you to keep a confidence for me. And keeping this confidence may demand that you lie for me. If you find that morally or ethically objectionable and unacceptable, I completely understand. So then, I'm going to give you a choice here. If you find that, in good conscience, you cannot continue to work for me and, at the same time, be expected to lie for me, then you may feel free to tender your resignation."

Phyllis huffed loudly and exclaimed, "Mr. Lang!" She had more to say but Richard was not finished. He raised a hand to silence her.

"Please! I am not done yet. Hear me out. After today, indeed after this meeting, the subject of where I was and what I was doing yesterday, and the conversation we are having right now, is to be considered forgotten. More than that, this conversation never happened. Frankly, Phyllis, I don't trust you. So understand that if you do bring it up, in any context whatsoever – whether or not you are still in my employ – I will categorically deny any of it."

She squirmed and gasped in protest, but let him go on, all the while her hateful glare was silently trying to kill him. "So tell me, what is it going to be? Or do you need some time to consider your answer?" Phyllis spluttered furiously but could not cough up a coherent sentence. "Very well, take some time. You can tell me your decision tomorrow. Now I'm going to have to ask you to go back to your desk, because I need to get ready for a meeting." He got up, took her arm, helped her to her feet, and literally showed the shocked and angry woman the door. He watched her sit down at her desk, her fists clenched, her mouth twitching, and thought, 'I don't believe I just did that'. When she loudly and dramatically burst into tears, he quietly closed the door and sneaked guiltily back to his desk.

It had all happened so spontaneously that it took him as much by surprise as it obviously had Phyllis. He couldn't ever remember speaking to a woman like that. He'd been raised to be respectful of women. It was not like him to show a woman that hard-nosed part of his personality. That was a male thing.

But where had the words come from? How had he found such eloquence in the midst of so much inner turmoil? He wasn't exactly proud of himself, but he had to admit it felt really good to have finally put her in her place. How could he have been such a wuss, such a wimp, for so long? Come Monday he might be interviewing for a new office manager. So what was the bad news? And to think, he had been prepared to offer her a raise.

A Kind of Vertigo of the Soul

TEN

He knew he was lying on his back. And he knew that his name was being called, over and over. He also heard a low buzz of unintelligible conversation going on in the background. It was unintelligible, but the buzz was all about being very concerned and insistent that Andy wake up. Eyes closed, he nevertheless knew exactly where he was, who was around him, and what had just happened to him. A gentle slap on his face jarringly brought Andy back to full hyper-consciousness. His physical body shivered as his other bodies slammed back into it and into realignment. Instantly reintegrated into total fight-or-flight alertness, he cleverly and cautiously remained prone.

He decided feigning unconsciousness was unnecessary, so he opened his eyes and saw Lohr and Reiko looking down at him with calm concern. In a voice loud and strong, respectful but with just a touch of annoyance in it, he said to them, "I would like this experience modified, please."

Lohr responded immediately. He knelt beside Andy and spoke forcefully, "With our sincerest and deepest apologies, it is done." Reiko added, "Forgive us. We grievously underestimated the power of your psychic link with Kahr. I am sure he meant you no harm." Lohr tried to reassure him further, "You are not hurt, Andy. I can assure you it is not possible to be physically harmed in this density. Well, *seriously* physically harmed anyway."

"Tell that to my gut."

The sarcasm zinged right by Reiko, who took him literally and placed a hand over his solar plexus. Though she did not touch him, he felt a cool heat soothing the spot. He breathed into it and in seconds his discomfort was gone. But Reiko only wanted to get the meeting going, so she asked sweetly, "Do you feel better? May we proceed with the introductions? Do you feel up to it?"

"Oh, yes, by all means, let's proceed with the introductions. Shall we?" Lohr was already helping Andy to his feet. "Just breathe, dear one, and we'll get you pumped right back up." Whispering discreetly in his ear, Lohr offered another piece of advice, "I would advise you not to rely too heavily on sarcasm or any other form of irony here. I, myself, enjoy and appreciate it – in fact, I love it – but, you see, some of them would need it translated. Sorry, but it's really not clear communication. You do understand, don't you?"

Andy nodded that he got it and said, "Thank you. I'll try to behave myself." He took three quick, deep breaths and felt his prana fountain begin to flow again. Three more breaths and Andy felt like he was back and, if possible, even more fully present than before. Like an actor whose stage fright disappears once he's on stage, he now felt truly in character as the Guy From Planet Earth. What's more, the attack had given him an edge of anger. No longer so blithely bedazzled by the whole experience, he was wary, ready not only for introductions, but for confrontations. He brushed himself off with a little help from Reiko and straightened his clothes. He may have imagined it, but he thought he heard something like a cheer of hurrah from the whales. Yes, he was quite ready. Go ahead, bring on the introductions! He led Lohr and Reiko into the room on top of the pink pyramid.

Once inside the thirty-foot square, he stopped to look around and to take in the meeting place. He noticed all kinds of details he hadn't been able to or hadn't the time to notice before, such as woven runners on the floor. The rugs were pale-yellow ochre with thick piles, and were decorated with unreadable hieroglyphic designs the color of umber. There were massive, but delicately-carved, pink alabaster benches and chairs lavished with black, magenta, and turquoise cushions. And there were three wells in the middle of the room, probably eight feet apart, each a circular hole five feet in diameter, each surrounded by a low, wide wall of the same pink alabaster stone from which the pyramid had been fashioned. Aligned left to right, one contained a fire, another held water and in the third one, the center well, there seemed to be nothing at all. It was impossible to know how deep its darkness went. A big cat, a spotted South American jaguar, lounged on one of the benches in typical regal, feline disdain. On the other side of the room, from the plains of Africa was a cheetah, watchful, but similarly sedate. Andy imagined that the magnificent cats had just been fed, and he was correct. The outsized snowy owl had flown to a perch on the back of one of the chairs, where the figure in green now sat. The owl still looked unnaturally large. And there were other animals present.

Flanking the figure in the purple robe, who also was now seated in a stone chair, were two smooth, shorthaired, muscular dogs. Andy recognized the breed, the long, graceful legs and neck, the tapering muzzle, the sharply pointed and erect ears: they were Salukis, the royal household dogs of the Pharaohs of Ancient Egypt. One of them sat on its haunches and the other reclined, sphinx-like, front paws extended. Both the figure in green and the figure in purple sat upright, alert, and perfectly still, calmly watching Andy with great curiosity. They were definitely human in appearance, at least from twenty feet away they looked human. But there was something about the figure in purple that Andy was sure he recognized. He was a strange-looking human with a very long face, pronounced cheek bones, heavily-lidded eyes, and thick lips. When he turned his head to one side, glancing at his cohort, his features were startlingly leonine. The hood of his robe had fallen back and Andy saw that his bald head was encircled with a hammered, golden crown of simple design.

The crown was a band two inches wide. In the middle of the forehead, a great widening took place that formed a convex curve, a shield that swept back far enough to encase part of the figure's large, hairless cranium. The only adornment to the shield was a polished disk that nearly filled the curved plane. The disk was a different, warmer shade of gold. Andy studied the man. It took a moment to coax the identification. Could it really be so? Was this figure merely a look-alike or was he actually in the presence of the Pharaoh Akhenaton? In his art history books, he had seen sculpted stone portraits of this man, also known as Amen Hotep IV. During his brief reign as Pharaoh of All the Egypts, painting and the plastic arts attained a level of realistic representation hitherto unparalleled in the ancient world. This radical departure in the arts was attributed to the encouragement of the god-king, Akhenaton. Even more importantly, this great leader had introduced monotheism to ancient Egypt. In a way, it was not a surprise to see him here. His odd, other worldly features had always indicated to Andy that the Divine Pharaoh was, in all likelihood, an extra-terrestrial. Whether or not this was indeed the god-king before him, Andy was already feeling humbled and intimidated by the powerful, yet benign, aura of energy coming off the one in green.

But it was the third figure, the figure in blue, that made Andy the most uncomfortable. Its emanation was both powerful and dark. The mysterious figure had removed itself to the opposite doorway, almost as far away from Andy as it was possible to be and still be present on the pyramid. Andy sensed that it – no, not an 'it,' but a 'he' – Andy sensed that he was sulking. The hood of his robe covered most of his face, so Andy was spared the full impact of the hideous, scaly countenance. This grotesque he-creature was the 'monster from outer space' that Andy had imagined he might one day meet on a flying saucer. Still he shuddered at the glimpse of the pointed snout, the mouth partly opened revealing sharp, snaggled, dagger teeth. It was a truncated version of an alligator's maw. And he was not only hideous, but radiated a dangerous hostility. He had viciously attacked Andy's body through an unusually vulnerable place: his psyche. Fortunately he had not yet laid a claw on him. Now the third figure, the one hooded in green, stood and came forward to greet him, drawing his attention away from both the god-king and the beast. Though he first sensed an androgynous being, as 'it' approached, 'it' turned out to be a 'she.' At first he thought her to be a male-to-female transsexual, but then he saw before him a tall, sturdy, attractive woman, a handsome, blond Amazon. Her large, moist, lapis-blue eyes radiated the same happy, "fear not, for you are beloved to me," greeting that he had received from Lohr and Reiko. Her chiseled, manly features were softened by her wide smile and a set of charming dimples. Her luxuriant, straight hair, of palest corn silk, fell to her shoulders. She stopped before him and they gazed at each other in a kind of mellow wonderment. Speech did not seem to be necessary and so they said nothing aloud to one another, but instead conversed telepathically.

Their silence, far from awkward, was ripe with the richness of the transmissions between them. Once Andy got over the initial novelty of 'hearing' her voice directly in his head and not through his ears, he assumed everyone else was hearing her greeting to him. Without really thinking about it, he assumed she was speaking aloud for all to 'hear.' He was partly correct. Although she was not speaking aloud, indeed, everyone could 'hear' her. Telepathy was the preferred method of communication here. No translation was necessary.

"Ahn Dee, at last we meet. I am Aya. My home is in the Pleiades star system, but I am a priestess of Gaia. Your planet is as beloved to me as my own. That is because your Goddess and my Goddess are one and the same. And the Goddess has need of me here on Earth.

"If you are confused because I look like one of your species and not like a creature from an alien world, I assure you there are many species in the cosmos that look like we do. You truly are not alone. But your desire was to communicate with others not like yourself. And there are many species that fit that description as well. Your first experience of conscious contact will be sufficiently rich if I present to you only one example. You are indeed a brave soul to initiate this inter-dimensional visit, and we honor you for your courage. However, at this time, we feel that exposing you to any more than one such species would prove too much of a shock to you. Forgive our presumption, but we have experience in these matters and ask that you trust us to have made the proper decision. Depending on how well this experiment goes, quite possibly you will be returning to this dimension again, and therefore, you will subsequently be introduced to other members of our Galactic Federation.

"And so, before I introduce you to Kahr, perhaps an explanation is in order. Kahr is a reptiloid, of a reptilian race that has been working behind the scenes of your planetary history for the last twenty-six thousand years. Some call them the Anunnaki, the alleged enslavers of the races of Earth. Like everything deemed of the Darkness, their work had its higher purpose. However, you yourself, like most of the incarnate of your planet, have a dread of and a deep-seated hatred for the Anunnaki. I am not here to defend them, or to bring reconciliation, that is – in part – why Kahr is present today. I am merely explaining the profound psychic link, indeed the racial cellular memory of past atrocities, that caused your gut level reaction to your first sight of Kahr."

Andy looked into Aya's radiant face, captivated by her perfection, by her holiness. Yes, she was holy. There was no other word. She was without guile. She was wise, loving and understanding beyond any other in Andy's experience, both in this and his earthly life. She was simply a greater being. And he knew that because – well, he just knew, that's all, like he knew what she was saying – it was there inside him. He knew that what she said was true, even when he didn't want to believe it. He trusted her unquestioningly. If there were some good reason for the presence of a reptiloid, then he would accept that. At least they hadn't introduced him to any of the Greys. He felt transcendently safe as long as he could see himself reflected in her eyes.

But then she turned her gaze to one side, and Andy followed it. And there, suddenly beside her, was Kahr. Andy looked right into his eyes. He just stared at the eyes, not daring to look at the rest of the creature, who stood on two legs like a human being, stood perhaps only five feet away. They were not human eyes. They were alligator eyes, reddish, unblinking eyes. Amazingly, there was emotion behind those eyes! Forked lightning crackled inside them, the threatening front of a deadly storm of rage. This creature, the one with a name like a snake's hiss, looked at Andy with contempt and defiance. Andy was rattled and unnerved, yet fascinated at the same time. He could not look away, and as he looked deeper into the bestial eyes, he saw something else. Even more astonishing, he saw there a brooding intelligence! Not a simple creature intelligence, but a human intelligence, cunning and complex!

Andy felt Lohr and Reiko press in protectively beside him. Now curiosity compelled him to look deeper and deeper into those eyes. And the thing that finished him off was the flood of awareness that he was not just looking at some other being, but surprisingly, an aspect of himself! This was the Darkness that lives in every soul, the evil that turns ordinary people into cold-blooded, genocidal murderers. Although it still shocked him to look it in the face, after lifetimes of madness and cruelty, of shame and guilt, he could no longer hate it, or fear it, or wish it dead. It was a part of him. He knew he had been a willing participant in the atrocities as surely as he had been a victim of them. There was nothing left to do but accept it, albeit painfully and grudgingly. With acceptance came the objectivity for that most difficult of resignations: forgiveness. But it would be hard won.

He looked at the seething hatred in the belligerent eyes of the evil reptile, and he could not let himself look away. He stared at Kahr tenaciously, even when the pictures of the unspeakable atrocities ran themselves across the back of his mind. And even when he saw the relentless carnage of bodies, the ghastly pantomime of snuffed-out lives, playing like a movie behind Kahr's mind too, he would not look away. He stood fast against the sheer horror of the vision. A part of him was in desperate agony and he wanted to leave his body to escape, but he forced himself to stay present.

A hand placed in gentle support on each of his shoulders helped. And all the while it was as if Kahr were showing him, forcing him to face just how awful they were, he and Andy both. His heart ached and throbbed and Andy felt himself expand into pure emotion. But instead of exploding, he found himself crying again. It was dry, silent, bitter crying, and he shook from the effort to hold it in check. And when he finally let it loose, a long, loud cry of anguish and frustration, of regret and heartbreaking remorse, he heard an answering cry from the beast, the demon spark went out of the eyes before him and the lizard dropped his head to his chest. As Andy shrank back into his body, he heard Kahr say, "It is finished. We are dead. He understands. I must go." The lizard-that-walks-like-a-man turned and the hooded figure in blue simply vanished.

"Wait!" Andy called after him. "I didn't mean to hurt you!" Staring at the spot in the air from which his antagonist had disappeared, his expression a mix of painful confusion and utter astonishment, Andy now spoke quietly, plaintively, to himself, "We didn't have a choice. We were swept away. I didn't mean to hurt you."

Reiko whispered in Andy's ear, "Do you know what you have done? Do you feel it? The healing has begun. Compassion has triumphed. I salute you." She kissed his cheek. He turned to answer and was surprised to see in her face a fleeting resemblance to the reptiloid until her features morphed back into her strange hybrid beauty. He moved his mouth to speak but was too overcome to say anything. It didn't matter because everyone 'heard' the thought, "Yes, I understand. But we did what we had to do. And we spent many lifetimes damned to hell. No, thank you. I don't want to be saluted."

He looked from face to face. Each in its way honoring the gravity of this moment of atonement. For what seemed to Andy to be a very long time, a desolate silence hung in the room on top of the pyramid on the island in the ocean inside the starship a long way out in space.

Then finally Aya spoke aloud to him, which give substance and weight to the thought and thus added reassurance. "Kahr is humbled but you have not hurt him. Perhaps on another day the two of you will meet again as friends. Perhaps not. But he was correct. It is finished. For you and for him the cycle is broken." This pronouncement was followed by another long, silent pause as Aya watched Andy carefully. She observed as the wrenching reconciliation filtered down through his various bodies – the etheric, the mental, the emotional, the physical – until he was settled into his new awareness, at least enough to continue the meeting. When she was satisfied this was so, she again spoke aloud.

"You must share this experience with others needing to reconcile. You must find the way. It will save lives." Andy breathed in her words and nodded that he understood, even if he didn't know how to do what she commanded.

She continued telepathically, "And now come and behold the future contained in the past. I will present you to His Holiness, Ankh-Ra, Divine Scientist and Metaphysician, from the Sirian star field." She took Andy by the hand and brought him to one of the high-backed, carved stone chairs positioned next to the well of fire and at a right angle to the purple-robed figure. Now, to his left, perhaps three feet away, sat the one he believed to be Akhenaton. Even seated, or more properly, 'enthroned,' he seemed tall. Though called by another name he was every inch the god-king. Here was an entity whose aura outshone them all. The dogs stirred a bit, both coming to attention beside their master. They were alert, quietly, aggressively ready to guard without seeming ready to attack. Aya indicated to Andy that he may sit and then crossed over to her own chair, which faced his from beside the well of water. Lohr and Reiko made themselves comfortable on cushions on the wall of the well of air.

The Ageless One regally, slowly cocked his head to observe Andy. Andy returned his curious gaze, but found that he could read nothing in the exotic, kohl-lined eyes. He surrendered to the inspection Ankh-Ra was giving him. The demigod said nothing for a very long time. Andy began to wonder if he was supposed to be the first to say or do something. He looked to Aya now instead of Lohr or Reiko for his clue. Aya closed her eyes and with a subtle nod let him know that nothing was expected of him. He returned to Ankh-Ra's eyes. This time he looked deeper and he began to feel dizzy. It was a kind of vertigo of the soul. He was on the verge of swooning and falling into the depth of wisdom in those intensely serious eyes. To save himself, he reacted quite involuntarily by jerking his head back. He gave an amused snort, and burst into a huge grin. The divinity surprised him by returning an even bigger grin and an even louder snort. Andy's startled face only caused Ankh-Ra's grin to widen into an open-mouthed, ear-to-ear smile. From there the smiles between them escalated into chuckles, which were rapidly piled one on top of the other until they collapsed into gales of laughter. Ankh-Ra's first gasped words to Andy were, "Now I remember you! But ... but .. but, I had forgotten how funny you are!" Andy couldn't talk but he answered by pointing back at His Silliness as if to say, "You too!" They slapped their knees and rocked back and forth, they held their sides and their stomachs, and of course, the more they tried to stop laughing the more they laughed. They laughed until they cried and when Andy saw black kohl running down the royal cheeks, he somehow managed to cry out, "Oh, my, your holiness, your mascara's running!"

They both shrieked and howled and moaned and wiped the tears from their eyes. Andy dabbed his eyes with the hem of Ankh-Ra's robe. Which caused more laughter. It became so painful they both had to turn away from each other. They looked down at the floor, gasping like fish out of water.

172

Gradually, and with great effort, they brought themselves under tenuous control. Then, coincidentally at the same time, they both looked over at the others. Aya, Lohr, and Reiko were sitting perfectly still, watching them with cool, slightly bemused, highly dignified detachment. Seeing the trio's wan smiles, weary from indulging their idiot children, only set them off again. And Aya's, Lohr's, and Reiko's exasperated groans of, "Oh, come on you two!" did not help them gain control of themselves. But finally they did, as they each dried the last tear, coughed and cleared their throats to signal that they were both once again ready for a decent, adult exchange.

"I have not laughed like that in a long time, Ahn Dee. Thank you. But forgive me. This is a meeting with a most serious agenda. You have honored us with your presence and your willingness to participate in a momentous experiment. I am afraid I have not conducted myself in a manner befitting this history-making event. Today a citizen of Earth meets citizens of the Galactic Federation. For now, it occurs on a starship. Within a few years, it will occur on Earth. And you will have helped that to happen. By virtue of the wisdom and compassion you have already demonstrated both here before us and in your life itself, and especially by your capacity for mirth, I deem you a most worthy receptacle for and carrier of our messages to the people of Earth."

Andy wasn't sure he liked the sound of that last part. But he was curious about these messages. And remembering that he had been instructed to keep his questions to a minimum, he decided to hear them out before speaking up. As if in answer to his unvoiced skepticism, Ankh-Ra said, "Your time with us is limited. We will discuss the role we expect you to play in as great a depth as your timing will allow, for soon we must return you to your home planet. Before that there is much to tell you. So let us begin."

"And the whales sang that it was good."

ELEVEN

Ankh-Ra sat back in his chair and pulled his robe around himself with the long, tapering fingers of his large hands. Before beginning, he paused, head down, as if to gather his thoughts or his energy or both. Andy followed his lead and made himself comfortable too. He willed his mind to become a blank screen or a blank page upon which Ankh-Ra could write. A small gust of breeze stirred the air inside the room and the firelight flickered on all the glowing faces waiting expectantly. The eminence nodded as if he had gotten a signal telling him to begin. He leveled a heavy-lidded gaze directly at Andy and began to speak out loud.

"To you, Ahn Dee, and to all the people of Earth, we of the Galactic Federation ask your indulgence in hearing what we have to say. When we speak to you, we are speaking both to your individual and unique integrity and to the collective you, those of like-mindedness who are aligned with our words. We do not ask that you embrace and believe the letter of these words but, rather, their spirit in truth. We trust that your own innate powers of discernment will serve you well and should be your final guide in all decisions regarding acceptance of what we are about to tell you. Our intention is not to be followed blindly. We ask of you no particular reverence, rather we encourage your irreverence. We claim no exalted status. However, we view your world from a different perspective, one which your limited reality cannot readily distinguish. For the time being, it is not

174

necessary that you believe us or even that you believe we exist. But some day, in the not too distant future, you will.

"Enormous challenges loom on your event horizon. Astounding changes are headed your way. Advance warning will prove vital to meeting, merging with, and riding the wave of the future. But this is only one aspect of our message. We begin with the announcement of a crucial astronomical event.

"There is a band, a ring of photon energy, approaching the Earth. It is already arriving in fragments or incoming waves. Your outer planet, Pluto, became immersed in the energy in 1972. Some of your scientists are already aware of this energy, however, they understand neither its origin nor its significance. The psychically gifted among you might detect this wave of energy as a Violet or Purple Ray. If it is not otherwise detected, its effects most certainly will be. When it fully arrives and the Earth is first enveloped in a Null Zone of seeming destruction, you will be told it is the end of the world, but it is not. It is the Beginning of the World, the world the way you have been asking for it to be for the last twenty-thousand lifetimes.

"Because the Photon Belt comes from Prime Source , it has the unlimited power to destroy the planet. However, for many years agents of the Galactic Federation have been preparing the Earth for this event. With our insight and our technology, we are here from the future to shape the now, your present, so that it is even better than intended. New power vortices have been created on Earth, old ones retuned, blocked ones re-tapped. The planetary energy grids have been enhanced, and in some cases, retro-fitted, in ways designed to protect Earth from those annihilating aspects of the Photon energy. And so, ultimately, the Earth will be cleansed and purified by immersion in the photon energy. Life will not be extinguished, but amplified. The power behind the Photon Belt will shift the planet, and all that dwell thereon, into the Fifth to the Seventh Dimensions. It will cause changes in all molecular and electromagnetic structures, within the realms of the animate and inanimate alike.

"As the planet itself is rejuvenated and transformed, so will it bring about a great evolutionary leap for the human race, and a change in thinking so vast, so profound, that many will be unwilling or unable to accept it. Many souls will choose to leave the planet at this time for a parallel Earth where Evil may continue its vain struggle with Good for the Illusion of Supremacy. These souls may not even be aware that anything has happened.

"For those who remain, for those who are Aware, the New Birth will not be an easy one. It may, indeed, give every appearance of being what some among you call 'The End Times.' But the Photon Belt is not ego-driven. It is not being brought because the Wicked need punishment and the Virtuous need to be exalted. This is why we are eager for you to tell all those with ears to hear, how this Shift, this Planetary Ascension, will be accomplished. It is for all those with open minds and open hearts to discern for themselves the Truth of our message. Each of you must decide what this information means to you and how you will or will not use it in the days ahead. Our intention is to help as many as we can to understand what will be happening to them. It is not to extort blind obedience or morally straight behavior from souls who already know better. It is not to frighten, or threaten with death, for truly, to die before one lives eternally is not necessary.

"Planetary Ascension is inevitable. It is part of a grand, eternal cycle as rhythmic and natural as the ocean's tides. We, your galactic brothers and sisters, are not here to make it happen. We are here to shape the experience and help it happen in the most expeditious and beneficial way possible. The Great Shift will occur over the course of seven says. As Time is already speeding up on your planet, these days will be as seven hours and not the twenty-four you might expect. The Photon Belt will be completely enveloping the Earth in the year 2000. This timing can and may be altered. Much depends on the Mindscape of the Mass Consciousness. But the Photon Belt will arrive and when it does, prepared or not, you will experience the changes. Hold thought steadfastly to the Good. Awake, O Humanity! On Earth as it is in Heaven!"

Andy was awake, alright. This was too astounding to miss! He watched the firelight dancing off the opaque eyes and, in his hyper awareness, the totality of his being was focused on the storyteller. As Ankh-Ra spoke, Andy saw the features of his face waver and subtly change. The Egyptian was showing Andy all the incarnations that he, Ankh-Ra, had ever experienced. In one dazzling minute his face rapidly morphed from one person, one gender, one species, to another. This was Ankh-Ra's way of proving to Andy who he was; these faces, these life forms, these lives were his credentials. It was an exquisite honor unlike any ever bestowed upon Andy. The spell was cast. Andy was enthralled. Only later would he remember that he had felt as if he too were morphing right along with him. And he would wonder what his own 'credentials' looked like to Ankh-Ra.

On the blank screen of Andy's mind there was a moving holographic picture illustrating everything Ankh-Ra was telling him. At times it took on the same dry, pedantic quality of an instructional film. At other times he would be swept away by the picture's sense of virtual reality. Andy was conscious of receiving at least two distinct but overlapping versions of the same basic message. One was rendered in words and the other in pictures. This did not distract Andy. His mind could and did take all of it in without missing a single detail. It all seemed perfectly natural. Just as in the dream-state, Andy accepted without question his ability to fly, so too now he accepted this expanded, dual-consciousness, this multiple awareness.

Ankh-Ra continued, "On the First Day, yes, there will be Fear. As the Earth enters the Null Zone, the outer edge of the Belt, you will feel the atmosphere grow heavy and oppressive. You will sense that something great and terrible is imminent. You will want to be on your best behavior. You will be told that the end of the world is at hand and that you should Repent. You will feel that whatever business you have left unfinished with Prime Source, you would like to make amends. Very quickly. And Repentance is not a bad idea. As the uneasy feelings stretch into hysteria, know that Fear will be left behind in the Third Dimension. If you have not already found your haven, then on this day you may be drawn to different communities, different places of sanctuary, so that you will have sustenance and nurturance. Follow your inner knowingness."

The words and the accompanying visions, random glimpses of the scenario Ankh-Ra was spinning for Andy, took on a heavy turbulence in his mind. His heart was stirred as if in a thick, chaotic stew, and what Andy saw was indeed fearsome. Great crowds of people in abject terror surging through streets full of burning rubble. And he asked Prime Source for mercy as the sights and sounds grew more and more terrible. And yet he knew it could not have been worse than the world has ever been. Certainly he and Kahr had conjured no worse. Blessedly, these flashes were relieved by tableaux of communities of the prayerful opening their doors to the tempest-bruised wayfarer.

"On the Second Day there will be bloating of the body. You will need a pure water supply. Your bodies will be redesigning themselves with water so that you can sustain the coming electromagnetic changes. Be forewarned: the Secret Governments of Earth will try to shape this scenario to their advantage. Their efforts to control your minds, to keep you subservient, their feeding on your negative emotions, will not be relinquished without a ferocious struggle. Indeed, they will only intensify their efforts, for they are pledged to do whatever is necessary to hold and extend their power in the three dimensional affairs of the planet. And they are so drunk with their own corruption, they believe they can actually stop the Procession of Ascension from happening. Need we say it? Don't give them any more power."

Andy saw an immense bank of machines, electric coils crackling and bursting with lightening flashes. Concave dishes were arrayed around large cities, and the power of these rays was thrust into full throttle until people

178

were clutching their heads and ears, writhing on the ground in agony. This symbolic vision was all the more terrifying for its silence. Then this mad, last-ditch effort to control humankind, even if it meant destroying people, was suddenly shut down. In the vision, the power was drained from the engines of mass mind control, a master switch was thrown, and the light faded to a dark and bloody brown. "Fear not. When you meet the strangers, ask them if they are aligned with the Light. Challenge their authority to do you harm. They must and will back down. So it is spoken, so it is done."

"On the Third Day you will find that nothing will work – cars, TV's, lights, cell phones, anything driven by electricity will cease functioning. Even batteries will be useless. Plastics of every kind will disintegrate into dust in 32 seconds. This will mean that clothing made from synthetics will fall to dust; better switch to cotton, linen, or wool. Plumbing, car parts, furniture, consumer goods packaging, shower caps, spatulas, Monopoly hotels, CD's, even computers, will seem to self-destruct. Do not give in to despair. Have faith that civilization will be restored. A replacement substance for plastics, one that is completely organic, will be brought to Earth in mass quantities six months after the changes."

A replacement for plastic? Now this struck Andy as silly. If it was an attempt to elicit a glimmer of humor from these dire warnings, it was only partly successful. Andy smiled, but weakly. And, at this point, he noticed that Ankh-Ra's telling was not half so dramatic as the images it brought to Andy's mind. In fact, he spoke with such purposeful evenhandedness and compassion for his listener, that it was as if someone or something else was orchestrating the visions that were streaming into Andy's consciousness. Perhaps it was a pre-recorded visual program used to reinforce the aural program being downloaded into Andy's head.

"And on this day, a large portion of the planet's population will 'depart.' Panic and Chaos will take their toll. Many will embrace their fear, expecting the planet to implode. They will be the ones who wanted to be rescued, who expected to be rescued. Indeed, that may be exactly how it seems to them, that they are being rescued. Whether or not they die by their own hand, they will not leave their bodies behind, and they too will disintegrate. Or so it will seem as they will simply disappear when they are taken onto the parallel, three-dimensional Earth being prepared for them."

A torrent of horrible images, images of a mass self-extinguishment, definitely at odds with the benign tone of Ankh-Ra's words, rushed over Andy and threatened to overwhelm him. And he saw people screaming but could not hear them. Slowly at first, it was one person at a time just vanishing in a split second, like a rapid film fade. Then with ever increasing momentum, scene after scene of mass suicide and death, busloads and carloads and planeloads of people crashing and burning. He saw individuals stepping off into air from bridges, from the tops of buildings, crowds of people throwing themselves into water from boats and from docks, body after body falling through the air, sinking beneath the waves. He saw people drinking elixirs of death and embracing their loved ones as they die, their darkened souls rising to form a ghastly shroud over the planet.

"On Day Four will come the Twilight Time. The sun will appear to fade. The stars will also begin to fade. The planet will be enshrouded in mist. It will be as though Nuclear Winter has befallen the Earth. As the temperature drops the winds will rise. There will be winds in excess of 175 miles per hour on the coasts, 125 inland. There will be destruction of epic, even biblical, proportions. Yes, a sense of humor will be absolutely essential. Your survival will depend on it. Remember this valuable advice: "Don't panic." Rest assured, elements will be brought to Earth to keep the planet warm enough to survive while the sun is not visible. Hugs will be needed more than ever, because you will be grieving for those who did not stay."

In spite of these relentlessly dismal prospects, Andy was sensing an underlying mood of hope. His knowingness told him that he would not be among those meeting their end. He realized that in the telling was the

180

presumption that this catastrophe was unequivocally survivable. If not, there would be no point to a warning. But things were bound to get worse before they got better.

"On Day Five the world will be plunged into total darkness. The darkness and the fog are to protect you from seeing the changes that will be taking place. We will shield your star system for its trip through the galaxy to be repositioned in the Sirius system. On this day (and on the Sixth) you may feel as if you have died. But you will have much love and support from many species. Do not despair. Do not be discouraged. If you have made it this far, you are a true Ascensionist and Light Worker. And, in various forms, our agents will be present to assist you. Even now, they are on your planet and are being briefed on how to help you."

Shock was added to shock. The entire solar system was going to be moved? The realization arrived like a thunderclap. A sonic shock wave of incredulity jarred Andy's brain. This was inconceivable. "I may feel as if I've died?! May?," he says. Ankh-Ra misread the sarcasm but registered the shock, so he hastened to reassure Andy that everything was being done, and would be done, to get those who had thus far survived, through this Great Tribulation.

"Either at or before this time, you will all have an implant, which will last three days, to help you endure these changes. It will help to stabilize the body and relieve the distress of changes in molecular structure. And you will have the vibrational support of the Cetaceans. Whales and dolphins, you see, are of a higher spiritual intelligence than their human counterparts. They do not have logic, however, because they do not need it. They exist and function without thinking about it. They are pure Being. By giving forth the steadying vibration of unconditional love and balance for all species, and for the planet, they are and will be here to assist you. And with you too, will be your guardian angels. They will be walking you through this, and you will not only feel their connection, but you'll begin to see them as well.

"A common reaction to the total darkness will be to want to find something to eat because that's what happens when your emotions are triggered. Bear in mind that, like plastics, food with synthetic preservatives will also disintegrate. Stock up on those naturally dried fruits and vegetables now. At this time you may find yourself in the company of some who still do not have full awareness of what is happening. Obviously they will be distressed and you will be moved to help them. The best way will be with your words. Though you won't be able to see, you can soothe with your voice, with the spoken word. If you use your other senses, the darkness will not be a problem. You will know instinctively what to do because, even now, you are already learning to listen to your inner selves. Remember to let those who are slow to awaken do so in their own timing. You can help, but you cannot help anyone against his or her will. You cannot impose awakenings on them, but you can offer your understanding and awareness of what is going on. Point people toward their inner light. That can be your gift to them.

"On Day Seven the stars will reappear in the sky. They will not be the same familiar stars you now see in your night sky. This may be confusing at first. And then you will notice more changes. The Light will Dawn again and there will be a second, lesser sun overhead. You will feel as though you have awakened into a new Genesis. Every living thing will be greatly invigorated. You will find no pollution, no fear, no rage. You will run the gamut of emotions. You will find other beings of the Galactic Federation, beings you never even imagined before, who will have for you, and bring to you, only Love, Balance, and Acceptance. They will be the intergalactic version of the U.S. agency known as F.E.M.A., only they might be called the Federation Emergency Management Agency. And you will be visited by your ancestors. Yes. This will be the Great Reunion you have longed for all your lifetimes since Lemuria. At last all the abandonment issues you have suffered since the Great Departure, will be resolved and healed. You will feel reunited with Prime Source. At last you will be Home. At last you will know Heaven On

Mother Earth. You will have gone through changes so vast, you will awaken as a new species of humankind. Yes, Ahn Dee, all this will happen to you, too.

"And what of these great changes about which we speak; what are they and how will they affect the people of New Earth? You will all experience phenomenal spiritual growth. You will all feel (and you will be) so complete, you will no longer accrue karmic debt. You may never feel the need to incarnate again. All knowledge will be given to you at your asking. Dimensional portals will be open to you, portals transcending time and space. For you, the New Human Race, travel to other planets and galaxies will be instantaneous. Do you think we really need spaceships to span the light-years? The spaceships are a dimensional bridge. This too you will come to understand.

"These miracles will be made possible because the physical body will be reconstituted. You all will be taller, which you might not notice at first except for the way your clothes fit. Two ribs will have been restored to your body. Your body will be less dense. There will be more space between the molecules. You will see light through your body, much as you, Ahn Dee, see your own body now become lighter. Only it will be more. People will be fading in and out until they master their new bodies. It won't take long until you will see each other as you now see our bodies glow and shine. Instead of two strands of DNA, your body's cells will have twelve, or six pairs of two. This will enable your body to become a Light body, or a semi-etheric body, which, like a thought form, can be changed, rejuvenated, or recreated in response to your conscious thoughts. There will no longer be such a thing as Lack. You will no longer be subject to disease, withering age, and death. You may choose death and rebirth, but it will not be preordained.

"This new structure will mean that you will recover your lost consciousness abilities. You will be that spark of the Creator you were never able to be before. Your chakra system will expand from seven centers to twelve, the highest chakra connecting you to the farthest reaches of the metaphysical universe while still remaining a part of Gaia. You will be able to tap into and use the full power of your magnificent brain. Along with clairaudience and clairvoyance, you will know and practice telekinesis. You will supply your needs based on thought alone. Whatever you need will be made manifest through the power of your mind. One of the effects of the Photon Belt will be to pull all of your simultaneous lives together into the Now. In your Light Body, all your past and future lives, all your lives in parallel universes, will be integrated. All this will bring you to the knowledge of who you really are; the full grandeur of your many incarnations; the full realization of your connection to the Godhead."

Andy was aglow in his heart and mind with the beautiful pictures Ankh-Ra was painting. But when the immortal of many lifetimes and many personalities paused, Andy's elation tripped and fell. It was all too good to be true. He didn't exactly want to cry, but he saw his child-like naiveté sitting in the dust, pouting, with a ferocious frown on its cherubic face. Once again forgetting that his thoughts were transparent, he was surprised when Ankh-Ra leaned forward, reached out and patted his hand.

"Oh, my poor child! You have a question that needs to be addressed. You want to believe me. But you want to know who I am. Who is telling you these unbelievable things? When they ask you on whose authority you learned these things, what will you tell them? As you have so correctly surmised, the pharaoh you mistook me for is but one aspect of my being. I am here before you today as a scientist. This is perhaps my greatest aspect. What kind of scientist am I, you ask? Aya has called me a Divine Scientist. I suppose you could call me a meta-scientist, although your scientists of Earth, would probably declare me a pseudo-scientist, if they could imagine me. You know, Ahn Dee, there is such a thing as an unhealthy skepticism."

Andy was amused by this comment on 'unhealthy' skepticism. It made Ankh-Ra seem more human. His cosmic mentor continued, "But I think what

184

you wish to ask is, what is my authority, what are my 'credentials' for imparting this scenario to you? You are wondering if I am to be believed. You are wondering if everything will happen exactly as I say.

"And I will tell you first, that I am not only a god-king of so-called ancient Egypt. I have shown you the many faces of my many incarnations, but I appear before you now in my most important manifestation. I am as Shiva, both the Creator and Destroyer of matter." Here he swiftly morphed into the traditionally portrayed image of the Hindu God, paused for effect, then morphed back into his Ankh-Ra incarnation.

"And yet, to put it somewhat more humbly, I am a gardener, a bioengineer, a builder of planetary-scale ecologies. Is Earth the only planet to pass through the crucible of the Photon Belt? No. As an immortal, I have seen this scenario played out many times. Are the details of what I tell you immutable? Again no. Your planet's Ascension will be uniquely its own. The story I have given you is not so much a script, but a plan. Everyone needs the structure of a plan. And I believe you have a saying, "plans are made to be broken." It implies that plans are not immutable, but subject to change. And so what I have told you is only an Idea, an idea of what may happen. But it is not necessarily what will happen.

"Like us, the species and planetary cultures represented in the Galactic Federation, each of you, incarnate now on planet Earth, are ideas in the Mind of God. Each of you is a unique and precious jewel. No two of you will experience this phenomenon the same way. But the paradigm must be set in place. The seed must be planted. The foundation must be laid. First comes the Intention, the Dream, the Plan, the Awareness of what you wish to accomplish or what you wish to avoid. Then comes the Manifestation. Do you begin to see what I am telling you? Good. And now we can go on to our next order of business."

It was now Aya's turn to speak. By way of introduction, Ankh-Ra simply turned his gaze to Aya. Andy slowly shifted himself and his attention to her.

She began and the first thing he noticed was a difference in the color of her thoughts. It was momentarily difficult to change gears to accommodate her way of teaching. He quickly picked up on the fact that Aya informed his being with abstract images of pure color and not the realistic, filmic dramas that were Ankh-Ra's style. And her speaking style was different too. Her words reverberated pleasingly in his head. The sounds of the words took on other additional meanings, as if he were hearing her in two harmonious languages simultaneously.

"Ideas, concepts, paradigms: we have many seeds to plant. There is more to our warning than cosmic rays and mass destruction. Before Paradise can be reached, conditions must be met. Each of you currently living on the Earth is responsible – like it or not, aware of it or not – for the future course your planet and your species will take. You can no longer claim ignorance as an excuse for not supporting the advancement of your species. Truly it can be said, you are all in this together. Your life – each individual life – is what your thoughts make it. That is a spiritual law each of you must come to understand and use in the present. No one will be allowed to remain unconscious.

"You all must learn – although it is really 're-learn' – to feel first instead of think first. Because if you think first, you will think first of yourself, and in linear time and space – in the third density where survival of the soul and the body are one and the same – that means you will become a predator. Now, to be a predator requires a victim, and once there is a predator and victim, it no longer matters which one you are. The roles are two sides of the same coin. You already know that you reap what you sow. The only way to stop this cycle is to break it. Pain and suffering, death itself, will never end until each one of you reweaves your personal web and lets go of a belief in enemies.

"But if you feel before you think, if you use your intuition and your compassion, you will know how to respond to each other effortlessly. If you

186

trust yourself, you can meet each other without fear, in an atmosphere of mutual respect. You cry out, "Can't we all just get along?" And you can, if you respect and honor and trust yourself. "To thine own self be true, and it must follow as the night the day, thou canst not then be false to any man." Your first allegiance is to yourself, the self that is the spark of Prime Source. Your responsibility to each other is your 'respond-ability,' your ability to respond to all that is life-affirming and sacred in each other. It begins by honoring the sacred in yourself. Just as the cruel and the base is a part of your being, so too is the divine. You merely have to choose to express the divine, to place it at the forefront of your life and being, and to renounce the lower ego."

Aya's statement was punctuated by a brilliant wash of color and musical tonality that surged through Andy and thrilled him beyond goose bumps. Andy gasped, "Aha! Yes!" But there was also a little grumpy man, a frowning gnome, that he saw out of the corner of his eye. There and gone in a scant three seconds, it was time enough for the grotesque cynic in him to put in an appearance and to raise his doubts. Andy sighed. But of course, Aya had read his thoughts.

"And when you tell them that is our message to humankind, and when they scoff at you and say, "How ridiculous! How simplistic!" then you must tell them, "Of course it is simplistic, but it is not simple. If it were simple, would we not have already achieved Heaven On Earth?" And, yes, it is obvious, as obvious as the Golden Rule. Then you may ask them, "Do you know a better way?" And you must understand, Dear One, that the scoffers are not the ones who have truly heard what you have said. They are the ones who will perversely continue to think first and not listen to their feelings.

"So you must not be concerned with everyone 'getting it,' because not everyone will get it. Not everyone is intended to get it. It is only necessary that a certain critical mass of the population receive our message. Each one who does get it, however, will hold the energy of the paradigm and some will actually pass it on. In this way, the few will influence the many. You need only be concerned with delivering the messages we have given you in whatever way you deem best."

Andy frowned. Aya stopped as if interrupted. Then, as if in answer to a complaint Andy did not even know he had made, she strongly declared, "Shaping your reality is not dishonest, you yourselves do it every day."

Ankh-Ra quickly interjected, "Yes, we know you have reservations. It has to do with sharing what we have presented to you with the rest of the world, doesn't it? Now is the time to hear those reservations. Go ahead and respond to what we have told you. Speak to us what is in your heart and your mind."

Aside from the glimpse of the misshapen little man, Andy had not been aware of having any reservations. Certainly they had not coalesced into worded thoughts. He was intent on absorbing the multi-leveled presentation, so he had to stop and switch gears again, from listening and taking in, to thinking and introspecting, to speaking and putting himself out there to be listened to and understood. He was now required to be an active participant in what was becoming a discussion. When he began to talk, he happily discovered he had a newfound eloquence.

"Thank you. I know and understand the truth of what you are asking me to say. I believe in the purity behind your intent. Or rather I want to. But, yes, I have doubts, many doubts. Foremost among them is: How can I possibly be the one to impart these messages? Who will listen to me? From what podium? I have no fame or celebrity which might cause people to listen to me. I have no special credibility among my species. First of all, I am an agnostic. I have not pledged myself to follow the teachings of any of the world's religions, instead, I have chosen not to honor one god over any other god. So I do not belong to any of the commonly accepted communities of faith. I am therefore considered godless. And that makes me a flawed vessel of spiritual truth. Yes, I believe in the Spiritual Path, I believe in striving for Personal Enlightenment that the One may benefit the Many, and I believe in a Supreme Being, be it God or Goddess or both, maybe even in Prime Source.

"But I am no authority, I am not holy, I have no credentials. I cannot claim the Moral High Ground. I am essentially a sinner like everybody else, but maybe worse because – do you know what I am, do you really understand it? – I am a homosexual. On this planet that fact alone makes me illegal and immoral in the eyes of the vast majority of my fellow planetary citizens. They do not see me as a magical blend of genders. They see me as a perverse deviation from the norm. What I am saying is, I am a societal anomaly, and in a society that fears diversity, a pariah. I frighten and confuse people. They hate me. They really hate me!"

Aya said, "Yes, we know very well what you are and who you are. If you think we overestimate you, perhaps you underestimate yourself. Throughout all of your known history, have not all prophets believed themselves unworthy?"

"Oh, no! Please! I am not a prophet! I will not accept that, nuh-uh, no way, no how! And if you want to talk prophet, well then, you'd better remember that bit about prophets never being recognized or honored in their own time or among their own people or country, whatever that saying is. Not to mention that charming trait we humans have: if we don't like the message, we kill the messenger!"

"You will not be killed," asserted Ankh-Ra.

Andy shot back, "Can you guarantee that?"

Ankh-Rah smiled at Andy's spunky retort. But it was Aya who answered, "To accomplish the task we ask of you, we offer all the protection and assistance you may require. Those who guide you even now, from every level of every dimension, are pledged to you and this mission. They will not fail you. We will not fail you. You cannot fail for, truly, yours may be considered a divine mission."

"So I'm on a mission from God. Fine. So were the Blues Brothers. So was Jesus Christ and look what they did to him. And I'm no Jesus Christ! But do you deny that I would be taking a great risk? Maybe even placing my life in jeopardy?"

Aya patiently continued, "There is an element of risk involved with all endeavors. To try is to risk failure. It is also to risk success. That is another choice you have to make. I know it seems harder to choose success, but if we did not have the utmost faith in you – you and your integrity and your creativity – your divinity – indeed, the holiness which you deny – you would not be here now. We believe in you. We have absolute faith in your respond-ability."

Andy knew such faith, from such higher realms and such greater beings, was not to be taken lightly, it could not be scoffed at. He was humbled. He was touched. For a moment it truly gave him pause. He could find neither the words for speech nor the thoughts for telepathy. He shook his head as if to clear it, and by allowing himself to be in the emotion of the moment, was able to continue.

"I suppose I should thank you. Okay, thank you. But I just have such a hard time seeing myself being listened to by millions of people. And how am I supposed to reach all these millions? How am I to gain their attention, let alone be heard by them?"

Ankh-Ra casually crossed his right leg over his left knee and fielded this question. "It is wise to express your doubts and fears, Ahn Dee. We heartily encourage you to do so. But we will also say, do not concern yourself with that now. You can say no to us here and now. That is perfectly appropriate and is alright. After your return to your life in San Francisco, you will take the time to think about all that we have told you. And when you have thought it through, when you have examined all the emotions this experience has brought forth, you will achieve emotional balance regarding this mission. Your contact with us will clear the way for contact with others. This is your purpose this time. This is why you are incarnate on Earth at this particular moment. You are a living link to the future. It is a life and a mission you have already accepted. And you are not alone. There are millions more like you now alive on the planet. They are the Light Workers, the Star Born. And when you have achieved this balance, you will come to accept consciously what you have already accepted subconsciously. Acceptance will bring clarity. Conscious acceptance will bring commitment. Commitment will bring the knowledge, the ideas, the wherewithal, every tool you need to accomplish this task. And you will see and know how we are with you every step of the way. Think about what we have told you before you decide whether you can or can't. You, Ahn Dee, already have such power; you have only to claim it."

"So I don't have to say "yes" right now? I don't have to give you any answer at all yet? Is that right?"

"That is correct," Ankh-Ra replied.

"And remember, this is a free will universe," said Aya. "You are a free agent. If you refuse, you must not consider that a lesser decision. You are free to refuse. You are free to modify any and all situations in which you find yourself. It could not otherwise be so. Understand that in saying no there is to be no shame, regret, or guilt. Our love and respect for you – no matter what you decide – is, and will remain, unconditional. You have already served the Ascension and helped to bring it to fruition, simply because the paradigm is now a part of you. So you see, there is no failure, you can't do it wrong."

That was an enormous relief. He breathed deeply and sighed. His prana fountain bubbled happily. For the first time since Ankh-Ra had begun his talk, Andy looked at Lohr and Reiko. She was reclining against him, his arms around her, and they were smiling back at him like proud parents, their eyes moist with the loving pride welling up inside them. He looked all around, reacquainting himself with the room and those present. The smiles Aya and Ankh-Ra were directing at him were pleasant and warm, but generally unreadable. The owl's big-eyed curiosity seemed to be about what Andy's decision would be, but it wasn't demanding one of him. The cats and the dogs were sublimely unfazed. Andy placed his hands on his head and began to move them around, checking himself, patting himself, taking the gauge of his hat size. His head outwardly felt no bigger, but inside, he felt, was the data equivalent of the New York Public Library. He was suddenly very thirsty and without having to ask, Aya produced a cup-sized ladle and dipped it into the well of water. The ladle was magically bottomless, and Andy drank and drank and drank until his thirst was quenched. And the whales sang that it was good. It was very good.

"a slimy, nasty man, who happened to be a reptile."

TWELVE

Andy awoke from his nap refreshed. When he saw the time he knew why. It was after six o'clock. Usually when he slept that long in the middle of the day he woke up groggy. Not this time. He sat up, swung his legs over the side of his bed, and was going to reach for his pants, when he noticed two things: his headache was gone and he really had to go to the bathroom. The pants could wait. On his way back to the bedroom his door buzzer went ballistic and startled him so badly he clutched the door frame and spat his favorite 'F-curse.' Somebody was laying on the button downstairs. He sneaked out into the hall to try to get a discrete look through the window in the front door. Whoever it was began to punch the button impatiently. Who was this 'A-curse' maniac? Andy leaned over the stair railing, craning to see down the three flights of stairs to the front door. He might have known. It was Richard and he was now letting himself in with his key. He charged up the stairs and, at the bottom of the last flight, froze for a moment when he saw Andy.

"Thank God you're alright!" He bounded up the rest of the stairs and stopped on the landing. "Where are your pants?" Andy bristled and glared but said nothing. Richard ignored the stone-cold silence, went right by the pants issue and urgently into his own story.

"I tried to call you about a half-hour ago from the office to see if you wanted to go to Dave and Chuck's for dinner. Some very disturbing 'funny stuff' has been happening and I was worried when you didn't answer. So anyway, I'm driving over and about half way here I notice this limo is following me. It's a classic black '59 Caddy, you know, with the rocket fins, and it speeds up to tail me really close. Do you want to go in and put some pants on?" Andy shrugged indifferently but turned and went back inside his apartment with Richard tailing him really closely. He followed him into his bedroom and stood talking all the while Andy was putting on his pants.

"So, every time we come to a stoplight I try to see who is behind the wheel but the glass is tinted so dark it's impossible. I'm getting very edgy because of the 'funny stuff' I mentioned, like the call I got at work from some guy, who claims he's a colonel in the Air Force, telling me – threatening me, actually – to keep quiet about yesterday in Mount Shasta, and I'm wondering if this is related. I decide I'd better try to shake this Caddy because I don't want to lead them – whoever 'they' are – to you, right? So I take them on a tour of Japantown and Hayes Valley and the Mission, only I can't shake 'em, so down on Potrero and 16th I decide to park and see what they'll do. Are you listening to this?" Andy nodded almost imperceptibly. He wasn't looking at Richard, instead he was randomly cleaning out his jeans pockets.

He was pissed off and trying to give him the cold shoulder. But Richard rambled on excitedly. "Anyway, they drive by, make a U-turn, come back, and pull into a spot across the street from me. I'm just sitting there in my car watching to see what's going to happen next when the back door on the driver's side opens. Now, I'm expecting to see somebody in an Air Force uniform get out, but no, uh-uh, this very tall, very skinny, goofy-looking guy in a black overcoat and hat pulled down over his ears to the top of his sunglasses gets out and starts to walk toward my car, only, ... only, he's not exactly walking. It's more like he's got an artificial leg or something because he's kind of loping, kind of sliding, swinging across the street toward me, and ...." By now, Andy had been sucked in and, even though he was still mad

194

at Richard, as he put on his socks and Reeboks, he was paying close attention to his tale. In fact, he urged him to, "Go on."

"Well, this is going to sound weird, but ... I don't think the guy was ... I mean, I think maybe he was ...."

"What you are trying to say is, you think he was an alien creature of some kind who was only masquerading as a human being."

Richard was flabbergasted. "Yes! That's right! That's exactly it! But how did you know?'

"It's a commonly reported aspect of the close-encounter phenomenon. They're called Men-In-Black, and they often show up after someone has witnessed a UFO or been abducted to try to scare witnesses or abductees into keeping quiet about their experience."

"Oh. But why are they after me? You're the one who had the close-encounter experience."

"I wouldn't be too sure about that if I were you. What about the lost half hour on Shasta? Anyway, go on with your story. What happened next?"

Richard frowned, thinking about what Andy had just suggested, but only for a split second. "Well, he comes up to my window and just stands there looking in at me. I don't exactly know why, but I am scared shitless and beginning to seriously freak. I lock my doors but they won't stay locked. Anyway, I don't want to show fear, so I roll down my window a crack and ask him what he wants. And he pretty much said – in this crazy-sounding, mad-as-hell accent – what you just said. He says to me if I was to tell anyone about the sighting – he called it a 'sighting' – that I will be killed. It was that simple: no innuendo, no beating around the bush, just an out and out threat. The second one today –which I don't take to very well – so I call him a few choice names and tell him to get lost. I think I actually said 'Why don't you go back where you came from!' Oh, I don't know, man, it is all so weird! So weird! I felt kind of strange the whole time too, kind of fuzzy, like I was in a dream. Or a nightmare. It was SO WEIRD!" Richard, his stomach trembling, abruptly sat himself down on the bed next to Andy and bent forward, hands on his knees. He leaned over even farther, his head between his knees, as if to keep from passing out. Andy put his arm around him and asked, calmly and quietly, "Are you gonna yak?"

"No," Richard replied, looking at his feet.

"Good. So just take it easy a minute and relax. Listen, I've already had a couple of run-ins with them myself. I think they're all bluff, more annoying than dangerous. I really don't think they'll do anything. But we have to keep our wits about us, okay? Are you going to be alright?"

"Yeah, I'm okay."

"And the man in black, what happened to him? Did he leave? He didn't follow you over here, did he?"

Richard dramatically and laboriously pulled himself back up into a normal sitting position. He slowly exhaled all his held breath.

"Yes, he left and, no, he didn't follow me. I swear he was trying to do some kind of mind control thing on me. Just so freaking weird, though, man! You know? It gives me the creeps, that's all."

"I'm sorry they're doing this to you too. I don't like it that you're being harassed. But I don't want you to get all bent out of shape over this, okay?"

"Alright. I'm not. Honest. I'm okay. But I don't want you to be harassed either. And that guy from the Air Force knew your name. That worries me. That worries me a lot."

"Yeah, what's that all about?"

"I'm afraid they may try to scare you too. And I don't know how serious they are with their threats. Maybe more serious than these Guys In Black."

"Tell me about the call from the Air Force."

"Not now, maybe later. Maybe at Dave and Chuck's. How about it? Do you want to have some dinner with us? Chuck is fixing salad and some kind of exotic veggie pizza. Are you hungry? Does that sound good?"

Andy gave it some thought then began tentatively, "Well, yes, I am hungry. And yes, it sounds good." He hesitated, then added vehemently, "But, if I go, I want it understood, I'm not going to talk about what happened to me, you got that? You can talk about your creepiness all you want but I'm not going to say a thing. Understand?"

"That's entirely up to you."

"You're damn right it is! Wait a minute. What's this? No pressure?"

"No, none. I promise."

"You're sure?"

"Absolutely."

"Alright, what have you done with Richard?"

"No, really, I mean it."

"Okay, then, I'll go. As long as you understand that I'm not going to talk about this, not now, not yet. Maybe not ever. You got that?

"Yes, I got it."

"It embarrasses me, and I don't know how I feel about it or what I want to say about it. I just need to figure it out first. Or try to. And it's got nothing to do with the threats."

"I understand."

"You do?"

"Yes, I do."

Now Richard was so fully recovered from telling his own shocking story, so newly self-possessed, that Andy had to look askance at him all over again. He was not quite sure he believed him. And he couldn't make up his mind whether or not he was willing to give him the benefit of the doubt. Richard met his skepticism with a playfully quizzical and impossibly innocent look. It was his patented 'have-I-done-something-wrong, I'm-sorry-please-forgive-me' look. He let it register on Andy who was still suspicious. Then he asked, "Would you kiss me?"

"What, right now?"

"Yes. Please?"

"No. I'm still mad at you."

"Maybe later?"

"Stop it."

"Shall we go then?"

"You drive me nuts."

Chuck and Dave's sprawling, fifth floor condo on Vallejo near Polk had a great, panoramic view from Ghirardelli Square and Aquatic Park, to Fisherman's Wharf and Alcatraz, all the way to Coit Tower and the Transamerica Pyramid. It was handsomely decorated in much the same manner as Richard's house, with comfortable contemporary furnishings. The objet d'art and tchotchkes, mostly framed photos, were minimal, avoiding any tendency toward clutter. There was nothing 'precious' about either abode. Each was quietly masculine in a welcoming and easy-to-live-in style, richly appointed yet neither ostentatious nor flamboyant.

Dr. Dave greeted them at the door. He was in his kick-back, after-work, casual dress: starched white shirt, no tie, pressed blue jeans, and white cotton socks, no shoes. He didn't need to remind Richard and Andy to leave their shoes on the plastic mat by the door, it was part of the drill. Chuck and Dave's New Year's Eve party was the only catering gig Andy had ever had where everybody, catering staff included, were wearing hospital slippers. Tonight Dr. Dave seemed shorter to Andy than he'd appeared to be at the office that morning, but maybe that was because they were both definitely less serious and more relaxed. Andy was rested. Dr. Dave had a glass of Chardonnay in his hand.

Chuck burst out of the kitchen, where he had just slipped the pizza in the oven, to greet his guests with his usual big-hearted gusto. A beefy, former pro football player, now Esalen-trained massage therapist, he was taller than Richard and massively muscled. For all his exuberance and the power of his physique, his bear hugs were surprisingly tender. After an afternoon of massages, the ruggedly handsome Polish-American was still dressed in his sweat pants, yin yang T-shirt and, of course, his stocking feet. He took their drink orders, one diet cola and one tonic with a twist, and hustled back into the kitchen.

Dr. Dave escorted Andy and Richard into the living room where he began the small talk with the seemingly innocuous question, "How did the rest of the day go for you guys?"

Andy and Richard exchanged a quick, cautionary look before Andy began with the equally innocuous, "Well, I had a good, long nap this afternoon so I'm feeling much better. And I got rid of my headache."

Chuck came in then with the drinks but only heard the word 'headache' so asked, "Do you have a headache? I can give you a quick neck and shoulders massage before the pizza is ready, if you want."

"No, no thanks, my headache's gone. I'm fine. But maybe Richard would like one. He's had an 'interesting' afternoon. Haven't you?"

Richard frowned and growled, "We aren't talking about it, remember?"

Chuck asked, "What aren't we talking about?"

Dave, with a questioningly suspicious look on his face, spoke up, "Richard and Andy came to see me at my office this morning. I know what Andy doesn't want to talk about. But what's this about an 'interesting' afternoon, Richard?"

Richard tossed off his discomfort and annoyance by glaring at Andy and fumbled around for a safe response. He came up with what he thought would be an acceptable alternative story to tell them, one that even Andy hadn't yet heard. "It's nothing much, really. It's just that Phyllis was being an unusually big pain in the butt this afternoon, and I did something I've never done before. I'm not exactly proud of it. Well, maybe I am a little bit." Richard paused, "But I shouldn't be. I was a bastard."

Chuck, all sympathetic sincerity, interjected, "You were a bastard to Phyllis? Stop it! I don't believe it! Are you kidding?"

Dave asked impatiently, "So come on, tell us. What happened?"

"She was just sticking her nose in my personal business, like she tries to do all the time, but I just decided I'd had enough."

Andy couldn't resist and piped up with, "You mean you got fed up with being manipulated and bossed around by that pushy old Phyllis? Gee, do you think there's a personal message for you in there somewhere?"

Richard took what was coming to him and kept his mouth shut.

Chuck gestured for a time-out with his hands, "Okay, okay, penalty flag. No bitchy, unspoken subtexts allowed! House rules. Now you guys have to tell me what we're not talking about." He looked from Richard to Andy to Dave but they all looked at each other, each one expecting someone else to speak first. Chuck sat back in his chair, crossed his legs, folded his massive arms over his barrel chest, and continued, "Well, I can wait, but somebody better spill or you'll all be going out to eat."

Dave stared hard at Andy. Andy stared back and finally said, "Go ahead, tell him what we came to see you about this morning."

"Are you sure you want me to tell this?" Andy nodded his assent. Then Dave looked to Richard. "If it's okay with him, it's okay with me. You might as well. Chuck's right, it's rude not to let him in on it."

Dave thought he could just say it but he clutched for a moment and said, "Wow! Now I know how you guys must feel. Where do you begin with something like this?"

He turned and faced Chuck across the coffee table, opened his mouth to speak, and still could not come up with the proper opening line. He just laughed nervously and scratched his head. Chuck looked at his wrist watch. "Just in case you're interested, Sweetheart, the pizza starts burning in about three minutes."

"Alright. Okay. Well, of course this is strictly confidential."

"Understood. Go on."

"Yesterday, about 4:00 a.m., Andy disappeared from his flat. Richard found him on Mount Shasta about ten hours later. They believe Andy was taken on board a UFO where he met . . . extraterrestrial . . . beings. That's basically it, right, guys?"

They mumbled in the affirmative and Dr. Dave went on, "I gave him a medical checkup just to be certain there had been no foul play. And we're going to follow up on the possibility of a head injury or some other neurological malfunction. Would you guys say that was accurate?" They hesitantly nodded, yes, and the room became totally, and very awkwardly, silent.

Chuck looked thoughtfully at his ankle, sucked in a breath through his teeth, exhaled slowly, and finally said, "Oh. I see." He thought about it some more while Richard, Andy and Dave tried to fill the quiet by shifting, squirming and otherwise repositioning themselves in their seats. Then Chuck felt obliged to add, "Well, that's nothing to be ashamed of."

Richard and Dave enthusiastically agreed. Andy rolled his eyes. The oven timer dinged and it couldn't have been more loud or startling if it had been the starting gun at a race. "Oh!" Chuck bolted and was half way to the kitchen before he announced, "Pizza's ready!"

Around the dining room table Chuck, Dave and Richard got caught up on which of their mutual friends they had seen or talked to and what they were doing. They made an attempt to include Andy by asking about his job which he always found boring to talk about. The best stories usually involved the appalling behavior of some of his customers but that quickly degenerated into Andy's whining and bitching. He therefore had very little to say about Coffee A-Go-Go. So it was back to plans for the Pride Parade and which out-of-town guests were arriving when and staying until when. And by the way, they were all invited to a cookout after the parade at the Lesbian Brothers' home in Noe Valley. The double couple, aka the Muffin Girls, (the polite nickname the Boys gave them instead of the rude one the ladies pretended to hate which was the Four 'Muff'keteers) always put on a great feed and Andy was assured a good time. He committed himself to go while planning to find an excuse to get out of it later.

After the local dish, discussing the national news, including the latest developments in the O.J. Simpson trial – "Just wait until they present the gloves in evidence," – got them through the rest of dinner, but it was clear to Andy that avoiding the topic on everyone's mind was becoming a strain. By the time dessert and coffee were served they were boring each other with tired old topics like Greg Louganis's coming out, the Unabomber striking again, and how terrible the Oklahoma City bombing had been. When the January earthquake in Kobe was mentioned, prompting the same old stories about 'where were you in '89?' when the Loma Prieta Quake shook the Bay Area, Andy decided they were plotting against him. At any rate, he'd had enough.

"I wasn't even in San Francisco in '89. I was still living in Chicago and dating my last lover who ended up dying of AIDS. Let's just cut out all the B.S. and get back to the topic you really want to talk about. Shall we?" He said it as sweetly as he could, with a smile on his face, but it was still quite the effective little conversation stopper. There were embarrassed murmurs of half-hearted protestation which quickly faded to guilty silence. But Andy knew that, like Sarah, these guys needed at least a crumb of information about his experience. And he especially owed something to Richard, who had strangely backed off on the subject since his introduction to the Men-In-Black, and who was now looking at him lovingly, with a kind of defiant pride, sending him the message that he didn't have to tell them anything if he didn't want to. And curiously enough, in the expectant silence around the dinner table at Chuck and Dave's, Andy decided he could believe this Richard. He could trust this Richard. Well, he could try and see how far he got.

202

"First, I want to say how much I wish I could tell you that it was all just a dream. In fact, part of me is still holding out for, even insisting on, the dream theory. But I have to be honest: this was like no other dream I've ever had. It was too detailed and so vivid that I have total recall. When I couldn't sleep last night, I reran the whole thing through my mind. It was like being able to remember what I'd had for dinner every night for the last month. Besides, a dream can't explain how I ended up on Mount Shasta. And unfortunately I can't either."

Chuck wanted very badly to know, "Were you abducted?"

"No. You see, over the last few years I've been doing a lot of meditating, a lot of pretty deep inner exploration and, I like to think, healing. I know this will sound silly, and probably pretentious too, but for the longest time I've had the desire to – to talk, to actually speak, in a dialogue – even if it was in my head – with others not from this world, with someone from another plane of existence altogether. In a sense, that's exactly what I've been doing for the last two years with Sarah and Riegel. I know that. But I wanted to do it on my own. And face to face. I don't know why it's been so important to me, but it has. Almost an obsession.

"So, once a week, in one of my sittings, I would mentally ask for connection. I visualized a landing spaceship and an opening door and myself, waiting to welcome the visitor from another world. There were a few times, in the last couple months, during meditation, when I would hear things or see images in my receptive, altered state, which I believed were return attempts to contact me. At first I was reluctant to share this with Richard, even now it embarrasses me, because I was self-conscious and I know how crazy it sounds. There is a part of me that is cynical and skeptical about all this, what Richard calls my 'X-Files shit.' You have to keep your perspective. I know that. You have to be discerning and responsible. So I was cautious, as I always am, about the possibility of self-delusion. I checked myself. I questioned. I'd get scared but I kept going back, back to that place inside where I felt these stirrings of connection. But I never felt like I was going out of control. I was always very careful about that. Then the night before last .... Well, let me just say that I was not exactly prepared for what happened to me."

When Andy paused to sip his decaf' coffee, Dave prompted quietly, "What did happen to you?"

Dave and the others waited expectantly, patiently, while Andy carefully considered just how much to reveal. He didn't have any idea how to edit this. He only knew he should try to keep it short. They were looking at him. Even the silence was begging him. He decided to trust his instincts and wing it.

"I was talking to Richard on the phone when they arrived. I didn't know who 'they' were. 'They' hadn't told me 'they' were coming. It all happened very quickly. I was surrounded by swirling light particles. Somehow I was levitated out of my bedroom, through my roof and into, for want of a better term, a flying saucer. I know, I know! Believe me I know how incredible that sounds. I don't know 'how' it happened, I just know it did. I never lost consciousness. I remember looking down at the City and wondering if anyone could see me riding this beam of light up into the sky. Even now I wonder if anyone saw a UFO over Potrero Hill early Wednesday morning."

"This would have been what time?" Dave asked.

Richard answered, "He called me about a three forty-five, so this would have been a little after four in the morning."

Dave nodded letting Andy know it was okay to continue with his account.

"On board I was greeted by Lohr, this big, good-looking guy in drag – at least he was in drag at first – who became my guide. We went to his room and he changed clothes. He gave me some 'guy' clothes to wear since I was naked and he briefed me about meeting the Contact Committee. Then he and Reiko, a woman friend of his, took me to meet them, this committee. It was on top of a pyramid, in another dimension, maybe even on another planet, I don't know. It was so fantastic it might very well have been a dream, except that I was so conscious – more conscious, more alive – than I've ever been before. Anyway, there were three beings in this committee, at least three that were visible. Although I had the feeling there were others there as well who were invisible, who were disembodied, pure Light energy. Anyway, except for one of them, they looked just like human beings. One was a gorgeous Amazon, as beautiful as a goddess, another was a very wise man who looked like an Egyptian pharaoh, and the third one, who I'm glad to say didn't hang around very long, was a ... man ... a kind of slimy, nasty man, who ... just sort of happened to be a reptile. You know, like an alligator man."

Andy winced while he paused to see what the response was going to be to that particular bombshell. His rapt audience let their jaws drop ever so slightly but, not wanting to miss a bit of this, kept their consternation tightly capped. In the effort they squirmed or shifted in their seats. Chuck tried to cross his legs and kicked the table leg. Dave sat back and folded his arms across his chest and Andy thought he detected a slight frown and wrinkling of his brow. And what about Richard, leaning forward, elbows on the table, did he really look lost or was he just straining to keep up? Andy assumed he was losing them.

"Of course you don't know. What am I saying? Anyway, after he – the alligator guy – left, the other two talked to me about the future and showed me a possible scenario that they want me to share with the rest of the people of Earth. I haven't agreed to this yet so don't ask me about it. There's a lot more to it than I can tell you right now. I just want to be brief. It would all sound too fantastic anyway. And this is freaky enough as it is." It suddenly seemed very warm in the dining room. Andy thought he was sweating and dabbed his brow and wiped his face with his napkin. His mouth felt dry. He took a long drink from his water glass.

Chuck asked, "Was the scenario, was it like some kind of Armageddon thing? Are they here to stop us from blowing up the planet?"

"Well, sort of, but not really. It's complicated. I mean there's some good news and some bad news. And I can't explain it in a few words, or confirm it or otherwise make it sound rational. Then there's the whole multiple dimensions thing and the Galactic Federation thing. That's why I don't want to go into it right now." Andy frowned and twisted his napkin. He took another nervous swig of his water. He was feeling conflicted and getting frustrated. Should he blow off telling the rest of the story? When it looked as though he was about to, Richard spoke up.

"Tell us what happened after your meeting with the Contact Committee?"

"Well, Lohr told me that we were going to go to a ... it was originally supposed to be a party .... Oh hell, forget it."

Chuck implored, "No, no, tell us. Please. We want to know all about it."

"It was like a dance club. I mean it *was* a dance club. It was a very good dance club too." Andy felt himself stretching out much too far and part of him was pulling back from the telling of the story. It became physically uncomfortable. He was becoming panicky, desperate that they believe him. He decided he needed to lighten up a bit. He ended up trying to be entertaining and it wasn't quite the right tone. He had already lost control. He saw the wall approaching but he couldn't stop himself.

"I mean it was incredibly high tech and the sounds were the best I've ever heard. They had effects you will never see or hear in the clubs South of Market. The Beat absolutely took control of your body. And there was the most amazing crowd there too. It was very gay and yet it was very mixed."

"Mixed how?" Chuck asked. "Do you mean gay and straight?"

"Chuck, I don't mean for this to sound sarcastic, but I'm afraid I could not read the predominant affectional preference of the crowd." Andy thought, that wasn't me talking, that couldn't be me talking. I sound like one of Skyler's twenty-year-old twinkette friends. Andy could count the bricks in the wall which was now rushing to meet him. Chuck didn't take the least offense. He apologized sweetly, "Of course, I'm sorry. So was it mixed genders?"

"Genders? Honey, it was mixed species. And for once the gay boys were not the best dancers."

Dr. Dave stiffened, sat up, clasped his hands together, leaned over the table and stared directly into Andy's eyes. He looked more than a little miffed. He cleared his throat and lowered his voice to its most fatherly, condescending tone, "Andy, I am sincerely trying to understand what happened to you. Like I told you at the office this morning, I genuinely want to help you make sense of your experience. And I still mean that, but, do you really expect me to believe you went 'partying' on a spaceship? Super intelligent beings from another galaxy have nothing better to do than 'get down'? I don't think I deserve to be insulted like that in my own home, now do I?"

"Take it easy, Dave." Richard interjected.

"David, let him continue. I believe him." Chuck defended.

This wasn't quite the wall Andy had expected but the impact still effectively shattered his ego defenses. He was taking this too personally and he knew it. If only he had the perspective he'd had on the spaceship. But he couldn't seem to locate his higher self. Under attack, he responded in the moment, this moment, the only way he could. His temper came to his defense. He too stiffened and sat up to face off with Dr. Dreamboat.

"I am telling you what happened. And I am not making this up. Perhaps it loses something in my telling. But I am not trying to insult your intelligence. If 'my experience' is not everything you would like it to be, then I suggest you get your own 'experience.' Richard, would you please take me home now?"

Richard and Chuck rushed to placate Andy, begging him to stay, to go on with his story, to just ignore Dave's rudeness. The clamor was so great Dave had to shout them down to apologize.

"Alright! Alright! I'm sorry. Maybe I jumped to the wrong conclusion. It just sounds trivial to me, that's all."

Chuck leaned over, clapped an arm around his partner's shoulder, and pulled him closer. "It's okay, Dave, but just let him finish, that's all."

"Yeah, hear him out before you judge him like that." While it was meant to be supportive, it was the wrong thing for Richard to have said.

Andy stood up abruptly and angrily fired back from his hurt feelings, first at Richard, "Or how about hearing me out and not judging me at all?" And then at Dave, "Or keeping your judgment to yourself?" Almost as soon as he'd said it Andy regretted it. And he was in the awkward position of standing there after his outburst with nowhere to go. A wave of shame washed over him. Fortunately the clamor resumed instantly, with all three of them apologizing and asking him to please sit down and please stay and please forgive them and go on with his story if he wanted and Richard reached out his hand. Andy took it to steady himself as he sank back down into his seat. His stomach churned and he momentarily felt nauseous.

That was all the warning he got. The nausea was quickly followed by one huge painful throb in the middle of his head, like someone had smacked him from the inside with a baseball bat. Not hard enough to do harm, just hard enough to get his attention. He covered his forehead with one hand and leaned over the table, supporting himself on his elbows. The pain drained away slowly but, gratefully, it did go away, and in a few seconds it was gone.

He must have looked awful because then everyone became quiet. Richard stood up and stepped behind Andy's chair. He bent over, wrapped his arms around him and whispered into his ear, "I'm an ass. Please forgive me. I'll take you home now if you want to go." It felt good to be in Richard's arms. His embrace and his words were surprisingly comforting. The sick feeling passed. He nodded in the affirmative. Although physically restored, Andy was still mortified and in his head he pleaded, "get me out of here, and hurry!"

Richard seemed to answer him, "Okay, right now, let's go." He gave him a peck on the cheek, unwrapped his arms, and stood up straight and tall. But he continued to stand protectively behind Andy's chair. Andy pulled himself together and spoke, "Sorry you guys. Thanks for taking an interest but I knew it wouldn't work. I'm really sorry I was such a jerk."

Dave tried his hand at patching things up, "Nobody meant to be a jerk, Andy. Especially me. I'm sorry too. Do you need anything? Can I write you a scrip for the pain?"

Andy was embarrassed that Dr. Dave had noticed his attack. He hastened to assure him, "No, thank you. It passed very quickly; I'm fine now."

Then Chuck asked, "Are you sure you won't stay? We're all feeling very contrite. I know if I was any more contrite my pecker would disappear." That got a smile out of everyone, even Andy. But he insisted that he should leave.

"Thanks, but no. I really need to call it a night. I have to get up early, I'm going in to work tomorrow morning." He started to get up and Richard pulled his chair back for him.

Chuck and Dave somberly walked Richard and Andy to the door. There wasn't any small talk as they watched them put on their shoes. Then they all exchanged their regrets again, and after hugging each other good night, Richard and Andy left.

Fortunately there was no one on the elevator. Just now Andy needed air. He couldn't have endured riding silently with a stranger in an enclosed space. Richard asked, "What was that about the pain? Are you okay? Should you be going to work tomorrow?"

"I'm okay. I got a sharp pain in my head, but it went right away. I feel fine now. I'll be alright tomorrow. Really. I will."

Richard wanted to believe him. He looked fine now. He certainly looked relieved to have the ordeal behind him. But he didn't like to see his baby in pain.

Out on the street, the sun had just set but the fog piled up outside the Golden Gate made it darker than it ordinarily would have been at this hour. Richard once again put his arm around Andy, this time partly for warmth. They walked slowly uphill on Vallejo to the car parked half a block away. A streetlight went off as they walked by it. Andy noted it in his head. It was something he'd been observing for a year or more: streetlights blinking off when he was around. It could be mere coincidence but it happened with an eerie and mysterious frequency. If Richard noticed the light going out he didn't mention it. So Andy kept quiet. Soon Richard wormed his way into the silence with a comment about the fresh, night air. But he had more to talk about than the microclimate of Russian Hill.

"I'm sorry it went so badly, babe. For what it's worth, I have a much better understanding of what it must be like for you. If you want to talk about it, fine. I'm here for you. I hope you know that. If you don't want to talk about it, that's fine too. But we are in this together. Don't forget that."

"Thanks. That's sweet. And thanks for rescuing me back there. But I'm afraid what happened tonight does not make me want to open up. And I should. I know that, dammit! I should be more open, less defensive, about it. I made a scene and I hate scenes. I'm going to be so embarrassed to see Chuck and Dave again. I really am sorry."

"Forget about it."

"But they're your friends and ...."

"They're your friends too. Look, it's okay. We're all adults. We're over it. Now you get over it too."

They separated and Andy walked up the sidewalk to his car door, while Richard went out into the street and around to unlock the doors from the driver's side. They both opened their door simultaneously, but Andy stopped them from getting in. He had one more apology to make.

"Richard, look, I'm also sorry for trying to set you up back there."

"Set me up? How do you mean?"

"Mentioning your 'interesting' afternoon. Remember?"

"Oh, yeah, that. Nice try." The two of them slid into their seats. The doors thudded shut together. Fastening his seat belt Richard muttered, "Ah, the joys of getting to know your boyfriend. Don't take this the wrong way, but you've been a real prick today. You have quite the little mean streak in you, don't you?"

"Yeah, well ...."

"It's okay, it's just that I've never seen that side of you before."

"You mean the Dark Side?"

"I'm not sure I'd call it your 'dark' side," Richard responded a bit apprehensively. He was going to say that Andy was cute when he was angry but checked himself. That would probably be the wrong thing to say. No, not 'probably,' it would definitely be the wrong thing to say. He started up the engine and checked the rearview mirror.

"Each of us is capable of anything." Andy injected ominously. "What we think, what we say, what we do. We are compassionate, selfless saints and we are cruel, sadistic satans. And everything in between. Like uncivilized, unsophisticated children, and we never seem to grow up."

Angry Andy was attractive but morose Andy was not. However that wasn't what concerned Richard just now. "I'd say you're still pissed off at me. Am I right? In fact, I'll bet I'm not out of the craphouse yet, am I?"

"You got that right." Andy had nothing more to add to that. Still, he had to smile at the man's self-absorption. Sometimes it was actually useful. Like right now it got Andy out of his own self-absorption. It was hard for him to stay mad at Richard. But Andy was damned if he'd let Richard know that.

Richard pulled the car away from the curb, drove a block and turned right on Hyde, deftly maneuvering around a clanging cable car. They drove in silence until they reached the Civic Center. Andy commented on how much he didn't like the architecture of the new library. Richard agreed perfunctorily but took advantage of the fact they were talking again and went right on with his agenda. "So what is it? Is it because I dragged you to see Dave or is it about not staying over last night. That's it, isn't it? At first it was the check-up but now it's the other thing."

"What other thing?"

"The fact that I didn't want to sleep over with you last night."

"Richard?"

"Yes?"

"Shut up."

"C'mon. We should talk about it. Let's clear the air."

"I don't think ...."

"Look, I'm sorry if I was turned off thinking about some slimy aliens having their way with you. But I'm over that now. I really am."

"So that was it! You couldn't stand to make love to me; you could not bring yourself to touch me, thinking I'd had sex with ETs? You pompous shit!"

"Aw hell, Andy! Give me a break, cut me some slack, would you?"

"You're over it so I should be too, right? Is that how it works? Okay, alright, fine! Here's a deal for you: how about I cut you some slack if you cut me some slack too?"

"Alright, Andy. Will you just calm down, please?"

"I'm thirty-seven years old. I already told you I'm not a virgin! What do you want from me? I just spent ten hours on a spaceship…"

Richard interrupted, "Yeah, yeah, yeah, I know, and all you got was a lousy T-shirt." Man! Andy was pissing him off. He was glad he hadn't told him he was cute when he was mad before, because he sure wasn't so cute now and he would have had to take it back. When he glanced over, Andy was looking right at him, his mouth wide open, his expression one of shocked, bemused surprise.

"What?" he asked Andy.

"That was very funny. Thanks, I needed that."

"I know what you need. You need a good spanking."

"Hey! I told you that *doesn't* turn me on. By the way, mentioning the T-shirt reminds me, there's something you probably should know. My ET-shirt is gone."

"What?" Richard slowed the car, pulled over to the curb, and stopped. He had pulled into a bus stop which was illegal but that was the farthest thing from his mind.

"You're kidding, aren't you?"

"No, I'm serious."

"Now let me get this straight. You didn't lose it, did you? I mean, when you say it's gone, you mean it just disappeared?"

"Yes. It was right on the chair beside my bed but, when I went to take a nap this afternoon, I noticed it was not there anymore."

"That's incredible! I can't find the tape to my answering machine either! It was the tape with you calling me the night you disappeared. Remember how you went on and on into my machine, trying to wake me up? Well, after you vanished I took that tape out of my machine for safe keeping. I thought it might be evidence. Anyway, it was in my jeans pocket the whole day when I went to Shasta to find you. These very jeans, the ones I'm wearing right now. After work and before I came over to get you to see if you wanted to have dinner at Dave and Chuck's, I went home to change. That's when I noticed it was gone, but I was in a big hurry, and then the alien guys in the black Cadillac followed me, and threatened me, and by the time I got to you, I'd forgotten all about it. As evidence my tape isn't much, but your shirt, that was some major proof! What do you think is going on?"

"I really don't know. But I've asked for my ET-shirt back."

"Asked who?"

"The Universe."

Richard did not want to go anywhere with that topic. He just wasn't ready to find out what Andy was talking about. He was too confused as it was.

"Well, do you think you'll get it back?"

"Yes, eventually I will. If I really need it."

"And my tape? Will I get my tape back?"

"I don't know. Maybe."

"Man! I don't believe all this stuff is happening to us! Things – solid, three dimensional things – don't just vanish into thin air. Even magicians don't really make things disappear. It's not magic, there's no such thing as magic, it's all trickery. It's just an illusion."

Andy just looked at Richard. He didn't want to go anywhere with that topic. He didn't feel like trying to convince Richard to loosen his grip on the third dimension, even though the third dimension was loosening its grip on both of them. Still they were bound by the rules; the laws of physics had not been voided completely. And, as if they needed to be reminded of that, the headlights of one enormous, fully three-dimensional Muni bus filled the car. It came barreling across Market, aimed right for them. Richard saw it bearing down on them in the rearview mirror, made the necessary instantaneous calculations regarding any other oncoming traffic, turned the wheel, gunned the gas, shot away from the curb, and took off down 8th Street headed into the heart of the South of Market area of town.

They fled in grim silence, crossing Mission, Howard, and Folsom. This was the way through SoMa Richard always took to get to Andy's, the way he drove the morning before last, when Andy vanished. He felt a similar urgency growing now, a gathering claustrophobia. He sensed this evening was going to end badly but he couldn't tell just how or why. They continued across Harrison, Bryant and Brannan. When 8th ended in a 'T' at Townsend he turned right, jogged left on Division, then right again onto Henry Adams, which became Kansas, which he took up Potrero Hill. He took a right on 20th and went a block and half. The parking goddess was not with him tonight. He double parked in front of Andy's building and they sat for a minute in silence. There were too many things they wanted to say and too many they didn't even want to think about saying. Andy had already decided that, tonight, any further conversation was risky. Richard didn't know if he should turn off the engine or leave it running. He left it running. The tension became unbearable.

Finally Andy turned to Richard and spoke, "Well, I guess I'd better go in." Richard's face took on a pained expression and he held on to the steering wheel for dear life. He could not stop himself from asking. He put all his effort into keeping the desperation he felt out of his voice. Without looking at Andy, he blurted, "Do you want to break up with me?"

It had the sound of a simple question, but it completely detonated the emotionally charged atmosphere in the car, and the explosion took Andy completely by surprise. It shook and shocked him so badly, leaving him so dizzy and disoriented, that he could hardly believe what he heard himself say, "I think maybe I do." It felt honest but it also felt like a mistake. He pictured debris landing miles away.

Richard sucked in air like he'd been punched in the gut, but the macho man was tough, he had too much practice at this sort of thing to lose it in front of Andy. "That's what I thought."

"No, wait, this is all wrong. I don't want to make that decision tonight. That's not fair. I don't want to make that decision at all. In case you hadn't noticed, I'm having a hard time dealing with all this. On my own I'm not doing so badly, but around you, and apparently around your friends, I'm edgy, thin-skinned, and a real bitch. I'm so moody it's beginning to scare me. I'm like this loose cannon and I can't help going off on you and I hate me doing that. You were right, I have been a prick, and you don't deserve that. But I don't know when I'm going to be able to settle down and get a grip on my life again. And in the meantime I can't seem to deal with you. I don't see how I can be part of a couple: I can't take care of 'us' because, right now, I can barely take care of me."

Richard turned off the engine. They sat in melancholy silence for a minute until a thoughtful and serious Richard asked, "Why do you have to take care of 'us'? Why can't I take care of you? What do you want? What do you need from me? Do you want me to go away and not come back? Am I supposed to wait in the wings until you give me my cue and then come running back to you?"

"I'm sorry, babe. I really am."

"Because if that's what you need I'll give it to you."

Andy couldn't reply. He looked away. He thought, "Oh, damn! I'm not going to cry again! I refuse. I will not humiliate myself further."

Richard continued, "Okay, let's take a week off and see where we stand. Call me if you need me, please, because I love you and I don't want you to feel like you can't lean on me. But I won't call you until next Thursday. How's that? Does that sound alright?"

"Can't we take it a day at a time? Can't we talk on the phone just to see how we're doing?"

"Yes! Of course! Anything you want! But you call me. I won't call you. I don't want to be putting any pressure on you."

"Then let's take a week off, but I'll call you tomorrow night. I mean maybe I'll call you tomorrow night. Maybe I'll call you on Saturday. Or Sunday. Or not. Maybe I won't call you until next week sometime. I'll just see how it goes."

"Fine, great. Whatever. But just one more thing."

"What is it?"

"Oh, hell! Never mind."

"No, c'mon, what is it?'

"It's nothing, forget it."

Andy looked at Richard who was looking at his hands on the steering wheel. He knew what he meant to ask. By now he knew the guy well enough for that. He needed reassurance. He wanted Andy to say he loved him. In his heart of hearts he did love Richard. But he was also ambivalent. And he had to be honest about that.

"Alright, I'll say it. Yes, I do."

"You do? Wait a minute, what are we talking about?

"You want to know if I love you. That's what you were going to ask, wasn't it? And the answer is, yes, I do. I love you. Is that better?"

Richard grinned sheepishly and nodded that it was. But Andy was quick to add, "But I still need my space." He got out, shut the car door and turned around. He leaned over to look through the window and tried to smile reassuringly as he waved, good night. Richard started up the engine, waved back, put the car in gear, and took off. Andy watched him leave. A twinge of separation anxiety painfully pinched his heart. "Why does love have to be so tortured?" he thought, then he turned and marched himself down the sidewalk to his door and went inside.

It was a little past 9:00. Richard noted the time and decided it was too late to go to an AA meeting. But he needed to talk, so on the car phone he dialed Dr. Dave, who, needing a minimum of explanation, extended an invitation to come right over. Richard headed for Van Ness, turned left onto Division and took it to 12th, tossing an affectionate, half wistful, salute toward the Eagle, San Francisco's premiere leather bar, as he drove by. He wanted a drink. He wanted a cigarette. He wanted a man to hold onto.

THIRTEEN

Andy sat on the top step of the pyramid, idly stroking the neck and shoulders of the jaguar stretched out beside him. As he lovingly petted the beautiful beast with the bass note purr, he thought to himself, "So, do you have a boyfriend?" The cat turned its head and looked squarely at Andy, as if to say, "What are you talking about? Shut up and just keep petting me."

"Sorry. I don't even know if you are a male or a female. Or if that even matters. I have a boyfriend. It matters to me. That he's male, I mean. He's not exactly a boy, although sometimes I wish he would grow up a bit." The big cat shook itself and used a hind leg to smack Andy's thigh lazily a couple of times. The message was clearly, "Knock it off. I don't care about your boyfriend."

"Alright, alright. I get it. You like this, though, don't you?" In place of a sigh, a long, contented moan came out of the cat's chest and throat, and the deep purring grew louder for a moment before fading away to a kitten-like yelp.

"You know, – now don't let this upset you – I'm actually more of a dog person. But this is nice. I'm enjoying this too."

Under the stars of an unknown galaxy, in an eternally tropical night, in an unknown dimension, Andy listened to the purring, the distant surf, the breeze in the rain forest and he expanded into a reverie of Oneness with All Creation. It was a ravishing feeling. Completely relaxed, completely authentic, yet psychedelically attuned to the vibrational nuances of All-There-Is, he was experiencing the highest high of his life. And it all seemed as natural and unpretentious as organic beets. If most men lead lives of quiet desperation, he would have to characterize his right now as one of quiet joyfulness.

And he thanked all his guides and guardians, all the saints and apostles and avatars, all the bodhisattvas, Jesus, Buddha, Mohammed, God, the Father, Mother, Creator and Moving Spirit, the Blessed Virgin Mary, Gaia, the Goddess, the Fates, Prime Source and whatever other powers that might be, that were responsible for this splendid, rapturous moment. And as he breathed in the Love and Light and exhaled the Divine Purity he was brought one whimsically insignificant yet profoundly appropriate word. That word was: *CHARMED*.

He saw it. He spoke it. "***Charmed***." It hung for a moment in mid-air. He examined it. It disappeared. He concluded, "I am ***charmed***." He was very amused by that. He just had to say it again, "***Charmed***." He shook the cat's forepaw and added, "I'm so sure." He stared at the spotted coat of the cat and felt the warmth and power underneath the fur as he stroked the living creature. It didn't surprise him at all to get a sensation that there was a kind of female 'person,' or 'personality,' somewhere under that pelt. The unabashed pleasure he was bestowing, and in which the cat was completely immersed, was not far from erotic.

But Andy noticed nothing unusual in their intimacy. Placid, unconcerned, his thoughts wandered back to the committee which was still inside the room behind him. They had asked him to wait outside while they conferred privately. The jaguar was the only animal to have joined him on the step.

"I wonder what they are talking about in there?" he thought silently to himself. The jaguar gently stole away his focus as it slowly, luxuriously stretched, yawned, then rolled onto its back asking Andy to rub its stomach. "Oh, you are a female. You are 'woman.' But that's okay, I don't need to hear you roar. The purring is fine. You just can't get enough of this, can you?"

"Of course not. When he's stroking you, do you ever get enough?"

"I haven't yet. So I guess I see your point."

"Delicious, isn't it?"

"Oh, yeah. Very delicious. Hey! Wait a minute! Here's a question for you. Speaking of delicious, if you weren't already fed and satisfied, would you eat me?"

"Not unless I were starving and then only if you gave me permission."

"That's good to know."

"Would you kill me for my coat or for sport as a trophy?"

"Certainly not. You're much too beautiful alive."

"That's good to know too. By the way, I know what they are talking about."

"You do? Can you tell me?"

"Mm-m-m-m, a little lower and a little harder, please. That's it. Ooh! That's right, that's pur-r-r-r-fect."

"Yeah? You were saying?"

"After meeting you and getting a clearer picture of your character, they are re-evaluating your case."

"Oh? And what's the verdict? Can you tell me that?"

"Why don't you ask them yourself?"

Andy looked over his shoulder. In the doorway to the pink alabaster room he saw Lohr and Reiko beaming at him. One of the salukis squeezed between them and barked at him. If their smiles and the dog's happy tail wagging were any indication, it must be good news. He got up and the jaguar waited a few moments before rousing herself to follow.

As soon as he stepped back inside the room, he noticed a change in the atmosphere; indeed, there was a change in the population. There appeared nine columns of light, not like the bright vortex that brought him on the ship but pale, nearly imperceptible light. The gossamer columns wavered and shimmered. There were no opposing currents roiling around within them. They independently glowed brighter then dimmer, pulsing as if to a quiet cycle of breathing. These lights shone with a softly reassuring, sentient tranquility. Each was a different pastel shade of pink, gold, blue, green, and lavender. They stood between Andy and the others like a colorful forest of ten-foot, truncated, transparent tree trunks. Aya beckoned to him, and as he started to make his way through the columns of light, they parted to let him through. Their energy was happy. He was tickled by it as he sensed an almost childlike, whimsical delight emanating from them. They knew a secret and they were bursting to tell it.

The others took their seats and Ankh Ra motioned for Andy to come over and once again sit beside him.

"Thank you for your gracious patience. We have been discussing the possibility of making a change or two in the shape of your visit today. Before I begin, I believe you know the other guests who have just joined us."

Andy looked around to find the 'other guests' and knew immediately that Ankh Ra was talking about the columns of light. Then he realized who the 'other guests' were and he broke into a huge grin. In his enthusiasm he practically shouted the name, "Riegel!" Without the vocal assistance of Sarah, their response was not 'spoken,' of course, but nevertheless clearly resonated in Andy's head.

"Ahn Dee," they harmonized. In this dimension the 'voice' of Riegel, reflecting their multiple-entity status, had the quality of nine-part, close harmony, half spoken, half sung. The vibration literally tickled his inner ear.

"Ah, recognition. Very good," Ankh Ra smiled. Then he continued, "They have brought some important information that we will share in a moment. But first, we have been petitioned by two entities who wish to speak with you. Because it is only while you are in this altered state that you are afforded access to their dimensional reality, we would like to grant their requests. However, the chosen meeting ground will include some of those Federation life forms from which we had planned to shield you. It is hoped that the atmosphere in which you will be meeting these entities will be sufficiently entertaining to disarm any possible shock or fear on your part. As we mentioned earlier, we did not wish to cause you psychic overload, but we have altered that directive. Seeing you in communion with Mae-Rao, our feline friend from the animal kingdom, only confirmed our faith in you. If you can talk to Mae-Rao, you can surely communicate with those you are about to meet. So you see that we can be flexible and that we are not, after all, quite the 'control freaks' you might have thought us to be."

The twinkle was back in Ankh Ra's eyes, for the first time since their earlier introduction and laughing fit. Andy smiled and made a little bow of thanks. He was excited to think that at last he would be meeting some real, live extraterrestrials. He immediately had fifty questions he wanted to ask but it was Lohr who spoke to Ankh Ra.

"Then are we going to Deck Nine, sir?"

"Yes," was the sage's reply.

Lohr smiled and bowed to Ankh Ra, more in gratitude than reverence. Andy was attuned to Lohr's unspoken excitement. He could tell that this Deck Nine was a favorite spot of Lohr's. It must be quite the place. He was eager to go himself without knowing why.

Ankh Ra continued, "But before we adjourn, Riegel brings you a message. Please pause to accept." Everyone mysteriously closed their eyes and Andy was hit with a vision. Their combined energies were formidable and gave him quite a shock. It was a good thing he was sitting down. To receive their transmission, his body involuntarily went ridged along the spine. Ramrod straight, his eyes remained wide open and he saw before them, as if on a TV screen in midair, a picture of Richard driving on an Interstate highway. Also in the picture was a majestic, snow-covered, mountain peak which he understood was Richard's destination.

Riegel's vibration, now more serious and thoughtful, intoned, "You see, Ahn Dee, at this moment in time, he is on his way to meet you. You will soon be reunited. As we speak, however, many other events are unfolding in your timing. Interruptive forces are gathering and converging on the mountain. The window of opportunity for exchange is narrowing. Consider and heed our admonition. Thank you. This concludes our message. Good-bye."

The vision was switched off. Andy's body relaxed. The bright and loving presence of the group of entities was gone in an instant, so fast their departure left a noticeable vacuum. A gust of ethereal wind rushed in to fill it. The fire flamed higher for a moment. And everyone opened their eyes as if waking up to the urgency of Riegel's message.

Aya stood and held out her hand beckoning Andy to, "Arise, Ahn Dee, my Love. Our meeting is concluded. One more meeting awaits you before your return to Earth. This exchange has been an honor and a privilege. Remember, we are with you always." She kissed her fingertips and touched them to the top of his head. Then Ankh Ra stood also to pronounce his benediction, "Think about what you have learned here. In the fullness of time, you will make the correct decision, and you will use this lesson to the benefit and glory of the Light Which Dwells in Everyone. Until we meet again, Ahn Dee, my Funny Friend, trust yourself, love yourself, respect yourself. You are beloved." The maker of worlds bowed deeply to Andy who was full of the bittersweet emotion of good-bye.

With nothing more to say, Aya, Ankh Ra and the animals began to walk away. With a slow grace and dignity the entourage moved themselves out the doorway of the room on top of the pink pyramid. Without looking back, when they came to the first step, they paused, then, as the great white owl launched itself into flight, they took the step and silently descended until they were out of sight. Andy, Lohr, and Reiko watched them go as if watching a particularly poignant sunset. Andy especially did not want them to leave. He wanted to ask questions, to just talk, to just be with them a little while longer. He despaired that he would ever be able to do what they had asked of him. He raised his hand in a plaintive little wave of reluctant good-bye, but Reiko and Lohr were there to buoy the sinking feeling and get him going again.

"There is no time to linger," the pragmatic Reiko reminded.

"Yes, we must go now," added Lohr.

Andy shook himself and agreed, "Alright, I'm ready. Let's go."

Reiko said to Lohr, "I think the well would be the quickest way back. What do you think?"

"Yes. And also the most fun. Are you going with us?"

"No, but I will try to meet you there. Save a dance for me. You too, Andy." She turned and walked out the opposite doorway. Before she too disappeared down the stairway, Lohr stepped up on the rim of the central well, the well of air, and bid Andy join him.

"What are we doing?"

"We are going to Deck Nine where the party is already in progress."

"The party? The one you told me about back in your room?"

"Yes. Well, one very much like it."

"Can I go dressed like this? I thought we were going to get dressed up."

"That was the plan at the time. And believe me, I'm just as disappointed as you. I was very much looking forward to giving you a makeover. However there is no longer sufficient time for all that. Please, I'm very sorry, but there just isn't. Oh, now look at you. Let me remind you. We are adaptable. We are flexible. What about all that 'respond-ability?' Hmmm? There, there, that's the brave soldier, carry on. Now, hurry. Step up here with me."

Andy did as he was told. "How do we get there? Are they going to beam us up, or down? Or what?"

"Well, we could do something like that but I think Reiko was right. We'll take the well. It will be fast and fun. It's like a slide, like an amusement park ride. You'll enjoy it."

224

Lohr positioned himself behind Andy and put his arms around him. Before Andy had a chance to protest, he was lifted up in Lohr's embrace, and they jumped into yet another kind of abyss.

Richard left Dave's about 10:30 P.M. After their talk he was calmer but no less pessimistic about his future with Andy. He was almost fifty years old and, even though he knew he still looked good, he was no longer the young stud who tricked every night with all the best looking guys in San Francisco. Sure, sometimes he wanted to relive his hedonistic past, the sex and the drugs, but that Richard was gone forever. He had survived all that. He now valued his health, his very life, above the seeking of pleasure, even though that pleasure was a siren song he could still hear, and which could still draw him to the rocky shoals of certain death. But no, like it or not, he had matured. Maybe he regretted his lost youth and maybe he didn't, but he was sure of one thing: even if he had the desire, he just didn't have the energy to play the hunt and chase game. No, it wasn't about scoring anymore, it was about companionship.

Companionship included hot sex of course, but companionship that stayed at home, companionship that shared a common life together, in one place. It bothered him that Andy was so damned independent. He insisted on working and maintaining his own living space. They might not ever agree on a mutually acceptable lifestyle together. Maybe Andy wasn't the right one. Maybe there was no 'right one.' Did that make him the 'one' by default? Well, it wouldn't make him the right anything unless he wanted to be with Richard. And right now he didn't. Would he change his mind about that? Or would this trial separation confirm it for Andy?

Richard pulled his car up to his garage door and pushed the opener button. He did not even notice the figure sitting in the car parked a half block away on Montgomery Street. Driving into the garage, he realized this circular thinking was getting him nowhere. And as much as he disliked coming home to an empty house, he knew he needed to be more upbeat. Oh, well, as Doris Day once sang, "Que Sera, Sera." He disarmed the security alarm, unlocked the door from the garage into the house and let himself in. He reset his alarm system and went into the living room.

A light from the hall allowed him to navigate his otherwise dark house. He paused to look out beyond his deck to the lights of Oakland and the Bay Bridge. He loved that view; so did Andy. On nights when Andy stayed over he often got hung up on the view. Sometimes they sat together on the sofa and watched the lights, talking about nothing, joking and teasing each other. Richard looked at his favorite photo of Andy and wished for such a moment right now. "Missing him already?" he asked himself. "Better get used to it. There's at least a week to go on this separation deal."

The pain of that disturbing thought drew forth some deeply embedded anger. Andy could be so damned 'high maintenance.' "And do you know what else?" he said aloud to the picture. "I just don't get it. I just don't get you. When you're around this stupid, way out, supernatural crap, you are so serene, so trusting, so confident. But when it comes to me, when it's about relating to me, you are so damned .... You're there and then you're not there. You just tune me out. I don't know, when it comes to love, you're just not very tough. You bruise too easily. And I don't want to hurt you. I don't mean to hurt you."

He decided to have that smoke. He'd picked up a pack of cigarettes on the way home rationalizing that he'd earned it. He opened the pack, snapped one out and put it in his mouth without lighting it. He felt around in his pants pocket for the complimentary book of matches. Stepping up to the sliding glass door that let out onto the deck he thought of the lyric that said, "The future's not ours to see." Was that really true anymore? Hadn't he seen at least a part of the future when he saw Mount Shasta, right before his eyes, right here in this house, thirty-six hours ago?

He looked at his reflection in the glass. Did he really want to start smoking again and have to give it up in a week when Andy came back to him? And if he didn't come back, would he end his days racked by lung cancer or emphysema, blaming Andy for walking out on him? A vision is one thing, imagination is another. Maybe he read the future that one time, but that was probably a fluke.

No, Doris was right, "What will be, will be." And Dave, too, was right when he told him he, Dave, couldn't possibly see where this was going to end up with Andy. Hadn't he and Andy already broken up several times in the three months they'd known each other? He had no control over it, only how he thought about it. He must not let despair get the best of him. He should keep thinking positively. Besides, maybe Riegel could offer up some insights for him. Maybe – "Damn!"

The doorbell rudely interrupted his meager attempt at a 'positive' thinking process. He snatched the cigarette out of his mouth. It was almost 11:00. Who would be calling at this hour? How did they know he was home? Given the events of the last two days, he wasn't sure what to do. The bell rang again. He froze. For a moment he thought that he might just ignore it and the intruder would go away. But no, whoever it might be had probably seen him come home, and besides, he was much too curious. He set the cigarettes and matches down on a side table and moved cautiously from the living room to the front hall. He could see no one through the frosted glass panel to the left of the door. He crept up to the door and peered out the one-way peephole. There was a silhouette but it was impossible to see who it was without turning on the outside light. He hesitated to do that but the visitor knocked very loudly in his face and made him jump. He muttered some choice curses but he had made up his mind. He boldly and quite purposefully flicked the switch.

The light startled and blinded the visitor, who stepped back and tried to shade his eyes. Richard could now see a blond man out there but had no idea who it was. He made sure the alarm was off and the chain was hooked, then opened the door a few inches. The guy was sure easy on the eyes. But he still didn't have any idea who he was or what he wanted.

"Yes?" he challenged.

The solidly built hunk with the platinum blonde buzz cut grinned sheepishly. "It is you! I wasn't sure if that was you who just arrived or not. Or if this was the house that went with the garage. These houses are packed together pretty close, aren't they?"

Richard only had to hear the voice to recognize Officer Travis Wilson. Without the helmet, sunglasses, and the rest of his uniform, he would not otherwise have had a clue. Well, maybe the dimples, but that was iffy. He stared at him, now dressed in jeans and a flannel-lined canvas jacket, with no apparent shirt on underneath and hoped he wasn't going to drool.

"Do you know who I am, Mr. Lang? It's Travis Wilson. Remember? The cop from Mount Shasta, the cop who —"

"Sure, yes, I remember you."

"Am I interrupting anything? I can go if I am."

"No, no you aren't. It's just, I'm surprised to see you, that's all"

"I'm sorry. I know this is crude of me. I swear I don't usually do this kind of thing. But I really need to talk to you. Look, maybe I should just go. Can I see you tomorrow though?"

"Well, of course, but really, I mean, as long as you're here. Why don't you come in?"

"Oh, wow, that would be great, thank you, thank you very much!"

Richard started to take off the chain then stopped, "You are alone, aren't you? Nobody followed you here, did they?"

"Huh? Yeah, I'm alone. I don't think anybody followed me. I didn't really notice, I wasn't paying any attention, I guess. Damn! I didn't think of that! Stupid! Stupid!"

"Hold on, take it easy, it's alright, just come on inside." He finished taking off the chain and Travis squeezed in before Richard could fully open the door. Travis brushed against him and he caught the subtle scent of his body odor mixed with some faded after shave. It was a very pleasant combination. He indicated the path to the living room and Travis walked directly into the center of the room and stood there. Richard relocked the door, reset the alarm system, then followed the younger man to the edge of the room, but did not enter.

"Great view you have here. Is that Oakland?"

"Thanks. Yes, it is. Can I get you something to drink? I'm afraid I can't offer you an alcoholic beverage, but I can make some coffee, decaf if you prefer, or I can get you a soda."

"No, thanks, I'm fine. But thanks."

"Why don't you have a seat?"

"Oh, okay, sure, thanks." Travis moved directly to the sofa and sat down on the end where Andy usually sat. Richard noticed that. He eyed his surprise guest with some suspicion. Travis sat on the edge of the sofa seat, as if he didn't want to get too comfortable, and leaned over, his elbows on his knees. His hands were clasped in front of him while his thumbs bumped each other, keeping time to some insistent, internal beat. Why was he so nervous? It made him nervous that Travis was so nervous. What was behind all this self-conscious urgency? It had to have something to do with their roadblock encounter but what?

"So what's going on, Officer Wilson? Richard strolled over to the matching armchair but remained standing, his arms folded over his chest. Travis had to strain to look up at him.

"You can call me Travis."

Richard was touched by the vulnerability in his eyes. The guy was placing an awful lot of trust in him. But why? They were strangers to each other.

"Okay, Travis. You can call me Richard. So what is it? Is this strictly a social call, or are you here on official police business?"

He only paused a moment before he replied, "Well, it's not exactly police business, because I got suspended yesterday. For two weeks. Without pay. Besides, I'm supposed to keep the whole Shasta thing to myself. 'We didn't see anything up there, just a lot of delusional people.' That's the line we're supposed to give."

"Mass hysteria?" Richard offered.

"That's right, a clear case of mass hysteria. I tried to tell them that I saw the flying saucers too but they told me I didn't and that I'd better not tell anyone that I did. They said because I let you go through the roadblock, maybe I was in cahoots with you. 'Course, they wouldn't say about what, but they made it real clear that I needed to take some time off and think about what I'd done."

"And what had you done?"

"Breached security, I guess. I can't tell exactly because they were the ones asking all the questions. Or I should say giving all the orders. I'm real mixed up about it. None of 'em will tell me anything. When I tried to ask a question they threatened me with more suspension time. They just kept telling me to keep my mouth shut and just pretend like nothing happened."

"Who are 'they?' If you don't mind telling me."

"Which 'they' do you mean? The Highway Patrol? The United States Air Force? Or those funny guys in the old black cars? In the last two days I've been threatened, busted, threatened again, and otherwise harassed. They told me if I talk, they'll just say I'm crazy and fire my ass. Excuse me. That's why I'm here, I guess. Maybe I am going crazy but I had to find out what happened to you. Did you see the flying saucers? What about your friend? What did you guys see up there on the mountain? Could you see anything in that cloud? Why didn't you want to talk to the doctors? Why did you ask me just now if I was alone or had been followed? Are they harassing you, too?"

Richard had to interrupt. "Now slow down, take it easy. We'll get this sorted out, don't worry." Officer Wilson's story had shocked Richard even while he heard his own experience being validated. And he had a few questions of his own to ask. For instance, what cloud? And yet he still wasn't sure just how far to trust this guy. He sat down in his favorite armchair.

"I'm sorry, there I go again. I'm not usually like this, honest. I'm not mental. I swear. I don't have a gun or anything." Richard smiled a little nervously, noting the man's youthful shyness, his eagerness to please. It was all very disarming to Richard. He genuinely wanted to believe this guy.

"Travis, just try to relax. You've got to understand, you've really surprised me here, and I need a little time to… "

Travis stood up abruptly, "You're right. I should go. I've intruded enough on your evening. Thanks for seeing me."

Richard jumped to his feet as well, but Travis was already on his way to the door. From across the living room he heard him say, "Good night. You've been very nice and I don't want to get you in any trouble."

Rattled to speechlessness by the impulsive behavior, he hurried to catch up with him at the door, where Travis had stopped and stood with his back to Richard waiting to be let out. He seemed strangely frozen to the spot on the threshold of Richard's front door. Richard came up behind him and for another awkward moment or two said nothing. Was he reading the situation correctly? He thought he knew the subtext but he couldn't quite be sure. It had been a long time since he'd found himself in this position. Then he made the commitment to find out so he just came out with, "Where will you go? Where are you staying tonight?"

Travis turned around slowly, he looked scared to death, and for a fleeting second, Richard thought he was going to cry. Then he took a deep breath, sighed, and said, "I don't know, man. I didn't have that part of it thought out either. I better just go and find a hotel room and leave you alone."

"I think you should stay here tonight. With me."

Travis was stunned, relieved and confused. Richard could read the tug of war in his face. Finally he stammered, "I don't know if I should do that. Are you sure, sure you have room? I don't want to put you to any trouble."

"It's no trouble. Believe me, I want you to stay."

"I could probably sleep on that couch, I won't bother you."

"Don't worry, we'll work something out. We have a lot to talk about. And besides, maybe I want to be bothered."

FOURTEEN

At first, the drop into the well was, like the flying episode, a surprisingly buoyant sensation. In this other reality, with its lightness of being, it felt more like stepping onto a bubble of air. It was dark inside the well, but there was a rhythmic pulsating glow within the dimness that Andy thought of as passing lighted floors on the way down. Then the diameter of this air-cushioned 'elevator shaft' contracted and a vacuum formed which took them faster and faster down the shaft. The pulsing light quickened and Andy noticed the artificial gravity increasing subtly, packing his molecules a little closer together. This slight compression caused him no discomfort, although he had little time to notice it. Protected by Lohr's embrace, he was not frightened even when their descent accelerated to what he could only guess was seventy or eighty miles an hour.

Then, what had been like a downhill luge ride, became a spiraling, looping, over and under zip through a giant, twisty straw, and just as Lohr had described, Andy now found himself on a thrilling roller coaster ride. By the time it spat them out onto a huge pile of cushions, both of them were yelling, laughing and screaming, breathlessly giddy and eager to go again. Gravity still being lighter than on Earth, when they hit the pillows they actually bounced twice before coming to rest. Once they stopped laughing, Andy extricated himself from his guide's embrace. It took some rolling and crawling to get off the mound of cushions, before they found their footing on the purple, carpeted floor of a round room almost as large as the one Andy

233

saw upon his arrival. It was the intersection of eight dimly lit corridors, and it would turn out to be the central court of a kind of mini mall of entertainment and recreation, a multiplex of clubs, bars, gyms, libraries, theaters and restaurants. Although there was nothing to distinguish one path from another, Lohr, of course, knew which one to take and Andy followed.

"Is this what you called Deck Nine?"

"Yes, it is. This is the recreation deck for the crew of the ship. You can meet your friends here, get a drink, a bite to eat, play games, participate in group meditation, exercise, see a show, perform your own show, do just about anything you can think of to amuse yourself. We're going to a club called the Cloud Chamber, one of the dance bars."

"I love to dance. I don't go out very much anymore though. Well, to be honest, I don't go out at all. The clubs are way too loud and smoky and I don't do drugs anymore, so it's not the same."

"Then there is also the risk factor, isn't there?"

"Risk factor? What do you mean? AIDS?"

"The risk that you might actually meet someone and fall in love with them."

"Are you being sarcastic?"

"No, but the syndrome is ironic, isn't it?"

Andy frowned, unhappy to have his foibles and idiosyncrasies so blithely exposed. Unwilling to continue this particular discussion yet unable to think of another subject, he fell silent.

Lohr did him the favor and went on with, "Well you won't find those nasty conditions in any of these clubs. The music is loud but not ear-splitting. There is, of course, no smoking, although we have areas for both those who are addicted and those who just like an occasional smoke. You see, for some of these entities it is physiologically impossible to become addicted to nicotine, although what they get out of it otherwise is quite beyond me. And of course there are other substances to be inhaled besides nicotine."

"I would have thought you were all beyond such vices as smoking."

"Most of us are, but it is always a choice, and we can't claim ignorance here. The risk of overindulgence is a balancing factor in any life, for every life form. Life without risk is flavorless. Personally, I think it is part of the nature of Prime Source. Always a little imperfection, a little irreverence, a margin for error must be allowed. It is one of the ways Prime Source can know Itself, just as we come to know ourselves by making mistakes or so-called 'wrong choices.' But listen to me talk, I can offer no credence for such claims other than my own experience. No single entity, especially yours truly, holds THE Truth. However each of us holds a piece of it. And even the Lie is part of the Truth. You could not have one without the other. We are each the Answer to the Question and we are also the Question. But I am rambling on. I often find that philosophizing ultimately becomes mental masturbation, boring masturbation at that. Thankfully, we have reached our destination."

They stopped in front of an open, eight-foot arched doorway, another tunnel in the series of tunnels on Deck Nine. Andy heard a faint, thudding, boom-box throb coming from deep inside the passageway. He thought he could make out the ambient murmur of a crowd. He also thought he could smell popcorn but all of these sensory impressions were very subtle, at least until they journeyed deeper into the tunnel. As they passed the abstract sculptural wall fixtures, the indirect lighting caused their white clothes to glow in vivid neon colors, a different color reflected with each light. The passionate beat of the music, growing in volume, raised the hairs on the back of his head in anticipation. He was itching to boogie.

Thirty feet ahead two figures, who had stopped under one of the lights, seemed to see them coming and skittishly moved on. It was too dim and the figures fled too quickly for Andy to have seen very much. It only told him they were not the only ones going 'out clubbing' tonight. But wait a minute, Andy realized he had lost all track of time. It could not possibly be nighttime.

It was just that going out was something one did at night. Then again, outer space is perpetual night. Whatever. The long walk down the entrance hall was only building suspense, drawing out his eager anticipation to the point where once again he began leading Lohr.

The music was getting louder. The popcorn smell was getting sweeter, more like caramel corn. They arrived abruptly when the passageway wheeled them around to the left and in that moment the volume of the music was bumped up a hundred and fifty percent. The beat hit them square in the face and Lohr and Andy were compelled to stop in deference to it. Andy's eyes opened wide and he thrilled to the sight of the midnight-blue room with stars and moving cloud simulations overhead. It was another huge, round, domed space, and in the center of it, spotlights were dancing over and under a crowd of several hundred. Now the entire color of the room blended into a dark magenta. The clouds moved through purple into pink.

The dance area was defined on four sides by upholstered-step-bleachers which held another two hundred enthusiasts sitting this one out. The floor was alive with dancers, bouncing to a sinuously funky groove. As Lohr had promised, it lacked smoke and ear-damaging decibels. There was also plenty of room on the dance floor and the dancers were using it to creative advantage. Andy hated a tightly packed dance floor so this was another improvement. But aside from these pluses, it was not so unlike the dance clubs Andy knew on Earth. And the music was so very danceable, so irresistibly danceable, that Andy was immediately captivated by the rhythm. He looked up at Lohr and grinned, and they both started to rock and bounce in place. Lohr nodded and gestured toward the dance floor, asking Andy in pantomime if he wanted to join the throng. He tried to say, "No, thanks. Not yet," but had to raise his voice just short of a flat-out yell.

Lohr yelled back, "What are you waiting for, a good beat?" They looked at each other, laughed and then Lohr surprised him by 'speaking' to him using telepathy,

236

"You see, we don't really have to shout. Telepathy works just fine over even the loudest sound waves. Just pay attention by looking at me when you want to send and be sure you have my attention as well so I can receive."

Andy nodded then tried it, "I just want to scope out the crowd a bit first, so just give me a minute or two, okay?"

"Of course. Tell me what you see."

"Men and women dancing. Some same sex couples. Lots of same sex couples. And they certainly do know how to dress. Even the heterosexual couples. Some very sexy. Some very elegant, though many are dressed like we are. You were right when you said this was pretty much the uniform around here. There seems to be quite a range in heights. And who are those guys way over there with the headgear?"

Andy looked harder through the acid-green darkness while waiting for Lohr to answer. When he didn't, Andy turned his head to look at him and saw him smiling back at him. "Well, who are they, Lohr?"

"Take another look. And while you are looking, tell me about that group of diminutive, synchronized dancers over there to the far right."

Andy directed his attention to the right and found a group of ten short people. They were dancing together in close formation, performing what was obviously a well rehearsed routine. It was a little bit like line dancing but the choreography was much more complex. Andy noted how their movements were controlled, precise, yet remained loose. The flashing lights and the intervening dancers obscured his view. He instinctively tilted his head sideways to get a better look. Were they children wearing sunglasses? No, that's silly, besides children don't have command of their bodies to that degree. Do they? He leaned back and forth and to each side straining to get a better glimpse. And then it hit him.

"Oh! Oh, no! I don't believe this." Andy frantically looked back to the first group, the tall guys with the strange headgear. Now he saw that it was not headgear at all. Those were their heads! He whipped his head back to take a second, still disbelieving, look at the little people and, indeed, they were not children wearing sunglasses! And now that his eyes were opened, everywhere he looked he saw another strange variation on the human form. There were glistening, scaly reptiloids like Kahr, and cloven-hoofed porcinoids. There were insectoids too, although, fortunately, they resembled praying mantises and not cockroaches. And even some of the ones who looked like 'regular' human beings displayed some unusual feature: overly large hands or feet, an enormous mouth, or no apparent mouth at all. Gender was not always discernible but, when it was, it was apt to be unmistakable. Whether pale, translucent skin, or dappled, camouflage pigmentation, big hair or no hair, the diversity before him was formidable.

To Andy, the epitome of outlandishness had to be what he would later describe as 'The Bug Man in Drag.' Quite unexpectedly and without warning, this eight-foot tall, (the wig alone accounted for a foot of that height) mantis-headed, stick figure in red, four-inch heels, tottered off the dance floor and came over and stood not five feet from him. Andy shrank back, pressing himself against Lohr, and tried to have it both ways — he pretended that he didn't see it and he also tried not to stare.

The creature was all exoskeletal limbs and barrel-chested thorax. It wore a tiny red halter top stuffed with something which gave it torpedo breasts and a matching slit skirt that somehow stayed up on virtually non-existent hips. It had a most un-humanoid set of two spindly arms and four spindly legs. The arms, wrist and hands were certainly not hands in the humanoid sense. They seemed cast and set, posed permanently in a mincing, limp-wristed attitude of prayer. Set off by clunky, jangly bracelets, these 'hands' resembled scoop-like pincers and one of them was larger than the other. The smaller 'hand' pinched the strap of a shiny, red vinyl purse. The purse was open and the creature dipped its larger 'claw' into it and pulled out a portion of caramel corn, spilling a good deal of it on the way to its mouth.

Glancing at the floor and the mess it was making, Andy noticed the heels of its four shoes were actually a spiky part of its foot that protruded through the heels of the satiny pumps. Lohr nudged Andy and said, "Go ahead, talk to him. I think he wants to dance with you." Andy looked at Lohr as if he were mad. When he saw the teasing smile and got the 'joke,' he said, "Get out!" and tried to shove him with both hands. Lohr couldn't be budged. But he laughed out loud at the attempt. "Hey, take it easy. I'm only half kidding you. I really do think he wants to dance with you. Talk to him. Go on, give it a try."

"How do you know that? How do you even know it's a guy?"

"If you don't believe me, then you find out. Just use telepathy. See what you can do with it. You said you wanted to meet a real extraterrestrial. Well, here's your chance."

From somewhere inside his fear of and distaste for approaching this ugly creature from an alien world, Andy was smacked with his own bigotry. Whenever he himself had been approached in the bars by someone 'N.P.A.' (Not Physically Attractive), Andy had always tried to be civil while he struggled with his guilt over having to reject a fellow gay man, a human being probably vulnerable like himself, with feelings of zero sexual self-worth. He knew, all too well, the pain of a brush-off based solely on standards of superficial sex appeal, and he knew he should be ashamed of himself right now. But a fellow human being was one thing and this was something else. It was a creature to Andy. Not human at all, not even gendered, despite the hair, false bosoms and skirt. In fact, if it were not for the drag, he would have had nothing whatsoever in his past experience to relate him to this gigantic creepy crawly. He groaned and gripped Lohr's sleeve, "Oh, no! Please tell me it –'he'– couldn't read my thoughts just now."

"No, he couldn't. You were not addressing him directly and you were also unconsciously guarding your thoughts. He can sense your reluctance, however, so you had better try to smooth things over a bit, don't you agree?"

Lohr was right, of course. Oh, what the hell, he could do this. Andy pumped himself up, turned his body toward his admirer, but he had trouble taking the first step. He steeled himself and commanded his foot to move, lurching free, launching himself away from Lohr's protective side. It only took two steps to put them as nearly face-to-face as they could be, given the disparity in their heights. He looked up at the inscrutable mantis face with the lurid makeup and found himself holding his breath, smiling through clenched teeth. "Breathe, Andy, breathe," he told himself. "If you ever needed that prana fountain, you need it now."

Andy's next lesson was the difference between breathing to raise one's light energy and hyperventilating. Staring at the grotesque insectoid, Andy was puffing like a steam engine, when he noticed that the bug man's thorax was emitting a high-pitched fluttering vibration that Andy sensed more than he actually heard. He forced himself to breathe faster to keep up, and he closed his eyes and thought, "Hello. My name is Andy." In his head he heard a very unpleasant scraping shriek that ended in a rapidly rising, tremulous musical scale, the upper limit of which was beyond Andy's perception. But it was more than an unpleasant noise – it had an embedded message, which was a revelation. Andy was taken by surprise. All of his own anxiety melted when he heard those tones because he now understood that it was trembling fear he heard in the Bug Man's transmission. He was as afraid of Andy as Andy was of him!

He opened his eyes and, just short of passing out, brought his breathing exercise to a gasping stop. Trying to get his breath back, he kept looking at the creature while sending a conciliatory message, "Don't be afraid. Please, don't be afraid. I won't hurt you. I'm a friend. I'm a friend from the planet Earth. My name is Andy. Ahn Dee?"

The music ended, the lights calmed down, the room was once again deep blue in color and everyone left the center of the dance floor to stand around the periphery or sit on the bleachers. Others departed the room altogether, through additional passageways, for places unknown. When quiet descended and he had calmed himself and his breathing, Andy noticed the bug man moving his arms and claws in tiny circles. He was also swaying and leaning first to the right and then to the left. Now Andy heard in his head the sound of his name, Ahn Dee. The bug man was 'saying' his name, although it really sounded more like someone very far away was screaming it. And in that same distant scream came the words, "I am friend. I am friend of Ahn Dee."

Andy nodded in happy astonishment, thrilled that he could understand. The bug man's nervous little dance continued with the addition of some subtle skittery motions of his feet. He was trying to tell Andy his name, but this communication was not as successful. To Andy's inner hearing, the name he gave was little more than a series of practically irreproducible clicking sounds. Andy's brow dramatically plunged into a severe frown. "What?" he said out loud. "What did you say? Call you what? I don't understand."

The bug man repeated it with renewed bodily emphasis and a resulting amplification in Andy's head, which Andy still could not fully understand, but from which he latched on to his own version of the name. "Okay, okay, I still didn't get it. But I got something here. I'm going to call you Deek. How's that? May I call you Deek?

"Deek?"

"Deek" took a step back, distancing himself from Andy, and dropped his arms to his sides. More caramel corn spilled onto the floor. The insect face was expressionless. But Andy read dismay in the gesture. He feared that perhaps he had unwittingly offended the timid giant, just the thing he didn't want to do, and he braced himself for the expected negative reaction. The bug man began doing a lateral two-step, back and forth. To Andy this looked a lot like agitation. He prayed the reaction wouldn't be violent.

"What's the matter? Did I say it wrong? Deek, I'm sorry. I..."

Still moving, the bug man made tiny two-step movements forward and back, raising his purse and extending it toward Andy at the same time. The distant voice in Andy's head said, "Call me Deek. Deek friend to Ahn Dee. Have take Deek eat treat." Somewhat clumsily, Deek was offering his caramel corn to Andy, who, at this overt sign of acceptance, felt he could relax now. He smiled and was just about to reach out and take some of the caramel corn when Lohr touched him gently on the shoulder. Andy turned to look at Lohr, and Deek wrenched himself around and, taking big, skittery steps, quickly vanished, exiting via the nearest connecting tunnel.

Andy did a perfect one-hundred-eighty-degree Spanky McFarland double-take, before spluttering, "What do you ... ? Hey! Where's he ... ? What's going on? What did I do ?"

"I'm sorry. I'm afraid I frightened him off. And you were doing such a good job, too. But I needed to warn you about eating the caramel corn. Food in the stomach does not travel well between dimensions. It could cause you distress when you return to Earth."

"Oh? Alright. That's alright, thank you," Andy replied relieved.

A single, steady, electronic beat had been hovering in the background and now it was building in volume and tempo. Counter rhythms and soaring chord harmonics were being layered onto it and, as a driving bass line joined in, the party entities began flocking to the dance floor. Just as infectious as the earlier music, this one also had Andy and Lohr bobbing and nodding and toe-tapping to the beat. As the crowd rushed onto the dance area, it was plain this was a very popular dance mix. The bass line dropped off and bongo and conga drums pushed the tempo up another notch. It had a distinctly Latin flavor and a delighted Andy asked, "What planet is this music from?"

Lohr grinned and replied, "Planet Miami Beach. This is music that has not yet been created on Earth but I imagine that by 1999 this will be a big hit in the South Beach clubs. Would you care to, what is it you say, "bust a move'?"

Andy replied, "Oh, yeah! This is the one. Let's go!"

Lohr took his hand and led him through the dancers to a spot near the center of the floor. And as he had observed earlier, some of the dancers were in groups, but most were in twos, threes or fours. He had to dodge a few arms and legs as they made their way, and he was utterly fascinated and amazed at the close up sight of these intergalactic beings performing their exotic movements. Some moved in a slow, counter rhythm and others were flailing and thrashing at peak tempo. Although a few seemed out of control, no one was actually bumping into anyone else. They all seemed to have a sixth sense concerning the respect of personal space. Lohr stopped and spun Andy into a facing position. He looked deeply into Andy's eyes signaling his intention, and in four rapid beats, they were locked in a wildly fast, hip-swiveling rumba. With complete and utter spontaneity, Andy followed Lohr's lead and they danced with the ease of seasoned professionals. Lohr turned him out to spin him around and brought him back to dance cheek to cheek, their butts stuck out, their crotches as far away from each other as possible, in an exaggerated display of the ambivalent sexual nature of their alliance. Lohr flung him out again, drew him back and dipped him, and Andy, oblivious to the precision and total concentration usually required for such dancing, happily followed his lead. They were a natural team. Whatever one wanted to do the other sensed and responded instantaneously.

So in synch were they that Andy felt his prana fountain gurgling and giggling like a baby. He felt that high again: he was connected to more than just the moment and, at the same time, he was supremely in the moment. And it was as effortless, as easy as the flying had been. Then Andy felt inspired, took the lead and introduced Lohr to the Bump. Playing off each other, they melded seamlessly, effortlessly, alternately bumping hips, shoulders and butts. They seemed to be bouncing off each other while actually barely touching. Their performance was flawless. On any other dance floor they would have stopped the show.

And when the music did stop abruptly for a count of eight before starting again, they knew instinctively, as did the other dancers, to freeze before throwing themselves back into the dance. The music stopped again for eight beats then resumed in the form of a percussion break accompanied by strobe lights. The crowd erupted in a vocal crescendo of cooing, whistling, squealing and hooting, wildly toning its appreciation. The lights strobed first from overhead, then from the side and finally from underneath, catching the dancers and suspending their movements in a stop-time ballet of mind-bending beauty. All the diverse and disparate styles of dancing were now united in one seething, roiling, living sea of, one might want to say humanity, but the correct word doesn't exist. It was way cool; it was totally awesome and then some. Andy experienced goose bumps all over his body. The foot stomping beat shook the floor. More notes, tones and counter rhythms were added, building a dense and unstoppable wall of sound. Then, in a plainly calculated measure, the sonic juggernaut faltered, the music went off the beat, stopped again, and the strobe lights went dark. The room was in absolute blackness and silence for four beats.

The crowd gasped. Screams of delight punctuated the void. Then hundreds of smaller lights were unleashed and darted through the crowd like frantic fireflies. The sound monster recovered and lurched forward, stronger and more relentless than ever. The tempo rose with each four-bar phrase until the unbearable excitement generated by the music crested and the tidal wave broke. The explosive sound settled over the dancers like water seeking its own level, viscerally washing them down from head to shoulders to waist, legs and feet. It let them all down gently but firmly, coming to a stop with two long and five short skiddery sonic blasts, and an extended fadeout chord.

244

Andy and Lohr, breathing hard but not quite out of breath, joined the crowd in letting go a long, loud sigh and a whoop of collective ecstatic exhilaration.

As usual, Andy was ready to go again, but Lohr took his arm and directed him off the dance floor. On their way to the bleachers through the dispersing crowd, Andy enjoyed exchanging smiles with his fellow revelers. The sharing of such joy was beyond price. Just as in the heyday of Disco, when the dance floor brought together gays and straights, whites and blacks, rich and poor, so too in this inspiring moment, species from many galaxies and star systems mixed and mingled in a cosmic Unity that Andy felt to his core.

"This is so great! I haven't had so much fun since the summer of '89," he gushed.

"Oh, really? And what was so special about that summer?" Lohr asked.

Andy had the feeling Lohr already knew the answer to that but he went ahead with his explanation, "I used to go dancing a lot that summer. This reminded me of it. That's all."

"And what else?" Lohr prompted. "Come on, don't be coy. There isn't time for that. That's when you chose him, isn't it?"

"You're referring to Jeffrey, aren't you? Jimmy Jeff. You know about him, don't you?"

"Oh, yes, indeed I do, but I want you to tell me about him."

"How do you know about him?"

Lohr sat down on the bleacher seat and motioned for Andy to join him. "That's irrelevant, but please continue. I believe we were in a dance club in Chicago. On Halsted, wasn't it?"

"Yes, it was."

"And do you recall the name of that club?"

"Of course, I do. It was ... Oh!"

"Yes?"

"It was called Contact."

"How interesting. Mere coincidence?"

"I don't think so."

"Actually, in this instance, it is a mere coincidence, but do go on." Andy caught the twinkle in Lohr's eye and got the joke. He smiled and said, "I don't believe you. It's significant to me."

"So it is. You were telling me why."

"Yes. Well, that's where I met Jeffrey. Jeffrey James Peter Parker Clanton or Jimmy Jeff as his family called him. He was from Texas originally. Houston. He'd been in Chicago for ten years but he kept his drawl. I am such a sucker for Southern accents. And hairy redheads. Anyway, he smiled, we danced, we talked, he told me he had AIDS (even though he looked in the peak of health), and I asked him to come home with me. He assured me we would be safe, and I knew we would. I was sober; I knew we would be alright. And emotionally, well, I thought I could handle that too. We made out a little and he threw up in my bath tub, (he was sicker than he looked) so I called him a cab and he went home. That was it. Hardly an auspicious beginning. I didn't expect to see him again but I did. I also didn't expect to fall in love with him but I did that too. We had one pretty good year together and one really horrible one, his last. I knew it was risky and crazy, I'm not stupid. Besides, everybody told me so, but I could not help myself. Our relationship seemed preordained somehow. And I found a lot of ways to accept that, both rational and delusional."

"And where is he now?"

The question shocked and angered Andy and he spat his reply, "He's dead, Lohr! How the hell should I know where he is? When they're dead, they're dead. They're gone. Forever."

"But you have an expanded awareness, an expanded consciousness, you are not unfamiliar with the concept of an afterlife."

"Oh, sure, but that doesn't mean Saturday nights he sends me messages on the Ouija board. The Veil may be thin but from this side, the side of the living, it might as well be the Great Wall of China. Death is final. It's a no-return trip to another country. He wasn't coming back. I wasn't going to see him anymore. It took me three months to finally get that. And for a while after he died, I desperately longed to see him again. I just wanted him to give me a sign, maybe visit me, in a dream or something, and tell me he was alright now, that he was happy and healthy again, that he really was in a better place. It didn't happen. Oh, I saw him in my dreams, but only twice and only briefly. He never spoke to me, he just smiled, then turned and walked away. And I would wake up, with tears in my eyes, missing him all over again."

"Well, he would like to speak to you now. He has something he wants to tell you. Would you like to see him?"

Andy was surprised but not incredulous. He had sensed this was coming. Besides, at this point, anything was possible. He looked around, searching for his former love, and asked, "Where is he? Is he here somewhere?"

"He is close by, but he wants to be sure you want to see him again. Can you tell him that?"

Andy gently bit his lower lip, dropped his chin and looked at the floor. After a moment weighing all the implications of that, he knew he did, and he said quietly, "Of course, I want to see him again."

"Good. Then come with me. We just have to go up one level, to the Observation Lounge."

"Are we walking or flying?"

"Oh, very good! Get that sense of humor going."

"What sense of humor? I'm serious. How are we getting there?"

"Well, it's pretty low tech, but we're going to take the stairs."

They arose and Lohr headed into the nearest tunnel, followed dutifully by Andy, who expected another long trek but was surprised when, almost immediately, they came upon a wide, sweeping, spiraling staircase. The stairs were busy, several parties of entities, all of very humanoid appearance, were climbing or descending. There was a strange light from above that bathed the stairs in a soft foggy glow. As they walked up Andy felt the slightest sensation cross his face, as if he had walked through an invisible cobweb. He wiped at his face, but there was nothing there.

Lohr volunteered the answer to his unasked question, "You have just entered reality number three. It is a somewhat fragile, rarefied atmosphere. Do you still feel light, as if your physical body was delicately expanded, as if there was more space between the molecules?"

Andy said, "Yes, it feels great, too. I love being lighter. It made dancing with you, like climbing these stairs, virtually effortless."

Lohr smiled and replied, "Good."

Andy wondered if there were more explanations to follow, but Lohr added nothing.

"Thank you, Lohr. You are a master of understatement."

F♦F♦EEN

At the top of the stairs they surfaced in another domed room of grand proportions. Glass surrounded them with a 360 degree panoramic view outside the spaceship. Ahead of them the Earth was featured prominently against the backdrop of stars. Andy followed the view to his left and twisted around to look behind himself. He silently mouthed one word, "Wow!" when he saw, just as he thought he might, the crescent moon, appearing to be nearly as big as the Earth. As if that wasn't "Wow!" enough, there was a vast field of flying saucers tapering back toward the Moon. He thought there must have been at least one-hundred-fifty of the space vehicles. There was a variety of shapes, but all were variations on the flying disc design. He did not have to ask the questions before getting the answers from Lohr.

"No, those are not all the starships of our flotilla and, yes, we are completely undetectable from Earth." If this really were, as indeed it seemed to be, a combination lounge and observation deck, and not some holographic simulation, Andy was hopelessly disoriented. For one thing, he had no idea they were so near the top of the ship, although with artificial gravity they could be upside down for all he knew. But here he was, Alice through the looking glass, and he quickly gave up trying to make any sense of this multi-dimensional wonderland. But top or bottom, there was the Earth and there was the Moon and there were all those stars and flying saucers. And this room was clearly something more than a lookout post. It was a sumptuous, all white, Art Deco nightclub. Except for that sci-fi view, it could have been a set for an Astaire and Rogers musical. Andy liked that. It appealed to his love of 'The Movies' and the culture of Hollywood in its 'Golden Age' that so fascinated him. Patrons were seated either at small tables around the perimeter or at large, semicircular, plush booths surrounding the raised circular bar in the center of the room.

The room was more than half full of guests but, even so and despite the high ceiling, oddly quiet. For a moment Andy thought his hearing was off. But no, just finely tuned to the serenity. Big band instrumental versions of the romantic songs of the Thirties and Forties were playing softly in the background. In this relaxed, sophisticated ambiance, conversations were subdued, discreet. The romantic lighting came from the starry night outside and the small, boudoir lamps placed at each table or booth. Five bartenders, three male and two female, in red service jackets, white tuxedo shirts, red bow ties, and black pants, were mixing and serving colorful drinks of huge proportions which they placed on trays which were then whisked to tables by similarly attired waiters and waitresses. The patrons were dressed in period evening clothes, the period ranging from the Thirties to the Fifties.

As he and Lohr stood waiting to be seated, Andy scanned the room for Jeffrey but did not see him. He did, however, notice that there were no distracting 'creatures' here. The patrons and the staff represented many races but they were all most definitely humans and all radiantly attractive. Some of them could have been his movie star portraits come to life. There was a Randolph Scott look-alike standing by a table, talking with twins of Tyrone Power and Dorothy Lamour. Doubles of the young and glamorous Fred MacMurray, Carole Lombard and Paulette Goddard shared a booth. Ann Southern and William Holden look-alikes were being seated on the main floor a few tables from clones of Linda Darnell, Jon Hall, and Rita Hayworth.

As Andy continued to survey the crowd, he noticed many of those in attendance were stunningly handsome or breathtakingly beautiful examples of both pure and mixed racial and ethnic types. It reminded him of Reiko. He missed her at the disco. Would she show up here? She certainly would fit in. She could wear a Givenchy gown with the best of them. It seemed a terribly romantic, glamorous and upscale place, but then it was just the kind of rendezvous spot Jeffrey would have chosen.

Surrounded by the most beautiful people he'd ever seen, in their beautiful clothes, some in shades of white, with pastel accents, others in vivid Technicolor hues, hearing the quiet murmur of their conversations, and contemplating his home planet from a hundred thousand miles in space, Andy didn't need to be told he'd been neatly folded and tucked into another dimension. It was both as subtle as the cobweb, and as obvious as the contrast between the serenity of this room and the exhilaration of the dance club he had just left. He marveled that this transition to another level of reality had been the easiest one yet, a simple walk up a flight of stairs.

Presently, a zaftig platinum blond hostess in diamonds, white opera gloves and a floor-length, strapless evening gown the pale green color of celadon pottery, approached and greeted them with a wry, warm-hearted smile on her Jungle Red lips and asked them where they would like to be seated. Lohr pointed to an empty booth nearby on the second tier. She led them to it and, as they sat down, placed menus in front of them. As soon as she left, Lohr excused himself and got up again. Andy only had to wonder to himself where he was going before Lohr answered, "I'll be at the bar. He'll be here very soon and I want you two to be alone. And remember, no food or drink."

Andy frowned as he watched him walk away. He did not like being left alone. To kill time he looked at the menu. It was in neat but illegible hieroglyphics. He tossed it aside and looked at the Earth. He saw the Great Lakes and blue, phallic shape of Lake Michigan and the megalopolis of Chicago at the southwestern tip of it. He saw the snow-capped Rockies to the left of a very long line of thunderstorm clouds over the Great Plains. But the coastline of California next to the vast blue of the Pacific was, visually dead center, the closest, most prominent feature. He easily found the Bay Area and the San Francisco peninsula. He suddenly felt just a little bit homesick, not for Chicago or San Francisco, but for Earth. When he thought about it he also felt really small, unattractive, underdressed, and out of place.

A lot of conflicting feelings collided in him at this moment. After everything he had seen and heard so far during this fantastic adventure, after everyone he had met and spoken to, waiting for his dead lover to make an appearance had to be the most unbelievable part. And maybe the most challenging. Where was Jeffrey? Still running on Gay Standard Time? He knew Andy hated to be kept waiting but Jimmy Jeff, as his family and most of his friends called him, was never punctual in life, so why should he be in death?

"Hello, Sweet Pea. I'm Sorry I'm late." The honey-coated drawl preceded him. The boyishly handsome redhead was not there and then he was there, appearing in front of Andy as if someone had pulled a magic cape off him. He stood unveiled in a bright salmon pink, short-sleeved, silk shirt and coral red linen pants. The glowing golden fuzz on his forearms and the even redder golden chest hair were the first features to catch Andy's attention. He looked up into the beaming face and couldn't speak. He was, if possible, even more handsome, more beautiful, than Andy remembered him to be. And there was around him a shimmering pink and gold aura of perfect health and blissful happiness.

Andy could only manage to speak two words, "You ... look ..."

"Divine? I know! That is what you were going to say, isn't it?" Jimmy Jeff's insouciant twinkle was unmistakable and unmistakably his alone.

Andy knew, without a shred of doubt, that this was no shade or simulation, but the totally miraculous resurrection of his former lover.

Andy looked back at him with recognition in his eyes, then grinned and returned the gleam. "I was going to say 'You look a helluva lot better than the last time I saw you.'"

"I should hope so! A catheter, a respirator, and three IV's, are certainly not my idea of a fashion statement. How the hell are you? You look good, too. Really good. Love the Luke Skywalker outfit. May I sit down?"

"Oh! Well, yes, I think you'd better."

Jimmy Jeff eagerly scooted into the both, sitting to Andy's left, but being careful not to sit too close. They looked at each other and into each other's eyes searching for the words to convey the way they felt. Finally it was Andy who tried to speak his heart.

"I can't believe it's you. I thought I would never see you again … like this. I thought I was resigned to that, but now that you're here …." He could not finish it. His eyes misted up and he tried to swallow the lump in his throat. Jimmy Jeff looked at him with heartbreaking tenderness. He raised his hand and reached toward Andy as if to stroke his cheek then snatched his hand back. And his eyes too brimmed fleetingly with tears as he said, "I can't touch you. It's not allowed. I want to, but I can't. Hell! I want to make love to you. But I can't."

Andy winced painfully, "Oh, terrific! That's great! Just like when you were alive. How enchanting! We get to relive our relationship complete with all the frustration and regret of our past? Who thought up these rules?"

"I'm sorry, sweetheart, I don't know who makes up the rules. It's some sort of dimensional thing. I don't understand it myself. They told me I could not touch you, that it would only be painful to try. So let's not go there. Let's spend our time together on the good stuff, okay?"

"Like the good stuff we never had? Or the good stuff where you turned into a vegetable and then left me?" Jimmy Jeff's bright aura did a brown-out and Andy instantly regretted his remark. He quickly added, "I'm sorry. I'm so sorry. I didn't really mean it. I thought I was over all that too. But it hurt. I guess it still hurts. I apologize."

"That was the way it had to be, darlin'. That was all part of our agreement. And you more than fulfilled your part of the bargain. When you get over here, to the so-called After Life, you'll understand. Believe me. But I'm the one that owes you an apology. That's one of the reasons I had to see you. I wanted to say to you, that I'm sorry I hurt you. I wanted to tell you that you were really good to me, and I will always–always!–love you for what you gave me."

"And what was that? Some inept nursing?"

"Now quit. You were a wonderful caregiver, the best. But you gave me something even more precious. You were there for me. Even at my worst – especially at my worst – you were there. Do you know the thing I was most afraid of, the thing I didn't know how I would face, the thing I could never bring myself to tell you?" Andy shook his head, no. "I didn't want to die with nobody around to hold me."

Andy's eyes brimmed over at that pronouncement, and he wiped the tears away from his cheeks as he answered in a steady voice, "But I couldn't hold you. At the end, I couldn't even do that for you. And those last few months, you were usually in so much pain you didn't want to be touched."

"Ah, but you were there, always there. You held my hand. Remember? And you put the ice pack on my forehead. And you touched me in a hundred other ways. You supported me, figuratively, just as surely as if you had held me literally. That's what really counts. I wanted you to know that. I never gave you the credit you deserve. And I wanted you to hear that from me. Okay?"

Andy nodded, yes, still wiping away the tears that ran down his cheeks.

"Are you okay?" Andy again nodded yes and forced a smile to prove it. "Good. And there's some more. Another thing I wanted to tell you is," – and he hesitated just a second before going on, – "that I have a partner over here.

And we are very much in love and very happy. We might even go into our next lifetimes together. That remains to be worked out, of course, but that is a distinct possibility."

"That's great," Andy snuffled and wiped his eyes with a starched linen napkin. "I'm very happy for you."

Jimmy Jeff cocked his head and arched an eyebrow, "I would like to believe you, but, Felix, don't pee on my leg and tell me it's rainin'!"

Andy rolled his eyes, "I am so sorry I ever told you my real first name! No, really, I am. I'm very happy for you and ... whatever his name is."

"You are not! You're jealous! I can tell. I can always tell."

"Of course you can. You had plenty of practice because you gave me lots of opportunities to be jealous."

"Oh, darlin', I wish you would get over that! That was just sex. It had nothing to do with you. A man's gotta do what a man's gotta do."

"Now who's peeing on whose leg? Haven't you learned anything since you've been dead?"

"Sorry, just a knee jerk reaction. I was a slut. I admit it. Had to do it. Couldn't help it. You should hate me. I deserve it."

"Oh, now you quit it! You couldn't help it and I'm not jealous. Let's just go on from there. Why change our little lies now?"

"Well butter my butt and call me a biscuit! Where did you get all that gumption? Hmmm? Never mind, it looks good on you. But they aren't lies, you know. They're the parts we chose to play. And while I'd love to talk to you about it some more, and drag up and re-hash every single particle of our mountainous pile of relationship dirt, there really isn't time for that."

Andy grinned and wiped away the last vestige of a tear. "You're absolutely right. Those are places we don't need to revisit."

"Let me see if I can get back on track here." Jimmy Jeff kept count on his fingers as he continued, "I wanted to tell you how much I love you and all you did for me and I did that. And I wanted to tell you about how I've moved on. And I did that, too. Let's see, what else was there? There was one other thing. Very important. What was it? Oh, yeah. But, Sweet Pea, I also want to know that you've moved on, too. I want to know that you're alright. I suppose what I'm getting at is, are you are happy, sweetheart?"

"Me? Happy? I don't know. I guess so. If you call ambivalent and coasting through life without a plan, happy... then yeah, I'm happy."

Jimmy Jeff threw his head back and laughed. "God, it's great to hear you bitch again!" And Andy smiled with the pleasure of how great it was to hear that laugh again. "But don't be so coy, Pumpkin Patch, I happen to know that you have a boyfriend too."

"Oh? And how do you know that?"

"I can see you. Sometimes. Not all the time. I'm getting better at it though. I watch you and I send thoughts to you. Sometimes I am even right beside you. You don't realize it, I know, but I'm still a part of your life. Just because I'm dead doesn't mean I don't care about you anymore. So, yeah, I know you have a boyfriend. And a damned cute one too."

"Then you know his name is Richard?"

"I know a helluva lot more about him than that. And I'm still happy for you." Jimmy Jeff could not stifle his own amusement at the joke he'd just dropped.

"Do I detect a note of jealousy in your dry wit?"

"Maybe just a tad. But I am trying to tell you that I have moved on and you should too. And this guy is good for you. I know you have mixed feelings about him, and it's not for me to try to sell him to you, – that's supposed to be Billy's job – however, I can also ...."

"Billy?"

"My new significant other. But I can also see that, when it comes to your new significant other, you are draggin' your feet, darlin'. You are sittin' on the dock of the bay, watchin' the tide roll away. There's a hole in your bucket, dear Liza, dear Liza, and you are ...."

256

"Wait a minute. Your new boyfriend is Billy?"

"Yes, Billy. Haven't you heard a word I've said?"

"Yes, of course I have, but Billy? Not Richard's Billy? The one who was killed by gay bashers?"

"Yessiree Bug, that's the Billy we're talking about alright. Surprise! Surprise! Surprise! I told you the two of you had a lot in common."

"And I grow weary of hearing my name taken in vain. May I join you now, por favor?"

Disembodied voices no longer fazed Andy, but he was still astonished by rapid materializations. Without waiting for permission, Wilhelm Alessandro Kreisler y Montoya announced himself telepathically then appeared standing to Jimmy Jeff's left. The broad-shouldered, slim-hipped, wiry Argentine, with the slicked back, dark blond hair, wore a severely tailored, white dinner jacket with a brilliant magenta silk bow tie and matching cummerbund. He paused to give everyone a good look at his magnificence, and had time to look down his aquiline nose at his rival, before sliding into the booth with feline grace to take his place next to his querido. He boldly drew Jimmy Jeff's face to his and kissed him lingeringly on the lips. Once he was certain that he had made the impression he intended, he smiled unctuously at Andy, extended his left hand and said, "You must be Felix. It gives me great satisfaction to meet you." He reached across Jimmy Jeff who intercepted the hand and lifted it to his own mouth and kissed it.

"Now, now, My Little Tango Tart, you know we aren't allowed to touch them. Have you forgotten? You promised me you'd behave. Have you decided to be a bore?"

"Ah, forgive me. I do not wish to be a bore. Anything but that! I believe you were talking about me when I so rudely interrupted. I apologize. Please, go on with your fascinating conversation."

"We were talking about moving on, about finding other partners, like you and I have. And yes, I was mentioning you to Andy. I said that you would be happy to tell him about Richard, about what a great catch he is."

"Catch? Happy? You say I would be 'happy' to tell him about Richard? That would be Richard, Richard the Great Catch, my Richard? Oh, my Tejano Longhorn, but you are so positive! Isn't he positive? Always he tries to say the most positive thing. He is such a positive influence on my life. Or perhaps I should say afterlife. Should say? Alright, then, I will say. You are such a positive influence on my afterlife, James. Thank you, gracias, gracias, muchas gracias, mil gracias!"

Andy and Jimmy Jeff stared blankly at Billy, blandly letting his tirade of mock gratitude wash over them. Andy was trying to keep his uncharitable thoughts to himself. Jimmy Jeff's abundant Texas charm bubbled over as he said with a big grin, "Wilhelmcita, he doesn't have a lot of time with us, so let's just get on with it and cut out all the bitchy, snotty crap, shall we?"

Chastened, Billy sat up straight, folded his hands together and placed them on the table. He looked down at them thoughtfully, gathering his dignity. Andy perceived the surrender, saw the demeanor change and the fiery aura flicker and dim. In fact, Billy momentarily grew transparent as if he had been drained of his aristocratic arrogance. But he came back and his aura took on a turquoise hue, then violet, gradually growing brighter but remaining soft and misty. He lifted his head and looked directly at Andy. The penetrating gaze from his ebony eyes was riveting. Ready to dismiss him a moment ago, Andy was now completely focused on Richard's ex-lover. The becalmed Billy began, minus the Fernando Lamas accent, "What can I tell you? You probably know all about us. You probably know more about me than I know about you."

"No, I doubt that's true," Andy quietly interjected. "I've seen pictures of you. I've asked him about you. Several times. But he hasn't told me anything, really. Just that you were together seven years and that you died in his arms after the two of you were attacked. He always changes the subject. He doesn't seem to want to talk about you at all."

Billy quickly looked down at his hands to hide the look of disappointment on his face. But Andy sensed his hurt and understood the reason for it.

"It's not as if he's forgotten you; he still wears your ring on a chain around his neck. It's just that, or so I've gathered, it's still too painful for him to talk about. Neither one of us has shared much about our pasts. What he's told me is really about as much as I've told him about Jeffrey. When it comes to old boyfriends, I think 'don't ask, don't tell' is the best policy. But if you would like to share something of what you know about him, – something private, but not too personal, – I'd be happy to listen. I'm sure you must know him better than I do."

"How long have you been seeing each other?"

"About three months."

Taking that into account, Billy gave the request some thought before he came up with what he hoped would be an unknown fact. He said, "Alright, let's try this one. Do you know that he is part Italian?"

"Yes, I do know that."

Jimmy Jeff couldn't resist interjecting, "I'll just bet he does, and I'll bet he knows which part, too!"

"James, eh, how you say in Dixie? Hush up." Jimmy Jeff pantomimed zipping his mouth shut and raised both hands over his head signaling his surrender to Billy's wishes.

"Do you know he was a Marine in Viet Nam?

"Yes, but not much more than that. He doesn't have much to say on that subject either."

"Do you know he has a brother and a sister? Have you met them?"

"I haven't met them. I know the brother, Robert, is a flaming homophobe, although his wife, Allison, and the kids seem to treat Richard pretty decently."

"And the sister?"

"Haven't met Annie yet either. They seem to like each other, they talk on the phone about once a month. I guess you know she's an ob-gyn in Colorado. What I don't get is why she still hasn't come out to anyone, especially her own gay brother."

"You're kidding! She still hasn't come out? Unbelievable! Is she still in practice with her lover?"

"Do you mean Doctor Gloria Dennis? Isn't that her name? Does that sound right?"

"Oh, my god! Then she's still with Denny?"

"So it would seem."

"Well, that's nice, I'm happy for them, but not to confide in Richard, that is despicable. What is the girl thinking?"

"I don't know but I think it may have something to do with Joan. She and Annie are barely speaking, and Annie knows Richard and Joan are tight, so she probably feels betrayed."

"Ah, Joan. La Jefe. She hated me. Absolutely despised me. Always the cold shoulder from her. And his father too, although he wanted to like me, I could tell, but he was so uptight about the gay thing. He avoids me even now, even over here. They hurt Richard so deeply! And it is all so unnecessary, the homophobia. Que lastima! Ignorant, hard-headed, hard-hearted people, I cannot forgive them! Do you get along with Joan?"

"Yes, I do."

"And how do you manage this?"

"I don't know. She's kind of crusty but I think she must have mellowed since you knew her."

"Like one of her fine wines, no doubt. Although if what you say is true, it is a miracle. I have heard of vintage wines turning to vinegar but never the other way around."

"Well, I'm sure you have your reasons, but I kind of like her."

Billy shrugged. Jimmy Jeff had been listening patiently to the exclusive conversation and took advantage of the lull to say, "I don't really have a lot to contribute here, so, if you two will excuse me, I think I'll go join that fellow at the bar, the one you came in with, Andy. Is that alright with everyone?" They both nodded their agreement and Billy slid out of the booth, standing to let Jimmy Jeff out. As they passed each other, he leaned close to Billy's ear and murmured, "Will you miss me?" Billy kissed him on the cheek and said, "Desperately, querido, every moment you are gone will be sheer agony."

Jimmy Jeff looked back at Andy and grinned, "See that? Move on. Get some of that lovin' for yourself." He winked and started off to the bar. Seeing him go, seeing him walk away again, Andy suddenly felt a painful twinge of regret, and paying no mind to the scene he had just witnessed between the two lovebirds, interjected urgently and loudly, "Will I see you again?"

"Yes, of course. Don't worry, I'll be back to say good-bye. You two talk. Get to know each other. You know, share, make nice. Okay?" Both Andy and Billy nodded obediently, then watched him walk around the empty booth beside theirs and up the five steps to the bar on the top level. They sat in awkward silence for a moment. Then Andy opened with, "So you two are crazy about each other, huh?"

"Yes, we are. I have not felt so much in love, so utterly captivated by another man, since Richard. Richard and I had a wonderful, full life together. It was the best and most magical relationship I had ever known. Certainly over the last few lifetimes. And I know we left our imprint forever on the eternal sands of the Island of Love. When James and I incarnate again, it will be the same love, taken to a higher level. You must tell Richard that my love for him lives on, that I am with him always. Will you do that? Please?"

Andy nodded his agreement. Then Billy continued, "Especially tell him it is all the same love and it doesn't die. And tell him also for me that I got the little bastards."

"The little bastards?"

"The little punk bastard homophobes who killed me. Three teenage boys from the East Bay. They couldn't have been more than sixteen, the evil little 'S.O.Bs'. But Richard and I were stoned, and happy. We had just made love. Our guard was down, we were careless, we didn't see them until it was too late. Tell him I felt no pain. I left my body instantly. Anyway, tell him I got them. Well, I didn't actually get them but I followed them, hounded them, to their fate."

"And what was that? What was their fate?"

"Two of them died within a year of my death, in the fiery crash of a car they had stolen together. The third, the one who swung the bat, he joined the Navy and was beaten to death for being gay."

"Geez! Talk about your instant Karma."

"I think Richard would want to know this, so will you tell him, please?"

"Sure I will. But Richard is going to have a hard enough time dealing with my being here on an interdimensional spaceship, meeting with extraterrestrials, let alone talking to you. Why would he believe me? Is there something I can tell him that would prove I talked to you?"

"I don't know. Do you mean besides the part about our being stoned, or the three juvenile murderers?"

"Well, he did tell me it was three teenage boys who attacked you. And I could have guessed about your being stoned."

"I see. Something else then, that only I know. Hmmmm. I'll have to think about that. But first, I want you to tell me something. Do you love Richard?"

"Of course I do."

"You say yes, but I sense that you are unsure. Why?"

"I don't know. I could probably give you a hundred reasons."

"Give me just one."

"We seem to be locked into this strange dynamic where he is always coming on to me, always in pursuit, always the testosterone driven 'man,' and that means I am always the 'woman,' having to keep him at arm's length, fighting to maintain my own masculine identity, to keep from being devoured by his relentless ardor."

"Yes, Richard is a man of enormous appetites and desires."

"And a man often heedless of personal boundaries."

"Would you rather he were cold and indifferent to you?"

"No. Not that. I have to confess, I do like being adored. Up to a point. But it becomes too one-sided. I mean, you know, sometimes I would like to do the pursuing. He doesn't give me the chance to adore him back."

"Have you made this clear to him?"

"What? Oh, good grief! And you claim to know the man?"

"I'm sorry. Yes, of course, I understand. But do you not believe he could change? Do you not believe he is capable of moderating this behavior?"

"Frankly, I don't know. How did you deal with it?"

"Ah, well, you see, here is the difference between us. I did not usually object to his rampant sexuality. I did not mind that he was unfaithful, as long as he came home to me. And when I did object, then, let's just say that perhaps I was – I am – more strong-willed than you."

Andy grew uncomfortable with the tone the conversation was taking. He knew he was being dissed, but that's not what bothered him. It was the hint of possible infidelity that struck a nerve. "What are you saying? That he's not a monogamous type of guy?"

"Certainly it was not in his make-up when we were together. It has become a cliché, I know, but you have to understand what an intoxicating, non-stop party the Castro was in the 1970's: the wonderful freedom, the easy camaraderie, the sheer numbers of gorgeous, available men, the drugs. We all made pigs of ourselves. One does not just drop that cold-turkey for monogamy. For us, an open relationship worked very nicely. At least at first. By the time we realized how deeply in love we were, the drugs, the tricking and the unspoken jealousy, were already tearing us apart."

"But you were together seven years. How? Why?"

"How? I don't honestly know. It was the roughest, bumpiest, most painful, and yet the most exciting, exhilarating, bronco ride of my life. But I stayed on. Why? Well, we had a lot of fun together. But also I think because I cared more about 'us' than about 'me.' Although, not to sound boastful, I had my share of extramarital dalliances myself. I gave as good as I got. As to why he stayed on, you'll have to ask him. Somehow I think his answer would be, 'we stayed together because we wanted to.'"

"I know that was supposed to be encouraging, but …. Listen, I've already had the bronco ride. Several of them, actually, including that handsome Texan at the bar. No offense. I don't know if I want another ride on the bronco. I don't know if I can stand another one. Or maybe I'm just not ready to get back in the saddle."

Billy's aura turned the color of spilled blood. He stiffened, glaring at Andy, his nostrils flaring. He gripped the edge of the table with both hands, squeezing hard to keep his anger in check, and slowly, almost imperceptibly, pushed himself away from Andy, distancing himself as if he'd just discovered Andy had a loathsome disease. "No, perhaps you are not ready."

"Excuse me for overworking the horseback riding cliché. But don't misunderstand me. I'm grateful to Richard, grateful *for* Richard. He puts up with an awful lot from me."

"Yes, I'm sure he does."

"Maybe I don't even deserve him."

"Then it would seem my job here is done." Billy let go of the table and looked around anxiously, hoping to get James's attention so he would return and get him out of the awkward spot in which he now found himself.

Andy continued to dig himself deeper, "I honestly don't think I'm man enough for him. Wow! Where did that come from? Do you know I've never told that to anyone before? Probably because I never thought of it before. Tell me, did you ever feel that he was more man than you could handle?"

Billy looked askance at Andy as if offended by the question. But he answered honestly, "Yes. Sometimes. But I handled it."

Before Andy could ask him how he handled it, Billy turned on him. Drawing himself up to his full, aristocratic haughtiness, his voice dripping with disdain, he proclaimed, "I have just decided that our conversation is over."

Andy's jaw dropped pulling his face along with it. Billy began to slide himself out of the booth. But Andy demanded, "Wait! What's the matter? Why are you leaving?"

"Because you are a silly twit and I no longer care if you ever get your life together, with or without Richard."

"Hey! I thought we were bonding here! Oh, you are treacherous! Damn! And I am not a silly twit! Just because I'm unsure, just because maybe I'm not yet ready to commit to him, doesn't mean I don't love him and it sure as hell doesn't mean I'm a twit!"

"Twit."

"Don't call me that!"

"Twit."

"Stop it!"

Both of them were startled into silence when Jimmy Jeff, a big, expectant grin on his face, suddenly appeared at the table to ask, "How's it going? You two okay? Are you making nice?"

They both responded in a sing-songy unison that sounded like children caught with their hands in the cookie jar, "Oh, yes, very nice. We're fine, thanks."

"Is he giving you some good advice, Andy?"

"Yes. Yes, indeed he is." Andy forced himself to smile at Billy who returned the cloying, mocking grimace.

"Thanks for sharing, Billy," Andy mocked.

"Thanks for creating the space for me to share, Andy," Billy returned. Whether or not the sarcasm registered with Jimmy Jeff, he was there to deliver a message, "Well, Lohr says we have to wrap it up, so make it quick. He said take five more minutes. I'll see you both then."

They smiled after him as he walked away, then faced each other to finish their confrontation. Andy opened his mouth but didn't get to speak.

"Don't say another word," Billy threatened. "You wanted me to tell you something about Richard which would make him believe you had spoken with me, didn't you? Well, didn't you?"

"You told me not to speak!"

"Then listen to this. Ask him about his 'film career.' About the 'movies' he made in the Seventies before he met me. Ask him about Rod Reams, Ricky Dick, and Rocco Palazzo."

Andy got the picture, alright, literally, right in his head. And it was rated triple-X. His lover was a former porn star! He shouldn't have believed it, but his gut-level reaction, told him it was true, and he groaned out loud without realizing it. Then he saw the superior smirk on Billy's face and he got mad. That's when he tried to launch his counter attack.

"You know what your problem is?" Andy goaded.

"Don't tell me what my problem is! I don't need you to tell me what my problem is, I already know what my problem is: I'm dead!"

"And I'm not! And I have Richard and you don't. Okay, William Jorge Fritz Chrysler Montego, or whatever your name is, it's so obvious to me that you are just plain old, green-eyed jealous!"

"And why shouldn't I be? I still love Richard deeply, passionately, unequivocally, to this day, this hour, FOREVER! I too am grateful for my time with him. Yes, I am jealous! But not in the way you think. We had a turbulent life together, yes, but it was also a life that found its bliss. Since that life was taken from me, I have watched him try to make another start with many lovers, from the weak and ineffectual, to the dangerously sociopathic. It has not been easy seeing him make a fool of himself, putting himself in jeopardy. And for what? For someone who cannot fully appreciate what the man has to give him?

Billy continued, "He loves you very much, – why he does so is beyond me, but he does. He loves you with a ripe, mature passion, a richness that he and I never knew. Perhaps if I had lived, if we had been given the time, … but that's only speculation. What I am saying to you is that you are getting the best Richard that he has ever been. Whether you can appreciate that or not. So if I am jealous, it is because he is giving to you what he never could give to me."

Andy was stung, his face as red as if Billy had actually slapped it. And of course this was the moment both Lohr and Jimmy Jeff chose to return to the booth. When he looked up to find Lohr directly beside him, he also noticed how large the Earth had become. A sun-drenched Gaia completely filled the panoramic view before him and northern California occupied dead center. Little shocks to his sensibilities began to snowball. Time began to speed up and crumble at the same time. Everybody wanted something from him and they wanted it now. Billy had just pronounced him an ungrateful ass. Jimmy Jeff announced that it was time for him to say good-bye. Lohr said that it was time for Andy to return to Earth.

Andy and Billy slid themselves to the opposite ends of the booth seat and stood up. Andy looked at Jimmy Jeff and saw his own sadness there.

"Will I ever see you again?" Andy asked, his shaky voice struggling to mask his hurt and confusion, and to hold back the tears.

"Not for a long while, partner. If I'm still here when you pass over, well, for sure, we'll see each other again. Otherwise it might take a couple of lifetimes. But remember me. Please. I may look different the next time we meet. So remember my essence. Remember my gifts. Remember that I am always with you. I will be watching out for you. Be very good to yourself. I love you."

Once he and Billy began to dematerialize they faded quickly. Ironically, it was the wistful sadness, maybe even regret, in Billy's eyes that was the last thing Andy saw of the two of them. Once again the Veil was drawn, the illusion of the finality of good-bye was devastatingly complete. Once again he felt as if a piece of his heart had been taken away from him.

Lohr's large hand gently covered the center of Andy's back, miraculously holding him together, keeping Andy from caving in to his shredded emotions. "Come along, dear one, we must hurry to get you back. Your newly beloved is leaping hurdles to reach you. And in the third dimension, time is running out."

Lohr pulled a small crystal vial from his pocket, and pulled out the diamond encrusted stopper from the top. "I must apologize to you. There is no time to waste. So I have to use this." He wafted the open vial under Andy's nose several times. Andy caught a whiff of a delightful scent, a sweet floral, like jasmine or gardenia. It set off a subtle vibration in his sinuses that rippled up through his head and down to his shoulders. It quickly dispersed and Andy was left smiling as the pleasurable sensation faded away. And yet he had the odd feeling that he was being sedated. "Don't worry. This will have no effect on your recall. You will remember everything you have experienced on board this ship."

Lohr wrapped one arm around Andy and held him to his side. He walked him to the back of Richard's car where the door to the back seat was open. "Then why don't I remember this fog?"

"It is only the cloud we created over the mountain to shroud your return."

"Why don't my feet touch the ground? What happened to my boots? And my pants? I can't go home without pants."

"I'm afraid you cannot return with souvenirs from the ship. It's a law. In fact I'm going to have to take your tunic."

"Aw, c'mon Lohr, it's cold! There's snow on the ground, for cripe's sake!"

"Alright, alright, I suppose you can keep the shirt. For a little while anyway. I can always retrieve it later. Now will you please get inside the car?"

"Lohr, I love you, man. You're the best dancer. You're the most beautiful woman and the handsomest man. You're the one that I really want. You know that?"

"Thank you. I love you too. May you some day know how precious you are to me. And I want you too, but it will have to be some other time. Let go. Let go. Good. Now sit down. Sit. Sit! There. Now stay put."

Andy said, "Am I there yet?" but Lohr was already gone.

S:XTEEN

Indeed, and amen, why must Love be such torture? Before Jimmy Jeff, Andy had not had any better luck with relationships than he was now having with Richard. He hadn't had a single one that he wouldn't call Love/Hate. Was he so hopelessly codependent? Or was ambivalence simply the true nature of the Game? By the time Andy had dragged himself up the stairs to his apartment he was absolutely certain the trial separation was a mistake. And he was also absolutely certain that it was exactly what he needed.

He let himself in and went to the kitchen for a bottle of club soda. His message machine light was blinking. He had four messages. He was very relieved that the intergalactic mafia hadn't left any of them. Two of the messages were offers of catering gigs coming up in the next week. He knew he had his rent money, but the practical part of his nature said he should take them. He hated to turn down too many. The summer slump was here and opportunities had dwindled. Besides, he always worried that the calls would stop if he didn't keep accepting them. He needed to be seen as reliable and making himself available was the best way to do that. But tonight he didn't care about that. He couldn't see himself passing one more tray of tapas, serving one more table of eight, slopping one more trough for the hogs. He let loose a loud and long groan of exasperation. Tonight he felt like he needed a very long vacation. So he hated to do it, but he called them back and declined the offers. The other two messages were from friends in

Chicago. One was from Martin Kovak, aka Marty, aka The Widow Kovach. Marty was Andy's age. They had met and become good friends in a grief counseling support group. The other message was from Patrick ('Patty') Cakely, probably Andy's best friend in Chicago. Patrick had the rarely bestowed distinction of having two 'drag names.' His lover of ten years, who went by the name of Chai, gave him the other name, the one that Andy actually preferred, Kitty. Both Patty and Kitty Cakely could always be counted on to make Andy laugh. He and Patrick had been awkward lovers briefly, years before Jeffrey. He was a fellow waiter from Andy's days at Chez Rouge. That their friendship survived working together, was a testament to the strength of their bond. But it hadn't served to encourage Andy to have an affair with Sky. Since moving to San Francisco, Andy missed Kitty very much and he could certainly use a laugh, but he just didn't feel up to giving him the latest news. Not tonight.

The emotional overload of the last two days left him exhausted and bereft. He felt very alone and isolated, adrift in his sea of ambivalence. Of course, being all of those things, he didn't like it one bit. Edgy, moody, volatile, he was unfit company even for himself. While he recovered his center from time to time, he was just as likely to go off again. He felt very 'off' right now and he could not make himself be 'on' for Kitty or anybody else. The words "edge of nervous collapse" came to his mind. Is this what he had been asking for when he wished to make contact with ETs? As wonderful and amazing as it all been, he had no idea it would also turn out to be such an enormous burden. Why had he been asked to tell the world of its coming transformation? "Why me?" he thought. "Why must I be their pawn? Why must I be Richard's pawn for that matter? Why? Huh? Why?"

Wanting answers where there were none, he almost relented and reneged on his deal with Richard so that he could call him, but talked himself out of it. Wanting guarantees where there were none, he thought maybe he should talk to Sarah but decided it could wait until tomorrow. Needing to be reassured, to feel approved of, he wanted to confide in Sky but decided that would be inappropriate. To love or not to love. To pursue or not pursue. To tell or keep silent. To accept or reject. As if he really had any choices. He admitted to himself that he was no stranger to this ambivalence, his own inner knowingness told him he was, yet again, like it or not, right where he was supposed to be: on the fence, teetering on the brink.

How many times had he felt as if some of his circumstances in life were fated? Fate was not to be resisted. It always won in the end. How many times had Life dragged him kicking and screaming down his Spiritual Path? But couldn't Fate just as readily be Doom? Well then it was all in how you looked at it. And he needed to look at it, to take a long and hard look at it, in all its permutations.

First of all, how was he going to make this tale of his believable? And who was he supposed to convince? He tried a left-brain approach: he sat at his desk and made notes, drew outlines, charted each course of action and the possible consequences, planning what he thought was every possible scenario. Every path led back to either a terrified or a humiliated Andy. He could find no satisfying answers to release him from the agony of indecision. It would take a miracle to turn him into a hero without turning him into a martyr. And as for Richard, maybe he *was* just too much for Andy to deal with after all.

For two hours he paced his apartment, bouncing himself back and forth between thoughts about his relationship with Richard and about his 'mission,' and how to make both of them work to his satisfaction. They seemed to be connected somehow even if he could not exactly put his finger on it. Was he destined to succeed or doomed to failure? He thought about these things until he felt he would scream. And always, whether he liked it or not, it seemed to him as though his fate was sealed. He was caught in a maze and couldn't find the exit.

The hour grew very late. The clock on the wall in his office read 1:00 a.m. and he was desperate for oblivion. In four hours he had to be up. He brushed his teeth, peed, undressed, set his alarm clock, then crawled into bed praying he would quickly go to sleep and wake refreshed enough to go to work. After three deep and only semi-relaxing breaths, he tried visualization. He pictured himself in a thermal pool, immersed to his neck in warm, soothing, buoyant water. He imagined this pool to be on a bluff overlooking the ocean, and he was watching the sun slipping beneath the horizon. It didn't seem to be working. Finally he was forced to command himself, to will himself, to sleep. The thought that he must be really getting good at entering altered states of consciousness briefly rippled through his mind as, amazingly, instantly he felt himself begin the slide into the longed for state of unconsciousness.

He was gone not five minutes. He knew because when he looked at the lighted dial of the clock by his bed he saw that it was only 1:05. He sat up, more wide awake than ever. It had taken only five minutes to cross town, hover over Richard's bed, see what he had seen, and return to his own bed and body. He knew what he had just done, but to his knowledge, he had never done it before. Yes, it was amazing but mostly he felt confused and a little bruised by the betrayal he had just witnessed. He did not want to believe it, yet he could find no solace in denial. He slid back down under the covers, his heart so heavy it pinned him to the bed.

His brain had finally overloaded and short-circuited. If only he could blame all this on insanity. Maybe he really was insane because he could not squeeze out another tear drop, he could not strike out and hurt something, destroy something – do anything – to erase the burden of knowingness, lift the weight, and make the agony in his soul go away. Maybe he really should see the shrink Dr. Dave recommended. He bet, if he played it just right, he could get some good drugs from him. That was supposed to be a joke, he told himself. But it was at times like these, times of extreme emotional distress and confusion, that he not so half-heartedly wished he could get high again. He wanted to get silly and stupid, just like in the old days before he had consistently abused his substances until they no longer delivered him away from care but into care's very lap. Admittedly that had never been a really good solution, but it had been a damn good distraction. Now maybe he didn't really want to be sedated, but he sure could use a little help. That was a pure motive, wasn't it? "Help," he sighed. "Please?"

And so he heard a now familiar voice in his head speaking quietly but insistently to him. It was the voice of one who cared for him. Lohr reminded him, **"The shortest way out is always through."** He told him to allow himself to feel the pain, to immerse himself in it, and see what it was all about. And the mere suggestion made it so, because that's when Andy passed out and sank into the 'dream-sequence.'

It started out as a black and white dream, a black and white movie. He was on a Hollywood soundstage of infinite proportions. It was very dark. The set was a road on a low hillside of dead trees. A heavy, waist-high mist hung over the mock landscape and spilled over onto the floor of the soundstage. Yards away was the camera crew and the Director. He could not see the Director's face, only his silhouette against a dim stage light. Stock footage of a full moon, alternately hidden and revealed by scudding clouds, was projected in an endless loop on a huge backdrop. And in the middle distance of the projected film was the burning model of a windmill. The shout of "Action!" set everything else in motion.

First he heard the tramping of feet and then saw the actor-villagers, their stage-craft torches still blazing, rise up over and descend the fake hillside toward him, mumbling congratulations to themselves. The mob of twenty-five or so barely made it over the crest of the hill before another shout rang out.

"Cut! Cut! Cut!" the Director yelled furiously. The moon and burning windmill disappeared when the endless loop ended. The mumbling turned to grumbling and groaning in a much livelier, exasperated tone. But the Director did not care to hear it.

"We will do this again! And AGAIN! Do you understand? You are a HAPPY MOB! You have just KILLED THE MONSTER! You are SAFE once more. What's the matter with you? Are you going to sleep? Well, WAKE UP! Because we will do this as many times as it takes. You WILL GET IT RIGHT! Now back to your places! And give it more LIFE! BE – 'ACT' – HAPPY! GODDAMMIT!"

The bitching ceased as the exhausted and browbeaten extras resigned themselves to the fortieth take – their doom, their circle of hell – and reversed direction to trudge back up and over the plaster and plywood hill. One of the women turned to look directly at Andy. Under her babushka he saw that it was a young and girlish Judy Garland. Being a dream, this seemed perfectly natural. Of all the extras, she alone was not tired. She smiled at him, which did nothing at all to diminish the manic intensity in her furiously blinking eyes, as she stammered, "Hello, D-Darling. Welcome to M-M-Metro-Goldwyn-N-Nightmayer. See you in the r-rushes." Then she turned away, took off like a bullet and scampered off ahead of everyone else into the distance.

There was the dream-state equivalent of a wipe dissolve and he was sitting by himself in a smoky screening room. The reel began with Judy and Mickey, at the peak of their formidable performing skills, whipped into a frenzy for what the clapboard said was the fifteenth take of their wildly animated Conga Number. These were rushes in several senses of the word, fed by the throbbing, insistent beat of the conga music. They were performing with frightening abandon. Andy was afraid they were going to hurt themselves, but as consummate pros, they made it through without missing a step or a beat. They struck their pose at the finale grinning demonically as the camera zoomed in on a tight double close-up. It took Andy's breath away, right down to the little pinwheels spinning in their eyes.

With all the seeming irrational randomness of any dream, the next clip brought Maria Montez face to face with Maria Montez as her own evil twin. Andy's beloved Maria! She could not act her way out of a paper bag and here she was, typically trapped in that bag and acting as hard as she could yet remaining strangely wooden. Maria, as the murderous, tyrannical Cobra Queen who had deposed Maria, the good and true Queen, seemed to struggle to remember her line, then, brow furrowed from the effort, she demanded petulantly, "Gif me dat Cobra Jool!"

The next dissolve brought an extreme close-up of Dorothy Lamour's face. She was silently emoting out of every pore and, being a much better actress, she was poignantly, wordlessly projecting her vulnerability, – the fragile, bruised exotic Orchid, waiting, praying, begging for love in the glow of a tropic moon. Then she became the tigress of passion, nostrils flaring, seething lustily and defiantly, looking off-screen, playing to something or someone just out of range of the camera. The clip was silent, probably Miss Lamour's screen test. There was not even a note of music to underscore her performance, just the distant, muffled clackity-clack of the film reels running through the projector. She existed, hermetically, on the silver screen, her face forty feet tall, all the while she shimmered and glowed, a creature of pure light and shadow, breathtakingly radiant, staggeringly gorgeous, frame by flowing frame, caught forever on film in the prime of her youth and beauty. Her heavy eyelids and lush, moist lips, her shining eyes and black, shining hair, were epically huge and luminous, the attributes of a divinity, shadow-play facsimiles of the Goddess, Herself.

But now Andy thought he could hear her breathing. Was there a live soundtrack to this scene? If so, it was soft, barely audible, even as it increased in intensity. And then she was ravished, plundered. She writhed and shuddered in a quietly rendered, exquisite orgasm that, in a slow lap

276

dissolve, seemed to set off the filmic, montage version of the 1906 San Francisco Earthquake. The low, mournful groan of the Screen Goddess was drowned out as the cross fade brought the destruction of old San Francisco into sharper focus. The sound rumbled up in crescendo as the chandelier in one shot first swayed then shook violently and plaster began to fall. In the next shot, the ground opened up, water mains broke, building facades crumbled exposing the terrified inhabitants clinging to shaking furniture, to the side of the building.

Quick, flash cuts caught multiple fragments of destruction. The face of catastrophe was just as riveting as that of the great beauty. From this stunning studio recreation of the 1906 San Francisco cataclysm there was now a further dissolve into another montage of catastrophe. This time it was 1953 Los Angeles and the invaders from Mars had begun the War of the Worlds in terrifyingly garish Technicolor. The unstoppable machines of conquest floated in horrific majesty above the street lamps of a city in flames, spewing their fiery rays of death and destruction, the toppling buildings catching crowds of fleeing people, crushing and burying them under mountains of debris. People ran for the presumed safety of a church, crowding inside to pray for some miraculous, last-minute salvation. Would God intervene on behalf of humanity? The eyeless, telescopic gaze of one of the Martian war machines seemed to follow them into God's House.

Did it really think about it for a split second, perhaps actually weighing the moral, the theological implications of what it was about to do? Did it perhaps have a pang of conscience? Was it going to change its mind and spare these people? But no, it was merely taking aim. The death ray powered up to full intensity, fired, and leveled the church with one screeching blast, incinerating everyone inside. ("Hmmm," Andy thought, "That's not how it was in the original release.") With an overlapping, linking soundtrack of crowd panic, there was a quick draining of color and then a fade to black before a slow fade up on another scene of mass hysteria. Kevin McCarthy was frantically trying to stop traffic and warn us about the Pod People. But suddenly the sound was cut and he was now disturbingly silent. His fear grew to gigantic proportions as his face filled the screen and magnified the terror which viscerally pulled at Andy. Parts of this dream were beginning to duplicate his experience with Ankh Ra adding a whole new dimension to the panic which now took control of Andy, drawing him out of his seat and thrusting him into the movie.

There was a silent, explosive flash, as if from a sloppy jump cut, and Andy was on his feet. He was not in the screening room any longer. He was in a hot, moist greenhouse surrounded by huge plant pods and he looked down at himself and saw that he was without color. In the gray, eerie half-light of a full moon shining down through the humidity-fogged glass of the greenhouse, he realized he was in a movie of his own making. He again heard Lohr murmur his advice for Andy to see where exploring his feelings would take him.

As soon as he mentally agreed a fearful premonition descended from his mind down through his body. He stiffened. He could not help himself, he was powerless not to look at what he sensed was behind him. He turned slowly, filled with dread, to confront a slimy pod that was growing rapidly before his eyes. Out of the eerie silence came a small, sporadic heartbeat that steadily grew in strength and volume. He watched terror-stricken as the huge fetal being developed quickly in a process of cross dissolves and frame-by-frame, stop motion. The naked man inside was struggling more and more violently to free himself and, when he tore off the last confining, sticky, translucent leaf of the birth pod and peeled the last layer from his face and emerged gasping for breath, Andy soundlessly screamed, "No!"

It was Richard. And he was sexually rampant. He stepped down off the box-like planter and staggered for only a couple of steps, quickly becoming accustomed to his legs. His eyes locked on Andy's, the gaze of hungry, naked lust sending a potent, electrified current of both fear and desire through Andy's quivering body. He was the deer in Richard's headlights. The leering, primal, alien Richard advanced menacingly, stalking his prey, never taking his eyes off his quarry. Andy was frozen in place.

Andy tried again and again to run, to scream, but no matter how hard he struggled, he could not move, not a sound came out of his mouth. The loudly beating heart was now the sound of his own. Suddenly a strong wind came up, blowing the moonlit greenhouse away, abruptly changing the scene, and transferring both of them to the bleak, sepia-toned landscape of Dorothy's Kansas where the cyclonic storm was just beginning. Unfazed, the sadistically grinning, Richard drew closer, rubbing his hands over his slippery wet body, radiating sexual heat. Now, along the horizon, the clouds began to spawn one tornado after another. Richard, the sex beast, was momentarily distracted by the ominous weather. He stopped. He and Andy were surrounded by funnel clouds dangling suggestively to the ground where they whirled and raked, sucked up and spit out the landscape. Richard refocused on Andy and took a step. But the scene morphed once more, again drawing out the suspense and prolonging Andy's anguish.

Now the lush greenery and giant flowers of Munchkinland in Oz swelled and everything burst into vibrant, full-Technicolor form around them. This only seemed to pump up Richard, exciting him even more. His sweaty flesh glowed, tinged with a lurid pink from the blood surging through his veins. He opened his mouth, licked his lips lasciviously and took another step. He looked at Andy's crotch and must have noticed that as the scenery grew and swelled so did Andy. Andy felt the painful tightening in his pants, heard a familiar cackle in the distance, then saw in the now brilliant blue sky behind Richard, a flying broomstick trailing black smoke and spelling out, **"Surrender, Andy."**

"Yes!" he breathed, "I want to. Anything to end this tacky dream, but ...." But nothing! A hot slap to his face knocked him into another movie entirely and back to black and white. Richard was gone and before him, so close he could feel her breath on his face and smell the tobacco mixed with her Evening In Paris perfume, stood Joan Crawford. In her heels she was as tall as Andy, padded shoulders draped with a dark fur coat. She was even more terrifying than Richard, if that were possible. He saw her silhouetted against darker shadows, simply but exquisitely lit with a band of light across her eyes. Grim, disgusted, repulsed, she twitched and quivered, barely controlling her smoldering anger, her large eyes moist with the pain of her betrayal. He could feel that her fury was about to explode.

Apparently Andy was now Ann Blyth to Joan's Mildred Pierce and she spewed all of her pent-up, bilious rage at him in one line, "Veda, you little SLUT." It was a knockout delivery of a knockout line. Literally. He both saw and heard the slap coming again, but this time the sound of the crack, and the stars he saw from the blow, became the bridge to another scene.

The cartoon stars disappeared as he shook his head to clear it and discovered he was sitting with one of his idols, the late, great female impressionist, Craig Russell. Backstage after a performance, Craig sat at his dressing table, clothed in a silk kimono, his stage make-up intact, brushing his real hair, with several moist wigs sitting on stands on the vanity before him. Andy sat beside him and listened to his sisterly advice. They looked at each other in the mirror. "Of course you're crazy," he told Andy. "We're all crazy in this crazy world. The key is to accept it, embrace it, work with it. Go on. Just say it. 'We're mad.' Say it with me, say it like Tallulah, 'We're maaad, dahling! Maaad! Do you hear me, maad!' No, no, shake your head more. And give it more vibrato. Deeper. Say it from down here, from the gut. 'Maaad!' 'Maaad!'"

Andy woke himself up saying it out loud, in his deepest, most resonant Tallulah Bankhead voice, "Maaad, darling, maaad! Maaad!" It was still very dark outside. He looked at the clock. It was 4:55, pre-dawn, just about time for him to get up anyway. He rolled over, turned off the alarm, rolled back and took a moment to wake up while he lingered in the warmth of his bed.

He stretched and yawned. He didn't want to open his eyes. He didn't want to get up. Then he said it again, "Maaad! Maaad! Maaad!"

As tired, angry and defeated as he felt, he couldn't help but smile at himself when he thought, "I sound like some kind of goofy, homosexual ram … having an anxiety attack."

The Coffee A-Go-Go that Andy managed was a storefront, wedged between a bank and a Pottery Barn, in the Financial District across from the Embarcadero Center. The shop space itself was a high-ceilinged ten by fifteen feet, decorated in Semiotic Italian Post-Modern Chic, a term that Andy felt sure he had made up. There was a combination office, prep and pantry area in back connected to the front by double doors and a service window.

Out front, two cash registers flanked a ten foot long counter that topped a display case for the food. The customers liked to wash down food with their lattes, espressos, and cappuccinos, almost as much as they liked the drinks themselves. It was a proven marketing ploy and Coffee A-Go-Go served some of the best coffee-bar food in the City. For the breakfast crowd, cakes, nut breads, cookies, scones, muffins and assorted pastries would fill the case. Later, for the lunch bunch, panini sandwiches, pasta and green salads, kept in their own refrigerated case, would be added to the fare. Most of the coffee and food was carryout and the space was designed for just that. There was room for only a few patrons to sip and munch while sitting on stools that stood along the chest-high counter shelves on either side of the door.

But in the morning most people were on their way to work and not interested in eating there. In the morning it was much too crowded for that. By 6:45 there would be eight servers behind the counter (nine, counting Andy), and a line of well-dressed caffeine addicts would be stretched out the door.

According to the posted hours, the shop opened Monday through Friday at 6:30 a.m. (closed on Saturday and Sunday). Andy couldn't rely on public transportation to get him to work that early so he always took a taxi. When it rounded the corner of Battery and Sacramento at 6:10, he smiled to see his trusted cohort, Skyler Bluestone, already rolling up the protective aluminum grating that covered the glass facade. The former preppy, now turned gay punk, could really fill out a white dress shirt and a pair of jeans. He was very easy on the eyes and Andy always enjoyed the view when Sky was around.

As the cab took off and the awnings were cranked down, Sky said, "Hi," in his usual flat delivery. But Andy knew his friend well enough to hear the concern in that one word even before Sky added, "So where the hell have you been?"

"Good morning. Thank you very much. It's good to see you, too," he playfully mocked Sky's insistence on getting right to the point. Andy kissed him on the cheek and they went inside together. Ordinarily they went straight to work making the first urns of coffee, but today, they paused as Sky caught Andy's arm, stopped him and turned him around so he could give him a firm embrace. Andy melted a little in the warmth of that hug.

"I really missed you, man. You kind of scared the crap out of me for awhile there, you know that?" He held on until Andy gently pulled himself away.

"I know. I know I did. Sorry."

"Are you alright? You look like hell."

"Oh, great, complimentary insults. Or do I have to pay? Thanks again for your concern but, I'm okay. I just had a restless night."

"So tell me about it. About your mysterious disappearance. Tell me about what happened to you last – when was it? – Tuesday night? And make it snappy, the crew will be here in fifteen."

"Yeah, okay, I will, but we need to get set up."

Talking as they got the place ready was their routine. Sharing the calm before the coming onslaught was a favorite time for both of them. They had separate chores in separate parts of the store so they usually had to speak up to share their banter. Sky started the coffee while Andy prepped the cash registers and the countertops. Sky unloaded and arranged the boxes of scones and muffins delivered earlier that morning. It took a few minutes for both of them to get things going, and Andy, pretending to be focused on his tasks, was not forthcoming. But he did ask Sky how Carlos was.

Sky groaned. "Yeah, well he turned out to be married. To a woman."

"Ouch! Sorry, babe. How'd you find out?"

"He let me drop him off at his house and his wife was waiting up for him. And she was really agitated. I never even got out of the car, let alone in the door. She was screaming at him – and at me – in Spanish and crying and all that ugly scene stuff that is so not how I like to end a date."

"So what happened?"

"He sweet talked her out of it; eventually she calmed down. Apparently she falls for it every time. It wouldn't work on me though." He was thoughtful for a moment then went on with, "You know, I forget there's this whole category of straight guys who think cheating with a guy isn't cheating. That is so perverted. But let's change the subject before I say something politically incorrect and ethnically biased and go off on the whole macho part of Hispanic culture."

"Oops, close callpre. But, hey, for what it's worth, I'm really sorry."

"Well, it was only our second date. As if it hurt much. Anyway, that's all there is to tell about it, so let's change the subject."

There was a short pause while Sky stared at Andy from the back room through the service window and waited for him to explain what had happened to him over the past two days. Andy appeared not to notice and since he was still not forthcoming, Sky piped up with a more blatant cue.

"Okay, Andrew, dude, enough stalling. So like what's your story?" he asked loudly from the work area.

"As far as Feltscher and the rest are concerned, I got up in the middle of the night, fell and knocked myself unconscious. I took myself to the hospital and when I got home I took a nap and forgot to phone in."

"Very good, very nice. Sounds reasonable. But what are you gonna do about a doctor's slip?"

Andy pulled Dr. Dave's note out of his pocket and waved it so Sky would see it from the back of the shop. "Got it covered. From Richard's friend, Dr. Forsyth."

"Dr. Dreamboat? Cool."

"Also, I predict that, because I may have received a mild concussion from my fall and am currently still suffering from a recurring headache, this headache will in fact recur at 10:45 this morning and I will be forced to leave work today by 11:00."

"Do you have a headache?"

"No, not now, but I had a whopper for about twelve hours. I'm taking off and meeting Sarah for lunch."

"Got it. Okay. So if you weren't at the hospital or taking a nap when I called you like fourteen times, what really happened?

This time it was only marginally easier for Andy to jump into the story. He prepped himself silently in his mind and on the count of three he began, "I was taken aboard a flying saucer and given a message for the people of Earth from extraterrestrials. Ten hours later I was let off on the slopes of Mount Shasta in northern California, where Richard had been told to pick me up." He winced, waiting for the bomb to blow up in Sky's head, praying there would be no flack, no fallout and no permanent damage.

Without missing a beat, Sky replied loudly, "I figured it was something like that. Did you bring back any proof?"

Andy sighed his relief. Sky always took him seriously. Crush or no crush, Sky consistently believed him, ... well, at least more than Richard did. He had to smile at the guy's nonchalance, his genuinely uninvolved cool. He wasn't messing with Andy. Although he was gradually catching on to camp, Sky had maybe two ironic bones in his body. What he said, he meant. Sky's honest, trusting and generous response encouraged Andy. He felt he could level with him.

"Yeah, but they took it back already."

"Really? I was thinking they probably inserted a microchip homing device or something but why would they take it back so soon?"

"It wasn't a microchip. Nothing – I repeat, nothing – was inserted. It was a T- shirt they took back."

"Why would they want that back?"

"Something about being against the laws of inter-dimensional interaction, I think. I'm not sure. Maybe they don't want me to be able to prove it. Maybe I have to find my own way of proving it. I'm sure I don't know."

"So how are they going to be able to track you? How are they going to be able to find you again?"

"Oh, don't worry about that. They are never very far away."

"Really? Did they give you some sort of special powers, like, can you see them when we can't?"

"I hadn't thought of that before, but in a way, you may be right. I feel like all my senses have been fine-tuned up a notch. Do you realize that last night, for the first time – at least that I'm aware of – I had an out-of-body experience?"

"Oh, man! Why doesn't that sort of stuff ever happen to me?"

"Maybe because you are such a little hedonist," Andy teased.

"Yeah, well, what can I say? When you're hot, you're hot. Besides, I am "just a material girl living in a material world." So you astrally projected? How cool was that?"

"Not as cool as you think."

"Don't be modest. Did you, like, hover over your bed? Could you see yourself down on the bed?"

Andy didn't want to get into that part of it and, fortunately, he didn't have to. The confidential part of their conversation was now over. The first two members of today's morning shift, Chrissy and Nicole, walked in the door. They carried in with them two more large, awkward boxes of fresh-baked breakfast pastries dropped off outside the door just minutes before. Dressed in the required jeans or khakis with white shirt and tie, they exchanged greetings and asked if Andy was feeling better before going into the back to get their aprons and sign in.

Sky came over to Andy to ask in a secretive whisper, "We have got to get together later outside of work to talk about this."

"Sure. When? Tonight?"

"I was thinking more like right after work. I'm heading to Bolinas tonight for the weekend. Lance said I could use his place. He's going to the Russian River until Sunday night. I was going to take Carlos along but he's obviously history. So I'm just going to chill out by myself. I don't suppose you could tear yourself away from your old man long enough to spend the weekend with me in Marin, could you?"

Andy loved Bolinas, the little hippy town on the coast that time forgot, but he interpreted the invitation in a highly charged sexual way, and it surprised him. Sky's invitation may have been completely innocent but Andy's reaction to it hadn't been. This had him flummoxed so Andy stammered, "Oh, geez, I don't know, I mean, yes, that would be nice, that would be great, but. ...."

"Not even for one night? I'll bring you back to the City tomorrow if that's what you want."

"Sky, Richard and I ...."

286

"Alright, alright. If he wants to come too, I guess he can. As long as he doesn't stay the whole weekend and you and I get some time to ourselves."

"No. No, that's not it. Well, it is it, I guess, but you don't understand ...."

Both disappointed and disgusted, Sky shook his head and frowned at Andy. "Man! You are so whipped. You know that?"

"Don't start with me! And what is that on your neck, another hickey? Is that a Carlos hickey?"

"No! That's a lonely little Eugene-from-Stanford-at-the-bar-last-night hickey."

"Veda, you little slut, go put your tie on. And put a band aid on that thing."

They were once again interrupted by two more arriving crew members, Domingo and Sherry, who did what Nicole and Chrissy had done and asked if Andy was feeling better before getting their aprons. They were immediately followed first by George, then Akira and the first two customers, who in turn were followed by three more customers. Chrissy and Nicole stationed themselves at one cash register and began service. Tina, the last crew member to arrive, scurried in behind customers six through ten. The rush was on and Andy and Sky would have to finish their conversation later.

It had been a restless and mostly sleepless night on Telegraph Hill too. About the time Andy and Sky were opening Coffee A-Go-Go, Richard was waking up to an empty bed. Groggy from a total of three hours of sleep, he knew something was wrong. The bed hadn't been empty when he dozed off. "Where is he? What happened to him? Did he freak out and split? Damn these skittish first-timers!" He pulled on his Calvins, threw back the covers, grabbed his robe and got up to go looking for his overnight guest. He scuffed into the bathroom to relieve himself and while he stood over the bowl, concluded the guy wasn't in the bathroom. "Better check the rest of the house. But first some coffee."

Richard was headed straight for the kitchen when Travis came inside through the sliding doors to the deck. He was wearing a pair of Richard's gym shorts and one of his Bay To Breakers 10K race sweatshirts. He was wearing his own sneakers without socks, the laces tucked inside, but shucked them as he spoke.

"Good morning. Great deck! Great view too. I hope you don't mind, I turned off the alarm system so I could take a walk."

Richard frowned. He wasn't quite sure how he felt about that. He squinted at Travis questioningly, "Did you now? How, may I ask did you know...."

"Oh, it's police stuff I learned. Don't worry, though. I didn't see anything suspicious out there. Here, I'll turn it back on." He did so and resumed his conversation. "I didn't realize the hillside was one big garden. I walked down those wooden stairs and back and then up to the tower. What's its name?"

"Coit Tower."

"Right. I really like your house and this hill. What's it called?"

"Telegraph Hill."

"Right. This is a great place, isn't it?"

"Yeah. I like it. Do you want some coffee?"

"Oh, yeah! That would be great!" Richard filled the coffee-maker reservoir with enough water for six cups.

"It's damp outside. Did you hear it rain last night? I didn't."

"No, that's from the fog."

"Really? That's great! I like the cool, damp air. It gets so dry and hot up north. I like this weather. Is it like this all the time or are you having a cool spell?"

"No, this is pretty typical."

"Well, it's great! I love it!"

Richard wished he would tone down the exuberance just a bit. What was that T-shirt Andy wore sometimes, **"Thank you for not being perky"**? The big kid enthusiasm with the bass baritone voice was something he was just not ready for this early in the morning. He put in the last scoop of coffee and pushed the 'on' button. "It'll be ready shortly. It just takes a minute to brew."

He got down two mugs, set them on the kitchen counter, then walked into the living room. He sat down in his easy chair, leaned back, crossed his legs, and carefully pulled the hem of his robe over his exposed knees and thighs. The last thing he wanted to be this morning was seductive. Travis stood with his back to the outside deck and its 'great view,' his legs slightly apart, his hands gripping each other behind his back in the pose known in the military as 'at ease.' Except he was anything but. He kept shifting his weight from one bare foot to the other, then lifting his weight up and down on the balls of his feet. He eyed Richard's gesture of modesty, then smiled nervously, when he noticed Richard was looking at him as he looked at Richard's legs.

"Why don't you sit down, Travis, you're making me nervous again."

"Oh! Sorry. Okay." He sat on the far end of the sofa, Andy's spot again.

"It's really foggy over the Bay. I could barely see Alcatraz. That is Alcatraz, isn't it? Over there. That way." He pointed in the proper direction and Richard nodded.

"Sorry but I've only been to San Francisco once before. It was with my folks. I was about six. I don't remember it very well. To be honest, I don't remember a thing."

"Well, I had never been up in your neck of the woods until Wednesday. So we're kind of even, don't you think?"

Travis smiled the shy smile again, showing off his dimples. "Damn!" Richard thought, "I'm just trying to be nice and he laps it up like a love-starved puppy." The puppy sat on the edge of the seat smiling awkwardly at Richard, and eyeing the end of the sofa nearest to his host.

After a minute of uncomfortable silence, Richard said, "Sorry, but I'm not much for conversation in the morning until I've had my coffee."

"That's alright, I understand."

The coffee maker sputtered and sighed, signaling the end of the process. Glad to hear it, Richard immediately stood and headed back to the kitchen. "Come with me and fix your coffee, I don't know what you take."

Like a coiled spring, Travis leapt into action and tailed him, as though he was afraid of being left behind. In the kitchen he stood very close to Richard, watching his every move with a deep, outlandish sincerity. Richard filled the two mugs with the dark, steaming brew, opened the refrigerator, took out a carton of half and half, smelled it to see if it was still good, and added some to his mug. "Want some?"

"Yes, thank you. With a couple of spoons of sugar, if you don't mind." Richard rummaged in a cabinet, got out a sugar bowl and another spoon and set them on the countertop next to the Half-and-Half. "Help yourself," he said and took his coffee back with him to the living room.

Travis came back with his coffee and sat down again, this time on the end of the sofa nearest to Richard. They sipped in silence for a minute. For the moment, Richard ignored Travis's move to get closer and savored his morning elixir. It worked fast. He was feeling better, more clear-headed.

"Good coffee," Travis offered.

"Thanks," he replied. He sipped some more. There was more silence. He caught Travis looking at him again, longingly. He decided it was time to clear the air.

"Travis, I think we need to talk about last night."

"Okay. So do you think those phone calls were from the weird guys in black or from the Air Force?"

Though he was obviously being evasive, he referred to the still pertinent fact that, three times during the course of the night, phone calls had awakened them both. Richard had felt compelled to answer them because his message recording tape still had not been replaced. And this morning he made himself a mental note to call Phyllis today and have her get another one for him. If, that is, she was still working for him.

290

"It's pretty hard to tell from static and breathing."

"You should really get caller ID."

"Maybe so, but that's not what I want to talk about."

"Yeah, I know. You mean about sleeping together don't you? It's alright. I understand. You were just being nice to me."

"It was more than that. I mean it was worse than that. I was being selfish, too. I want to apologize for letting things go a little too far."

"No, don't apologize for that. Please. I'm the one that should apologize to you. I know what a lousy lay I was. I'm sorry. But honest to God, it was my first time, with a man, and I wanted to be with somebody – I mean I wanted to be with YOU – because of all the, you know, but I just, I really didn't know what to do, because I wanted you and I wanted you to teach me and, but the phone rang and spooked us and, I couldn't relax and, well, hell! At least it was safe. It was safe, wasn't it?"

Richard silently cursed him for making this so difficult. What do you do with a man so unspoiled? How do you tell him, "Look, I think you are incredibly handsome, naive, and sweet, but I can't be what you need me to be." How do you tell him you only wanted to screw him because he is incredibly handsome, naive and sweet, and he made himself available to you? How do you tell him you took him to bed to prove something to yourself, then changed your mind at the last minute when the phone rang and you thought it was your lover.

"Oh, yes. It was safe, alright. Very, VERY safe."

Travis nodded. There was more coffee sipping. The air did not yet seem particularly clear to Richard. He sat across from temptation and it didn't seem to be planning on leaving any time soon. Was it time to start dropping hints already? But no, the guy was too vulnerable right now. Maybe after breakfast. Richard drained his mug and put it on the end table. He stood up and announced, "I'm going to take a shower."

"May I take one too?"

"Yes, of course."

"I mean right now, with you."

"No! Listen Travis, you do remember that guy who was with me in the car at Mount Shasta, don't you?"

"Yes, of course, I do. Although you never told me why he wasn't wearing any pants. But that's when I knew you were probably, you know, gay. Or hoped you were."

"Oh, for ... ! Never mind that. His name is Andy and he is my "buddy," my "significant other," my "lover," the guy I would marry if it were legal to do that. Do you understand?" Richard watched the subtle play on Travis's open-mouthed, attentive face, registering in rapid succession, recognition, disbelief, hurt, a little disgust and disbelief again.

"Then why did you let me ... ?"

"I'm sorry. I truly am. I had a moment of weakness last night. That's all. That's all it was. I didn't want to be alone either. You needed a place to stay. You're a very attractive guy. And I told you I was selfish. What more can I say? I hope you can forgive me."

Travis blushed. Then, a by now familiar look of panic animated his face and he put down his mug, popped up from his seat and took off for the front door saying, "I guess I really better go then."

Richard nonchalantly stuck out his arm and caught him as he tried to rush past. He offered no resistance whatsoever and stopped abruptly at the touch of Richard's hand on his shoulder. Then he looked at Richard with precisely the needy look of desire Richard didn't want to see. For a second Richard was afraid Travis was going to try to hug him, or, even worse, kiss him. He put his other hand on Travis's other shoulder and, with both hands, held him firmly at arm's length.

"Now relax, would you please? You're not running out of here like that. Besides you're wearing my clothes. Why are you wearing my clothes?"

"Oh, yeah. I don't know. I just wanted to."

"Well never mind that. Where are you going to go, anyway? Back to your empty cabin in the woods?"

"I don't know that either. I don't really want to go back there. Not yet."

"Then you might as well stay here, at least until you know what you want to do next. Don't worry, I'll find you a place to stay here in the City. But remember, we're not fooling around any more, okay? You got that?"

"Okay. I got it. I don't want it but I got it."

"I'm afraid that could pretty well describe the situation for all of us. Now sit down, have some more coffee, and after we get cleaned up, we'll go get some breakfast."

Richard retrieved his own mug and took it to the kitchen sink. While he rinsed it and put it in the dishwasher, Travis obediently sat back down, clicked on the TV and got the local news.

"And elsewhere in California, tragedy struck our sister station in Redding when its NewsCopter crashed killing everyone on board, including reporter and weekend anchor, Paula Perez. Eyewitnesses said the copter seemed to disintegrate in midair shortly after take off from the station at 7:39 p.m. last night. There were no fatalities on the ground. The cause has yet to be determined but officials are looking into the possibilities of either mechanical malfunction or pilot error. The crew was on the way to cover a report of an alleged carjacking on Interstate 5. Tragically, that report turned out to be false. Next up, a look at today's weather forecast following this message. Stay tuned."

As Richard came back through on his way to the bathroom, he was just in time to hear Travis's exclamation, "Holy sh ... ! I don't believe this!"

"What? What is it?"

"Remember that television crew up at Shasta? Well, they just killed 'em off in a fake helicopter accident." Travis clicked off the TV.

"WHAT? You're kidding!"

"No, sir, I am not kidding. You think that's a coincidence? I don't."

"Did they report on the UFOs? I mean, did it make the news up there in Redding?"

"No, it didn't. There was not one word about it on TV or on the radio or in the papers."

"Well, that's not one-hundred percent true. While driving up there I was listening to a call-in show on the radio and people were talking about the lights they saw as it was happening."

"That may be but there was no other coverage. At least I never ran across any. And I looked for it."

"Incredible! So all of sudden nobody saw anything? That's impossible! Who the hell's conspiracy is this? You saw 'em, didn't you?"

"Sure did."

"We aren't crazy, are we?"

"No, sir, we are NOT crazy."

Something moved outside. Both men noticed it. Both men snapped their heads a quarter turn to look out to the deck. The light was changing. The sun was shining through patches of blowing fog. The rose bushes, the giant begonias, the ornamental pear trees, swished and shook in a gust of breeze. They looked at each other without speaking, a little too spooked to mention it. It was Travis who had to break the silence and offer the reassurance they were not crazy. "Only a shadow."

Richard felt compelled to agree even if he didn't quite believe it either. He nodded and said, "Right. Just a shadow."

It was way too quiet but neither of them knew what to say or do next. So they both jumped when the phone rang and pretended they hadn't. Richard covered up his jump by using it to propel himself to the phone where he snatched the handset from the cradle and angrily snapped, "Hello!" He shocked his caller who immediately went on the defensive, "Well, I'm terribly sorry to bother you this early, Mr. Lang, but ..."

"Phyllis?"

"Yes, but I just ..."

"Holy Mother of ... ! Phyllis, you just scared the ... Well what is it?"

"I said I'm sorry, but I just wanted to catch you at home to get the model number of your answering machine. See I thought if ..."

"Hold on, hold on, I'll look."

" ... if I could catch you early enough I could stop on my way to work and get a tape for it and give it to you at work so you'd have it and you could get messages again on your machine at home. Hello? Mr. Lang?"

"Yes, yes, thank you. Here it is." He rattled off the manufacturer's name and the model number so quickly that he had to repeat it for her. But his annoyance fell away and he found himself adopting the tone he had used with her yesterday afternoon. "Oh, and, Phyllis, while I have you on the phone, I have some business to attend to with an out-of-town client so I don't know when I'll be coming into the office today. Can you handle things for me?"

"Yes, of course, I can, you know I can." was her tight-lipped reply.

"Good. Then does this mean you have decided to keep your job with All The Best Realty?"

"I will be in the office today at 9:00 a.m. with your replacement tape, Mr. Lang. Which you may pick up there at your convenience. I will 'handle things' for you today, Mr. Lang, as I always do, but as for the future of my employment with All The Best Realty, I cannot honestly say that I have made up my mind one way or the other."

"Uh-huh. I don't think I need to remind you that I gave you until today to make that decision. So I know you will either tell me or leave written notification for me by the end of the day, won't you?"

"If you insist, then yes, I will."

"And I do insist, so thank you in advance."

Too mad to say anything, Phyllis kept her mouth shut, but Richard felt the heat in her roiling, toxic silence. This was not the way he wanted to see her go either. He didn't want to have to fire her outright.

"Phyllis, I want you to know that, if you can abide by the conditions we talked about yesterday, then I really do want you to stay."

The silence continued. Richard thought he noticed a change in it, a softening perhaps. Maybe it was less roiling and more throbbing. He couldn't be sure. "Just so we're clear on that," he added. He waited.

She finally responded with an unreadable, "Yes. I believe we understand each other."

"I hope so. Now if you'll excuse me. Thank you and good-bye."

"Good-bye."

Travis was staring at Richard. He didn't have a clue what was going on. He was too polite to ask.

"That was my office manager. We are trying to reach an understanding."

Travis nodded as though he understood but he really didn't and he wasn't sure he wanted to.

SEVENTEEN

Andy could tell you the time of day by the ebb and flow of the customers encountered at Coffee A Go-Go. In the morning it was tied to the times people were due at work. Customer surges happened on the half hour from 6:30 until 9:00. Then, like late students who should have been in class five minutes ago, the last wave of office workers scattered and disappeared into their high-rise 'classrooms.' The streets of the Financial District were magically empty by 9:05. The next mini rush would be around 10:00 as 'first period' ended for some and the coffee and cigarette breaks began. So at 9:10, with the lines gone, Andy granted Chrissy, George, Domingo and Nicole the first morning break, with the next break for Sherry, Akira, Tina and Sky to follow at 9:30.

Andy was an attentive, hands-on manager. Not much ever got by him, so he noticed that the crew was really on top of things today. Today there had been only two major spills: one by a customer, and one by a worker. Both spills had been attended to quickly and efficiently and the lines kept moving without interruption. Miraculously, both spills had somehow missed splashing on any customers. Thankfully, no one (or their clothes) had been harmed in the dispensing of caffeine on this particular morning.

Neither had any of his crew been mistreated, nor themselves baited into abusive behavior this morning. The customers had been extraordinarily well-behaved. Some of the high-powered 'suits' they usually served didn't need any caffeine. Men or women, they were often so stressed out or gym-pumped

297

before they ever got to work that they came in with a chip on their shoulder. And on Friday mornings especially, with everybody jockeying to meet deadlines and get out of the office early to start the weekend, things had been known to get ugly. In fact, by this time of the morning it was not unusual for Andy to have witnessed or mediated five or six examples of coffee-consumer rage. Today there had been only five or six frowny faces and not one threat of a lawsuit.

Sky's bicycle courier pals were also often tightly wound up when they stopped by. As they went about getting a caffeine jump-start on their adrenalin-fueled day, they could become overly aggressive, and the playful hi-jinks could turn nasty. But of all the customers, they were probably the happiest to see Friday roll around. Having already survived four days of the work week, they tended to be on their best behavior on Fridays. Like most of the other everyday customers – the occasional cop or bus driver, the retail clerks, the out-of-towners, the tourists from the nearby hotels, even the homeless folks, like their very own Flash Pan, the Natty Nutbar – the couriers were, for the most part, decent and civil. But today everybody was exceptionally nice. It was a Friday so harmonious that Andy was actually feeling glad to be back at work. If there had been any wood to knock on to keep that luck going, he would have.

Now the prolonged, frenzied waves of the early morning crush had been replaced by the abrupt tranquility of the mid-morning slump. Customers were still coming in, but they were few in number. Akira was easily handling the four who were ordering now. Tina bussed and picked up trash while Sherry wiped down all the countertops and restocked the napkins and the milk and sugar dispensers. They worked quickly, still caught up in the pace of the rush. But the noise level had abated dramatically and there was more room in the shop. The dancing around, the bouncing off or falling all over each other, had ceased. Andy fixed himself a regular, black coffee. Finally he had a moment to himself to think about something besides his crew and his customers. And what was it that his rest-deprived mind chose to ponder? He wondered what Richard was doing right now.

Oh yes, he knew they had an agreement not to contact each other. It was all his own bright idea, for cripe's sake. But that didn't give Richard the right to trick on him last night. If that is indeed what happened. Andy was shamefully willing to dismiss his out-of-body experience, to deny what he sensed was the truth, if it would cut Richard some slack and soften his own hurt feelings. He had been pretty stressed last night. It could have been a reaction to all that anxiety, part of a fever dream formed by his own pathetic insecurities. Oh, hell, who was he kidding?

Besides, whether it was or wasn't true, he was longing to see Richard, to talk to him. He most definitely was missing getting his 9:15 check-in call. This temporary separation thing was even tougher than he'd thought it might be. He didn't want to admit it but he was feeling needy and he hated that feeling. He knew the neediness was his ego talking. He'd been too preoccupied to notice he had an ego lately, so where the hell had 'he,' his ego, come back from? He thought they – he and his ego – had an arrangement, as in, "I'll take care of the whole of me and you quit bossing me around." But 'he' never seemed to go far away for long and now 'he' was back. And ego demands could only lead to more heartache. Still, it was better to embrace his ego than to deny it.

He, the whole of Andy, was mad at Richard and mad at himself. He was mad at Richard for making him mad at himself. And it upset him even further to think that, now that he had 'his space,' he wasn't so sure he wanted it. He was even mad at himself for not knowing what he wanted. Maybe he didn't know what he wanted, but he knew he didn't want to think about it right now. He wasn't a complete idiot, not yet. He could see that he was setting himself up again, just like last night. He didn't want to dissect any more dilemmas. He was much too tired. What he wanted was a break. He just wanted to sit on this stool in the morning sunshine and sip his coffee and watch Sky hose down the sidewalk outside.

And as he watched the waves of spray from the nozzle rhythmically sweeping the cement, he grew sleepy. Eyes wide open, he nevertheless blanked out for a second. He came out of it when he sensed he was being stared at. He looked up and down the street not sure what he was looking for. In the bustle of car and foot traffic he was drawn to what wasn't moving. Across the street was a tall, thin figure in a long, gray trench coat. The skinny guy wore a navy blue watch cap stretched down over his ears. Andy snapped to attention. It wasn't a guy, it was one of them. He stood up and rapped violently on the window to get Sky's attention.

"Sky! Look! Do you see that guy across the street? That tall guy, over there?" he shouted and pointed with an urgency that startled Sky. But it was to no avail because Sky couldn't see. He couldn't see the guy because, when Andy looked again, the guy wasn't there. Sky frowned at Andy and mouthed the words, "What guy?"

"Never mind."

Andy shrugged, smiled sheepishly and sat back down. Sky turned off the water and started winding up the hose. Andy settled back on his stool and into his disturbed thoughts. "Wow," he wondered, "Am I losing it or what?"

"Mr. Gage? There's a call for you."

"Oh! Okay. Thanks, Akira. I'll be right there."

Surprised by Akira's announcement, the first thought that came to him was, "Is it Richard? Did he called me anyway?"

On his way to the back of the shop he wondered what tone he should take with him. "Should I confront him or pretend like nothing is wrong?" He took a determined breath as he pushed through the swinging door to the back of the shop, and decided to wing it. He put his coffee down, composed himself, and picked up the receiver.

"Hello?"

"You tell last night. You tell this morning. Not smart. Very bad."

"Go to hell!" He slammed down the phone just as Sky appeared in the back room doorway. Sky took it in without saying anything. Their eyes met and Andy knew he'd been both seen and overheard. Sky's blank look assumed nothing, except maybe that he expected to be let in on the phone scene. He carefully let the swinging door close behind him, advanced a few steps then stopped and folded his arms over his chest.

"Telemarketers," was how Andy answered the patiently waiting look on his friend's face. His friend didn't really believe he would yell like that at a telemarketer. His friend's face just kept staring at him. But Andy refused to be stared down. "Man, I really hate them, don't you?" he added.

Neither was Sky about to back down. He stood firm. Andy offered nothing more. Finally Sky raised an eyebrow then shook his head and sighed.

"Hey," Andy challenged, "Don't look at me in that tone of voice."

"I know, but, telemarketers? As if. I thought it was your old man on the phone. He usually calls by now. He's late. What's going on between you two? Doesn't he want you to go to Bolinas with me?"

Andy steadied himself with one hand on the countertop and sank slowly onto a stool. "I haven't talked to him yet. In fact, I probably won't talk to him at all today." Sky said nothing, waiting patiently for the rest of the story. "It's okay, we're just taking a break from each other." Sky listened, and nodded, expecting more. He refolded his arms and shifted his weight onto his other hip, and waited. Andy raised his voice. "It's okay!" he barked dismissively.

Sky gave up. He nodded again, muttered, "Yeah, right," then turned and walked away. He punched open the door to the front of the shop, walked through it and shoved it back behind him as if he could slam it, leaving it swinging back and forth, sweeping the empty air, a fitting punctuation to his disgusted exit.

Andy groaned "Oh, man!" and covered his eyes with one hand. Things had been going so well this morning. But now that had flip-flopped too. Here he was basically lying to his friend, keeping him at arm's length, pushing him away. First Richard, now Sky.

He needed to talk to Sarah. He knew he could talk to her. He needed to unburden himself and she was going to hear the whole damned thing. He hoped she was ready for him. Maybe he should leave work now, take a long walk over to the bookstore where he was to meet her, and try to get back to his centered self. A walk always made him feel better. He certainly didn't need to stay here. The crew would do fine without him. He could just leave his note for Feltscher to pick up. He didn't need to give it to him in person. Besides, he didn't really feel like confronting that jerk anyway.

"You don't look sick to me."

Too late. Feltscher, the jerk, had oozed into the back room, arriving quietly as if hoping to catch Andy doing something illicit. The twenty-five year-old with the curly brown hair, his little pug nose perpetually stuck up, stared down at Andy, while sucking on a toothpick. It was a pity, everybody agreed: Feltscher would be cute if he weren't such a slime-ball. Andy, weary and defeated, looked up at him before launching his counter attack.

"Yeah? Well I am now. How are you doing, Alan? Having a prosperous middle management Friday?" Andy learned a long time ago, with Feltscher you had to meet cocky with cocky. It was the equivalent of dealing with certain queens where you have to meet bitchy with bitchy. He hated it. It was tedious. He could stand it for about five minutes.

Feltscher smirked, "You could say that. I have five more Coffees to hit before noon, but yeah. Not bad for a Friday. You got everything under control here?"

"I'd say so. Except for this pain in ... "

"Your butt?"

"I was going to say 'my head.' The pain in my butt is standing right here in front of me."

"You wish."

"No, I don't really, but sometimes I'd swear you wish. I've caught you looking at my ass before. Not to mention Nicoles's, Sherry's, George's, Chrissy's, and Sky's."

With anyone else, that would have been insubordination. Feltscher seemed to take it as a compliment. Even worse, he seemed to take it as a competition. He took the toothpick out of his mouth to snort and leer at Andy. Then he said, "Ooh, that's right, that Sky is a humpy little piece, isn't he? And I bet it makes you crazy with jealousy when I give him the once over, doesn't it?"

Worn down before his five minutes of tolerance were up, Andy couldn't help himself. He snapped. He stood up and let go loudly and furiously with, "You want to know what makes me crazy? Huh, Feltscher? I'll tell you what makes me crazy!" He sounded to himself like he was shrieking and it wasn't pretty. It was the rise Feltscher had been trying to get out of him all along. He was about to go off on his boss, really read his beads, but no, something told him to back off. He abruptly stopped it.

Feltscher, however, moved in for the face off, "Yeah. I wanna know. So? Why don't you tell me? What makes you crazy, Gage, huh? What? What is it?"

No words formed in Andy's head but his instinct took control and he literally separated himself from the situation. He took a step back and forced himself to grin at Feltscher through gritted teeth. And inside himself, he figuratively did the same thing. He took a cleansing breath. He watched as he saw, fleetingly, a phantom figure, in the form of a grotesque little gnome, separate itself from his body and disappear as it stomped angrily away from the confrontation. It must have been in Andy's head because Feltscher didn't seem to notice; he just continued smirking at Andy. It should have surprised Andy to encounter that phantom from a dual reality at work, in his waking world, but it barely registered on him. What surprised him was getting the perfect answer to his belligerent boss's goading and how easily it tumbled out of his mouth without stumbling over his grin. "Tyranny makes me crazy, Alan. Tyranny. Haven't a clue? Look it up."

Andy pulled out his slip from Dr. Dave and thrust it in Feltscher's bewildered face. "I believe this is all you're really looking for."

Feltscher looked at the slip, then plucked it gingerly from Andy's fist, to which Andy replied, "You're welcome."

Sherry poked through the door and announced, "Mr. Gage, there's somebody here to see you."

Elated at his own handling of Feltscher's harassment, Andy excused himself and started to follow Sherry back to the front of the store. Brimming over with pride and newfound self-confidence, he pushed the door part way open, before his boss, in a rush to get out of the shop, barged past. He nearly smacked Andy, barely missing him with the swinging door. Andy caught it, nonchalantly pushed it back the other way and stepped forward into the front of the shop. He wasn't at all prepared for who had come to see him. His only warning clue was the curious look he saw on Sky's face. He stopped and let the door swing back behind him when he saw who was waiting.

"I know, I know. I said I wouldn't call. But I never said I wouldn't stop by for coffee." Richard smiled at him from over the counter. He could see the surprise on Andy's face and he rushed on while he still had that advantage. "Believe me I wouldn't bother you like this, but I just heard some news that I thought you should know about."

Andy seemed more than surprised. In fact, he was stunned to the point of muteness. This time his instinct told him to say as little as possible. Even if he'd wanted to, he couldn't have said anything. He didn't know why, but he had never felt so self-possessed before in the midst of so much emotional turmoil. When he just stood there, blinking, wide-eyed, not saying anything, Richard grew very concerned. Andy seemed to be looking right through him and it was unnerving. Richard asked, "Are you alright?"

He was actually looking around Richard at the stocky, blond man standing behind him. Seeing the man was shocking too, but at the same time Andy felt so detached, yet so present, that he had no choice but to go with it. The last time he had been so calmly but vibrantly 'in the moment' was on the pyramid. He was present on several levels at once. He remembered how wonderful that had felt. And now it was happening again. It took Andy a moment, but he recovered from the realization nicely.

"Yes. I'm doing alright. Is that the man you slept with last night?"

It was as though Richard subtly had the wind knocked out of him. His gasp was almost silent. His unbelieving eyes widened then blinked furiously. He tried to speak but could only cough up one syllable, "Wha'?" He was acutely aware there were others nearby, other customers in the shop and they were being served by Sherry and Tina. And there was the Kid, too. Right next to them! He was too mortified to notice that everyone seemed oblivious to the drama going on beside them, the drama between him and Andy. Everyone that is except the Kid, Sky. He also froze. Andy looked at the blond man. He had to admire his youthful masculinity. Sky looked at the blond man too. He did his own admiring, then back to Andy.

Andy reached his hand over the counter and addressed himself to the stranger, "Hi. I'm Andy."

Travis stepped forward and introduced himself, "Hi. I'm Travis. Travis Wilson. Officer Wilson? With the California Highway Patrol. Remember? From Mount Shasta?"

"At the roadblock? I'll have to take your word for it. You were in uniform, and you wore a helmet and sunglasses."

Richard was utterly amazed. Andy was wary, but he didn't seem to be angry at all. How did he know? And why wasn't he angry? But the tension was broken, he could now cautiously put himself back into the scene and he did so by interjecting, "I know what you mean. I didn't recognize him at first myself."

"Pleased to meet you," Travis offered with a game smile.

Andy really wasn't quite sure he could say the same, but he didn't have to. Sky decided he definitely wanted to get to know this man a little better. He too reached over the counter and offered his hand, "Hi. I'm Sky. I'm the assistant manager." He didn't smile at Travis but his intense stare, which unapologetically and unashamedly announced his sexual interest, stopped just short of publicly mentally undressing him. Then he made a point of looking at Richard when he added, "and I'm a friend of Andy's too."

Being new to all this, Travis could only sense part of the multi-layered subtext of the situation. But he took Sky's hand and looked into his eyes and when he said, "Travis Wilson. It's a real pleasure," he could not have been more sincere.

Sky pulled out his own spontaneously formed agenda and went on, "I have the use of a house in Bolinas for the weekend. Andy and I were talking about going up there to chill out." Guilt free, but looking at Richard all the while, Andy hastened to insert, "I hadn't made up my mind to go." Sky continued, "Would you two like to join us?"

Richard held eye contact with Andy as he replied, "Oh, I think a little weekend getaway in Bolinas sounds very nice to me." To Sky he added, "If it's alright with Andy, then I think we would like that a lot. Wouldn't we, Travis?"

"Sure. I don't know why not. Sounds pretty good to me," he said with a bashful grin, hands behind his back, shifting his weight from one foot to the other, anxiously rocking back and forth. Even though he had never heard of Bolinas and had no idea whatsoever where it was, in his mind he was packed and halfway out the door.

Sky held eye contact with Travis and smiled seductively as he spoke, "Great, then. Sounds like we got ourselves a plan. I get off at three. Why don't we all meet at Andy's house and leave from there?"

Travis nodded as though he knew where to find Andy's house.

Andy said, "Fine with me. Whatever. Sky, you're on break now."

Sky took the hint and walked Travis down to the end of the counter while trying to sell him on the exquisite pleasures of caramel lattes. Richard kept looking at Andy who was taking obvious delight in watching the amusing 'new couple.'

"Do you know what just happened here?" he said to Richard.

"I hope you mean we just got back together."

"Oh, yeah, I guess that just happened too."

"Andy, I have so much to tell you."

"Well, then it's a good thing we have the whole weekend ahead of us, because I sure have a lot to tell you, too."

"Look, I'm going to take him to the office with me and see if I can find a place for him to stay for a couple weeks. Can you meet us for lunch?"

"Sorry, but I'm meeting Sarah for lunch. We'll talk later."

"Okay, then I'll see you at your house, say what time? About three thirty?" Andy nodded "okay." They had a date. Richard kissed his own finger tips and held them palm forward, a love benediction meant only for his partner. They were going away together for the weekend. How sweet! "Like buttah." The rollercoaster car of Andy's Friday was headed back up to the top. Even if it didn't stay there, even if the ride weren't over, all he could do was grin like an idiot.

E¡GH¡EEN

$\int$hortly after Richard pried Travis away from Sky, Andy left the coffee shop in Sky's capable hands and headed for his rendezvous with Sarah. On the way he took off his necktie, rolled it up and stuffed it in the pocket of his black leather, motorcycle jacket. He wore leather not because he had a desire to be part of the rowdy, raunchy biker brotherhood, but because, as vain and superficial as he knew it was, he loved how he looked in it. And he loved how he felt in it, like wrapping himself in maleness, or a magic cloak of invincible masculinity. With a pair of jeans and his black Doc Martin oxfords, it was the butchest gay uniform Andy felt he could pull off. But most importantly, Richard loved how he looked in it too.

And Andy loved San Francisco for having the climate that allowed him to wear leather year round. Just like today, windy and warm in the sun, cold in the shade, it was perpetual autumn here. He didn't miss Chicago's temperature-humidity index summers and wind-chill winters. Right now, right this minute, all of San Francisco was sun-soaked and Andy was in love with the City. And he was in love with Richard. Everything was going to be alright between them. He knew they could get back on track during this weekend getaway. He caught a California Street cable car and rode it up and over Nob Hill to Polk Street. Akashic Books and Tapes was a half block walk away.

The bookstore "for all things spiritual and metaphysical" had been around for a long time. It had been around long enough to have seen technology eventually force a name change from Akashic Records and Books to Akashic Books and Tapes. It would, no doubt, survive a similar reincarnation as Akashic Books and CDs. He arrived at a quarter past eleven and nodded to Edward, the pleasant looking, fiftyish, bear who was now on duty at the cash register, was familiar to Andy as one of the managers of the store. Edward smiled in recognition and nodded back. Andy stopped and took off his sunglasses. He let his eyes adjust for a moment to the dimmer, indoor lighting before he continued deeper into the vintage 1920's era store.

It was one long, high room with what appeared to be the original glass globe lighting fixtures hanging from the hammered tin ceiling. Displays and bookshelves six feet high ran down the center of the creaky, well-worn wooden floor. The walls held book shelves nine feet high, each side of the store having its own ladder on rails. All the wood was stained the color of walnut and darkened further by wax, dirt and age. There were also several locked, glass-enclosed cases and cabinets. Akashic Books and Tapes dealt in used as well as new books and in first editions and rare books as long as they had something to do with the esoteric, theosophical and metaphysical arts.

The business office was on a balcony at the back which overhung the tape and CD area and was reached by a cast iron, spiral staircase. A CD of Peruvian flute and guitar music played at a barely discernible volume. Norman, a balding but young looking forty year old man, familiar to Andy as Edward's partner, both in the bookstore and in life, was talking quietly on the telephone from the office above. There were several shoppers studying the shelves, browsing the titles or reading a particular book. None of them was Sarah, but then she wasn't inclined to be early like Andy.

He passed the community bulletin board, with its postings of AIDS services, ads for practitioners of a multitude of healing modalities, notices for free public programs given by psychics and mystics (both homegrown and imported), yoga and tai chi classes, life-enhancing herbal supplements, and a marketplace of pre-owned items, both mundane and unusual, offered for sale or wanted to buy. He glanced at one page, scripted large, with a fringe of phone numbers at the bottom, and had to admit to himself, "That's a great price for gravity boots." But he was not in need of gravity boots and headed instead for the self-help books section. Impatient to see Sarah, he found it difficult to focus on browsing. He saw nothing on the shelves relative to his specific crisis of belief anyway so he soon gave up and wandered over to the extensive UFO section. There were several hundred titles of books on UFOs and close-encounters of every kind, and he had scanned most of them during previous visits. In spite of his recent experience, he thought their titles looked even more laughingly unbelievable than ever. This was the lunatic fringe to which he must now add himself and it didn't seem so funny anymore. The street door opened and clanged the bell. Andy looked up. A shapely female was silhouetted against the bright sunlight on Polk Street.

The woman stopped still and took off her sunglasses. She folded them and placed them in the small, beaded handbag hanging from the long gold chain around her neck and over her shoulder. She wore a denim jacket appliquéd with colorful travel patches, and further decorated with hand-sewn, antique buttons, charms and rhinestones. This was worn over a turquoise, scooped-neck, French cut T-shirt whose snug fit did little to either conceal or subdue her ample bosom. Two large plastic clips were a little more successful at rounding up her explosion of blond curls. She wore several bracelets and rings and a dangly pair of amethyst crystal earrings inside another pair of hoop earrings. Tight, purple Capri pants did not make her shapely butt look fat because it wasn't and, with her gold satin, high-heeled Manolo Blahnik pumps, helped show off her gorgeous gams. Andy knew this was either Bette Midler's understudy or Sarah Fitzsimmons.

He rushed over to her and they air kissed both cheeks, laughed about it, and then gave each other their usual warm hug. "Good to see you!" she gushed, squeezing his arm and trying to keep her voice down in the library-like store.

"Yeah, likewise!" he answered back in a similarly muffled tone.

"So how's everything in outer space?"

His open face shriveled into a scowl as his index finger snapped to attention before his puckered lips and he shushed her as silently as he could.

"Oops, sorry," she said, then looked around before adding teasingly, "Any Men-In-Black in here?" She was kidding but Andy was not as he also looked around answering, "No, I don't think so, but I saw one this morning at work and they called me at work too."

"Oka-a-a-ay," she added, hesitantly. "So I guess you're still a little spooked, aren't you? I get the picture."

"I told them to go to hell. I have a feeling they might leave me alone now."

"I certainly hope so."

Changing the subject, Andy asked, "Did you want to look around here for a bit before we go to lunch?"

"Do we have time?"

"Oh, sure we do."

"Then, yes, I would like to browse. I don't get into the City much you know."

"Looking for anything special?"

"Not really. I'll leave that up to the Universe. Give me fifteen minutes."

Andy nodded and watched her walk away slowly and stealthily down the right aisle of the store. He chuckled to himself when he decided it looked more like she was stalking the books than browsing. He yawned and picked up a nearby photo book of sacred sites of the world to keep himself occupied. In the section on sacred mountains he got goose-bumps when he turned to the page on Mount Shasta. One large, full-page photo showed her majesty by day. Another smaller photo on the facing page showed the snowcapped peak lit by moonlight. All at once he became overwhelmed by so many mixed emotions that he simply had to dismiss them all and go on to the next page. But a strong feeling of wanting to go back to the mountain lingered. He flipped forward a few more pages, then flipped back for one more look at the magic mountain. It was definitely calling to him. He gave in, admitting that he probably would go back some time, then forced himself to go on and look at the rest of the book.

When he grew bored with the pretty pictures he looked for Sarah and saw her at the far end of the store. She was searching partially by reading the energy of the volumes. She held her hands over the top shelf of books in the center section and looked like she was going to play a very tall air piano. A quizzical expression fleetingly crossed her face then she looked at Andy and motioned for him to join her. "Oh, what now?" he thought, a trifle bothered. He didn't really feel like moving but he sighed and set off to see what she wanted. About twenty feet from her, a book dropped on his head, hit him squarely on the crown and flipped off onto the floor.

"Ouch!" he said very loudly, more surprised than hurt, causing everyone in the store to look at him. "I'm sorry. I didn't do that. It fell," he tried to answer their questioning, disturbed stares and be quiet at the same time. He gestured vaguely toward the ceiling, patted his head, then pointed toward the floor and noted the mixed reactions on the faces. Sarah had both eyebrows raised and her mouth open in genuine surprise. The rest of his audience was either indignantly annoyed or begrudgingly amused, mostly the former. He looked up to try to see where the book had come from. He could see no gap in the tightly packed books.

Edward, the store manager, called out softly, "Are you alright?"

Andy replied in a stage whisper, still trying not to disturb, yet loud enough for everyone to hear, "Yes, I'm alright, thank you." And to the few remaining onlookers, "Sorry. Sorry."

A highly amused Sarah came up to him and accepted his sheepish grin but

312

asked, "Aren't you going to pick it up?"

He retrieved the slim, paperback tome and turned it over. He made a face like he smelled something distasteful. Sarah watched him tilt his head and scowl skeptically at the cover. She had to ask, "May I see it?" He handed it over to her and she saw that it was a used book with the title, 'Riding the Coming Energy Waves: Earth Changes and How to Recognize Them and Work With Them Toward Personal Fulfillment.' It was by Desiado Lamour, as channeled by R.A. Hanks. It was copyrighted 1972.

"Looks interesting. Are you going to buy it?"

"I don't know. Should I?"

"Well, dear, I think it's obvious."

"Ever hear of this Desiado Lamour or R.A. Hanks?"

"No. There are lots of channels that get one book published and then are never heard from again. Doesn't mean the information isn't valid."

"Doesn't mean it is, either. But look at the copyright. It's old." He handed it to her and she turned it over to read the blurb on the back. She responded with, "Time and timing in the other realms is not particularly relevant to our conception of time as a cause and effect string of individual events happening consecutively in a line."

"Did you just make that up?"

"No, it says that right here, on the back. Look, if it doesn't speak to you on some level, don't buy it. But, Andy, it hit you on the head. I'd say there is a message for you in there somewhere."

"Okay, okay, I'll buy it. Haven't you found anything yet?"

"Well, no. At least nothing jumps out at me." She laughed at her own joke and shrugged. "But, seriously, I wondered if you'd seen this one." She pulled out another slim paperback with a provocative title. Andy looked at it. The color scheme of the cover spoke first and loudest to him.

"God, that's truly bad graphic design!"

"I won't argue with you there, but what about the title?" 'Time Is of the Essence: Easy Travel to Other Worlds' by Austin Wilmington.

Andy went a little spacey for a moment, as if he were taking a quick trip to another world, then answered Sarah as if she had been badgering him, "Okay, okay, I'll get this one too. Are you ready to mosey on over to the Green Goddess?"

Sarah nodded her assent and led him to the checkout counter. Edward, who was not unused to seeing books falling into customers' proverbial laps, smiled and quietly joked with them about the leaping literature as he rang up the sale. Andy took the change and the paper bag, said "Thanks," and the pair stepped out onto Polk Street. They put on their sunglasses and headed north. He began by telling her that he found it very difficult to talk about his experience. He hadn't yet told the whole thing to Richard and wasn't sure he should.

He was especially cautious after Dr. Dave's outburst at dinner last night and how ridiculous it made him feel. It made him uncomfortable even to think about sharing his story again. But he wanted to tell her, he wanted some validation. With that out of the way, he began with what it felt like to levitate in the vortex of light, the passing of his body through the roof of his flat, and being sucked into what he thought of as the bottom of the spaceship. He described meeting Lohr, the perfectly beautiful, shape-shifting, androgyny of his mentor, and how he felt as though he had somehow known him previously. His description of the spaceship's labyrinthine interior and Lohr's Spartan quarters overlapped his telling of the dimensional layers he experienced. Each fantastic facet of his story triggered his memory of yet another facet, and his unburdening began to take on a life of its own.

Encouraged by Sarah's lack of skepticism, he rushed out his tale in staccato bursts of barely coherent fragments. She listened intently as they walked, asking only the occasional clarifying question. They continued along upper Polk Street, the 'yuppified,' upscale Russian Hill part of the street, and almost to Ghirardelli Square before turning left on Bay Street. He told her of how, for a moment, he was afraid he was going to meet some of the loathsome Grays, of how Lohr communicated telepathically, and how he, Andy, had actually, really and truly, 'flown' in the rarefied atmosphere of a dimension that was both inside and outside the spaceship. They turned north again to follow Van Ness to the western side of Aquatic Park. He described Reiko and her otherworldly, terrestrial extraterrestrial hybrid beauty. They climbed the hill of Fort Mason together and wonder piled on wonder as he took her up the pink pyramid, step by step, reaching the zenith of his conscious connectedness to the Universe and All-There-Is, only to stop her dead still on the sidewalk with his chilling encounter with the reptilian, Kahr.

They both had to catch their breath. The mere telling of it was transporting them into a dizzying altered state. So they lingered here at the summit of the hill with a sweeping, 180 degree view of the Bay, Fort Mason at their feet, and centered themselves with several deep breaths. Before going on with the story, Andy tried to clear his head and vowed to restrain himself. But he warned her that he hadn't come to the most incredible parts of it yet. Sarah seemed oblivious to a couple joggers passing by them and to the movement of the leaves of the eucalyptus trees in the wind. She gave Andy her full attention as he told her of the holiness of Aya, the Pleiadian priestess of Gaia, of his seriously silly mind meld with the awesome, the multi-dimensional demigod, Ankh Ra, the Maker of Worlds and their entourage of sentient animal beings. He spoke of the playful telepathic conversation with the Jaguar, Mae Rao. And then he seemed to run out of steam and just stopped talking.

"What's the matter?" Sarah asked.

"This gets really difficult for me here. This is where they told me about the Photon Belt, the Earth changes, what my mission was."

"Your mission?"

"If I choose to accept it, yes, my mission. And it really does sound impossible. I'm supposed to tell the world of the coming Ascension of the planet and warn of the Earth changes and disasters it will bring."

"Oh."

"Oh? That's it? Just 'Oh'?"

"Well, what more can I say? We've heard of the Photon Belt before. And we've heard of the predicted Earth changes, which, in case you haven't noticed, haven't been happening. But why were you tapped to tell everybody? I thought it was information available for those who are supposed to know, for those who want to play in that realm of possibility. I didn't think it required a prophet."

Andy winced, "Don't say that! Don't even think of it like that! I hate that!"

"Sorry. So no kissing the hem of your garment. Okay, got it. But what are you allegedly supposed to do with this alleged information? Stand on a street corner with a sign on a stick - 'Repent! The Photon Belt is coming!' - and shake it in the faces of people?"

"Are you making fun of me?"

"No, of course not! I'm making fun of them, King Tut and the Karmann Ghia Priestess."

"Yes, but you think I made them up, don't you? You think this whole weird trip came out of my head, don't you?"

"Andy, that is just not true. It is NOT what I think and it is NOT YOUR IMAGINATION! Your head doesn't send your body on trips to Mount Shasta."

"How do you know that?"

"How do I know that? Andy, do you think I make up what Riegel tells people? Do you think I pull Riegel out of my head? Is that what you think?"

"No! I believe in channeling, it's been around for thousands of years. I believe that some people have the ability, the unique gift to channel. And you are one of them. I know Riegel. I know you! Of course, I believe you actually channel them! I know you aren't faking it!"

"But how do you KNOW THAT? How do you know I channel the thoughts and give voice to the thoughts of disembodied entities? Hard to believe, isn't it?"

"So is what happened to me."

"Yes, but it happened. Things like that DO happen, Andy. You and I know it and believe it, and more and more people every day are finding out that we are more than our physical body.

"Remember that quote you put on Jimmy Jeff's AIDS Quilt panel, 'We are not physical beings having a spiritual experience, we are spiritual beings having a physical experience'? Remember that? There is more to God's Universe than we are capable of experiencing with the physical senses. Life saving premonitions are miracles. Psychic crime busters and sunshine and rain are all miracles. Reality's a collective hunch. It's all phenomena. Or it's all illusion. Take your pick. It's all pretty unbelievable. Shit happens.

"You know it's true because you just KNOW, that's all. You can't prove it. That's what believing is. That's what faith is. You don't have to prove anything to me or Richard or anybody else. And if others scoff, if others don't share those beliefs, that's perfectly okay. It's a big Universe. A big, free will, free choice, Universe. There's more than enough room for every belief out there. And maybe you don't get any more 'out there' than what I'm saying, but God made Truth with many doors to open for every believer who knocks. And if that's not a direct quote from the Bible, it's damned close!"

Sarah paused just long enough for Andy to burst into exuberant applause. They laughed and hugged and laughed some more when they heard Sarah's stomach growl. They laughed even harder when they heard Andy's stomach growl in reply. "Come on, Space Boy, let's go get lunch."

"Okay, but I'm not finished. There's more, much more. Oh, and that was very cool how you brought the Bible into it. My Baptist grandmother is spinning in her grave."

"Yeah, and so is my Roman Catholic mother. And believe me, she could use a good spinning. Sorry, Ma, just kidding!"

Located on the Bay between Aquatic Park and the Marina, with barracks on the hill and docks on the water, Fort Mason was, during World War II, one of the major embarkation points for troops heading for the Pacific Theater. Today, as part of the Golden Gate National Recreation Area, its corrugated, galvanized tin-clad warehouses and piers are home to an arts enclave of business offices, galleries, studio spaces, theaters and exhibition halls. The Green Goddess Restaurant was this modern-day community's, and some thought even the Bay area's, vegetarian culinary crown jewel. All of its produce was said to be organically grown exclusively by a Zen co-op near Santa Cruz. The co-op's bakery also had a branch at the Green Goddess. Even non-veggie-heads ranked the cooking at four stars or better. Sarah and Andy were seated just where they wanted to be – by the window wall that looked out on the Marina, the Dome of the Palace of Fine Arts, the Presidio, the Golden Gate Bridge, the Marin headlands and Sausalito. They studied their menus in silence until Sarah mentioned, "I'm very hungry and it all looks so good, I have no idea what to order. Do you?"

"No, but don't get the tofu."

"What are you talking about? They make everything taste great here."

"Yeah, but do you know how they get tofu? Do you know what tofu is?"

Now Sarah caught on that he was joking and she played along. "No, I don't know how they get tofu. What is tofu? Please, tell me."

Andy beckoned her to lean forward and, in strictest confidence, shielded by their menus, he whispered conspiratorially, "It's whale snot."

Sarah sat, unmoved, blinking at him, waiting for him to admit it wasn't funny. Refusing to break character, he ignored her and went back to his menu. In self-defense she felt she had to say something. He must never be allowed to get away with nose humor either at the dinner table or in her presence. "So was that some of the celebrated gay wit I've heard so much about?"

"Hey, there's no reason to malign my people! Order the tofu, if you want to, go ahead. But don't come crying to me if you can't eat it. I'm getting the polenta." She grinned, shook her head and went back to her menu.

A tall, pale and pretty young blonde in white blouse, khaki chinos and navy bib apron embroidered with the restaurant logo, definitely in her twenties, and sufficiently pierced to be wearing three sets of stud earrings, appeared at their table and greeted them in a polite but low-key manner.

"Hello, my name is Vikki, can I get you a beverage to start?

"Iced tea with plenty of lemon for me, thanks," answered Sarah.

"And for you, sir?"

"Just water, thank you. With lemon, too, please."

"It comes with lemon, do you want extra lemon with your water?"

"Uh, well, I don't ...."

"We can put it on the side, if you like."

"Oh, okay, sure. Extra lemon will be fine."

"Are you both ready to order now or do you need a few minutes?"

Andy looked at Sarah who confirmed, "I'm ready."

Andy said, "Me too. Go ahead, Sarah."

"I'd like the house mixed greens salad and the sweet potato and black bean chili. Does that come with bread or crackers?"

"All our entrees come with a basket of assorted breads. In addition, the chili comes with blue cornbread"

"Blue?"

"It's made with blue corn and it's rilly, rilly good. It's very dense and moist, almost like cake. I think you'll rilly like it."

"Alright, then. Yum! I can't wait!"

"And what kind of dressing did you want for your salad? Today we have raspberry vinaigrette, honey mustard, creamy Italian, lite Italian vinaigrette, yogurt ranch, and lemon tahini."

"The raspberry vinaigrette, please."

"Thank you. And you sir, what will you have?"

"I'll have the house mixed greens salad too, but could you hold the radicchio and the cilantro, please? I'd like that salad with the lemon tahini dressing, and I'd like the polenta. Thanks."

Vikki jotted it all down on her tab, took their menus, thanked them and left to give their orders to the kitchen. Sarah commented on the ease with which Andy placed his order, "If I didn't know better, I'd swear you were born and raised in Marin County and not a Chicago boy at all."

"Do you think all we eat in the Midwest is hamburgers and fries?"

"Oh, you don't? Tell me, did you develop your taste for tahini at MacDonald's or Pizza Hut?"

"Don't get me started. Be nice, won't you? Besides, as a former Philly Bandstand Queen, you've got a lot of room to talk. See? I am such a bitch lately. Even when I think I'm relaxing, I'm on edge. I'm trying very hard to be nice. I'm just dying to rip into Vicky, who, by the way, probably spells her name with two "k's" and two "i's". She's very nice and a very good waitress but I am trying rilly, rilly hard not to be sarcastic. You know, sarcasm rilly, rilly isn't clear communication."

"Where did you learn that? On a spaceship?"

"Yes, as a matter of fact, I did learn it on a spaceship."

"Tell me more, tell me much more."

"So are you dating anybody?"

"You know I don't have time to date. I've got a steady clientele of people to channel for and frighten. Besides I've got two bizarro children to raise."

"You do have bizarro children. So smart, so humanoid. Of course I mean that in the nicest possible way."

"Yeah, yeah, yeah. Stop changing the subject and tell me what else happened on that spaceship."

"Well, if you insist. Funny you should mention Jimmy Jeff's Quilt panel. I saw him again. On the spaceship. They have this beautiful Deco nightclub. It's also like this observation deck with these windows and this 360 degree panorama of outer space … ."

"And you have the nerve to question whether my channeling is a mental aberration! But go ahead, this is rich."

"Maybe I should back up and tell you about the Bug Man in Drag that I met while I was dancing with Lohr in the ship's disco."

"Disco? Bug Man? In Drag? Not over lunch, but go on."

"We talked. Jimmy Jeff and I. He's doing well, very well. He looked gorgeous and …he's got a boyfriend."

"Get out!"

"I am out! I couldn't be more out in a dress!"

"Did you meet the guy, the boyfriend, too?"

"Uh-huh. And get this. Are you sitting down?"

Sarah looked puzzled for a moment, even she didn't always get Andy's non sequiturs. "Well, duh!"

"His new boyfriend is Richard's ex. The one that was murdered? Back in '83 or '84? Didn't I tell you about him?"

"Yeah, but only that you thought Richard still had a thing for his former significant other who had died. Some years back. I don't know when. But I know you never mentioned he was MURDERED!"

"It was a gay bashing incident. He still won't talk about it. But I met this guy. Billy, was – is – his name."

"Wow! So your dead ex- is hooked up with his dead ex-. Well, that's keeping it in the soul group. I guess that means Richard and you are meant to be a couple."

"Hold on a minute. I didn't exactly get their blessing from the Great Beyond, the Other Side of the Veil. In fact, Billy and I didn't get along at all. Oh, Jimmy Jeff wants me to be with Richard. That's just fine with him. Time to move on, get a love life, be happy, that sort of crap. But Billy was, well, just a thoroughly obnoxious, bitchy, jealous queen."

"Hey, there's no reason to malign your people!"

"Yeah, well if the spike-heeled, Joan Crawford, come-fuck-me pump fits … ."

"What did he do to you?"

"He read my beads! The evil little Argentine queen … !

"There's that Q-word again."

"… the arrogant, twerpy, freakin' Latin American, twink gigolo … !"

"No, no, don't hold back, tell me how you RILLY feel."

"… had the nerve to look into my soul and tell me that if I didn't get my act together, that maybe I wasn't worthy of Richard's love! I shouldn't have let it get to me, I know that, but he also told me about Richard's past and it just makes me furious when I think about it."

"About what? Richard's past or Billy's scolding?"

"Both! Oh, I deserved the scolding! He was totally, absolutely right about me, the prick bastard! But nobody likes to have themselves laid out like some tired, old rug!"

Andy abruptly clammed up when Vikki brought them their drinks and the dish of extra lemon slices. He and Sarah both smiled sweetly and muttered their thanks. Without a word, she turned and left the table as quickly as she had arrived and Sarah leaped back into the conversation.

"Like some "tired, old rug"? That's pretty harsh! Tell me something, was he cute? I'll bet he was cute."

"Of course he was cute! He was gorgeous! He was divine, he was heavenly! But he was dead! Anyway what difference does that make?"

"I think jealousy is a two-way street."

"Yes, it is and I was - I am - jealous."

"You're jealous of his looks? Why? You're a very attractive man. Okay, you're no Brad Pitt, but you ARE an attractive man. Maybe not conventionally attractive but … . Oh, hell! Look, it's sure not MY job to make you feel like a stud."

"Good thing too, thank you very much. I know what you're saying and that's not why I'm telling you this. I'm angry and jealous mainly because he told me something about Richard that I sure wish I didn't know."

"For crying out loud, what did he tell you? What was it?"

"He oh-so-very passive-aggressively let it slip that, back in the seventies, Richard used to star in gay porn movies."

"Wow! That's an eye-opener! But I believe it. He's a VERY good looking guy. He could probably still star in gay porn movies today. So what? What's wrong with that? You should be proud that you got such a sexy guy who is crazy about you."

"How do you trust a guy who is so hot he's been in porn? Those guys are all impossibly good looking! I could never measure up to them, never compete with them! And as you so astutely pointed out, he could still be humping anybody he wanted to today. What's wrong with that? What's wrong with him? Why is he saving my butt from mountain tops and then practically accusing me of screwing extraterrestrials while I'm out there in space. He doesn't trust me because he can't trust himself. He's the one who was a whore and he's accusing me of being one!"

Vikki brought their salads and bread and, once again, shut them up. Andy was too worked up to smile and mutter thank you. So was Sarah. She was concerned about her friend. And more than a little angry with him. But there wasn't anything she could say with Vikki at the table.

"Is there anything else I can get for you right now? Your chili and polenta will be right up."

They each shook their head no and did not look at her. Vikki seemed oblivious to the vibe at the table and was so busy she left without waiting for a reply. Sarah tore off some bread and buttered it vigorously. Andy stabbed his salad, loaded a forkful, and stuffed it in his mouth. He got a large amount of tangy dressing in that forkful causing him to swallow without chewing properly and he choked and coughed and had to chug some water to wash the greens down.

"Are you going to be alright?"

Andy, red-faced and eyes full of tears, nodded yes as he coughed and hacked some more and sipped a bit more water. Sarah saw her opening and moved in. "Well, sweetie, darling, you know I love you, but I have to say: you DESERVED TO CHOKE after that ridiculous rant! And don't act so shocked. Honestly! You men and your stupid competition! I will never get that about you guys! Notice I said 'guys' and not 'gays'? You're ALL competitive. And I don't even want to start on your sorry-assed looks-ism or your pathetic age-ism! Richard was distraught when he came to see me. He loves you, dammit. And if you don't know that, if you MUST feel sexually inferior, I'm afraid that's YOUR problem, darling. Don't take it out on Richard. Okay? I think the problem is: you don't trust yourself. You have to trust yourself, sweetie. You have to trust that you are good enough, cute enough, - whatever enough, - that you are enough for him. Has he ever given you any reason whatsoever to doubt his love, any reason to not trust his love for you?"

Andy, recovered from his choking fit, didn't miss a beat. "Frankly, yes!"

"Oh! Oh? Well, then…that's very different. Never mind." Sarah put down her fork and sat back in her chair, away from the table. "Don't you think you'd better tell me about it before I make a further ass of myself?"

"You're not an ass. You're absolutely right on all counts. I'm an idiot and I don't know what it's going to take for me to get over myself, but I have to play the cards I'm dealt, right?" Sarah frowned. She didn't necessarily agree, but she didn't want to argue the point, so she responded with a non-committal shrug.

Andy continued, "Which I know is difficult if you aren't always playing with a full deck. Richard showed up at Coffee A-Go-Go this morning with Officer Travis Wilson of the California Highway Patrol, who let Richard in and out of the roadblock at the base of Mount Shasta. It seems he lost his job because of that, or is on probation or something, anyway, he came to Richard for, God only knows what kind of comfort, which Richard apparently gave him last night, as well as a place to stay. Fortunately, Officer Wilson has switched his affection to my friend and co-worker, Sky, and poses no immediate threat. Let me emphasize, in spite of my highly volatile nature lately, I am *not* having too hard a time with this.

"Anyway, the four of us are leaving this afternoon to spend the weekend in Bolinas where I feel, positively, I might add, that we will all sort these feelings out like adults. Okay, I'll grant you, we are looks-ist, age-ist, think-with-our-dicks, male adults, but adults nevertheless. And I think I can bring myself to share the full details of my ET experience with Richard –even the part with Billy – and re-establish the trust between us that you so correctly brought up as vital to our relationship. Now that just sounded rather pompous, even to me, but that's just one more character flaw I need to deal with, okay? In the meantime, I am still trying to understand just what the hell I have been through." Andy noticed Vikki making her way to their table and stopped talking.

Their lunches arrived. Vikki asked if they needed anything more and was politely dismissed by Sarah. Andy continued, deftly changing the subject, "You know, Richard has been approached by the Men-In-Black, too."

"No! I didn't know."

"And no matter what I personally think of Travis Wilson, he is someone who experienced that whole incredible event with Richard and me. And it has affected him in strange ways too. Oh, before I forget, they told me something very interesting they heard on the news this morning. The news helicopter, with the same crew that covered the Shasta Incident, crashed last night, under mysterious circumstances, killing everyone on board. That gave me a chill when I heard it, I can tell you."

"That is eerie! Of course, the whole news blackout thing is very strange to me, extraterrestrials are the story of the Millennium, but the Media has refused responsible coverage of UFOs ever since Project Blue Book was closed. Although I don't like to play in the conspiracy theory sandbox, I think the government knows plenty that it isn't about to make public. But I get exhausted trying to figure out who must know what and why they are keeping quiet about it. The number of people who must know something has to be huge. I just can't imagine a conspiracy that large hanging together. And how do they get them all to keep quiet about it? And how many mysterious helicopter crashes can they get away with?"

Andy added, "And do they have help from the ETs themselves? Are the Men-In-Black working only for themselves or for the larger, shadow government, which has sworn to keep the conspiracy a secret and keep themselves in power? And which branch of the government has the power, which one is orchestrating it all? Could it be the Military? The State Department? The CIA?"

Sarah continued, "And the science community would have to be in on it too. Surely they must know something about UFOs or the Photon Belt that they aren't telling. But what? And why aren't they telling?"

"Scully, I think we're watching too much TV."

The chatty couple became silent as the enormity of their thoughts caught up with and overcame them. They took up their forks and spoons and began to eat their lunch. They exchanged pleasantries about how good the food was and how hungry they had been. They ate in silence until Vikki stopped by to see how everything was and got replies enthusiastic, if somewhat muffled by mouthfuls of food. Andy took up the conversation again when he thought of telling Sarah who else he had seen on the spaceship.

"I almost forgot to tell you, Riegel was on the spaceship too."

"Really? That's incredible!"

Andy rolled his eyes and said, "Could you please try not to use that phrase?"

"Oh, sorry, but you know what I mean. I think that's so neat! What did they look like?"

"Like you said you pictured them, columns of colored light. They had the same unmistakable loving and gentle energy. They were there on the pyramid and told me that things were transpiring rapidly back on Earth and that I would have to go back soon. I felt honored to see them there. Nice to meet old friends in a situation like that."

"I wonder if they'll tell me about it."

"That's partly why I asked you if you had heard anything about a UFO flap over Mount Shasta through your psychic friends' grapevine."

"Nothing yet, but I think I told you that I have a client coming tomorrow and I have a feeling his session might be revealing of something connected to your experience. He's a new client. His name is Doyle. He just wants a standard reading but he did mention something about extraterrestrial contact in the message he left on my machine."

"Did you talk to him?"

"No, I left a confirming message on his answering machine.

"When did he call you?"

"Thursday morning. The morning after you got back."

"Did he tell you how he heard about you?"

"Now that you mention it, he didn't. That's strange. I usually get that information. I'll ask him when we talk, either on the phone or at the session."

Sarah buttered a slice of her blue cornbread and took a bite. She chewed it thoughtfully then made a connection in her mind and squeaked, "Oh!"

"What?"

"I just remembered. He said he was an officer in the military. I don't think he mentioned which branch. But he made it clear that his visit was personal, that it was to be in a strictly civilian capacity. And he emphasized that it was to be kept very confidential."

Andy was shocked by the sudden realization that she had divulged some privileged client information. "Thanks for breaking his confidence for me," he said ironically.

"Geez! Why did I tell you all that? I never do that."

"I know. That's why I'm surprised. But that does sound promising, very promising. But I'd be careful, if I were you."

"You know, I have an intuition you were probably not the only one visiting that ship last Wednesday. Which reminds me, would you like the name of a bona fide psychiatrist who treats abduction victims?"

"I wasn't abducted!"

"Yes, but he would be someone sympathetic and more open to your story."

"Oh. Alright. I guess so. I don't know. Dr. Dave wants me to see a psychiatrist too. Do you think I should?"

"Only for your own peace of mind. The doctor I'd recommend is in Berkeley. His name is Pierce, Kevin Pierce. He hasn't published anything on the subject but he is supposed to be very interested and making room in his practice for people who have made contact. I've gotten some positive feedback from a couple clients about him. Might be worth checking out."

Andy looked at his plate and sighed. "Does he also do relationship counseling?"

"Honey, you and Richard will be fine. Just keep communicating; if you don't, that's when you lose that trust."

Andy looked out at the Marina and the Golden Gate. The sky was an intense cerulean blue. He didn't want to think about human relationships right now. He felt a strong yearning to be back on that ship with Lohr. He wanted to feel the connection he'd had to All-There-Is when he was on the pyramid. He wanted to stroke Mae Rao again. He could feel himself rush into his light body. Before he could say anything to Sarah he slipped into what he called his 'mind meld consciousness,' where he was fully expanded into the cosmos and also fully grounded to Mother Earth.

As he stared out the window, Sarah turned her attention outside too. She felt the sunlight on her face and sighed. She understood that her friend didn't really need her advice. She knew he would make his way through this in his own unique timing with his own unique set of strengths and talents, and in his own unique wisdom. She watched the boats moored at the Marina and the clear sky over the Palace of Fine Arts. She felt herself spacing out and she knew what that meant. She brought herself back to check on Andy.

He sat motionless and unnaturally erect in his chair. His eyes were moist and searching. They were not seeing the outer world, but looking at his inner universe. She knew he was in a trance and that she had to sit patiently and wait until he came out. She intuitively grasped her role as anchor for him with no sense of emergency, only feeling that she should protect him here in this place of public vulnerability. She sat back and neatly folded her napkin and placed it on the table.

Just when it became apparent to her that Andy had not breathed in a long time, he took a deep breath, a quiet gasp, and exhaled it loudly. He did it again, and a couple more times until he had a natural breathing rhythm going. Sarah began to get nervous that Vikki would come back with the check and break his connection. He made a raspy sound to clear his throat then sighed again. She leaned forward and asked, "Andy?"

He took a huge breath but quietly exhaled his answer, "Lohr."

"Andy? Do you know where you are? Can you tell me?"

He inhaled again and answered in a breathy, husky whisper, "Andy knows where he is." He inhaled again and quietly gave full voice to his next words, "I am Lohr."

"Lohr."

"Yes."

"Do you wish to speak to me or to Andy?"

"Both of you."

Sarah quickly gave the restaurant a once over for Vikki. She was not to be seen. "It's alright, go ahead. Tell us what you want to say."

"Encourage this one ... to use this gift. Remind him that he can speak to me directly and hear me directly whenever he needs me. But there are others who wish to speak through him. Teach him safety. This is enough. I will go."

Andy blinked several times and relaxed back into his body. He reached for his water glass and drank. He said nothing but returned his thoughtful gaze to the sky outside. He seemed to be looking for something out there.

"Andy?"

"Yes, I know. I heard him."

"Are you alright?"

"I feel fine." He did not look at her. She could not take her eyes off him. She did not know what to say. He was so calm about this. Then a big grin lit up his face and he sat up a little straighter.

"There it is!"

She turned her head to locate the object of his search.

"What? Where?"

He pointed and said, "That light in the sky over there. It's the ship. The one I was on. It's my spaceship."

She saw the light ten degrees above the north tower of the Golden Gate Bridge. She stared at it for signs of movement or a change in brightness. "How do you know that's not an airplane?"

"Because it's going to leave ... right .. . about ... NOW!"

Sarah gave a small gasp of her own as the light streaked away to the north right on cue and was gone so fast she almost wasn't sure she had seen it leave at all.

"Can I get you anything else?"

"Oh, good lord!" Sarah exploded at the surprise appearance of Vikki.

"I'm sorry. I didn't mean to scare you."

"That's okay. No, nothing else for us, thank you."

Andy added, "Just the check, please."

"Sure. Here you go. You can pay the cashier at the counter. Thanks. And have a rilly nice day!"

"Oh, there is one more thing," Andy blurted. "Would you call us a cab, please?"

"Just ask the cashier, sir, she'll be happy to call one for you. Bye-bye." Vikki smiled sweetly and headed for a trio of newly arrived diners.

"Sorry to break this up but I have to get back to my apartment and pack. I'm being picked up at 3:30. Can I drop you somewhere?"

She looked at her watch and said, "Yes, at Pier 39. If the cab gets here soon, I can get the 2:45 ferry back to Sausalito."

Andy paid the check and they stepped outside the restaurant to wait for the cab in the sunshine. Across the roadway was Building B of the Fort Mason complex. Sarah gave Andy a hug and remarked, "Thanks for a wonderful lunch. And especially for the freaky light show. Are you going to be okay with the channeling thing?"

"Do you remember that time I told you I had accepted an accelerated path, that I wanted to be part of this Ascension process?" Sarah nodded, yes.

"Well, this is it. Like it or not, I asked for it." He was surprised by his own reaction. He had never felt more at home in his own body.

"I'm here to help, guy. Don't forget that. I'll work on the channeling with you. Can't wait to hear who else will come through. And I sure hope I get to talk to Lohr again."

She watched the sheepish smile on her friend's face turn to a scowl as, once more, he looked at something behind her and out of her sight range. What now? she thought. She turned just in time to see the tailfins on a black 1959 Cadillac slowly disappear around the corner of Building B. She felt a momentary chill as she looked back at Andy. "Was that what I think it was?" she asked.

"Yes, indeed."

But Andy was perfectly calm, he got no chills from them now. They were one more piece of a fascinating puzzle, and the puzzle was his life. And there was no solution to that puzzle. There was only being and becoming on this journey. The lotus unfolds according to a plan, sometimes understood, often not. What other interesting obstacles would now appear to enliven the flow of his journey? This is one incredible movie, he thought. My life has become one amazing movie. He hugged Sarah and assured her, "It's going to be okay. I feel very peaceful and centered now. It is what it is. I am what I am. And I am becoming what I will become."

"Well, you know the old saying," Sarah told him, "Shift happens."

AFTERWORD

When Richard and Andy had finally finished their detailed account of the Shasta Incident, Joan Lang, that staunch Presbyterian matriarch, deep in thought the whole time, said to Andy, 'There's just one thing I'd like to know. Where is God in all this?'

Andy only hesitated for a split second before answering, 'Well, where *isn't* God in all this?'

ABOUT THIS BOOK

The author took the best literary advice and chose to 'write what he knew.' However, he denies ever being aboard a UFO. The writing of this book was actually finished in 2001. The author maintains that the story would be different if written today because of his own personal growth. The book is set in the year 1995 for a particular reason.

Originally envisioned to be the first of at least two, and possibly three, books, the story was designed to show how predictions, even by mystical beings supposedly blessed with future sight, are often imprecise and subject to correction.

At the very least, the author wanted to portray our three-dimensional reality as a fluid field of *possibility*, and not one of set-in-stone *probability*.

ABOUT THE AUTHOR

This is Jerry Thomas Boyd's first novel. It started as a short story in a writing class back in San Francisco in 1995.

Jerry Boyd knows who he is. He knows as a writer he is merely a dilettante. This doesn't bother him. He only wanted to tell an entertaining tale from a metaphysical perspective.

He lives in his home state of Indiana and is unlawfully married to a man and happier than he's ever been in his life.

His own story could have happened in any other time or place, but it didn't.

ACKNOWLEDGMENTS

The author wishes to thank …

… His partner in life, Dennis Kniat, who teaches him how to love and be loved and never waver, who keeps him grounded in that love. Because of Dennis, the relationship portrayed in this book would be different if written today.

… Elisabeth Y. Fitzhugh, his publishing mentor and friend of more than twenty years. She is much more a part of this book than words can say.

… Gerald (Jerry) Ramsey, who, besides being his friend of more than forty years, deserves thanks and praise for his editing skill. His additional eye as a proofreader for this book has been an invaluable gift to the author and a significant enhancement to the quality of the text. Of course, any errors, inconsistencies, oddities and so forth, are the author's responsibility alone.

… His immediate family, his parents, Madelyn and Warren Arthur 'Buck' Boyd, Sr., his brother, Warren Arthur 'Mike' Boyd, Jr., his sister-in-law, Betty Gowing Boyd, his totally awesome nephews, Tommy and David Boyd, his cousin Linda Kemp, his aunt and uncle, Bob and Donna Burnham, for their love and support, and his Grandpa, Donald H. Boyd, who is also much more a part of this book than words can say.

... His family of choice, brothers and sisters all, who bless him and honor him with their friendship, humor, understanding and love: most prominently, Molly Gorden, Geralyn Lutty and Doug Jones, Lorrie Lesher and Bill Hobler, Bernadette Aukward, Scott Sedar and Bari Biern, Jerry and Catherine Ramsey, Dennis Keithley, Steve and Diana McIntire, Francesca Drath, Charlie Reisdorf and Bob Fish, Larry Thwing, Pat Glenn, Michelle Matlock, and Nancy Hard.

... A special thank you to the intelligence known as Benu, as channeled through Karen Cook, for the unique perspective on the possible arrival and effects of the Photon Belt.

... The many unseen guides, guardian angels, visitors from other worlds and time-frames who influence our lives for the best and to the nature devas who keep us all going and growing.

... Mother Earth, for giving us someplace to stand, a home for the wondrous biodiversity of all the Nature Kingdoms and whose living being we either curse or bless with our words and deeds.

... The many others who inspire him, whether it is with their acceptance or rejection of him. He is grateful for the joys and sorrows of his life for awakening him to the possibility that Beloved I AM and Beloved We All Are. For that, he thanks Our Deity Which Art.

AND FINALLY

A Special Thanks…

The foundation for my personal understanding of an expanded awareness and my experience of a multidimensional reality, which is reflected in the pages of this book, derives from my cherished exchanges with the team of non-physical intelligences known as Orion (as expressed through Elisabeth Y. Fitzhugh). I took classes and seminars with Orion for the better part of three years in the late 1980s.

Although genderless, to me they are like beloved uncles who patiently, gently and lovingly challenged me and encouraged me to express the fullness of my being. In so doing, they profoundly influenced and shaped who I am today. In my portrayal of the collective character called Riegel, I acknowledge them with gratitude and honor them for their continuing contribution to my spiritual path.